The Belle of the Ball

Just this once, thought Miss Trent, I will wear my hair in ringlets. For the first time since I became a governess, I will unpack my orange gown . . . And if Sir Waldo asks me, I will waltz with him . . .

Heads turned at her radiant entrance to the party. Tongues wagged as that exalted gentleman claimed the very first dance with the Underhill governess. And before the week was over, every gossip in the district had it that the shameless Miss Trent had dared to set her cap for the leader of London society.

THE NONESUCH

A romantic comedy of manners set in England's elegant Regency age.

Bantam Books by Georgette Heyer
Ask your bookseller for the books you have missed

THE BLACK MOTH
THE CORINTHIAN
FARO'S DAUGHTER
FREDERICA
THE NONESUCH
POWDER AND PATCH

GEORGETTE HEYER
THE NONESUCH

BANTAM BOOKS
NEW YORK · TORONTO · LONDON · SYDNEY · AUCKLAND

This edition contains the complete text of the original hardcover edition.
NOT ONE WORD HAS BEEN OMITTED.

THE NONESUCH

A Bantam Book / published by arrangement with
E. P. Dutton

PRINTING HISTORY

Dutton edition published March 1963
Bantam edition published June 1969
7 printings through March 1990

ISBN 0-553-25382-4

PRINTED IN THE UNITED STATES OF AMERICA

KRI   10 9 8 7

CHAPTER I

THERE WAS A TWINKLE in the Nonesuch's eye as he scanned the countenances of his assembled relations, but his voice was perfectly grave, even a trifle apologetic. "I am afraid it is quite true, ma'am," he said, addressing himself to his Aunt Sophia. "I *am* the heir."

Since the question, so indignantly posed by Lady Lindeth, had been rhetorical, this very frank and manly confession surprised no one. They all knew that old Cousin Joseph Calver had left his fortune to Waldo; and when Lady Lindeth had summoned him to account for himself she had acted on the impulse of the moment, and with no expectation of hearing the news denied. Nor had she had any very real expectation of Waldo's renouncing the bequest in favour of her only child. She naturally felt that no worthier heir to eccentric Cousin Joseph's estate existed than Julian; and she had done her best to introduce the noble orphan to him, even enduring the rigours of a week spent at Harrogate, when Julian had been an engaging child in nankeens and a frilled shirt, and she had tried (quite unavailingly) to gain entrance to Broom Hall. Three times had she driven out from Harrogate, the bored but docile little boy beside her, only to be told, twice, by Cousin Joseph's butler, that the Master was not feeling clever enough to receive visitors; and, once, that the Master would thank her not to come pestering him, because he didn't want to see her, nor her son, nor anyone else. Enquiry had elicited the information that the only visitor ever admitted into the house was the doctor. Local opinion was divided, charitable persons maintaining that a disappointment suffered in his youth was responsible for this churlishness; others asserting that he was a muckworm who grudged every groat he was obliged to spend. Having had the opportunity to perceive the neglected condition of the grounds of Broom Hall, Lady Lindeth had ranged herself with the majority. A suspicion that Cousin Joseph might not be as plump in the pocket as

1

was supposed had occurred only to be dismissed: Broom Hall, though greatly inferior in style and size to young Lord Lindeth's seat in the Midlands, was a very respectable house, with probably as many as thirty bedrooms. It did not stand in a park, but its gardens appeared to be extensive; and she was credibly informed that most of the surrounding land belonged to the estate. She had left Harrogate much inclined to think that Cousin Joseph's fortune was considerably larger than had previously been supposed. She did not grudge it to him, but she would have thought herself a very unnatural parent had she not made a push to secure it for her son. So she had swallowed her resentment at the treatment she had received, and had continued, throughout the succeeding years, to send Joseph small Christmas gifts, and periodical letters, affectionately enquiring after the state of his health, and regaling him with accounts of Julian's virtues, beauty, and scholastic progress. And after all her pains he had left his entire estate to Waldo, who was neither the most senior of his relations nor the one who bore his name!

The most senior of the three cousins gathered together in Lady Lindeth's drawing-room was George Wingham, the son of her ladyship's eldest sister. He was a very worthy man, however prosy; she was not particularly fond of him, but she thought she could have borne it better had Cousin Joseph made him his heir, for she was obliged to acknowledge that his seniority gave him a certain amount of right to the bequest. Not, of course, so good a right as Laurence Calver. Lady Lindeth held Laurence, the youngest of her nephews, in contempt and dislike, but she hoped she was a just woman, and she felt she could have supported with equanimity his succession to a fortune which he would have lost no time in dissipating.

But that Cousin Joseph, ignoring the claims of George, and Laurence, and her beloved Julian, should have named Waldo Hawkridge as his heir was so intolerable that had she been of a nervous disposition she thought she must have succumbed to Spasms when she had first heard the incredible news. As it was, she had been unable to speak for a full minute; and when she did she had merely uttered Waldo's name, in a voice so vibrant with loathing that Julian, the bearer of the tidings, had been startled. "But, Mama——!" he had expostulated. "You *like* Waldo!"

That was perfectly true, but quite beside the point, as she

crossly told her son. She was, in fact, much attached to Waldo, but neither her fondness for him nor her gratitude for his unfailing kindness to Julian prevented her from feeling positively unwell whenever she thought of his enormous wealth. To learn that Cousin Joseph's estate was to be added to an already indecently large fortune did make her feel for a few minutes that so far from liking him she detested him.

She said now, in a peevish tone: "I can't conceive what should have induced that disagreeable old man to choose you for his heir!"

"There is no understanding it at all," Sir Waldo replied sympathetically.

"I don't believe you ever so much as *saw* him, either!"

"No, I never did."

"Well, I must own," said George, "that it was an odd sort of a thing to do. One would have thought—— However, none of us had the least claim on the old fellow, and I'm sure he had a perfect right to leave his money where he chose!"

At this, Laurence Calver, who had been lounging on the sofa, and moodily playing with an ornate quizzing-glass, let the glass fall on the end of its ribbon, and jerked himself up, saying angrily: "*You* had no claim to it—or Waldo—or Lindeth! But *I'm* a Calver! I—I think it *damnable!*"

"Very possibly!" snapped his aunt. "But you will be good enough not to use such language in my presence, if you please!"

He coloured, and mumbled an apology, but the reproof did nothing to improve his temper, and he embarked on a long and incoherent diatribe, which ranged stammeringly over a wide ground, embracing all the real and fancied causes of his sense of ill-usage, the malevolence of Joseph Calver, and the suspected duplicity of Waldo Hawkridge.

Until George Wingham intervened, he was heard in unresponsive silence. His oblique animadversions on Sir Waldo's character did indeed bring a flash into Lord Lindeth's eyes, but he folded his lips tightly on a retort. Laurence had always been jealous of Waldo: everyone knew that; and very ludicrous it was to watch his attempts to outshine his cousin. He was several years younger than Waldo, and he possessed none of the attributes which Nature had so generously bestowed on the Nonesuch. Failing to excel in any of the sports which had won for Waldo his title, he had lately turned towards the dandy-set, abandoning the sporting attire of the Corinthian for all the extravagances of fashion popular amongst the young dandies. Julian, three years his junior, thought that he looked ridiculous in any guise; and instinctively turned his eyes towards Waldo. They warmed as they looked, for to Julian Sir Waldo was at once a magnificent personage in whose company it was an honour to be seen, the big cousin who had taught him to ride, drive, shoot, fish, and box; a fount of wisdom; and the surest refuge in times of stress. He had even taught him something of his own way with the starched folds of a neckcloth: not the intricacies of the Mathematical or the Oriental Tie, but an elegant fashion of his own, as unobtrusive as it was exquisite. Laurence would do well to imitate the quiet neatness of Waldo's dress, Julian thought, not realizing that the plain, close-fitting coats which so admirably became Waldo could only be worn to advantage by men of splendid physique. Less fortunate aspirants to high fashion were obliged to adopt a more florid style, with padding to disguise sloping shoulders, and huge, laid-back lapels to widen a narrow chest.

He glanced again at Laurence, not so much folding his lips as gripping them tightly together, to keep back the retort he knew Waldo didn't wish him to utter. From vapourings about the injustice of fate, Laurence, working himself into a passion, was becoming more particular in his complaints. Any stranger listening to him would have supposed that Waldo was wealthy at his expense, Julian thought indignantly: certainly that Waldo had always treated him shabbily. Well, whether Waldo liked it or not, he was not going to sit meekly silent any longer!

But before he could speak George had intervened, saying in a voice of grim warning: "Take care! If anyone has cause to be grateful to Waldo, you have, you distempered young Jack-at-warts!"

"Oh, George, don't be a fool!" begged Sir Waldo.

His stolid senior paid no heed to this, but kept his stern gaze on Laurence. "Who paid your Oxford debts?" he demanded. "Who gets you out of sponging-houses? Who saved you from the devil's own mess, not a month ago? *I* know to what tune you were bit at that hell in Pall Mall!—no, it wasn't Waldo who told me, so you needn't cast any of your black looks at him! The Sharps tried on the grand mace with you, didn't they? Lord, it was all hollow for them! You were *born* a bleater!"

"That's enough!" Waldo interrupted.

"It is! More than enough!" said George rebelliously.

"Tell me, Laurie," said Waldo, ignoring this interpolation, "do you *want* a house in Yorkshire?"

"No, but—what do *you* want with it? *Why* should you have it? You've got Manifold—you've got a town house—you've got that place in Leicestershire—and—you ain't even a Calver!"

"And what the devil has that to say to anything?" struck in George. "What have the Calvers to do with Manifold, pray? Or with the house in Charles Street? Or with——"

"George, if you don't hold your tongue we shall be at outs, you and I!"

"Oh, very well!" growled George. "But when that ramshackle court-card starts talking as though he thought *he* ought to own Manifold, which has been in your family since the lord knows when——!"

"He doesn't think anything of the sort. He thinks merely that he ought to own Broom Hall. But what would you do with it if you did own it, Laurie? I haven't seen it, but I collect it's a small estate, subsisting on the rents of various farms and holdings. Have you a fancy for setting up as an agriculturist?"

"No, I have not!" replied Laurence angrily. "If that sneaking screw had left it to me, I'd have sold it—which I don't doubt *you'll* do—as though you weren't *swimming* in riches already!"

"Yes, you would have sold it, and wasted its price within six months. Well, I can put it to better use than that." The smile crept back into his eyes; he said consolingly: "Does it comfort you to know that it won't add to my riches? It won't: quite the reverse, I daresay!"

Mr Wingham directed a sharply suspicious look at him, but it was Lady Lindeth who spoke, exclaiming incredulously: "What? Do you mean to tell me that that detestable old man wasn't possessed of a handsome fortune after all?"

"Doing it rather too brown!" said Laurence, his not uncomely features marred by a sneer.

"I can't tell you yet what he was possessed of, ma'am, but I've been given no reason to suppose that he's made me heir to more than a competence—deriving, I collect, from the estate. And as you and George have both frequently described to me the deplorable state of decay into which the place has fallen I should imagine that the task of bringing it into order is likely to swallow the revenue, and a good deal more besides."

"Is that what you mean to do?" asked Julian curiously. "Bring it into order?"

"Possibly: I can't tell, until I've seen it."

"No, of course—Waldo, you know *I* don't want it, but what the dooce do *you*—— Oh!" He broke off, laughing, and said mischievously: "I'll swear I know, but I won't tell George—word of a Lindeth!"

"*Tell* me?" said George, with a scornful snort. "Do you take me for a flat, young sauce-box? He wants it for another Orphan Asylum, of course!"

"An Orphan Asylum!" Laurence jerked himself to his feet, staring at Sir Waldo with narrowed, glittering eyes. "So that's it, is it? What ought to be mine is to be squandered on the scaff and raff of the back-slums! You don't want it yourself, but you'd rather by far benefit a set of dirty, worthless brats than your own kith and kin!"

"I don't think you are concerned with any of my kith and kin other than yourself, Laurie," replied Sir Waldo. "That being so—yes, I would."

"You—you—— By God, you make me sick!" Laurence said, trembling with fury.

"Well, take yourself off!" recommended Julian, as flushed as Laurence was pale. "You only came here to nose out what you might, and you've done that! And if you think you're at liberty to insult Waldo under any roof of mine I'll have you know you're much mistaken!"

"Make yourself easy: I'm going, toad-eater!" Laurence flung at him. "And you need not put yourself to the trouble of escorting me downstairs! Ma'am, your very obedient servant!"

"Tragedy Jack!" remarked George, as the door slammed behind the outraged dandy. "Well-done, young 'un!" He added, with a grin that suddenly lightened his rather heavy countenance: "You and your roofs! Try telling me *I* came to nose out what I might—and see what I'll do to you!"

Julian laughed, relaxing. "Well, you did, but that's different! You don't grudge Cousin Joseph's property to Waldo any more than I do!"

"No, but that ain't to say I don't grudge it to those curst brats of his!" said George frankly. He was himself a man of substance, but he was also the father of a large and hopeful family, and although he would have repudiated with indignation any suggestion that he was not very well able to provide for his children, he had for years been unable to consider his unknown and remote cousin's problematical fortune without thinking that it would furnish him with a useful addition to his own estate. He was neither an unkindly nor an ungenerous man; he subscribed what was proper to Charity; but he did feel that Waldo carried the thing to excess. That, of course, was largely the fault of his upbringing: his father, the late Sir Thurstan Hawkridge, had been a considerable philanthropist; but George could not remember that he had ever gone to such absurd lengths as to succour and educate the lord only knew how many of the nameless and gallows-born waifs with which every city was ridden.

He looked up, to find that Waldo was watching him, the faintest hint of a question in his eyes. He reddened, saying roughly: "No, I don't want Broom Hall, and I hope I know better than to waste my time recommending you not to drop your blunt providing for a parcel of paupers who won't thank you for it, and, you may depend upon it, won't grow up to be the respectable citizens you *think* they will, either! But I must say I do wonder what made that old miser leave his money to you!"

Sir Waldo could have enlightened him, but thought it more tactful to refrain from divulging that he figured in his eccentric relative's Will as "the only member of my family who has paid no more heed to me than I have to him."

"Well, for my part I think it very unsatisfactory," said Lady Lindeth. "And not at all what poor Cousin Joseph would have wished!"

"You do mean to do that, Waldo?" Julian asked.

"Yes, I think so, if I find the place at all suitable. It may not be—and in any event I don't want it prattled about, so just you keep your tongue, young man!"

"Well, of all the abominable injustices——! *I* didn't prattle about your horrid brats: it was George! Waldo, if you mean to go north, may I go with you?"

"Why, yes, if you wish, but you'll find it a dead bore, you know. There will be a good deal of business to be settled with Cousin Joseph's attorney, which will keep me busy in Leeds; and whatever I decide to do with Broom Hall I must look into things there, and set about putting them in order. Dull work! In the middle of the Season, too!"

"Much I care! That's what *I* think a dead bore: going from

7

one horrible squeeze to another; doing the pretty to people I'd as lief never see again; showing-off in the Grand Strut——"

"You know, you're spoilt, Julian!" interrupted George severely.

"No, I'm not. I never did like going to parties, and I never shall—not these insipid ton parties, at all events. I like living in the country. I say, Waldo, I wonder if there's any fishing to be had near Broom Hall?" He saw that Sir Waldo was looking at Lady Lindeth, and added: "Oh, Mama don't object! Do you, Mama?"

"No," she answered. "You must do as you please—though it seems a pity you should go out of town just now. There's the Aveburys' Dress-party, and—— However, if you prefer to go to Yorkshire with Waldo I am sure I have nothing to say!"

There was a good deal of reluctance in her voice, which one at least of her audience recognized and appreciated. She was a devoted but not a foolish parent; and while, on the one hand, she was bent on thrusting her son into the heart of the ton, and (if possible) arranging an advantageous marriage for him; on the other, she had far too much wisdom either to try to drive him against his inclination, or to cast the least rub in the way of his allegiance to his cousin Waldo. It stood greatly to her credit that almost from the hour of her widowhood she had made up her mind that she must never keep Julian tied to her apron-strings. But although she had adhered strictly to this resolve she had suffered many qualms, fearing that the very sweetness of his disposition might be his undoing. He was a handsome boy, and one who had come into the world hosed and shod, as the saying was; and her dread was that he might be flattered and coaxed into such company as Laurence kept, with disastrous results. With Waldo he was not only safe but fortunate as well, since Waldo, taking him into his own circle, was introducing him to men of the first rank and character. That most of these gentlemen were addicted to the more dangerous, and (in her view) more degrading forms of sport, she did not allow to weigh with her. It was incomprehensible to her why any man should wish to risk his neck in the hunting field, or in a curricle race; or should derive the smallest satisfaction from *planting a flush hit* in the face of some unoffending acquaintance, encountered in Jackson's Boxing Saloon; but she was fortified in her acceptance of these peculiar activities by the knowledge that no female was fitted to be a judge of such matters; and by the realization that nothing was farther from her ambition than to see her son joining the ranks of those who abjured violent sports. Furthermore, however many pangs of jealousy she might have been made to suffer when, having failed to turn Julian from some adolescent and ill-judged start, she had seen Waldo blight it by the mere lifting of an eyebrow, she could still be thankful to him. His ideas might not coincide with hers; she might resent Julian's devotion to him; but while she knew his influence over her darling to be strong no maternal apprehensions seriously troubled her.

She met his eyes, and saw the understanding smile in them. He said: "I know, ma'am—but where's the use? I'll take good care of him!"

The annoying thing about him was that he did know, though never had she confided in him her ambition to see Julian achieve the social success to which his birth, his looks, and his fortune entitled him. She responded tartly: "He is of age, and very well able, I trust, to take care of himself! A very odd idea of me you must have, my dear Waldo, if you think he is obliged to ask my permission for anything he may wish to do!"

The smile touched his lips; he murmured: "No! The only idea I have of you, ma'am, is that you are a woman of great good sense."

As he turned away from her, Julian, whose attention had been diverted by a question addressed to him by Mr Wingham, demanded gaily: "Are you talking secrets? When do you mean to go Yorkshire?"

"I haven't decided the precise date, but sometime next week. I shall be travelling post, of course."

The expression of disappointment on Julian's face was ludicrous enough to make even his ruffled mother smile. He exclaimed impulsively: "Oh, *no*! You can't wish to be shut up in a stuffy chaise for—— Oh, you're trying to gammon me, are you? Waldo, you're a—you're a——"

"Gull-catcher," supplied George, on the broad grin.

Julian accepted this blithely. "Yes, *and* a regular dryboots! Curricle, Waldo, or phaeton?"

"I don't see how we can go by either when I've no horses stabled on the Great North Road," objected Waldo.

But Julian was not to be hoaxed twice. He retorted that if his cousin was such a nip-farthing as to grudge the expense of sending his cattle forward they would either hire job-horses, or proceed by such easy stages as could be managed by one team.

"I like young Lindeth," said George, when, presently, he walked with his cousin in the direction of Bond Street. "A very good sort of a boy: nothing of the rum 'un about *him*! But as for Laurence——! Upon my word, Waldo, I wonder that you should bear with him as you do! Well, I was used to think him more flash than foolish, but after listening to his damned insolence today I think him the most buffleheaded clunch I ever saw in my life! If there's *one* person anybody but a sapskull would have taken precious care not to rub against, it's you! Good God, where does he think he'd be, if you was to abandon him? Don't you tell me he hasn't cost you a small fortune, because *I'm* not a gapeseed! Why you didn't lose your temper and tell him he'd had his last groat from you I shall never know!"

"Yes, you will," responded Sir Waldo calmly. "I didn't lose my temper because that is precisely what I *had* told him."

George was so much surprised that he halted in his tracks. "You had? Waldo, you don't mean it!"

"No, probably not, but today's outburst shows that Laurie thinks I do. So now you know why I hadn't the smallest inclination to lose my temper. For how much longer do you mean to stand like a stock, attracting the attention of the vulgar? *Do* come out of your trance, George!"

Thus adjured, Mr Wingham fell into step again beside his tall cousin, saying earnestly: "I was never more glad of anything in my life! Now, don't waver from it, I beg of you! Damme if I wouldn't prefer to see you wasting the ready on a pack of ragged brats than on that young once-a-week man!"

"Oh, George, no!" expostulated Sir Waldo. "Coming it *too* strong!"

"Oh, no, I ain't!" said George obstinately. "When I think of the things he said today, and the gratitude he owes you——"

"He owes me none."

"*What?*" George gasped, once more coming to a sudden halt.

His cousin's hand, gripping his arm, forced him onward. "No, George: not again!" said Sir Waldo firmly. "I've done very badly by Laurie. If you don't know that, I do."

"Well, I don't!" George declared. "From the time he was

at Harrow you've positively *lavished* money on him! You never did so for Julian!"

"Oh, I've never done more for Julian than send him a guinea under the seal, when he was a schoolboy!" said Sir Waldo, laughing.

"So I knew! Of course, you may say he was pretty well-breeched, but——"

"I shan't say anything of the sort. I should have done no more for him whatever his circumstances might have been. By the time he went to Harrow I wasn't such a cawker as I was when Laurie was a boy." He paused, slightly frowning, and then said abruptly: "You know, George, when my father died, I was too young for my inheritance!"

"Well, I own we all thought so—made sure you'd play ducks and drakes with it!—but you never did so, and——"

"No, I did worse: I ruined Laurie."

"Oh, come now, Waldo——" George protested, adding after a moment's reflection: "Encouraged him to depend on you, you mean. I suppose you did—and I'm damned if I know why, for you never liked him above half, did you?"

"I didn't. But when I was—what did he call it?—*swimming in riches*, and my uncle was possessed of no more than an independence—besides being as big a screw as our cousin Joseph, and keeping Laurie devilish short—it seemed so hard-fisted not to come to Laurie's rescue!"

"Yes, I see," said George slowly. "And having once begun to frank him you couldn't stop."

"I might have done so, but I didn't. What, after all, did it signify to me? By the time I'd acquired enough sense to know what it signified to *him*, the mischief had been done."

"Oh!" George turned this over in his mind. "Ay, very likely! But if you think the fault is yours, all I can say is that it ain't like you to leave him to sink or swim now! What's more, I don't believe you would!"

"No, I was afraid he wouldn't believe it either," admitted Sir Waldo. "He seems to have done so, however, which makes me hopeful that the mischief has not gone beyond repair."

George uttered a bark of sceptical laugher. "He'll be gapped in some hell before the week's out—and don't tell me you've tied him up, because he ain't such a bottlehead that he don't know you'd never compel him to pay the forfeit!"

"I haven't, but I paid his gaming debts only on his promise that he would incur no more of them."

11

"His promise——! Good God, Waldo, you don't depend on that, do you?"

"But I do. Laurie won't go back on his word: witness his rage today, only because I've compelled him to pledge it!"

"Once a gamester always a gamester!"

"My dear George, Laurie is no more a gamester than I am!" replied Sir Waldo, amused. "All he wishes to do is to sport a figure in the world. Do believe that I know him much better than you do, and take that frown off your face!" He slipped his hand within his cousin's arm, grasping it lightly. "Instead, tell me this, old chap! Do you want Broom Hall? Because, if you do—and you need not fly up into the boughs! —I hope you know you've only to——"

"I do not!" interrupted George, with unnecessary violence. "Merely because I said I thought it an odd start in Cousin Joseph to have left his property to you—— By the bye, my aunt didn't like it above half, did she?"

"No—most understandable! But I really can't feel that Lindeth stands in the least need of Broom Hall."

"Oh, lord, no!—any more than I do! Bless the boy, he never gave it a thought! You know, Waldo, it's my belief he's going to cut up all her hopes! Ever since he came down from Oxford she's been trying to push him into the first style of fashion—*and* into an eligible marriage—and then, when there isn't a ton party he ain't invited to attend, what does he do but beg you to let him go with you into the wilds of Yorkshire! I promise you, I was hard put to it not to burst out laughing at the look in her face when young Julian said the Season was a dead bore! Mark me if she don't prevent his going with you!"

"She won't even make the attempt. She's by far too fond of him to try to thrust him down any path he doesn't wish to follow—and has too much commonsense as well. Poor Aunt Lindeth! I do most sincerely pity her! She was obliged to abandon her efforts to bring her husband into fashion, for he despised nothing more; and to discover now that Julian, who has all in his favour to blossom into a Pink of the Ton, is as bored by such stuff as ever his father was is really very hard."

"I think the better of him for it," declared George. "To own the truth, I always looked to see him trying to follow in *your* steps! Well, if she does let him go with you next week, take care he don't fall into mischief—unless you have a fancy for getting your eyes scratched out!"

"None at all! Are you apprehensive that he will form an

12

attachment to a milkmaid? Or set the countryside by the ears? You terrify me, George!"

"No, no!" George said, chuckling. "It's you who will do that! Well, I don't mean you'll set 'em all by the ears precisely, but, lord, what a flutter there will be when they find the Nonesuch amongst 'em!"

"Oh, for God's sake, George———!" said Sir Waldo, withdrawing his hand abruptly from his cousin's arm. "Don't talk such nonsense! If I were a betting man, I'd lay you odds against the chance that anyone at Oversett has ever heard of me!"

CHAPTER II

NEITHER PROPHECY hit the mark, but, in the event Mr Wingham came nearer to it than Sir Waldo. Broom Hall belonged to a country parish whose centre was the village of Oversett, situated in the West Riding, rather closer to Leeds than to Harrogate, and not above twenty miles from York; and although the majority of the Reverend John Chartley's parishioners knew nothing about Sir Waldo, and several elderly gentlemen, such as Squire Mickleby, took very little interest in any member of the Corinthian set, amongst the ladies, and the younger gentlemen, a good deal of excitement was felt. No one was acquainted with Sir Waldo; but several ladies had at some time or another spent a few weeks in London, and had had him pointed out to them in the Park or at the Opera as one of the leaders of the ton; and every budding young whip who prided himself on his light hands and the prime nature of his turn-out was torn between longing to see just how Sir Waldo did the trick and dread lest such an out-and-out top-sawyer should regard with contempt the efforts of his admirers to emulate his skill.

The first person to learn the news was the Rector, and it was his daughter who carried it to Staples, the most considerable house in the neighbourhood, where it was variously received. Mrs Underhill, who knew no more of Sir Waldo than the Rector's most illiterate parishioner, but understood, from the awe in Miss Chartley's face, that the news was remarkable, said, in a placid voice: "Fancy!" Miss Charlotte, a bouncing fifteen-year-old, looked for guidance at Miss Trent, her adolescent adoration of her young preceptress having led her to regard that lady as an authority on any subject which came under discussion; and Mrs Underhill's niece, Miss Theophania Wield, fixed her large, suddenly sparkling eyes on Miss Chartley's face, and uttered breathlessly: "Is it true? Coming to Broom Hall? Oh, you're shamming it, Patience—I know you are!"

Miss Trent, though the announcement had caused her to look up from her stitchery, her brows raised in momentary surprise, resumed her work, volunteering no remark; but Mr Courtenay Underhill, who had lounged in to pay his respects to his mama's visitor, exclaimed in the liveliest astonishment: "Sir Waldo Hawkridge? Old Calver's heir? Good God! Mama, did you hear? Sir Waldo Hawkridge!"

"Yes, dear. Well, I'm sure I hope he'll find it to his liking, though it will be wonderful if he does, the way Mr Calver let all go to rack and ruin! I don't seem able to recall him at the moment, but there! I never was one for remembering names —not but what you'd think I should keep that one in my head, for I never heard such a funny one!"

"They call him the Nonesuch!" said Courtenay reverently.

"Do they, love? That would be a nickname, I daresay. Depend upon it, it was given him for some silly reason, like the way your grandfather was used to call your poor Aunt Jane Muffin, all because——"

"Oh!" cried her niece, impatiently interrupting these amiable meanderings, "as though anyone was ever called that for a stupid joke! It means—it means *perfection*! Doesn't it, Ancilla?"

Miss Trent, selecting a length of silk from her skein, replied, in her cool, well-bred voice: "A paragon, certainly."

"Fudge! It means being the greatest Go among all the Goers!" stated Courtenay. *"Particularly* on the roads— though they say the Nonesuch is a clipping rider to hounds too. Gregory Ash—and he knows *all* the Melton men!—told me that in harness and out no man can do more with a horse than the Nonesuch. Well, if he is coming here, I won't be seen driving that chestnut I had from old Skeeby, that's certain! Mama, Mr Badgworth has a neatish bay he'd be willing to sell: beautiful stepper—carries a good head—just the right stamp!"

"Oh, pooh! As though anyone cares a rush for such stuff!" broke in Miss Wield scornfully. "Sir Waldo is first in *consequence* with the ton, and of the first style of elegance, besides being very handsome, and *hugely* wealthy!"

"Elegant! Handsome!" jeered Courtenay, mimicking her. "Much you know about it!"

"I do know!" she flashed. "When I was at my uncle's house in Portland Place——"

"Yes, you were as thick as inkle-weavers with him, of course! What miff-maff you do talk! I don't suppose you've ever so much as clapped eyes on him!"

"I have, I *have*! Frequently! Well, *several* times! And he *is* handsome and elegant! Ancilla, he is, isn't he?"

Miss Chartley, who was a very gentle, prettily behaved girl, seized the opportunity to intervene in what promised to develop into a shrill quarrel, turning towards Miss Trent, and saying in her soft, shy voice: "I expect you know more about Sir Waldo than any of us, for you were used to live in London, were you not? Perhaps you may even have met him?"

"No, indeed I have not," Miss Trent replied. "I never saw him, to my knowledge, and know no more of him than the rest of the world." She added, with the glimmer of a smile: "The company he keeps was quite above my touch!"

"I daresay you didn't wish for his acquaintance," said Charlotte. "I'm sure *I* don't: I hate beaux! And if he is coming here to hold up his nose at us all I hope he will go away again!"

"I expect he will," said Miss Trent, threading her needle.

"Yes, that is what Papa says," agreed Miss Chartley. "He thinks he can only be coming to settle with the lawyers, and perhaps to sell Broom Hall, for he can't wish to live in it, can he? Papa says he has a very beautiful house in Gloucestershire, which has been in his family for generations. And if he is so very fine and fashionable he must think this a dull place, I daresay—though it is quite close to Harrogate, of course."

"Harrogate!" said Courtenay contemptuously. "*That* won't fadge! He won't remain at Broom Hall above a sennight I'll be bound! There's nothing to make him wish to stay, after all."

"No?" said his cousin, a provocative smile on her exquisite countenance.

15

"No!" he stated, revolted by this odious self-satisfaction. "And if you think he has only to see you to fall in love with you you much mistake the matter! I dare swear he is acquainted with a score of girls prettier by far than you!"

"Oh, no!" she said, adding simply: "He couldn't be!"

Miss Chartley protested involuntarily: "Oh, Tiffany, how can you? I beg your pardon, but indeed you shouldn't——!'"

"It's perfectly true!" argued Miss Wield. "*I* didn't make my face, so why shouldn't I say it's beautiful? Everyone else does!"

Young Mr Underhill instantly entered a caveat, but Miss Chartley was silenced. Herself a modest girl, she was deeply shocked, but however much she might deprecate such vainglory honesty compelled her to acknowledge that Tiffany Wield was the most beautiful creature she had ever seen or imagined. Everything about her was perfection. Not the most spiteful critic could say of her that it was a pity she was too tall, or too short, or that her nose spoiled her loveliness, or that she was not so beautiful in profile: she was beautiful from every angle, thought Miss Chartley. Even her dusky locks, springing so prettily from a wide brow, curled naturally; and if attention was first attracted by her deep and intensely blue eyes, fringed by their long black lashes, closer scrutiny revealed that a little, straight nose, enchantingly curved lips, and a complexion like the bloom on a peach were equally worthy of admiration. She was only seventeen years of age, but her figure betrayed neither puppy-fat nor awkward angles; and when she opened her mouth it was seen that her teeth were like matched pearls. Until her return, a short time since, to Staples, where her childhood had been spent, Patience Chartley had been generally held to be the prettiest girl in the neighbourhood, but Tiffany had quite eclipsed her. Patience had been brought up to believe that one's appearance was a matter of no importance, but when the parent who had inculcated one with this dictum said that it gave him pleasure merely to rest his eyes on Tiffany's lovely face one might perhaps be pardoned for feeling just a trifle wistful. No one, thought Patience, observing herself in the mirror when she dressed her soft brown hair, was going to look twice at her when Tiffany was present. She accepted her inferiority meekly, so free from jealousy that she wished very much that Tiffany would not say such things as must surely repel her most devout admirers.

Apparently sharing her views, Mrs Underhill expostulated,

16

saying in a voice which held more of pleading than censure: "Now, Tiffany-love! You shouldn't talk like that! Whatever would people think if they was to hear you? It's not becoming—and so, I'll be bound, Miss Trent will tell you!"

"Much I care!"

"Well, that shows what a pea-goose you are!" struck in Charlotte, firing up in defence of her idol. "Because Miss Trent is much more genteel than you are, or any of us, and——"

"Thank you, Charlotte, that will do!"

"Well, it's true!" muttered Charlotte rebelliously.

Ignoring her, Miss Trent smiled at Mrs Underhill, saying: "No, ma'am; not at all becoming, and not at all wise either."

"Why not?" Tiffany demanded.

Miss Trent regarded her thoughtfully. "Well, it's an odd circumstance, but I've frequently observed that whenever you boast of your beauty you seem to lose some of it. I expect it must be the change in your expression."

Startled, Tiffany flew to gaze anxiously into the ornate looking-glass which hung above the fireplace. "*Do* I?" she asked naïvely. "*Really* do I, Ancilla?"

"Yes, decidedly," replied Miss Trent, perjuring her soul without the least hesitation. "Besides, when a female is seen to admire herself it sets up people's backs, and she finds very soon that she is paid fewer compliments than any girl of her acquaintance. And nothing is more agreeable than a prettily turned compliment!"

"That's true!" exclaimed Tiffany, much struck. She broke into laughter, flitting across the room to bestow a brief embrace upon Miss Trent. "I *do* love you, you horrid thing, because however odious you may be you are never *stuffy*! I won't admire myself any more: I'll beg pardon for being an antidote instead! Oh, Patience, are you positively sure Sir Waldo is coming?"

"Yes, for Wedmore told Papa that he had received orders from Mr Calver's lawyer to have all in readiness for Sir Waldo by next week. And also that he is bringing another gentleman with him, and several servants. The poor Wedmores! Papa said all he might to soothe them, but they have been thrown into such a quake! Mr Smeeth seems to have told them how rich and grand Sir Waldo is, so, of course, they are in dread that he will expect a degree of comfort it is not in their power to provide for him."

"Now, that," suddenly interjected Mrs Underhill, "puts me

17

in mind of something I *should* like to know, my dear! For when my Matlock told me I couldn't credit it, for all she had it from Mrs Wedmore herself. Is it true that Mr Calver left them nothing but twenty pounds, and his gold watch?"

Patience nodded sorrowfully. "Yes, ma'am, I'm afraid it is. I know one shouldn't speak ill of the dead, but one can't help feeling that it was very wrong and ungrateful, after so many years of faithful service!"

"Well, for my part, I never did see, and no more I ever shall, that being dead makes a scrap of difference to what you was like when you were alive!" said Mrs Underhill, with unwonted energy. "A nasty, disagreeable clutchfist he was, and you may depend upon it that's what he is still! And not in heaven either! If you can tell me who ever said one should speak respectfully of those who have gone to the other place, you'll have told me something I never heard before, my dear!"

Patience was obliged to laugh, but she said: "No, indeed, but perhaps one ought not to judge, without knowing all the circumstances. Mama, I own, feels as you do, but Papa says we can't know what may have been at the root of poor Mr Calver's churlishness, and that we should rather pity him. He must have been very unhappy!"

"Well, your Papa is bound to say something Christian, being a Reverend," replied Mrs Underhill, in a reasonable spirit. "The ones *I* pity are the Wedmores—not but what they'd have left that old screw years ago, if they'd had a mite of sense, instead of believing he'd leave them well provided for, which anyone could have guessed he wouldn't, whatever he may have promised them! How are they going to find another situation at their time of life? Tell me that!"

But as Miss Chartley was quite unable to tell her she only sighed, and shook her head, thus affording Tiffany an opportunity to turn the conversation into another, and, in her view, far more important channel. She asked her aunt how soon after his arrival she meant to call on Sir Waldo.

Mrs Underhill's origins were humble; with the best will in the world to conduct herself like a lady of quality she had never managed to grasp all the intricacies of the social code. But some things she did know. She exclaimed: "Good gracious, Tiffany, whatever next? As though I didn't know better than go calling on a gentleman! If your uncle were alive it would have been for him to do, if he'd thought fit, which I daresay he wouldn't have, any more than I do myself, because what's the use of leaving cards on this Sir Waldo if he don't mean to stay at Broom Hall?"

"Then Courtenay must do so!" said Tiffany, paying no heed to the latter part of this speech.

But Courtenay, to her considerable indignation, refused to do anything of the sort. Modesty was not one of his outstanding characteristics, nor were his manners, in his own home, distinguished by propriety; but the suggestion that he, at the age of nineteen, should have the effrontery to thrust himself on Sir Waldo affected him so profoundly that he turned quite pale, and told his cousin that she must be mad to suppose that he would be so impudent.

The urgency with which Miss Wield conducted the ensuing argument, and the burst of angry tears which ended it made Mrs Underhill feel very uneasy. She confided, later, to Miss Trent that she did hope Sir Waldo wasn't going to upset them all. "I'm sure I don't know why anyone should be in a fuss over him, but there's Tiffany as mad as fire, all because Courtenay don't feel it would be the thing for him to call! Well, my dear, I don't scruple to own that that's put me a trifle on the fidgets, for you know what she is!"

Miss Trent did know. She owed her present position to the knowledge, which had made it possible for her, in the past, to manage the wayward Beauty rather more successfully than had anyone else.

Miss Wield was the sole surviving child of Mrs Underhill's brother, and an orphan. The late Mr Wield had been a wool merchant of considerable affluence. He was generally considered to have married above his station; but if he had done so with social advancement as his goal he must have been disappointed, since Mrs Wield's brothers showed little disposition to treat him with anything more than indifferent civility, and the lady herself was too shy and too sickly to make any attempt to climb the social ladder. She had died during Tiffany's infancy, and the widower had been glad to accept his sister's offer to rear the child with her own son. Mr Underhill had already retired from trade with a genteel fortune, and had bought Staples, where his gentlemanly manners and sporting tastes were rapidly making him acceptable to all but the highest sticklers in the neighbourhood. Rejecting his elder brother-in-law's tepid offer to admit the little girl into his own London household, Mr Wield consigned her to his sister's care, thinking that if she and Courtenay, two years her senior, were one day to make a match of it he would not be ill-pleased. Contrary to expectation he had not married again; nor did he outlive Mr Underhill by more than a year. He died when Tiffany was fourteen, leaving his fortune, of which she was the sole heiress, in the hands of trustees, and his daughter to the joint guardianship of her two maternal uncles, the younger of these gentlemen having been substituted for the deceased Mr Underhill.

Mrs Underhill had naturally been much affronted by this arrangement. Like her brother, she had looked forward to a marriage between Tiffany and her son. Mr Underhill had left his family very comfortably provided for; no one could have said she was a mercenary woman; but just as Lady Lindeth coveted Joseph Calver's supposed fortune for Julian, so did she covet Tiffany's very real fortune for Courtenay. She said, as soon as she knew the terms of Mr Wield's Will, that she knew how it would be: mark her words if those Burfords didn't snatch the child away before the cat had time to lick its ear! She was right. Mr James Burford, a bachelor, certainly made no attempt to take charge of his niece; but Mr Henry Burford, a banker, residing in very good style in Portland Place, lost no time in removing Tiffany from Staples, and installing her in his daughters' schoolroom. The heiress to a considerable fortune was a very different matter from the motherless child whom Mr Burford had expected to see superseded by a half-brother: besides his two daughters he had three sons.

Mrs Underhill was an easy-going woman, but she might have roused herself to struggle for possession of the heiress if she had been able to suppress a feeling of relief at the prospect of being rid of a damsel crudely described by the rougher members of her household as a proper varmint. Neither she nor a succession of governesses had ever known how to control Tiffany, who, at fourteen, had been as headstrong as she was fearless. Her exploits had scandalized the county, and given her aunt severe palpitations; she led Courtenay and little Charlotte into hair-raising situations; she drove three of her governesses from the house in a state of nervous prostration; already as pretty as a picture, she could change in the twinkling of an eye from an engagingly affectionate child into a positive termagant. Mrs Underhill surrendered her without protest, saying that Mrs Burford little knew what she had undertaken.

It did not take Mrs Burford long to find this out. She said

(with perfect truth) that Tiffany had been ruined by indulgence; there was nothing for it but to send her to school.

So Tiffany was packed off to Miss Climping's Seminary in Bath, to be tamed, and transformed from a tomboy into an accomplished young lady.

Unfortunately, Miss Climping's establishment included a number of day-pupils, with whom Tiffany soon struck up friendships. She was permitted to visit them, and once outside the seminary considerably extended her circle of acquaintances. It was not until a billet from a love-lorn youth, addressed to Tiffany, and smuggled into the house by a venial servant, fell into Miss Climping's hands that the good lady realized that the unexceptionable visits to schoolfriends masked far from desirable excursions; or that a girl not yet sixteen could embark on a clandestine love-affair. Tiffany was a valuable pupil, her trustees paying for every extra on the curriculum without a blink; but had it not been for one circumstance Miss Climping would have requested Mr Burford to remove from her select establishment a firebrand who threatened to ruin its reputation. That was the arrival, to assume the duties of a junior teacher, of Ancilla Trent, herself a one-time pupil at the school. Bored by the reproaches and the homilies of what she called a parcel of old dowdies, Tiffany took an instant fancy to the new teacher, who was only eight years older than herself, and in whose clear gray eyes she was swift to detect a twinkle. It did not take her long to discover that however straitened her circumstances might be Ancilla came of a good family, and had been used to move in unquestionably genteel circles. She recognized, and was a little awed by, a certain elegance which owed nothing to Ancilla's simple dresses; and bit by bit she began to lend an ear to such scraps of worldly advice as Ancilla let fall at seasonable moments. It was no part of Ancilla's duty to admonish the older pupils, nor did she do so. She appreciated the humour of certain outrageous pranks, but managed to convey to the heiress that they were perhaps a little childish; and when informed of Tiffany's determination to marry into the peerage not only accepted this as a praiseworthy ambition, but entered with gratifying enthusiasm into various schemes for furthering it. As these were solely concerned with the preparation of the future peeress for her exalted estate, Tiffany was induced to pay attention to lessons in Deportment, to practise her music, and even, occasionally, to read a

21

book; so that when she left school she had ceased to be a tomboy, and had even acquired a few accomplishments and a smattering of learning.

But she was harder than ever to manage, and nothing was farther from her intention than to submit to her Aunt Burford's plans for her. Mrs Burford, launching her eldest daughter into society, said that Tiffany was too young to be brought out. She might sometimes be allowed to join a small, informal party, or be included in an expedition of pleasure, but she was to consider herself still a schoolroom miss. She would attend concerts and dancing-lessons under the chaperonage of her cousins' governess; and she must spend a part of her time trying to improve her French, and learning to play the harp.

Mrs Burford had reckoned without her host. Tiffany did none of these things; and at the end of three months Mrs Burford informed her lord that unless he wished to be plunged into some shocking scandal, and to see the wife of his bosom dwindle into the grave, he would be so obliging as to send his niece back to Yorkshire. Not only was she so lost to all sense of propriety as to escape from the house when she was believed to be in bed and asleep, and to attend a masquerade at Vauxhall Gardens, escorted by a besotted youth she had met heaven only knew where or how: she was utterly destroying her cousin Bella's chances of forming an eligible connection. No sooner did a possible suitor catch sight of Bella's abominable cousin, said Mrs Burford bitterly, than he had eyes for no one else. As for a marriage between her and Jack, or William, even had she shown herself willing (which she most certainly had not), Mrs Burford would prefer to see any of her sons beggared than married to such a dreadful girl.

Mr Burford was ready enough to be rid of his tiresome ward, but he was a man of scruples, and he could not think it right to consign Tiffany to the care of Mrs Underhill, who had already shown herself to be incapable of controlling her. It was Mrs Burford who had the happy notion of writing to beg Miss Climping to give them the benefit of her advice. And Miss Climping, perceiving an opportunity to advance the interests of Ancilla Trent, of whom she was extremely fond, suggested that Mrs Burford should try to persuade Miss Trent to accept the post of governess-companion in Mrs Underhill's household. Miss Trent, besides being a most superior female (no doubt Mrs Burford was acquainted with her uncle, General Sir Mordaunt Trent), had also the distinction of being the

22

only person who had ever been known to exercise the smallest influence over Miss Wield.

Thus it was that Ancilla became an inmate of Staples, and, within a surprisingly short time, Mrs Underhill's principal confidante.

Mrs Underhill had not previously confided in any of the governesses she had employed, for although she was a good-natured woman, she was quite understandably jealous of her dignity; and in her anxiety not to betray her origins she was prone to adopt towards her dependants a manner so stiff as to border on the top-lofty. She had been too much delighted to regain possession of her niece to raise any objection to the proviso that Miss Trent must accompany Tiffany; but she had deeply resented it, and had privately resolved to make it plain to Miss Trent that however many Generals might be members of her family any attempt on her part to come the lady of Quality over them at Staples would be severely snubbed. But as Miss Trent, far from doing any such thing, treated her with a civil deference not usually accorded to her by her children Mrs Underhill's repressive haughtiness was abandoned within a week; and it was not long before she was telling her acquaintance that they wouldn't believe what a comfort to her was the despised governess.

She said now, developing her theme: "She's no more than a child, when all's said, but with *that* face, and the things one hears about these smart town-beaux—— Well, it does put me quite in a worry, my dear, and I don't deny it!"

"But I don't think it need, ma'am: indeed I don't!" Miss Trent responded. "She may set her cap at him—in fact, I am tolerably certain that she will, just to show us all that she can bring any man to his knees!—and he might flirt with her, perhaps. But as for doing her any harm—no, no, there can't be the least cause for you to be in a worry! Only consider, dear ma'am! She's not a little serving-maid with no one at her back to protect her!"

"No," agreed Mrs Underhill doubtfully. "That's true enough, but—he might want to *marry* her, and a pretty piece of business that would be!"

"If he shows any such disposition," said Miss Trent, laughter warming her eyes, "we must take care to remind her that he is not a member of the peerage!"

Mrs Underhill smiled, but she sighed too, saying that she wished to goodness Sir Waldo wasn't coming to Broom Hall.

23

The wish was echoed, a few days later, by the Squire, who told Miss Trent that he heartily wished the Nonesuch at Jericho.

He had overtaken her on her way back to Staples from the village, and had very civilly dismounted from his hack to walk with her down the lane. He was thought by many to be rather an alarming man, for besides being a trifle testy he had an abrupt manner, and a disconcerting way of staring very hard at people from under his bristling eyebrows. Mrs Underhill always became flustered in his presence, but Miss Trent was not of a nervous disposition. She met his fierce gaze calmly, and answered the questions he shot at her without starting or stammering, thus winning his rare approval. He said she was a sensible woman: no namby-pamby nonsense about her! He wished he could say the same of some others he might mention.

In this instance Miss Trent responded only with a slight smile, which caused him to say, in a threatening tone: "Don't tell me *you* are in raptures over this Pink of the Ton!"

That drew a laugh from her. "No, how should I be? I am past the age of falling into raptures, sir!"

"Gammon! Chit of a girl!" he growled.

"Six-and-twenty!"

"Ay, so you may be: exactly what I thought! Wouldn't signify if you was six-and-fifty, either. Look at my wife! Killed with delight because this chuckfarthing fellow is coming amongst us! Means to give a party in his honour, if you please! None of your pot-luck mind! Oh, no! Shouldn't wonder if she sends out her cards for a turtle-dinner, and has a waltzing-ball to round the thing off in style! Ay, you may laugh, miss! Don't blame you! *I* shall laugh when the fellow sends his regrets—which he will do, if I know anything about these Town Tulips! I shall call on him, of course: can't but do the civil, though I'd as lief give him the go-by."

"Never mind, sir!" said Miss Trent encouragingly. "I daresay he will be gone again within a sennight, and he can't break any hearts in such a short time, surely?"

"Break any hearts? Oh, you're thinking of the girls! *They* don't bother me! It's our boys. Damme if I wouldn't be better pleased if he was a Bond Street fribble, for *that* wouldn't send 'em mad after him! The mischief is that he's a Top-of-the-Trees Corinthian—and I've seen what harm they can do to silly young greenheads!"

The amusement left her face; she replied, after a moment:

"Yes, sir: so to have I. In my own family—— But that was in London! I can't think that here, in such a quiet neighbourhood, the silliest greenhead could find the means to run into a ruinous course."

"Oh, I don't fear they'll do that!" he said impatiently. "Merely break their necks, trying to outdo their precious Nonesuch! Would you believe it?—even my Arthur, slow-top though he is, has smashed my phaeton, trying to drive through my west farm-gate with never a check—nor any precision of eye neither! As for Banningham's cub, riding that goose-rumped gray of his up the stairs at Brent Lodge, and your Courtenay hunting the squirrel on the Harrogate road —but mum for that! No harm done, and a rare trimming he got from old Adstock—for it was the wheels of *his* carriage the young chucklehead was trying to graze! Driving to an inch! 'You can't drive to an ell!' Adcock told him. But you won't repeat that!"

She assured him that she would not; and as they had by this time reached the main gates of Staples he took his leave of her, saying sardonically, as he hoisted himself into the saddle, that they might think themselves fortunate Joseph Calver hadn't gone to roost in the middle of the hunting season, when every cawker for miles round, after first pledging his father's credit for white-topped boots, would have crammed his horse at a stake-and-bound, and would have been brought home on a hurdle. "Mark my words!" he admonished Miss Trent. "You'll see Underhill rigged out in a coat with a dozen shoulder-capes, and buttons the size of saucers before you're much older! I told Arthur not to think I'd help him to make a cake of himself, aping the out-and-outers, but I don't doubt Courtenay will get what he wants out of his mother! All the same, you females!"

CHAPTER III

IT WAS PERHAPS inevitable that the Nonesuch's arrival at Broom Hall should fall a long way short of expectation.

Young Mr Mickleby, the Squire's son, was able to report to his cronies that Sir Waldo had sent his horses on ahead, for he had himself seen two grooms turn in at the gates of Broom Hall. But the horses they led were only coverhacks: goodlooking prads, but nothing marvellous, and no more than two of them. They were followed by a travelling-carriage, which was later discovered to contain only a couple of soberly-clad servants, and a disappointingly small amount of baggage. It soon became known that Sir Waldo was driving himself from London, by easy stages; and although this accorded, in the main, with the younger gentlemen's ideas of how a noted whip should travel, *easy stages* fell tamely on their ears, spoiling visions of some sporting vehicle, slap up to the echo, swirling through the village in a cloud of dust.

No one of more note than the ostler at the Crown witnessed Sir Waldo's arrival in Oversett, and his account of this momentous event was discouraging. Instead of a curricle-and-four, which even provincials knew to be the highest kick of fashion, Sir Waldo was driving a phaeton; and so far from swirling through the village he had entered it at a sedate trot, and had pulled up his team outside the Crown, to ask the way to Broom Hall. No, said Tom Ostler, it wasn't a high-perch phaeton: just an ordinary perch-phaeton, drawn by four proper good 'uns—a bang-up set-out of blood and bone! There was another gentleman with Sir Waldo, and a groom riding behind. Very pleasant-spoken, Sir Waldo, but not at all the regular dash Tom Ostler had been led to expect: he wasn't rigged out half as fine as Mr Ash, for instance, or even Mr Underhill.

This was dispiriting, and worse was to follow. The Squire, paying his promised call, was agreeably surprised by Sir Waldo: a circumstance which might please the Squire's contemporaries but which conjured up in the minds of Mr Underhill, Mr Banningham, and, indeed, Mr Arthur Mickleby as well, a sadly dull picture. No buck of the first head, it was gloomily felt, would have met with the Squire's approval. Arthur ventured to ask if he was a great swell. "How the devil should I know?" said his father irascibly. "He ain't all daintification, if that's what you mean." He eyed Arthur's exquisitely starched shirt-points, and the wonderful arrangement of his neckcloth, and added, with awful sarcasm: "*You'll* cast him quite into the shade! Lord, he'll be like a farthing-candle held to the sun!"

To his wife he was rather more forthcoming. Mrs Mickleby was as eager as her son to learn what Sir Waldo was like, and far less easy to snub. Goaded, the Squire said: "Fashionable? Nothing of the sort! Turns out in excellent style, and looks the gentleman—which is more than Arthur does, since he took to aping the smarts!"

"Oh, don't be so provoking!" exclaimed Mrs Mickleby. "My cousin told me he was of the first style of elegance—*bang-up to the nines,* he said! You know his droll way!"

"Well, he ain't bang-up to the nines. Not the kind of man to be cutting a dash amongst a set of quiet folk like us, my dear!"

Mrs Mickleby opened her mouth to utter a retort, saw the malicious gleam in the Squire's eye, and shut it again.

Pleased with this success, the Squire relented. "It's of no use to ask me what sort of coat he was wearing, or how he ties his neckcloth, because I didn't take any note of such frippery nonsense—which I *should* have done if he'd been sporting a waistcoat like that Jack-a-dandy one Ash was wearing the last time I saw him! Seemed to me he looked just as he ought. Nothing out of the ordinary!" He paused, considering the matter. "Got a certain sort of something about him," he pronounced. "*I* don't know what it is! You'd better ask him to dinner, and see for yourself. Told him I hoped he'd come and eat his mutton with us one day."

"Told him—— Mr Mickleby! You did not! *Eat his mutton with us*—! Of all the vulgar, shabby-genteel—— What did he say?"

"Said he'd be very happy to do so," replied the Squire, enjoying his triumph.

"Very civil of him! I shall hope to show him, my dear Ned, that although we may be *quiet folk* we are not precisely *savages!* Who is the young man he brought with him?"

But the Squire, beyond saying that Sir Waldo had mentioned that his cousin was bearing him company, was unable to enlighten her. He had not seen the young man, and it had not seemed proper to him to enquire more particularly into his identity. Indeed, as his wife told Mrs Chartley, in some exasperation, it had apparently not seemed proper to him to find out anything whatsoever about Sir Waldo. She was perfectly at a loss to guess what the pair of them had found to talk about for a whole hour.

The next person to see Sir Waldo was Courtenay Underhill, and in circumstances which set all doubts to rest. By a stroke of rare good fortune, Courtenay was privileged to witness the Nonesuch perform just such a piece of driving skill as he had yearned to see; and was thus able to reassure his friends. He had been riding along the road when he had seen Sir Waldo's phaeton approaching. He had known at once that it must be his, for he did not recognize the horses. "*Such* a team! I never saw such perfect movers! Matched to a hair, and beautifully put-together! I had a capital view, for it was on that long stretch half a mile short of the pike-road to Leeds. Well, the Nonesuch was coming along at a spanking pace, overtaking a farm-cart, which I'd just met. The fellow that was leading the horse made as much room as he could, but you know how narrow the lane is, and ditched too; I must say I thought the Nonesuch would be pretty well bound to check, but he kept on, so when he went past me I stopped, and looked back—well, to own the truth I thought he'd either lock his wheels, or topple into the ditch!"

"He gave the cart the go-by? On *that* road?" demanded Mr Banningham, awed.

Young Mr Mickleby shook his head. "I wouldn't have cared to attempt it: not just there!"

"I should rather think you wouldn't!" said Mr Banningham, with a crack of rude laughter.

This unkind reference to his late mishap made Arthur flush angrily; but before he could utter a suitable retort Courtenay said impatiently: "Oh, sneck up! He gave it the go-by just as though—just as though he had yards to spare! More like inches! I never saw anything like it in my life! I'll tell you another thing: he catches the thong of his whip over his head. I mean to practise that."

"Ah!" said Mr. Banningham knowledgeably. "Nervous wheelers! Cousin of mine says it's the quietest way, but there ain't many people that can do it. Shouldn't think you could. Was the Nonesuch wearing F. H. C. toggery?"

"No—at least, I don't know, for he had on a white drab box coat. Looked as trim as a trencher, but nothing to make one stare. Greg says the out-and-outers all have as many as a dozen or more capes to their box coats, but I didn't notice anything like that. No nosegay in his buttonhole, either: just a few whip-points thrust through it."

Meanwhile, the Nonesuch, as yet unaware of the interest he was creating, had found enough to do at Broom Hall to keep him in Yorkshire for much longer than he had anticipated. The house itself was in better repair than he had been led to expect, the main part of it, though sadly in need of renovation, being, as Wedmore anxiously assured him, quite dry. Wedmore made no 'such claim either for the eastern wing, which contained a number of rooms bare of furnishings, or for the servants' wing. Of late years, he said, the Master hadn't taken much account of them. There were slates missing from the roofs: they did the best they could with pails set to catch the worst leaks, but there was no denying those parts of the house were a trifle damp. "I only hope dry-rot may not have set in," said Sir Waldo. "We must get a surveyor to come and inspect it immediately. Did your master employ a bailiff?"

"Well, sir, no!" Wedmore replied apologetically. "There used to be one—Mr Hucking, a very respectable man—but —but——"

"Not of late years?" suggested Sir Waldo.

Neither the defective roofs nor the lack of a bailiff was any concern of the old butler's; but he was a meek, nervous man, and was so much in the habit of bearing the blame for every shortcoming in the establishment that it was several moments before he could believe that Sir Waldo really was smiling. Much relieved, he responded with an answering smile, and said: "The Master got to be very eccentric, sir, if you'll pardon the expression. Mr Hucking thought there were things that needed doing, but he couldn't prevail upon the Master to lay out any money, and he quite lost heart. He was used to say that bad landlords make bad tenants, and I'm bound to own—— Well, sir, I daresay you'll see for yourself how things are!"

"I've already seen enough to prove to me that I shall be kept pretty busy for the next few weeks," said Sir Waldo, rather grimly. "Now I should like to discuss with Mrs Wedmore what are the most pressing needs here: will you desire her to come to me, if you please?"

"Waldo, you're never going to lay out *your* blunt, bringing this rackety place into order?" demanded Lord Lindeth, as Wedmore departed. "I may be a green 'un, and I know I haven't sat in my own saddle for very long yet, but I'm not a *widgeon*, and only a widgeon could fail to see that this old lickpenny of a cousin of ours has let the estate go to rack! It's true we haven't had time to do more than throw a glance over it, but don't you tell me that old Joseph ever spent a groat on his land that wasn't wrenched from him, *or* that he hasn't let out the farms on short leases to a set of ramshackle rascals that dragged what they might from the land, and never ploughed a penny back! *I* don't blame them! Why—why—if *one* of my tenants was living in the sort of tumbledown ruin I saw when we rode round the place yesterday, I'd —I'd—lord, I'd never hold up my head again!"

"Very true: I hope you wouldn't! But with good management I see no reason why the estate shouldn't become tolerably profitable: profitable enough to pay for itself, at all events."

"Not without your tipping over the dibs in style!" countered Julian.

"No, Master Nestor! But do you imagine that I mean to throw the place on the market in its present state? What a very poor opinion you must hold of me!"

"Yes!" Julian said, laughing at him. "For thinking you can gammon me into believing you mean to bring the place into order so that you may presently sell it at a handsome profit! Don't throw your cap after *that* one: I know you much too well to be bamboozled! You are going to bring it into order so that it will support some more of your wretched orphans. I daresay it may, but I'd lay you long odds that it won't also give you back what you'll spend on it!"

"If only old Joseph had known how much after his own heart you were, Julian——!" said Sir Waldo, shaking his head. "No, no, don't try to mill me down! You know you can't do it—and we shall have Mrs Wedmore upon us at any moment! Take comfort from the thought that I haven't yet decided whether the place is what I want for my wretched orphans: all I *have* decided is that it would go too much against the pluck with me to shrug off this—er—honeyfall!"

"Honeyfall? An obligation, more like!" exclaimed Julian.

"Just so!" agreed Sir Waldo, quizzing him. "You've nicked the nick—as usual, of course! *No*, you pretentious young miller! Most certainly not!"

Lord Lindeth, his spirited attempt at reprisals foiled, said hopefully: "No, but I dashed nearly popped in a hit over your guard, didn't I?"

"Country work!" mocked Sir Waldo, releasing his wrists as the door opened. "Ah, Mrs Wedmore! Come in!"

"Yes, sir," said the housekeeper, dropping a curtsy. "And if it is about the sheet which his lordship put his foot through last night, I'm very sorry, sir, but they're worn so thin, the linen ones——"

"About that, and a great many other things," he interrupted, smiling reassuringly down at her. "Why didn't you confess like a man, Lindeth? Afraid to give your head to Mrs Wedmore for washing, no doubt! Go away, and I'll try what I can do to make your peace with her!"

"Oh, *sir*——!" protested Mrs Wedmore, much flustered. "As though I would think of such a thing! I was only wishful to explain to you——"

"Of course you were! It's quite unnecessary, however. What *I* wish is that you will tell me what must be purchased to make this house habitable, and where it may be most quickly obtained."

Mrs Wedmore could not remember when more welcome words had fallen on her ears. She gave a gasp, and said in a strangled voice that quite failed to conceal her emotions: "Yes, sir! I shall be most happy to—if you *mean* it, sir!" She read confirmation in his face, drew a deep breath, and launched into a catalogue of her more pressing needs.

The outcome of this interview would have vexed him very much, had he known of it; but as his staff at Manifold had always taken it for granted that whatever was needed in the house might instantly be ordered, and none of his neighbours considered anything less than the installation (by his mother) of the very newest and most revolutionary of closed kitchen-stoves to be worthy of interest, he had no idea that the *carte blanche* he gave the Wedmores would instantly become a topic for wonder and discussion in the district.

It was Mrs Underhill who brought the news back to Staples, after visiting the Rectory one day for a comfortable gossip with Mrs Chartley. Mrs Wedmore, of Broom Hall, and Mrs Honeywick, of the Rectory, were old cronies, and into her friend's receptive ear had Mrs Wedmore poured forth every detail of a never-to-be-forgotten orgy of spending in Leeds.

"And let alone all the linen, and the china, and such, he's got the builders at Broom Hall as well, looking to see what must be done to the roof, and inspecting every bit of timber in the house, so it looks as though he means to stay, doesn't it, my dear?" said Mrs Underhill.

Miss Trent agreed that it did.

"Yes, but on the other hand," argued Mrs Underhill, "he told Wedmore he wouldn't be entertaining guests, so he didn't want any smart footmen hired. Well, of course, he *is* a single

31

man, but you'd expect him to be inviting his friends to stay with him, wouldn't you?"

Not having considered the matter, Miss Trent had formed no expectations, but again she agreed.

"Yes," nodded Mrs Underhill. Her face clouded. "But there's something I don't like, Miss Trent—not above half I don't! He's got a lord with him!"

"Has he, indeed?" said Miss Trent, trying to preserve her countenance. "What sort of a—I mean, *which* lord, ma'am?"

"That I can't tell you, for Mrs Honeywick couldn't remember his name, so she wasn't able to tell her mistress: only that he's Sir Waldo's cousin, and very young and handsome. Well! The Squire's lady may be in high croak—which I don't doubt she is, for, you know, my dear, she does think herself the pink of gentility—but for my part I had as lief we hadn't got any handsome young lords strutting about the neighbourhood! Not that I don't care for modish company. When Mr Underhill was alive we were for ever increasing our covers for guests, not to mention going to the Assemblies in Harrogate, and the York Races, and I'm sure if I've passed the time of day with one lord I've done so with a dozen. What's more, my dear, for all the airs she gives herself, Mrs Mickleby won't set such a dinner before this one as I shall, *that* you may depend on! Yes, and that puts me in mind of another thing! She's sent out her dinner-cards, and not a word on mine about Tiffany! She told Mrs Chartley that she knew I shouldn't wish her to invite Tiffany to a formal party, her not being, properly speaking, out yet. Well, if that's what she thinks she's never seen Tiffany in one of her tantrums! It isn't, of course: she don't want Tiffany to be there, shining down her daughters, and I can't say I blame her, for a plainer pair of girls you'd be hard put to it to find!"

It was evident that she was torn between her hope of securing the heiress for her son, and a strong desire to out-do the Squire's wife. Her intelligence was not of a high order, but she had a certain shrewdness which informed her that the graciousness of Mrs Mickleby's manners was an expression not of civility but of condescension. Mrs Mickleby, in fact, was coming the great lady over her, and that (as she had once, in an expansive moment, told Miss Trent) was something she wouldn't put up with, not if it was ever so! Mrs Mickleby might be related to persons of consequence, and she certainly was the Squire's wife, but Staples was a far larger house than the Manor, and Mrs Underhill, however inferior her breeding, knew better than to employ a Female to cook for herself or her guests.

Miss Trent did not for a moment suppose that the issue was in doubt; so she was not surprised when Mrs Underhill launched immediately into a discussion on the number of persons to be invited to dinner; how many courses should be served; and whether or not the dinner should be followed by a dance. The question was, which would Sir Waldo prefer? What did Miss Trent think?

"I think that Sir Waldo's preferences don't signify, ma'am," replied Ancilla frankly. "It is rather which would *you* prefer!"

"Well, if ever I thought to hear you say such a nonsensical thing!" exclaimed Mrs Underhill. "When the party's to be given in his honour! Not that I should be consulting my own tastes however it might be, for you don't give parties to please yourself—at least, *I* don't!"

"No, indeed you don't, ma'am!" Ancilla said affectionately. The smile which made her look younger, and decidedly mischievous, danced in her eyes. "In general, you give them to please Tiffany! You should not, you know."

"Yes, it's all very well to talk like that, my dear, but I'm sure it's natural she should want a bit of gaiety, even though her Aunt Burford didn't see fit to bring her out this year. What's more, my dear—and I don't scruple to own it, for well I know I can say what I choose to you, and no harm done!—if Tiffany was to find it too slow for her here there's no saying but what she'd beg her uncle to fetch her away, which he *would* do, because it's my belief he didn't like sending her back to me above half—and no wonder!"

Ancilla hesitated for a moment; and then, raising her eyes to Mrs Underhill's face, said, a little diffidently: "I understand you, ma'am—of course! but—but do you think that Mr Courtenay Underhill shows the least disposition to—to fix his interests with his cousin? And—could you be comfortable with her as your daughter-in-law?"

"No, but that's no matter. It was the wish of both their fathers—and she's young yet! I daresay she'll grow to be more conformable," said Mrs Underhill optimistically. Her mind reverted to the more immediate problem; after pondering deeply for a few moments, she said: "Twenty-four couples could stand up in my drawing-room, and very likely more, but the thing is there *ain't* as many young persons in the district: not without I was to invite a set of company, like the

33

Butterlaws, which I wouldn't for my life do! It might be that Sir Waldo would as lief sit down to a rubber of whist, but then there's this young lord of his! It has me quite in a worry to decide what to do for the best!"

"How would it be, ma'am, if you were to make no decision, but to leave it to chance? Then, if you thought your guests would like to get up a set or two, I can play the music for them."

But Mrs Underhill would have none of this. "If I give a dance, I'll hire the musicians from Harrogate, like I did at Christmas," she declared. "There's never been anything nip-cheese about my parties, and nor there ever will be! What's more, I won't have you demean yourself, as if you was of no more account than that fubsy-faced creature that was here before you came to us! No: you'll take your place at the table, and help me to entertain my guests, like you were one of the family, which I'm sure I often feel you are, so kind and obliging as you've always been to me, my dear!"

Ancilla blushed rosily, but shook her head. "Thank you! You are a great deal too good, ma'am. But it would never do! Only think how Mrs Mickleby would stare! Charlotte and I will eat our dinners in the schoolroom, and I'll bring her down to the drawing-room afterwards, as a good governess should."

"Now, don't you talk flummery to me!" begged Mrs Underhill. "You was hired to be a governess-*companion* to Tiffany, and that's a very different matter, for all you've been so kind as to teach my Charlotte. And very grateful I am to you. I promise you."

"I don't feel I deserve any gratitude!" said Ancilla ruefully. "I haven't succeeded in teaching her very much."

"Oh, well!" said Mrs Underhill tolerantly. "I don't hold with keeping girls cooped up in the schoolroom; and to my way of thinking they don't need to have their heads stuffed full of learning. You teach her to be pretty-behaved, and you'll hear no complaints from me! And as for the Squire's wife, let her stare! Not that I think she would, for she's always very civil to you, on account of your uncle being a General. In fact, it wouldn't have astonished me if she'd invited you to her party." She stopped, the most pressing problem of all evoked by her own words. "That party! Oh, dear, whatever's to be done, Miss Trent? Tiffany will be as mad as Bedlam when she knows she's not to go! Such a dust as she'll raise! I own it puts me in a quake only to think of it!"

"She's bound to fly into a passion," admitted Ancilla, "but I believe I may be able to reconcile her. In a very improper way, of course, but it is never of the least use to appeal to her sense of what is right, because I don't think she has any —or any regard for the sensibilities of others either."

Mrs Underhill uttered a faint protest; but she found it impossible to deny that Tiffany, for all her caressing ways, had never yet shown the smallest consideration for anyone. She did not enquire into the methods Miss Trent meant to employ to keep that volatile damsel in good spirits; and Miss Trent volunteered no explanation. Her methods were certainly unorthodox, and must have earned the censure of any mother anxious to see her daughter grow into a modest female, with delicacy of character as well as prettiness of person. But Miss Trent had long since realized that her lovely charge was governed by self-interest. Perhaps, if she were to be deeply in love one day, her nature might undergo a change; meanwhile, the best that the most conscientious preceptress could do for her was to instill into her head the belief that elegant manners were as essential for social success as an enchanting face; to keep her from passing the line; and to prevent her setting everyone in the house by the ears whenever her will was crossed.

So when Tiffany came tempestuously into the schoolroom (as Ancilla had known she would), to pour out the tale of Mrs Mickleby's infamous conduct, she listened to her with an air of blank amazement, and exclaimed: "But——! Good heavens, Tiffany, you don't mean to tell me that you *wish* to go to that party? You cannot be serious!"

Tiffany's bosom was heaving stormily, but an arrested, questioning look came into her eyes as she stared at Miss Trent. "What do you mean?"

Miss Trent arched her brows incredulously. "*You* at such an insipid squeeze? Oh, dear, how *very* improper in me to say that! Charlotte, don't sit with your mouth at half-cock! You were not listening—and if you dare to repeat what I said I shall drag you through fields *full* of cows!"

Charlotte giggled, but Tiffany stamped her foot angrily. "It is a party for Sir Waldo and his cousin, and *everybody* will be there!"

"Exactly so! Now, don't eat me! If you indeed wished for it I'm sorry—but I must own it is not at all the sort of party at which *I* should wish you to make an appearance. You would be the youngest lady present, and you may depend

35

upon it that Mrs Mickleby, if she had asked you, would have taken care to have your place set as far from her distinguished guests as possible. I imagine you would have had Humphrey Colebatch to squire you, perfectly tongue-tied, poor boy! Another thing—which I know one ought not to consider, of course!—is that you couldn't wear the dress that becomes you better than any of the others:—I mean the one with the knots of ribbon and the sash exactly the colour of your eyes."

"Yes, I could!"

"Not in Mrs Mickleby's drawing-room!" Ancilla said. "Only think of all those green curtains and chairs! the effect would be ruined!"

Tiffany was beginning to look thoughtful; but she said, with a slight pout: "Yes, but I don't see why Mary Mickleby should be at the party, or Sophia Banningham, and not me! They aren't out either—at least, they haven't had a London season!"

"No, and I wouldn't wager a groat on the chance that when they get up from dinner Mrs Mickleby won't pack all the young people off to the morning-room, to play speculation, or some such thing. There is to be no dancing, you know: just a chattery evening, with a little whist for the gentlemen, I daresay."

"Oh, no! How shabby! Do you think it will be like that indeed? How bored Sir Waldo and his cousin will be!"

"No doubt they will be. And how agreeably surprised when they come to your aunt's party!"

"Yes, very true!" Tiffany said, brightening.

"Sir Waldo!" exclaimed Charlotte scornfully. "I think it's the stupidest thing!—Everybody running wild over him, except Miss Trent and me! *You* don't want to meet him, do you, ma'am?"

"No, not particularly, which is a fortunate circumstance, for I can't suppose that he would think me any more interesting than I think him," responded Ancilla cheerfully.

CHAPTER IV

IRONICALLY ENOUGH, the two persons who least desired the introduction were the first of the Staples household to meet Sir Waldo. Charlotte and Miss Trent, driving into the village in the one-horse phaeton originally bestowed on Mrs Underhill by her husband in the mistaken belief that it would afford her amusement to tool herself about the neighbourhood, were bound for the Church, with a basket full of flowers. Leaving the phaeton in the stableyard of the Rectory, they carried the basket through the wicket-gate into the Churchyard, and were employed in arranging lilies and delphiniums in two vases set on the altar when they were startled by a man's voice, saying: "But how charming!"

"Oh, how you made me jump!" exclaimed Charlotte involuntarily.

"Did I? I beg your pardon!"

Miss Trent turned her head, and saw that a stranger had entered the Church, accompanied by the Rector, who said: "Well met, Miss Trent! How do you do, Charlotte? Charming indeed, is it not, Sir Waldo? And, I think, unusual. We are indebted to Miss Trent both for the notion and for the execution of it. But you are not yet acquainted! Sir Waldo Hawkridge—Miss Trent, Miss Charlotte Underhill!"

Charlotte bobbed a schoolgirl's curtsy; Miss Trent, bowing slightly, critically watched the advance up the aisle towards her of this representative of a set she held in poor esteem. He carried himself with the natural grace of the athlete; he was certainly good-looking; and she was obliged to acknowledge that although it was evident that no provincial tailor was responsible for the cut of his coat he adopted none of the extravagances of fashion. He was dressed for riding, in buckskins and topboots, and he carried his hat and crop in one hand. The other, a shapely member, bare of rings, he held out to her, saying: "How do you do? May I compliment you? I have recently seen saloons and ballrooms decorated in this style, but not, I believe, a Church. It is altogether delightful!"

Their eyes met, both pairs gray, hers very cool and clear, his faintly smiling; she gave him her hand, and was aware of the strength latent in the clasp of his. She was a tall woman, but she had to look up to his face; and, as she did so, she became conscious of a tug of attraction. The thought flashed into her mind that she beheld the embodiment of her ideal. It was as instantly banished; she said, as he released her hand: "You are too good, sir. Mine was not the inspiration, however. In the parish where I was used to reside it has been the custom for some years."

It would have been too much to have said that Miss Trent's instinctive recognition of the ideal was reciprocated. The Nonesuch had been for too many years the target at which ambitious females had aimed their arrows to be any longer impressionable; and certain painful disillusionments suffered in his youth had hardened his heart against feminine wiles. He was not so much cynical as armoured; and at the age of five-and-thirty believed that he was past the age of falling in love. What he saw in Miss Trent he liked: the fine eyes which looked so directly into his, the graceful carriage, the indefinably well-bred air which distinguished her, and the absence of any affectation in her manners. He liked her voice, too, and the civil indifference with which she had received his compliment. It was refreshing to meet a marriageable female who did not instantly exert herself to win his admiration; it might be pleasant to pursue her acquaintance; but if he were never to see her again it would not cost him any pang of regret.

She turned her head away, to attend to the Rector, who was gently quizzing Charlotte. "I saw your phaeton in the yard, and was told by my good James that *Miss Charlotte* had driven in. Now, that I *didn't* see, which is a severe disappointment!"

"Oh, Mr Chartley, you *know*——!" protested Charlotte, overcome by blushes and giggles. "It was Miss Trent!"

He laughed, and glanced at Sir Waldo. "Not even Miss Trent, who, I must tell you, is a very pretty whip, and a pattern-card of patience besides, has succeeded in curing this foolish child of a profound mistrust of even the sleepiest cart-horse! Eh, Charlotte?"

"Well, I *don't* like horses!" she said boldly. She cast a defiant look at Sir Waldo, and added: "and I won't pretend I do, because I hate shams! You can never tell what they mean to do next! And if you pat them, they—they *twitch!*"

This was rather too much for the Rector's and Miss Trent's gravity, but Sir Waldo, though there was a laugh in his eye, replied gravely: "Very true! And when you stretch out your hand only to stroke their noses they toss up their heads, as though they supposed you meant to do them an injury!"

Encouraged, Charlotte said: "Yes! Though my brother says you should take hold of the bridle before you do so. But if they think you mean to hurt them, when they are for ever being cosseted and cared-for, they must be perfectly addle-brained!"

"I'm afraid they haven't very much intelligence," he admitted.

She opened her eyes at that. "But *you* like them, don't you, sir?"

"Yes, but there is never any accounting for tastes, you know." He smiled at Ancilla. "I collect that we share that particular taste, ma'am?"

"Mr Chartley has misled you, sir. I'm the merest whipster. Charlotte, we must not stand dawdling any longer!"

"But you will take a look in at the Rectory before you go, won't you?" said the Rector. "Sir Waldo has been admiring our little Church, and I have promised to show him the twelfth-century piscina—our greatest pride, is it not?"

He moved away, and Sir Waldo, with a smile and a bow to the ladies, followed him. But when the flowers were arranged to Ancilla's satisfaction, and she picked up her basket, nodded to Charlotte to come away with her, the Rector joined her, and the whole party left the Church together. Ancilla found herself walking beside Sir Waldo down the path leading to the Rectory; declined his offer to carry the basket; and asked him civilly how he liked the Yorkshire scene.

"Very well—as much as I have seen of it," he replied. "As yet, that's not very much: I have been spending most of my time in Leeds. I hope presently to see more of the country-side. My young cousin has been exploring far and wide, and is enthusiastic; says it is finer by far than his own county. That's because the Squire has put him in the way of getting some excellent fishing."

She laughed. "I hope he will enjoy good sport—though my small experience informs me that *catching* fish is not neces-sary for your true angler's enjoyment."

"Oh, no! But to *lose* a fish is quite another matter!"

"Certainly! One cannot wonder that it should cast even the most cheerful person into gloom, for it is always such an enormous one that escapes!"

"I begin to think you are yourself an angler, ma'am: you are so exactly right!"

"Indeed I am not! I was used to accompany my brothers sometimes, when I was a girl, but I very soon discovered that it was not at all the sport for me. When I caught nothing—which was in general the case—I found it a dead bore, and when a fish did get on my hook I was at a loss to know what to do with it, because I can't bear handling fish! They wriggle so!"

They had reached the wicket-gate; he held it open for her, saying gravely: "They do, don't they? So slimy, too! Almost as disagreeable as Miss Charlotte's twitching horses!"

She stepped past him into the garden, but paused there, waiting for Charlotte and the Rector to join them. "Poor Charlotte! It was too bad of Mr Chartley to poke fun at her, for she has tried so hard to overcome her fear of horses, and is secretly much ashamed of it. Pray don't laugh at her!"

"You may be sure I shan't. I should be far more likely to recommend her not to give the matter another thought. Now, why do you look surprised, ma'am?"

She coloured faintly. "Did I do so? Perhaps because it *did* surprise me a little to hear you say that—being yourself, so I'm told, such a notable horseman."

He raised his brows. "But must I therefore despise those who don't care for horses?"

"No—but I have frequently observed that gentlemen who are addicted to sporting pursuits are prone to despise those whose interests are quite different." She added quickly: "It is very understandable, I daresay!"

"I should rather call it intolerably conceited," he replied. He regarded her quizzically. "Furthermore, ma'am, I have a notion that it is you who despises those of *us* who are addicted to sport?"

"That's to say I'm intolerably conceited," she countered, smiling. "I am afraid I deserved it!"

They were interrupted by the Rector, who came up with Charlotte at that moment. He suggested that Sir Waldo should return to the house with them, but this was declined. Sir Waldo took his leave of the ladies, and went off with the Rector towards the stables.

40

Charlotte was plainly bursting to discuss the unexpected encounter, but Ancilla checked her, begging her to reserve her remarks until they should be out of earshot of her very penetrating voice. She was obedient, and listened docilely enough to a warning against any indiscreet utterance; but Ancilla knew her too well to place much reliance on her assurance that she would mind her tongue. As soon as she became excited, she would blurt out whatever thought came into her head, infallibly incurring Mrs Chartley's deep, if unexpressed, disapproval. Mrs Chartley was a kindly woman, but her sense of propriety was strict. It was with relief that Ancilla saw her charge carried off by her friend and contemporary, Miss Jane Chartley, who came running down the stairs as soon as they had entered the house. No doubt the Rectory schoolroom would be regaled with Charlotte's opinion of the Nonesuch, but at least her governess would not be put to the blush by her forthright speech and far from retiring manners.

In the event, when she was ushered into the parlour, Ancilla found Patience alone. She was busy with some white work, hemming a seam with the tiniest of stitches, but she gladly laid it aside when she saw Ancilla. She was quite as eager to discuss the Nonesuch as Charlotte, but being a very well brought-up girl she was much less precipitate, and spent as much as five minutes talking on indifferent topics before saying: "I must tell you that we have had such an interesting visitor this morning, Miss Trent. Papa took him to see the Church: I wonder, did you meet him there?"

"Sir Waldo? Yes, we did. Indeed, we walked back together, all four of us, and parted at the gate. Your papa went off with him then to the stables."

"Oh, yes! He rode over to call on Papa, and then Papa brought him in to introduce him to Mama and me, and he was with us for quite half-an-hour. What did you think of him? Were you surprised? I own, I was—and Mama too, I think! All the gentlemen have been talking so much about his being such an out-and-out Corinthian that I had pictured something quite different—though I've never *seen* a Corinthian, of course. You have, I expect: is that what they are really like? Do you think he *is* one?"

"There can be no doubt he is: a very famous one! As for whether all Corinthians are like him, I can't tell, for I was never acquainted with one."

Patience said shyly: "I fancy you don't care for that set, and I must say I never thought I should either, for one hears

41

such things about them! But he is not in the least what I had imagined! Not proud, or—or what Dick calls *a dashing blade*! He was so easy, and unaffected, and well-informed; and he seems to feel just as he ought about serious matters: he and Papa talked a little of the dreadful hardships the poor people have been suffering, and I could see how pleased Papa was with him. What did *you* think of him, Miss Trent?"

"Oh, a diamond of the first water!" replied Ancilla promptly. "His air, one of decided fashion; his manners most polished; his address—perfection!"

Patience looked at her. "You didn't like him?"

"On the contrary! I thought him very amiable."

"Ah, that signifies that you think his *manners* amiable, but not—not his disposition!"

"My dear Miss Chartley, I know nothing about his disposition!"

"No, but—— Oh, I think I must tell you! It can't be wrong to do so! Sir Waldo hasn't mentioned the matter, even to Papa, and we believe he would as lief it were not known, because he told Wedmore that Mr Calver had privately desired him, when the precise state of his affairs should have been ascertained, to make provision for his old servants. Even Papa doesn't believe Mr Calver did anything of the sort! The Wedmores are to have a pension which will make them comfortable beyond anything they had hoped for: Mrs Wedmore came to tell Honeywick yesterday! You may imagine how much she was overcome—how thankful!"

"Indeed! I am very glad to know that Sir Waldo has done what he should."

"Yes, and of course it was expected that he would. You may say that he is so wealthy that it means no more to him than it would mean to me to give a penny to a beggar, but what strikes one so particularly is the *manner* of it. It was done with a delicacy that shows Sir Waldo to be a man of sensibility, not above considering what must have been the feelings of two such faithful people when they discovered how little their service had been valued!"

Ancilla acknowledged it; but murmured wickedly: "He has won your heart, I see! He has *great* address!"

"Oh, *no!*" cried Patience, quite shocked. "How can you——? Oh, you are funning, but indeed you should not! I hope my heart is not so easily won!"

Ancilla smiled at her. "I hope it may not be—and certainly

42

not by a Corinthian! Don't look distressed! I was only funning, of course: I don't fear for you!"

Recovering her complexion, Patience said: "We shall none of us have time to lose our hearts: he doesn't mean to settle at Broom Hall, you know."

"I should suppose not: he would find it very slow. Does he mean to sell the place?"

"We don't know. He didn't tell us what he means to do; and, naturally, one would not ask prying questions." She looked up, as her mother came into the room, and smiled, saying: "I have been telling Miss Trent how agreeable we think Sir Waldo Hawkridge, Mama; gossiping, you will say!"

"I suppose we all gossip about him," Mrs Chartley replied, shaking hands with Ancilla. "How do you do, Miss Trent? Yes, I must own that I was very pleasantly surprised in Sir Waldo. After the tales we have heard about *the Nonesuch* I had not expected to find that this Tulip of the Ton, instead of being a great coxcomb, is a man who wants neither sense nor feeling. I thought his manners particularly good, too: he has an air of wellbred ease, and no pretension—and as for his leading our sons astray, nonsense! I hope they *may* copy him! Indeed, I find myself regretting that Dick is at school, for he would be all the better for a little polish!"

"Town bronze, ma'am? Oh, no!" Ancilla protested.

"Oh, not à la modality! I meant only that it would do him a great deal of good to perceive that a man may be sporting-mad without advertizing the circumstance."

She said no more about Sir Waldo, and Ancilla made no attempt to bring the conversation back to him. His name was not mentioned again until Charlotte, seated beside her in the phaeton, uttered in awed accents: "Well! To think we should have been the first to meet Sir Waldo, and to talk to him! Oh, Miss Trent, wasn't it nuts for us?"

Ancilla burst out laughing, but protested as well. "Charlotte! Do you wish to see me turned off without a character, you abominable girl? *Nuts for us,* indeed!"

"As though Mama would! No, but *wasn't* it? Tiffany will be as angry as a wasp!"

Knowing that it would be useless to expect Charlotte to refrain from exulting over her cousin, Ancilla held her peace. She was justified by the result: Tiffany received the news with indifference; for while Charlotte had been making the acquaintance of the Nonesuch she had met and dazzled Lord Lindeth.

Whether the encounter had been by accident or by her own design was a point she left undisclosed. She had refused to accompany her cousin and governess that morning, voting the object of the expedition slow work, and declaring that nothing would prevail upon her to sit bodkin in a carriage designed to carry no more than two persons. Instead, she had had her pretty bay mare saddled, and had ridden out alone, declining the escort of the groom expressly hired to attend her. Since there was nothing unusual about this he made no attempt to dissuade her from conduct unbefitting her years and station, merely remarking to Courtenay's groom that one of these days, mark his words, Miss would be brought home with her neck broke, ramming her horses along the way she did, and thinking herself at home to a peg, which the lord knew she wasn't.

The latter part of this criticism Tiffany would have much resented; but she would have been rather pleased than annoyed at the accusation of ramming her horses along, which she considered to be exactly the style to be expected of one who took pride in being a hard-goer. Accustomed, as a little girl, to career all over the countryside on her pony, she had not as yet learnt to accept chaperonage; and although she was willing to ride with Courtenay, or with Ancilla, she found the presence of her groom irksome, and dispensed with it whenever she could. On this occasion she had an excellent reason for doing so: the Squire had let fall the information that young Lord Lindeth was going to fish the stream that ran through the grounds of the Manor; and Tiffany, by no means reconciled to her exclusion from Mrs Mickleby's dinner-party, had every intention of making his acquaintance. Miss Trent might be right in thinking that the party would not suit her; but even less did it suit her to be the last lady of consequence in the neighbourhood to meet the distinguished newcomers. No more than her aunt did she doubt that Mrs Mickleby's omission of her name from the elegant dinner-card sent to Mrs Underhill sprang from a jealous fear that her own two daughters would be cast into the shade by the appearance on the scene of an accredited beauty. Well! Mrs Mickleby, no doubt hopeful that Mary or Caroline would contrive to attract the interest of a titled gentleman, should discover that one at least of her exalted guests was in no mood to make either of these damsels the object of his gallantry. Lord Lindeth, if the beautiful Miss Wield could con-

44

trive it, was going to think the party very flat, when he looked in vain for her amongst the guests.

It was an easy matter to find Lord Lindeth. The stream he was fishing wound through a stretch of open country. Tiffany saw him from a distance, and cantered easily in his direction, neither so close to the stream as to make it apparent that she wished to attract his attention, nor so far from it that he would not hear the thud of the mare's hooves. It was a little unfortunate that his back should be turned towards her, but she felt sure that he would look round when he heard her approach. She reckoned without her host: Lord Lindeth was casting into a likely pool; he had got a rise; and he gave not the smallest sign of having heard the sound of a ridden horse. For a moment it seemed as though Miss Wield's careful strategy must be thrown away. She was a resourceful girl, however, and as soon as she realized that he was wholly absorbed in his sport she let her whip fall, and reined in, uttering a distressful exclamation.

That did make him look round, not so much interested as vexed. It was on the tip of his tongue to request the intruder to make less noise when he perceived that the rude interruption had come from a lady.

"Oh, I beg your pardon!" Tiffany called. "But would you be so very obliging, sir, as to give me my whip again? I can't think how I came to be so stupid, but I've dropped it!"

He reeled in his line, saying: "Yes, of course—with pleasure, ma'am!"

She sat still, serenely awaiting his approach. He laid his rod down, and came towards her. There was a slight look of impatience on his face, but this speedily vanished when he was near enough to see what a vision of beauty had accosted him. Instead of picking up the whip he stood staring up at Tiffany, frank admiration in his gaze.

She was dressed in a flowing habit of sapphire-blue velvet, a lace cravat round her neck, and a curled ostrich plume caressing her cheek. It did not occur to Julian that this undeniably becoming costume was scarcely the established country-mode; he thought only that never in his life had he beheld a more staggeringly lovely girl.

An enchanting smile made him blink; Tiffany said contritely: "I *am* so sorry! I interrupted you—but I can't mount without a block, so you see . . . . !"

He found his tongue, saying quickly: "No, no, you didn't, I assure you!"

45

A gleam shone in her eyes. "But I know very well I did!"

He laughed, flushing a little: "Well, yes! But you needn't be sorry: *I'm* not!"

"Oh, and you looked so vexed!"

"That was before I saw who had interrupted me," he retorted audaciously.

"But you don't know who I am!"

"Oh, yes, I do. Diana!"

"No, I'm not!" she said innocently. "I'm Tiffany Wield!"

"Tiffany! How pretty! But you make me remember an old poem: *Queen and huntress, chaste and fair*—though I rather fancy it was about the moon, not the goddess. But I know the title is *To Diana*, and the refrain, or whatever it's called, is *Goddess, excellently bright!* So——!"

"I don't think I ought to listen to you," she said demurely. "After all, sir, we haven't been regularly introduced yet!"

"There's no one to perform that office for us," he pointed out. "Do you care for such stuff?"

"No, not a scrap, but my aunt thinks I should! And also that I should *never* converse with strange gentlemen!"

"Very true!" he answered promptly. "May I present Lord Lindeth to you, Miss Wield?—he is most anxious to make your acquaintance!"

She gave a trill of laughter. "How do you do? How absurd you are!"

"I know—but what else was to be done in such a case? I was afraid you would gallop away!"

"So I shall—if you will be so very obliging as to pick up my whip for me, sir!"

He did so, but stood holding it. "I'm tempted to keep it from you!"

She held out her hand. "No, please!"

He gave it to her. "Only funning!" It struck him that it was strange that so young and lovely a girl should be quite unattended, and he said, glancing about him in a puzzled way: "Is no one with you, Miss Wield? Your groom, or—or——"

"No one! It's so *stuffy* to have a groom at one's heels! Do you think it very improper?"

"No, indeed! But if anything were to happen—some accident——"

"I'm not afraid of that!" She shortened the bridle. "I must go now. Thank you for coming to my rescue!"

46

"Oh, wait!" he begged. "You haven't told me where you live, or when I shall see you again!"

"I live at Staples—and who knows when you will see me again?" she replied, her eyes glinting down into his. "I'm sure *I* don't!"

"Staples," he said, committing it to memory. "I think I know—oh, I should have told you that I'm at Broom Hall, with my cousin, Waldo Hawkridge! Yes, and we are to dine at the Manor the day after tomorrow—some sort of a party, I believe! Shall I see you there?"

"Perhaps—perhaps not!" she said mischievously, and was off before he could demand a more positive answer.

CHAPTER V

LORD LINDETH, who had greeted with disapprobation the news that he was to be dragged out to a dinner-party, returned to Broom Hall after his encounter with Miss Wield in quite a different frame of mind. The first thing he did was to run through the various visiting-cards which had been bestowed upon his cousin; the next was to burst into the library, where Sir Waldo was frowning over his deceased cousin's rent-books, demanding: "Waldo, are you acquainted with anyone called Wield?"

"No, I don't think so," replied Sir Waldo, rather absently.

"Do pay attention!" begged Julian. "From Staples! Isn't that the place with the wrought-iron gates, beyond the village? They *must* have called, but I can't find any card!"

"Presumably they haven't called, then."

"No, but—— Of course, the name might not be Wield: she spoke of her *aunt*, and I suppose—— But there's no card bearing that direction that I can find!"

Sir Waldo looked up at this, a laugh in his eye. "Oho! *She?*"

"Oh, Waldo, I've met the most *ravishing* girl!" disclosed his lordship. "Now, think! Who lives at Staples?"

"Miss Wield, I collect."

"Yes, but—— Oh, don't be so provoking! Surely you must know who *owns* the place."

"I can see not the smallest reason why I must know—and I don't."

"I wish you may not have lost the card! You would suppose her uncle must have called, wouldn't you?"

"Well, I haven't so far given the matter any consideration," said Sir Waldo apologetically. "Perhaps he doesn't approve of me?"

Julian stared at him. "Nonsense! Why shouldn't he?"

"I can't imagine."

"No, nor anyone else! Do stop talking slum, and try to be serious!"

"I am serious!" protested Sir Waldo. "Quite perturbed, in fact! I have sustained an introduction to someone who, unless I am much mistaken, *does* disapprove of me."

"Who?" demanded Julian.

"A female whose name I can't recall. A remarkably good-looking one, too," he added reflectively. "And not just in the common style, either."

"She sounds a maggotty creature to me!" said Julian frankly. "Not but what I think you're shamming it! Why should she disapprove of you?"

"I rather fear, my fatal addiction to sport."

"What a ninnyhammer! No, but, Waldo, do think! Are you perfectly sure no one from Staples has been here?"

"Not to my knowledge. Which leaves us quite at a stand, doesn't it?"

"Well, it does—except that she may be at the party. She didn't precisely say so, but—— Lord, what a fortunate thing it was that we stayed with the Arkendales on our way here! I might not else have brought my evening rig with me!"

This ingenuous observation made Sir Waldo's lips twitch, for Julian's reception of the news that his journey north was to be broken by a visit to the home of one of the highest sticklers in the country would not have led anyone to foresee that he would presently think himself fortunate to have undergone a stay which he had stigmatized as an intolerable bore. Similarly, when he knew that he had been included in Mrs Mickleby's invitation to Waldo he had denied any expectation of enjoyment, saying that if he had guessed that he had fled from the London scene only to be plunged into a succession of country dinner-parties he would not have accompanied his cousin.

But all such unsociable ideas were now at an end; it was not he but Sir Waldo who deplored the necessity of attending a dinner-party on a wet evening: Julian had no doubt of its being a delightful party; and as for the ancient vehicle brought round from the coach-house for their conveyance, he told his cousin, who was eyeing it with fastidious dislike, that he was a great deal too nice, and would find it perfectly comfortable.

Miss Wield would have been pleased, though not at all surprised, to have known how eagerly his lordship looked forward to meeting her at the Manor, and how disappointed he was not to see her there; but if she had been an invisible spectator she would not have guessed from his demeanour that he was at all disappointed. He was far too polite to betray himself; and of too cheerful and friendly a disposition to show the least want of cordiality. It was a great shame that this ravishing girl was absent; but he had discovered her aunt's name, and had formed various plans for putting himself in this lady's way. Meanwhile, there were several pretty girls to be seen, and he was perfectly ready to make himself agreeable to them.

A quick survey of the drawing-room was enough to inform Sir Waldo that the beautiful Miss Wield was not present. Miss Chartley and Miss Colebatch were the best-looking ladies, the one angelically fair, the other a handsome redhead, but neither corresponded to the lyrical description Julian had given him of Miss Wield's surpassing beauty. He glanced towards Julian, and was amused to see that he was being very well entertained amongst the younger members of the party. He was not surprised, for he had not taken Julian's raptures very seriously: Julian had begun to develop an interest in the fair sex, but he was still at the experimental stage, and during the past year had discovered at least half-a-dozen goddesses worthy of his enthusiastic admiration. His cousin saw no need to feel any apprehension: Julian was enjoying the flirtations proper to his calf-time, and was some way yet from forming a lasting passion.

For himself, Sir Waldo was resigned to an evening's boredom, denied even the amusement of pursuing his acquaintance with the lady who disapproved of him. He had looked in vain for her, and was conscious of disappointment. He could not recall her name, but he did remember that he had been attracted by her air of cool distinction, and the smile which leaped so suddenly into her eyes. She was intelligent, too, and had a sense of humour: a rare thing, he thought, amongst females. He would have liked to have known her better, and had looked forward to meeting her again. But she was not present, and he was provided instead with a number of middle-aged persons, as dull as they were worthy, and with a sprinkling of boys and girls. Amongst the girls, he awarded the palm to Miss Chartley, with whom he exchanged a few words. He liked, as much as the sweetness of her expression, the unaffected manners which, in spite of a not unbecoming shyness, enabled her to respond to his greeting without blushing, nervously giggling, or assuming a worldly air to impress him. As for the boys, he would have had to be extremely dull-witted not to have realized, within a very few moments of entering the room, that most of them were taking in every detail of his dress, and, while too bashful to put themselves forward, were hoping that before the evening was out they would be able to boast of having talked to the Nonesuch. He was well-accustomed to being the object of any aspiring young sportsman's hero-worship, but he neither sought nor valued such adulation. Mr Underhill, Mr Arthur Mickleby, Mr Jack Banningham, and Mr Gregory Ash, bowing deeply, and uttering reverently *Sir*! and *Honoured*! would have been stunned to know that the only young gentleman to engage Sir Waldo's amused interest was Humphrey Colebatch, a red-headed youth (like his sister), afflicted with an appalling stutter. Presented by his fond father somewhat dauntingly as *this silly chub of mine*, and further stigmatized by the rider: *not of your cut, I'm sorry to say*! he had disclosed, in the explosive manner of those suffering an impediment of speech, that he was not interested in sport.

"He's bookish," explained Sir Ralph, torn between pride in his son's scholastic attainments and the horrid fear that he had fathered a miscreature. "Worst seat in the county! But there! No accounting for tastes, eh? Take my daughter, Lizzie! Never opened a book in her life, but rides with a light hand and an easy bit, and handles the reins in form."

"Does she?" Sir Waldo said politely. He smiled encouragingly at Humphrey. "Oxford?"

"Cam-Cam-Cambridge!" He added, after a brief struggle: "M-Magdalene. J-just d-down. Th-third year."

"Magdalene! So was I—Magdalen, Oxford, though. What do you mean to do next?"

"G-go up for a fourth year!" replied Humphrey doggedly, and with a challenging look at his father.

"Fellowship?"

"Yes, sir. I *hope*!"

But at this point Sir Ralph intervened, testily adjuring him not to keep boring on about his affairs; so he bowed awkwardly to Sir Waldo, and walked away. Upon which Sir Ralph said that scholarship was all very well in its way, but that if he had guessed that his heir was going to run mad after it he would never have let him go up to Cambridge at all. He showed a disposition to become even more confidential, asking to be told what Sir Waldo would do in such a case; but as Sir Waldo did not feel himself to be qualified to advise harassed parents, and was too little interested to bend his mind to the problem, he speedily extricated himself from this tête-à-tête. It spoke volumes for his social address that he contrived to do it without in any way offending Sir Ralph.

Meanwhile, those of Humphrey's contemporaries who had jealously observed his encounter with the Nonesuch pounced upon him, demanding to be told what Sir Waldo had said to him.

"W-wouldn't interest you!" responded Humphrey, with odious loftiness. "N-nothing about sport! We talked ab-about Cam-Cambridge."

This disclosure stunned his audience. Mr Banningham was the first to recover his power of speech; he expressed the sentiments of his boon companions by saying: "He *must* have thought you a slow-top!"

"N-not at all!" retorted Humphrey, curling his lip. "W-what's m-more, he's not such a c-c-cod's head as you l-led me to think him!"

At any other time so insufferable a speech must have goaded his childhood's playmates into punitive action. A sense of propriety, however, restrained them, and enabled Humphrey to saunter away, not only unmolested, but filled with the comfortable conviction of having, in a few heaven-sent moments, paid off all the scores of a short lifetime.

Since Mrs Mickleby seated the Nonesuch between herself and Lady Colebatch at her extended dining-table, it was not until much later in the evening that he made the acquaintance of Mrs Underhill. In the welter of introductions he had scarcely distinguished her amongst so many matrons; but Lord Lindeth had not been so careless. Undismayed by a gown of puce satin lavishly adorned with lace and diamonds, and by a headdress supporting a plume of curled feathers clasped by a glittering brooch of opulent dimensions, he had seized the first opportunity that offered of approaching Mrs Underhill, when the gentlemen joined the ladies after dinner; and it was he who made Sir Waldo known to her. Obedient to the summons telegraphed to him by his young cousin, Sir Waldo came across the room, and was immediately made aware of his duty.

"Oh, here is my cousin!" said his lordship artlessly. "Waldo, I fancy you have already been presented to Mrs Underhill!"

"Yes, indeed!" responded Sir Waldo, rising nobly to the occasion.

"Well, we were introduced," conceded Mrs Underhill, "but it wouldn't surprise me if you didn't happen to catch my name. I'm sure there's nothing more confusing than to be introduced to a score of strangers. Many's the time I've been in a regular hobble, trying to set the right names to the right faces!"

"But in this instance, ma'am, I have something to assist my memory!" said Sir Waldo, with admirable aplomb. "Did I not have the pleasure of meeting your daughter not so many days since? Miss—Miss Charlotte Underhill? She was helping another lady—a tall lady, older than herself—to deck the Church with flowers."

"That's right!" said Mrs Underhill, pleased with him. "And mightily puffed-up she's been ever since, you talking to her so kindly, as she tells me you did! As for the tall lady, that would be Miss Trent: her governess. Well, properly speaking, she's my niece's companion, and a very superior young female. Her uncle is General Sir Mordaunt Trent!"

"Indeed!" murmured Sir Waldo.

"Waldo!" interrupted Julian, "Mrs Underhill has been so kind as to invite us to attend the party she is holding on Wednesday next! I believe we have no other engagement?"

"None that I know of. How delightful! We are very much obliged to you, ma'am!" said Sir Waldo, with the courtesy for which he was renowned.

But afterwards, jolting back to Broom Hall in the late Mr Calver's ill-sprung carriage, he expressed the acid hope that his cousin was properly grateful to him for accepting the invitation.

"Yes, very grateful!" replied Julian blithely. "Not but what I knew you would!"

"Having thrust me into an impossible position I imagine you might!"

Julian chuckled. "I know, but—— She's that glorious creature's aunt, Waldo!"

"I am aware! It remains only for you to discover that your glorious creature is engaged to one of the local blades, and you will have come by your deserts."

"Oh, no! I'm tolerably sure she's not!" said Julian confidently. "Her cousin must have mentioned the circumstance, if—— Besides,——"

"Do you mean Charlotte? Was she there tonight?"

"Charlotte? No—who's she? Courtenay Underhill!"

"Oh, a male cousin! What is *he* like?"

"Oh—oh, very agreeable!" said Julian. He hesitated, and then said: "Yes, I know what you're thinking, and I suppose he is inclined to be what you'd call a coxcomb, but he's very young: hardly more than a schoolboy!"

"Quoth the graybeard!" said Sir Waldo lazily.

"Now, Waldo——! I only meant that I shouldn't think he could be twenty yet, and I'm *three*-and-twenty, after all!"

"No, are you? I'll say this for you then: you're wearing *very* well!"

The infectious chuckle broke from Julian again. He retorted: "I'm too old, at all events, to ape *your* modes!"

"Is that what Master Underhill does?"

"Corinthian fashions, anyway. He was looking you over so closely that I wouldn't bet a groat on the chance that he won't turn out in your sort of rig within the week. He asked me all manner of questions about you, too."

"Julian!" said Sir Waldo, with deep foreboding. "Tell me at once just *how* rum you pitched it to that wretched youth?"

"I didn't! I said *I* didn't know what larks you was used to engage in—which was true, though I know more now than I did yesterday! Waldo, *did* you once win five guineas by flooring the bruiser at some Fair in the second round?"

"Good God! How the devil did that story reach Yorkshire? I did: and if *that's* the sort of folly this chuckleheaded new friend of yours admires I hope you told him it was a fudge!"

"No, how could I? I told him to ask *you* for the truth of it.

He didn't like to approach you tonight, but I daresay he will, when we go to Staples next week."

"Before then—long before then!—I shall have sent you packing, you hell-born brat!"

"Not you! I'd rack up at the Crown if you cast me out! Only wait until you have seen Miss Wield! *Then* you'll understand!"

Sir Waldo returned a light answer, but he was beginning to feel a little uneasy. There was a certain rapt note in Julian's voice which was new to him; and he had not previously known his young cousin to pursue a fair object with a determination that brushed aside such obvious disadvantages as a vulgar aunt, and a cousin whom he frankly acknowledged to be a coxcomb. He set little store by his consequence, but Sir Waldo had never yet seen him either encouraging the advances of led-captains, or seeking the company of those whom he would himself have described as being not fit to go; and it seemed highly improbable that he would try to fix his interest with any girl, be she never so beautiful, who was sprung from the mushroom-class he instinctively avoided. At the same time, it would be unlike him to be thinking of mere dalliance. Under his gaiety, Sir Waldo knew, ran a vein of seriousness, and strong principles: he might (though his experienced cousin doubted it) look for amusement amongst the muslin-company, but it would be wholly foreign to his nature deliberately to raise in any virtuous breast expectations which he had no intention of fulfilling. He had once or twice fancied himself in love, and had paid court to the chosen fair; but these affairs had dwindled, and had died perfectly natural deaths. He had never dangled after any marriageable girl in the cynical spirit of the rake: his youthful adventures in love might be transient, but he had embarked on them in all sincerity.

"I like the Squire, don't you?" remarked Julian idly.

"Better than I like his wife!"

"Oh, lord, yes! All pretension, ain't she? The girls are very unaffected and jolly, too: nothing to look at, of course! I suppose the most striking, *au fait de beauté*, as Mama would say, was the redheaded dasher, with the quiz of a brother, but, for my part, I prefer Miss Chartley's style—*and* her parents! No pretensions *there*, but—I don't know how to express it!"

"A touch of quality?" suggested Sir Waldo.

"Ay, that's it!" agreed Julian, yawning, and relapsing into sleepy silence.

He made no further reference to Miss Wield, either then or during the succeeding days; and so far from showing any of the signs of the love-lorn entered with enthusiasm on a search for a likely hunter, under the aegis of Mr Gregory Ash; struck up a friendship with Jack Banningham's elder brother, and went flapper-shooting with him; dragged his cousin twenty miles to watch a disappointing mill; and in general seemed to be more interested in sport than in ravishing beauties. Sir Waldo did not quite banish his uneasy suspicion that he was harder-hit than his mother would like, but he relegated it to the back of his mind, thinking that he might well have been mistaken.

On Wednesday, when he saw Miss Wield at the Staples party, he knew that he had not been mistaken.

The hall at Staples was very large and lofty, with the main staircase rising from it in a graceful curve. Just as the cousins, having relinquished their hats and cloaks into the care of a powdered footman, were about to cross the floor in the wake of the butler, Miss Wield came lightly down the stairs, checking at sight of the guests, and exclaiming: "Oh! Oh, dear, I didn't know anyone had arrived yet! I'm late, and my aunt will scold! Oh, how do you do, Lord Lindeth!"

As conduct befitting one who was to all intents and purposes a daughter of the house this belated arrival on the scene might leave much to be desired; but as an entrance it was superb. Sir Waldo was not at all surprised to hear Lord Lindeth catch his breath; he himself thought that he had never beheld a lovelier vision, and he was neither impressionable nor three-and-twenty. The velvet ribbons which embellished a ball dress of celestial blue crape and silver gauze were of an intense blue, but not more brilliant than Tiffany's eyes, to which they seemed to draw attention. Pausing on the stairway, one gloved hand resting on the baluster-rail, her pretty lips parting in a smile which showed her white teeth, Tiffany presented a picture to gladden most men's hearts.

O my God! thought Sir Waldo. *Now we* are *in the basket!*

She resumed her floating descent of the stairs, as Julian stood spellbound. Recovering he started forward to meet her, stammering: "M-Miss Wield! We meet again—at last!"

Enchanting dimples peeped as she gave him her hand. "At last? But it's hardly more than a sennight since I disturbed you at your fishing! You were vexed, too—horridly vexed!"

"Never!" he declared, laughing. "Only when I looked in vain for you at the Manor last week—and I wasn't *vexed* then: that's too small a word!" He ventured to press her hand before releasing it, and turning to introduce his cousin to her.

Sir Waldo, who strongly (and quite correctly) suspected that Tiffany had been lying in wait on the upper landing, and had thus been able exactly to time her appearance on the scene, bowed, and said How-do-you-do, his manner a nice blend of civility and indifference. Tiffany, accustomed to meet with blatant admiration, was piqued. She had not sojourned for long under her uncle Burford's roof in Portland Place, but she had not wasted her time there, and she was well aware that, notwithstanding his rank, Lord Lindeth was a nonentity, when compared with his splendid cousin. To attach the Nonesuch, however temporarily, would be enough to confer distinction on any lady; to inspire him with a lasting passion would be a resounding triumph; for although he was said to have many flirts these seemed always to be married ladies, and the decided preferences he showed from time to time had led neither to scandal nor to any belief that his affections had been seriously engaged.

Dropping a demure curtsy, Tiffany raised her eyes to his face, favouring him with a wide, innocent gaze. She had previously only seen him from a distance, and she now perceived that he was very good-looking, and even more elegant than she had supposed. But instead of showing admiration he was looking rather amused, and that displeased her very much. She smiled at Lord Lindeth, and said: "I'll take you to my aunt, shall I? Then perhaps she won't scold after all!"

Mrs Underhill showed no disposition to scold, though she was quite shocked to think that two such distinguished guests should have entered her drawing-room unannounced. When, much later, she learned from her offended butler that Miss Tiffany had waved him aside, like a straw, she was aghast, and exclaimed: "Whatever must they have thought?"

Totton shuddered; but Tiffany, reproached for her social lapse, only laughed, and declared, on the authority of one who had lived for three months on the fringe of the ton, that a want of ceremony was just what such persons as Lord Lindeth and the Nonesuch preferred.

Lord Lindeth, too much dazzled to question the propriety of Tiffany's conduct in impulsively sezing his hand, and leading him up to his hostess, would have endorsed this pronouncement; Sir Waldo, following in their wake, reflected that he would have thought Tiffany's artlessness amusing, if only some other young man than Julian had been enthralled by it. He was in no way responsible for Julian; but he was fond of the boy, and he knew very well that his aunt Lindeth implicitly trusted him to keep her darling out of mischief. This duty had not, so far, imposed any great tax on his ingenuity: Tiffany would have been flattered to know that one glance at her had been enough to convince Sir Waldo that she repesented the first real danger Julian had encountered.

A swift look round the room informed Sir Waldo that the company consisted of the same persons whom he had met at the Squire's dinner-party, and he resigned himself to an evening's boredom, exactly as his hostess had foretold. "Because you can't conjure up persons which don't exist, not with the best will in the world you can't," she had said to Miss Trent. "Mrs Mickleby took care to invite all the genteel families she could lay her hands on, drat her! I daresay, if we only knew it, she thinks I'll make up my numbers with the Shilbottles, and the Tumbys, and the Wrangles, which is where she'll find herself mightily mistaken."

Miss Trent suggested mildly that the Shilbottles were very agreeable people, but was overborne. "Agreeable they may be," said Mrs Underhill, "but they're not genteel. Mr Shilbottle goes to Leeds every day to his manufactory, and I hope I know better than to invite him to meet a lord! Why, next you'll be telling me I ought to send a card to the Badgers! No! His lordship and Sir Waldo had better be bored than disgusted!" She added, on a hopeful note: *"One* thing you may depend on: they'll find nothing amiss with their dinner!"

The repast which she set before her guests was certainly enormous, consisting of two courses, with four removes, and a score of side-dishes, ranging from a rump of beef à la Mantua, wax baskets of prawns and crayfish, to orange soufflés and asparagus, and some atlets of palates: a delicacy for which her cook was famous.

Miss Trent was not present at dinner, but she brought Charlotte down to the drawing-room afterwards, and was instantly seen by Sir Waldo, when he came into the room with the rest of the gentlemen. She was wearing a dress of crape with lilac ribbons, with long sleeves, and the bodice cut rather high, as befitted a governess, but he thought she looked the most distinguished lady present, and very soon made his way to her side.

The room had been cleared for dancing, and the musicians from Harrogate were tuning their instruments. Mrs Underhill, explaining that she thought the young people would like to dance, had begged Sir Waldo not to think himself obliged to take part, if he did not care for it, which had made it easy for him to range himself amongst the elders of the party. He might be noted for his courtesy but he had not the remotest intention of standing up with a dozen provincial girls through a succession of country dances. But when the first set was forming he went up to Miss Trent, and solicited the honour of leading her into it. She declined it, but could not help feeling gratified.

"That's a set-down!" remarked Sir Waldo. "Are you going to tell me that you *don't* dance, ma'am?"

She was thrown into a little natural confusion by this unexpected rejoinder, and said with less than her usual calm: "No, thank you. That is, yes, of course I do, but not—I mean——"

"Go on!" he said encouragingly, as she stopped, vexed with herself for being suddenly so *gauche*. "You do dance, but not with—er—*gentlemen who are addicted to sporting pursuits!* Have I that correctly?"

She looked quickly at him. "Did I say that?"

"Yes, and in a tone of severe disapprobation. You did not *then* tell me you preferred not to dance with me, or course: the occasion hadn't arisen."

"I haven't told you so now, sir!" she replied, with spirit. "I said—I hope civilly!—that I don't dance at all!"

"After which," he reminded her, "you said that you *do* dance, *but not*——! Civility then overcame you, I collect! Quite tied your tongue, in fact! So I came to your rescue. I wish you will tell me what I've done to earn your disapproval."

"You are quite mistaken, sir. You must know that you have done nothing. I assure you I don't disapprove of you!"

"Just my imagination, Miss Trent? I don't believe it, but I'm very ready to be convinced. Shall we join this set?"

"Sir Waldo, you are labouring under a misapprehension! It would be most improper in me to stand up with you, or with anyone! I'm not a guest here: I am the governess!"

"Yes, but a *most* superior female!" he murmured.

She looked at him in some astonishment. "Did you know it, then? And asked me to dance? Well, I'm very much obliged to you, but I think it shows a strange want of conduct in you! To ask the governess rather than Miss Wield——!"

"My cousin was before me. Now, don't recite me a catalogue of the girls I *might* have asked to stand up with me! I daresay they are very amiable, I can see that one or two are pretty, and I know that I should find them all dead bores. I'm glad you won't dance: I had rather by far talk to you!"

"Well, it won't do!" she said resolutely. "I am quite beneath your touch, sir!"

"No, no, that's coming it much too strong!" he said. "When I have it on excellent authority that your uncle is a General!"

For a moment she suspected him of mockery; then she met his eyes, and realized that the laughter in them was at a joke he believed she would appreciate. She said, with a quivering lip: "D-did Mrs Underhill say that? Oh, dear! I shouldn't think you could possibly believe that she didn't learn about my uncle from me, but I promise you she didn't!"

"Another of my misapprehensions! I had naturally supposed that you introduced him into every conversation, and had been wondering how it came about that you forgot to mention him when we first met."

She choked. "I wish you will stop trying to make me laugh! Do, pray, Sir Waldo, go and talk to Mrs Mickleby, or Lady Colebatch, or someone! I might have twenty generals in my family, but I should still be the governess, and you must know that governesses remain discreetly in the background."

"That sounds like fustian," he remarked.

"Well, it isn't! It—it is a matter of social usage. It will be thought most unbecoming in me to put myself forward. I can see that already Mrs Banningham is wondering what can possess you to stand talking to me like this! Just the thing to set people in a bustle! *You* may stand on too high a form to care for the world's opinion, but I can assure you *I* don't!"

"Oh, I'm not nearly as arrogant as you think!" he assured her. "Setting people in a bustle is the last thing I wish to do! But I find it hard to believe that even the most deplorably top-lofty matron could think it remarkable that I should engage in conversation the niece of one of my acquaintances. I should rather suppose that she would think it abominably uncivil of me *not* to do so!"

"*Are* you acquainted with my uncle?" she demanded.

"Of course I am: we are members of the same club! I don't mean to boast, however! He is an older and by far more distinguished man than I am, and *acquaintance* is all I claim."

She smiled, but looked rather searchingly at him. "Are you also acquainted with his son, sir? My cousin, Mr Bernard Trent?"

"Not to my knowledge. Ought I to be?"

"Oh, no! He is very young. But he has a number of friends amongst the Corinthian set. I thought perhaps you might have encountered him."

He shook his head; and as Sir Ralph Colebatch came up at that moment she excused herself, and moved away to find Charlotte. She soon saw her, going down the dance with Arthur Mickleby; and realized ruefully, but with a little amusement, that while she had been engaged with the Nonesuch her enterprising pupil had contrived to induce Arthur to lead her into the set. Some mothers, she reflected, would have censured her pretty severely for not having kept a stricter chaperonage over a schoolgirl admitted to the drawing-room merely to watch the dancing for an hour, before going demurely upstairs to bed; but she was not surprised to find Mrs Underhill complacently eyeing her daughter's performance, or to learn that she had given Charlotte leave to dance.

"Well, I daresay I ought to have said no," she admitted, "but I like to see young people enjoying themselves, which it's plain she is, bless her! I'm sure there's no harm in her taking her place in a country-dance or two, for it's not as if there was to be any waltzing, *that* you may depend on! Nor it isn't a formal ball, which would be a very different matter, of course." She withdrew her gaze from Charlotte, and said kindly: "And if any gentleman was to ask you to stand up with him, my dear, I hope you'll do so! There's no one will wonder at it, not after seeing Sir Waldo going smash up to you, the way he did, and stand talking to you as though you was old friends!"

"He was speaking to me of my uncle, ma'am!" and Miss Trent, snatching at the excuse offered her by the Nonesuch, but flushing a little. "They are acquainted, you see."

"Ay, that's just what I said to Mrs. Banningham!" nodded Mrs. Underhill. " 'Oh,' I said, 'you may depend upon it Sir Waldo is acquainted with the General, and they are chatting away about him, and all their London friends! I'm sure nothing could be more natural,' I said, 'for Miss Trent is very well-connected,' I said. That made her look yellow, I can tell you! Well, I hope I'm not one to take an affront into my head where none's intended, but I've had a score to settle with Mrs B. ever since she behaved so uppish to me at the

Lord-Lieutenant's party!" A cloud descended on her brow; she said: "However, there's always something to spoil one's pleasure, and I don't scruple to own to *you*, Miss Trent, that the way his lordship looks at Tiffany has put me in a regular fidget! Mark me if we don't have him sitting in her pocket now, for anyone can see he's nutty upon her!"

This was undeniable. Miss Trent thought it would have been wonderful if he had not been looking at Tiffany with that glow of admiration in his eyes; for Tiffany, always responsive to flattery, was at her most radiant: a delicate flush in her cheeks, her eyes sparkling like sapphires, and a lovely, provocative smile on her lips. Half-a-dozen young gentlemen had begged for the honour of leading her into the first set; she had scattered promises amongst them, and had bestowed her hand on Lord Lindeth, taking her place with him while three less fortunate damsels were still unprovided with partners. But that was a circumstance she was unlikely to notice.

"Miss Trent, if he thinks to stand up with her more than twice that's something I won't allow!" said Mrs Underhill suddenly. "You must tell her she's not to do so, for she'll pay no heed to me, and it's you her uncle looked to, after all!"

Ancilla smiled, but said: "She wouldn't flout you publicly, ma'am. I'll take care, of course—but I fancy Lord Lindeth won't ask her for a third dance."

"Lord, my dear, what he'd like to do is to stand up with her for *every* dance!"

"Yes, but he knows he can't do so, and has too much propriety of taste, I'm persuaded, to make the attempt. And, to own the truth, ma'am, I think Tiffany wouldn't grant him more than two dances in any event."

"Tiffany?" exclaimed Mrs Underhill incredulously. "Why, she's got no more notion of propriety than the kitchen cat!"

"No, alas! But she is a most accomplished flirt, ma'am!" She could not help laughing at Mrs. Underhill's face of horror. "I beg your pardon! Of course it is very wrong—shockingly precocious, too!—but you will own that a mere flirtation with Lindeth need not throw you into a quake."

"Yes, but he's a lord!" objected Mrs. Underhill. "You know how she says she means to marry one!"

"We must convince her that she would be throwing herself away on anyone under the rank of a Viscount!" said Ancilla lightly.

The dance came to an end, and she soon had the satisfaction of seeing that she had prophesied correctly: Tiffany stood up for the next one with Arthur Mickleby, and went on to dance the boulanger with Jack Banningham. Lord Lindeth, meanwhile, did his duty by Miss Colebatch and Miss Chartley; and Miss Trent extricated Charlotte from a group of slightly noisy young people, and inexorably bore her off to bed. Charlotte thought herself abominably ill-used to be compelled to withdraw before supper: she had been looking forward to drinking her very first glass of champagne. Miss Trent, barely repressing a shudder, handed her over to her old nurse, and returned to the drawing-room.

She entered it to find that the musicians were enjoying a respite. She could not see Mrs Underhill, and guessed that she had gone into the adjoining saloon, where some of the more elderly guests were playing whist. Nor could she see Tiffany: a circumstance which filled her with foreboding. Just as she had realized that Lindeth was another absentee, and was wondering where first to search for them, a voice spoke at her elbow.

"Looking for your other charge, Miss Trent?"

She turned her head quickly, to find that Sir Waldo was somewhat quizzically regarding her. He flicked open his snuff-box with one deft finger, and helped himself to a delicate pinch. "On the terrace," he said.

"Oh, no!" she said involuntarily.

"Well, of course, they may have been tempted to take a stroll about the gardens," he conceded. "The terrace, however, was the declared objective."

"I collect it was Lord Lindeth who took her on to the terrace!"

"Do you? *My* reading of the matter was that it was rather Miss Wield who took Lindeth on to it!"

She bit her lip. "She is very young—hardly out of the schoolroom!"

"A reflection which must cause her relations to feel grave concern," he said, in a tone of affable agreement.

She found herself to be so much in accord with him that it was difficult to think of anything to say in extenuation of Tiffany's conduct. "She—she is inclined to be headstrong, and quite ignorant of—of—— And since it was your cousin who *most* improperly escorted her I think you should have prevented him!"

"My dear Miss Trent, I'm not Lindeth's keeper! I'm not Miss Wield's keeper either, I thank God!"

"You may well!" she said, with considerable asperity.

Then, as she saw the amusement in his face, she added: "Yes, you may laugh, sir, but I *am* Miss Wield's keeper—or, at any rate, I am responsible for her!—and it's no laughing matter to me! I must *do* something!"

She looked round the room as she spoke, a furrow between her brows. It was a warm June night, and the drawing-room was hot and airless. More than one unbecomingly flushed young lady was fanning herself, and several shirt-points were beginning to wilt. Miss Trent's brow cleared; she went up to a little group which included Miss Chartley, the dashing Miss Colebatch, and the younger of the Squire's daughters, with their attendant swains, and said, with her charming smile: "Dreadfully hot, isn't it? I dare not open the windows: you know what an outcry there would be! Would you like to come out for a little while? It is such a beautiful moonlight night, with not a breeze stirring, that I have ventured to direct the servants to bring some lemonade on to the terrace. But you must put on your shawls, mind!"

The suggestion was thankfully acclaimed by the gentlemen, and by the Squire's jolly daughter, who clapped her hands together, exclaiming: "Oh, famous fun! Do let us go!" Miss Chartley, wondering what Mama would say, looked a little doubtful, but decided that if Miss Trent was sponsoring this interlude it must be unexceptionable; and in a very few minutes that resourceful lady had assembled some four or five couples, dropped an urgent word in Totton's astonished ear, and had informed several matrons, with smiling assurance, that she had yielded to the persuasions of their various offspring, and was permitting them (under her chaperonage) to take a turn on the terrace, before resuming their exertions on the floor. She would take good care that none of the young ladies caught chills; and, indeed, must hurry away to be sure that they had put on their shawls.

Sir Waldo was an appreciative spectator of this talented performance; and when Miss Trent, having shepherded her flock on to the terrace, was about to follow them, she found him once more at her elbow, smiling at her in a way which was oddly disturbing. "Well done!" he said, holding back the heavy curtain that hung beside the long window of the saloon that gave on to the terrace.

"Thank you! I hope it may answer, but I'm afraid it will be thought very odd conduct in a respectable governess," she replied, passing out into the moonlight.

"Not at all: you carried it off to admiration," he said, following her. He raised his quizzing-glass, and through it scanned the scene. "I realize, of course, that if the truants have gone farther afield it will be my unenviable task to discover them, and——No, they have not been so imprudent. How fortunate! Now we may both be easy!"

"Yes, indeed!" she responded, with the utmost cordiality. "I was shocked to see you in *such* a worry, sir!"

He laughed, but before he could answer her she had stepped away from him to put a scarf round Tiffany's shoulders. Courtenay, who had been awaiting his moment, seized the opportunity afforded by the Nonesuch's being alone for the first time during the evening to approach him, asking very respectfully if he might procure a glass of champagne for him. He then added, in case the great man should snub him for presuming to address him: "I'm Underhill, you know, sir!"

Sir Waldo declined the champagne, but in a friendly manner which gave the lie to Mr. Jack Banningham, who had prophesied that any attempt on Courtenay's part to engage him in conversation would be met with a severe setdown. He said: "We met at the Manor, didn't we? I rather fancy I saw you on the Harrogate road the other day, driving a well ribbed-up bay."

No more encouragement was needed. Within a very few minutes Courtenay was subjecting him to a stringent cross-examination on his real and imagined exploits. He bore it very well, but interrupted at last to say: "But must you throw *all* my youthful follies in my face? I thought I had lived them down!"

Courtenay was shocked; but Miss Trent, standing within earshot, felt that her first favourable impression of the Nonesuch had not been entirely erroneous.

CHAPTER VI

IT HAD BEEN MRS MICKLEBY who had first had the honour of entertaining the Nonesuch and his cousin; but it was generally acknowledged that the event which started the succession of gaieties which made that summer memorable was Mrs Underhill's informal ball. Hostesses who had previously vied with one another only in the mildest ways became suddenly imbued with the spirit of fierce competition; and the invitation cards which showered upon the district promised treats which ranged from turtle-dinners to Venetian breakfasts. Assemblies and picnics became everyday occurrences, even Mrs Chartley succumbing to the prevailing rage, and organizing a select party to partake of an al fresco meal by the ruins of Kirkstall Abbey. This unpretentious expedition achieved a greater degree of success than attended many of the more resplendent entertainments which enlivened the month; for not only did the skies smile upon it, but the Nonesuch graced it with his presence. Mrs Banningham, whose daring Cotillion Ball had fallen sadly flat, for many days found it hard to meet the Rector's wife with even the semblance of cordiality; and it was no consolation to know that she had only herself to blame for the failure of a party designed to outshine all others. She was imprudent enough to exclude the Staples family from the ball, informing her dear friend, Mrs Syston, (in the strictest confidence) that Tiffany Wield should be given no opportunity to flirt with Lord Lindeth under her roof. Mrs Syston told no one the secret, except Mrs Winkleigh, whom she felt sure she could trust not to repeat it; but in some mysterious way Mrs Underhill got wind of Mrs Banningham's fell intention, and nipped in with some invitations of her own before ever Mrs Banningham's gilt-edged cards had been procured from Leeds. One of the under-grooms was sent off with a note to Sir Waldo Hawkridge, inviting him and his cousin to dine at Staples on the fatal day; and no sooner had his acceptance been received than the Chartleys and the Colebatches were also bidden to dine. Not a party, wrote Mrs Underhill to all these persons: just a conversable evening with a few friends.

"And if that don't take Mrs B. at fault, you may call me a wetgoose!" she told Miss Trent. "Done to a cow's thumb, that's what she'll be! She and her Cotillion Balls!"

Great was Mrs Banningham's chagrin when she received Sir Waldo's polite regrets; and greater still her rage when she discovered that all the absentees had been at Staples, eating dinner on the terrace, and then, when the light began to fail, going indoors, either to chat, or to play such childish games as Crossquestions, and Jackstraws. Her own party had been

65

distinguished by a certain languor. Everyone had been disappointed by the absence of the Nonesuch; and if the ladies were glad to find Tiffany absent, almost all the younger gentlemen, including Mrs Banningham's son Jack, considered any ball at which she was not present an intolerable bore. Mrs. Banningham was even denied the solace of picturing the Nonesuch's boredom at Staples, for Courtenay told Jack that the party had not broken up till past midnight, and that when it came to playing Jackstraws the Nonesuch had them all beat to flinders, even Miss Trent, who had such deft fingers. It seemed that he had challenged Miss Trent to a match, when he discovered how good she was at the game. Capital sport it had been, too, with Sir Ralph Colebatch offering odds on Miss Trent, and even the Rector wagering a coachwheel on the issue. Mrs Banningham could not delude herself, or anyone else, into thinking that the Nonesuch had been bored.

He had not been at all bored; nor had Julian found it difficult to persuade him to accept Mrs Underhill's invitation. The Nonesuch, who had meant to spend no more time in Yorkshire than might be necessary for setting in train certain repairs and alterations to Broom Hall, was lingering on, and under conditions of some discomfort, since the builders were already at work in the house. He had his own reasons for remaining; but if he could have placed the slightest dependance on Julian's going back with him to London he would have subordinated these (temporarily, at all events), for the sake of conveying that besotted young man out of danger. But when he had thrown out a feeler Julian had said, with studied airiness: "Do you know, I rather fancy I shall remove to Harrogate for a while, if you mean to go back to London? I like Yorkshire, and I've made certain engagements—and more than half promised to go with Edward Banningham to some races next month."

So he remained at Broom Hall, steering an intricate course between his own interests and Julian's. His trusting young cousin would have been astonished, and deeply shocked, had he known that Waldo's lazy complaisance masked a grim determination to thrust a spoke into the wheel of his courtship. His allegiance to Waldo was too strong to be easily shaken; he did not for a moment wish him otherwhere; but he was often troubled by vague discomfort; and although Waldo had not uttered a word in her dispraise he could not rid himself of the suspicion that he regarded Tiffany a little contemptuously, and too often treated her as though she had been an importunate child, to be tolerated but given a few salutory set-downs. And then, having infuriated her, he would relent, charming her out of her sullens with his glinting smile, and a word or two spoken in a voice that held a tantalizing mixture of amusement and admiration. Even Julian could not decide whether he was sincere, or merely mocking; Julian only knew that Tiffany was never at her best when he was present. He thought that perhaps she too felt that Waldo did not like her, which made her nervous and selfconscious. And when you were very young, and shy, and anxious to make a good impression on someone of whom you stood in awe it was fatally easy to behave like a show-off character in your efforts to conceal your shyness. It did not occur to Julian that there was not a particle of shyness in Tiffany's nature; still less that Waldo was deliberately provoking her to betray the least amiable side of her disposition.

But Sir Waldo, with fifteen years' experience at his back, had taken Tiffany's measure almost at a glance. It was not his custom to trifle with the affections of fledglings, but within a week of having made Tiffany's acquaintance he set himself, without compunction, to the task of intriguing her to the point of pursuing him in preference to Julian. He had had too many lures cast out to him not to recognize the signs of a lady desirous of engaging his interest; and he knew that for some reason beyond his understanding he possessed the wholly unwanted gift of inspiring débutantes with romantic but misplaced tendres for him. He had been on his guard ever since he had been (as he had supposed) paternally kind to the niece of an old friend. She had tumbled into love with him; and from this embarrassing situation he had learnt also to recognize the signs of a maiden on the verge of losing her heart to him. Since he had nothing but contempt for the man of the world who amused himself at the expense of a pretty girl's sensibility, it was his practice to discourage any such tendency. Had he detected in Tiffany the least indication of a romantic disposition he would have adhered to his rule; but he saw nothing in her but a determination to add his name to the roll of her conquests, and strongly doubted that she had a heart to lose. If he was wrong, he thought, cynically, that it would do her no harm to experience some of the pangs of unrequited love with which her numerous suitors were afflicted. He believed her to be as selfish as she was conceited;

67

and, while it was possible that time might improve her, he was persuaded that neither her disposition nor her breeding made her an eligible wife for young Lord Lindeth.

He had told Miss Trent that he was not Lindeth's keeper, and that, in the strictest sense, was true. Julian's father had left him to the guardianship of his mother, and had appointed two middle-aged legal gentlemen as his trustees; but Sir Waldo's shrewd Aunt Sophia had enlisted his aid in rearing the noble orphan at a very early stage in Julian's career, and he had progressed, by imperceptible degrees, from the splendid cousin who initiated his protégé into every manly form of sport (besides sending him guineas under the seals of his occasional letters, and from time to time descending in a blaze of real dapper-dog magnificence on Eton, driving a team of sixteen-mile-an-hour tits, and treating half-a-dozen of his cousin's cons to such sock as made them the envy of every Oppidan and Tug in the College) to the social mentor who introduced Julian into select circles, and steered him past the shoals in which many a green navigator had wallowed and foundered. He had come to regard Julian as his especial charge; and although Julian's years now numbered three-and-twenty he still so regarded him: Lady Lindeth could not blame him more than he would blame himself if he allowed Julian to be trapped into a disastrous marriage without raising a finger to prevent it.

To cut out a young cousin who reposed complete trust in him might go very much against the pluck with him, but it presented few difficulties to a man of his address and experience. Indulged almost from the hour of her birth; endowed not only with beauty but with a considerable independance as well; encouraged to think herself a matrimonial prize of the first stare, Tiffany had come to regard every unattached man's homage as her due. Sir Waldo had watched her at the Staples ball, playing off her cajolery in an attempt to attach Humphrey Colebatch; and he had not the smallest doubt that she did it only because that scholarly but unprepossessing youth was patently impervious to her charms. He was well aware, too, that while she would look upon her own capture as a resounding triumph he ranked in her eyes amongst the graybeards who had outlived the age of gallantry. There had been speculation, and a hint of doubt, in the swift glance she had first thrown him. She had certainly set her cap at him, but he could have nipped her tentative advances in the bud with the utmost ease. He would have done it had he not seen the glow in Julian's eyes as they rested on her ravishing countenance, and realized that that guileless young man was wholly dazzled.

Sir Waldo was neither dazzled by Tiffany's beauty, nor so stupid as to suppose that any good purpose would be served by his pointing out to Julian those defects in the lovely creature which were perfectly plain to him, but to which Julian was obviously blind. But Julian, under his compliance, had a sensibility, and a delicacy of principle, to which virtues Sir Waldo judged Tiffany to be a stranger; and nothing could more effectually cool his ardour than the discovery that in their stead she had vanity, and a sublime disregard for the comfort or the susceptibilities of anyone but herself. Julian might ignore, and indignantly resent, warnings uttered by even so revered a mentor as his Top-of-the-Trees cousin, but he would not disbelieve the evidence of his own eyes. So the Nonesuch, instead of damping the beautiful Miss Wield's pretensions, blew hot and cold on her, encouraging her one day to believe that she had awakened his interest, and the next devoting himself to some other lady. He paid her occasional compliments, but was just as likely to utter a lazy set-down; and when he engaged her in a little mild flirtation he did it so lightly that she could never be quite sure that he was not merely being playful, in the manner of a man amusing a child. She had not previously encountered his like, for her admirers were all much younger men, quite lacking in subtlety. Either they languished for love of her, or (like Humphrey Colebatch) paid no attention to her at all. But the Nonesuch, by turns fascinating and detestable, was maddingly elusive; and so far from showing a disposition to languish he laughed at her suitors, and said that they were making great cakes of themselves. Tiffany took that as an insult, and determined to bring him to her feet. He saw the flash of anger in her eyes, and smiled. "No, no! You'd be gapped, you know."

"I don't know what you mean!"

"Why, that you're wondering whether you might not make *me* a great cake. I shouldn't attempt it, if I were you: I never dangle—not even after quite pretty girls."

"*Quite pretty——?*" she gasped. "*M-me?*"

"Oh, decidedly!" he said, perfectly gravely. "Or so I think, but, then, I've no prejudice against dark girls. I daresay others might not agree with me."

"They do!" she asserted, pink with indignation. "They say —*everyone* says I'm *beautiful!*"

He managed to preserve his countenance, but his lips twitched slightly. "Yes, of course," he replied. "It's well known that *all heiresses are beautiful!*"

She stared up at him incredulously. "But—don't you think I'm beautiful?"

"Very!"

"Well, I know I am," she said candidly. "Ancilla thinks I shouldn't say so—and I meant not to, on account of losing some of my beauty when I do. At least, that's what Ancilla said, but I don't see how it could be so, do you?"

"No, indeed: quite absurd! You do very right to mention the matter."

She thought this over, darkly suspicious, and finally demanded: "Why?"

"People are so unobservant!" he answered in dulcet accents.

She broke into a trill of delicious laughter. "Oh, abominable! You are the *horridest* creature! I'll have no more to do with you!"

He waved a careless farewell as she flitted away, but he thought privately that when she forgot her affectations, and laughed out suddenly, acknowledging a hit, she was disastrously engaging.

Miss Trent, who had approached them in time to hear these last sallies, observed in a dispassionate voice: *"Quite abominable!"*

He smiled, his eyes dwelling appreciatively on her. She was always very simply attired; but she wore the inexpensive muslins and cambrics which she fashioned for herself with an air of elegance; and never had he seen her, even on the hottest day, presenting anything but a cool and uncrumpled appearance.

Sir Waldo, having cleared up one small misunderstanding, had contrived to get upon excellent terms with Miss Trent. His ear had been quick to catch the note of constraint in her voice when she had asked him if he was acquainted with her cousin; he fancied that she was pleased when he disclaimed any knowledge of Mr Bernard Trent; and he presently sought enlightenment of Julian.

"Bernard Trent?" said Julian. "No, I don't think—oh, yes, I do, though! You mean General Trent's son, don't you? I've only seen him by scraps: the sort of cawker who talks flash, and is buckish about horses!" He broke off, as a thought occurred to him, and exclaimed: "Good God, is he related to Miss Trent?"

"Her cousin, I collect."

"Lord! Well, he's the greatest gull that ever was!" said Julian frankly. "Crony of Mountsorrel's—at Harrow together, I fancy—and you know what a Peep o' Day boy *he* is, Waldo! Always kicking up larks, and thinking himself at home to a peg, which the lord knows he ain't, and going about town accompanied by the worst barnacles you ever clapped eyes on!"

"Yes, I know young Mountsorrel: one of the newer Tulips!"

"Tulips!" snorted Julian, with all the scorn of one who had been introduced, at his first coming-out, into the pink of Corinthian society. "Smatterers, more like! A set of roly-poly fellows who think it makes them regular dashes to box the Watch, or get swine-drunk at the Field of Blood! And as for being of the Corinthian-cut—why, most of 'em ain't even fit to go!"

"You're very severe!" said Sir Waldo, amused.

"Well, it was you who taught me to be!" Julian retorted. "Mountsorrel is nothing but a cod's head, I own, but only think of the ramshackle fellows he's in a string with! There's Watchett, for instance: he wears more capes to his driving-coat than you do, but you'll none of you admit him to the Four-Horse Club! Stone, too! *His* notion of sport is bull-baiting, and going on the spree in Tothill Fields. Then there's Elstead: he knocks-up more horses in a season than you would in a lifetime, and flies at anything in the shape of gaming. Thinks himself slap up to the echo. Why, when were you ever seen rubbing shoulders in one of the Pall Mall hells with a set of Greek banditti?"

"Is that what young Trent does?"

"I don't know: not a friend of mine. I haven't seen him lately: rusticating, I daresay. He didn't look to me like a downy one, so you may depend upon it he found himself in Tow Street."

Armed with this information, Sir Waldo very soon found the opportunity to set himself right with Miss Trent. Wasting no subtlety, he told her cheerfully that she had misjudged him.

They were riding side by side, Julian and Tiffany a little way ahead. Mrs Underhill felt herself powerless to prevent the almost daily rides of this couple, but she did insist on Ancilla's accompanying them, and was sometimes able to persuade her son to join the party. Occasionally Patience Chartley went with them; and, quite frequently, Sir Waldo.

Ancilla turned her head to look at him, raising her brows. "In what way, sir?"

"In laying your cousin's follies at my door." He smiled at her startled look, and betraying flush. "What happened to him? Lindeth tells me he's in a string with young Mountsorrel, and his set."

"He was used to be—he and Lord Mountsorrel were at school together—but no longer, I hope. His connection with him was ruinous."

"Ran into Dun territory, did he? The younger men don't come much in my way, but I've always understood that Mountsorrel has more money than sense, which makes him dangerous company for other greenhorns. Too many gull-catchers hang about him—not to mention the Bloods, and the Dashers, and the Care-for-Nobodies."

"Yes. My uncle said that, or something like it. But indeed I never laid Bernard's follies at your door, sir!"

"Didn't you? That's discouraging: I believed I had solved the riddle of your dislike of me."

"I don't dislike you. If—if you thought me stiff when we first met it was because I dislike the set you represent!"

"I don't think you know anything about the set I represent," he responded coolly. "Let me assure you that it is very far removed from Mountsorrel's, ma'am!"

"Of course—but you are—oh, the Nonesuch!" she said with a quick smile. "Mountsorrel and his friends copy you—as far as they are able——"

"I beg your pardon!" he interrupted. "They don't—being unable! Dear me, I sound just like the Beautiful Miss Wield, don't I? Some of them copy the Corinthian rig—in the exaggerated form I don't affect; but my set, Miss Trent, is composed of men who were born with a natural aptitude for athletic sports. We do the thing; Mountsorrel, and his kind, are lookers-on. Don't ask me why they should ape our fashions, when there is nothing more distasteful to them, I daresay, than the sports we enjoy, for I can't tell you! But you may believe that the youngster anxious to excel in sporting exercises is safer amongst the Corinthians than amongst the Bond Street beaux."

"Ah, yes, but—does it not lead to more dangerous things? To gaming, for instance?"

"Gaming, Miss Trent, is not confined to any one class of society," he said dryly. "It won't lead him to haunt the wine-shops in Tothill Fields, to wake the night-music, or to pursue the—er—West-end comets, to his destruction." He laughed suddenly. "You foolish girl! Don't you know that if he did so it would be bellows to mend with him within five minutes of his engaging in a little sparring exercise at Jackson's?"

"To own the truth, I had never considered the matter," she confessed. "Though I do recall, now you put me in mind of it, that whenever my brother Harry was engaged to play in a cricket-match, or some such thing, he was used to take the greatest pains not to put himself out of frame, as he called it."

"Wise youth! Is he too a budding Corinthian?"

"Oh, no! He is a soldier."

"Like your uncle!"

"Yes, and my father, too."

"Indeed? Tell me about him! Was he engaged at Waterloo?"

"Yes—that is, my brother was, but not my father. My father was killed at Ciudad Rodrigo."

"I am sorry." his tone was grave; but he did not pursue the subject, asking her instead, after a moment or two, if her brother was with the Army of Occupation. She was grateful to him for respecting her reserve, and answered far more readily than she might have done. She seldom mentioned her family, for Mrs Underhill was interested only in the General; and although Mrs Chartley sometimes enquired kindly after her mother, and her brothers, she rarely allowed herself to be lured into giving more than civil responses, feeling that Mrs Chartley could have little interest in persons with whom she was unacquainted.

Sir Waldo was much more successful in winning her out of her reticence; and it was not many days before he knew more about Miss Trent's family than Mrs Chartley, preoccupied with her own family and her husband's parish, had even guessed. He knew that Will—the best of all sons and brothers!—was the incumbent of a parish in Derbyshire, and already the father of a hopeful family. He had married the daughter of one of Papa's oldest friends, a dear, good girl, beloved of them all. Mama and Sally lived with him and Mary, and in the greatest harmony. Sally was the youngest of the family: only a schoolroom child yet, but already remarkably accomplished, and bidding fair to become a very pretty girl. Christopher joined them during the holidays, except when his uncle invited him to stay in London, and indulged him with all manner of high treats, from snipe-shooting in Regent's Park, or skating on the Serpentine, to Astley's Amphitheatre, and pugilistic displays at the Fives Court. Uncle Mordaunt had taken upon his shoulders the whole charge of Kit's education at Harrow. Nothing could exceed Uncle Mordaunt's goodness and generosity: in spite of possessing a fortune that was genteel rather than handsome he had been almost at outs with them all for refusing to live upon his bounty! But with Will so comfortably situated; and Harry now able (since he got his Company) to contribute towards the family funds; and Mama teaching Sally herself, which she was well qualified to do, being the daughter of a Professor of Greek, and (as they told her when they wanted to joke her) very *blue*! it would be shocking to be so much beholden.

"And the elder Miss Trent, I collect, doesn't choose to be in any way beholden?"

"No more than I need. But you mustn't suppose that I am not already very much obliged to my uncle and aunt, if you please! My aunt was so kind as to bring me out, as the saying is—and to spare no pains to get me eligibly riveted!" she added, a gurgle of laughter in her throat, "She had a strong persuasion that even though I've no fortune a respectable alliance might have been achieved for me would I but *apply* myself to the business! Oh, dear! I ought not to laugh at her, for she bore with me most patiently, but she *is* such a funny one!"

His eyes gleamed appreciatively, but he said: "Poor lady! Were you never tempted to apply yourself?"

"No, I was always old cattish," she replied cheerfully.

"Were you indeed? Did you remain with your uncle for only one season?"

She nodded. "Yes, but pray don't imagine that I might not have stayed had I wished to do so! To have done so when he has three daughters of his own to bring out would have been rather too strong, I thought—particularly when Bernard had got so shockingly into debt."

"So you became a governess! Not without opposition, I should suppose!"

"Oh, no! Will and Harry made a great dust, and even Mary said she took it very unkind in me not to wish to live at their expense. They all pictured me eking out a miserable ex-

74

istence on a pittance—and used as if I had been a slave into the bargain! The only comfort they could find was in the thought that I could return to them if I found my lot insupportable."

"Have you never done so?" he asked, looking rather searchingly at her.

"No, never. No doubt I might have done so, but I've been singularly fortunate. Miss Climping, dear creature, treated me as though I had been her niece rather than the junior mistress; and it was she who recommended me to Mrs Burford, to take charge of Tiffany."

"Good God, do you count that good fortune?"

"Most certainly I do! My dear sir, if I were to tell you what an enormous wage I'm paid it would make you stare!"

"I know very little about such matters, but I seem to have heard that an upper man can command a bigger wage than a governess."

"Ah, but I am a very superior governess!" she said, putting on an air of large consequence. "Only fancy! Besides such commonplace subjects as water-colour sketching and the use of the globes, I instruct my pupils in music—both pianoforte and harp; and can speak and read French *and* Italian!"

"I have no doubt at all that you earn every penny of your hire," he said, smiling.

She laughed. "The mischief is that I don't! My conscience pricks me very often, I promise you, for Charlotte has neither inclination nor aptitude; and Tiffany will do no more than commit to memory the words of an Italian song. I've convinced her that *some* skill on the pianoforte is an indispensable accomplishment for a lady with social ambitions; but nothing will prevail upon her to play the harp. She complains that it breaks her nails, and says that it is better to have pretty nails than to be able to perform upon the harp."

"I still maintain that you earn your hire, ma'am!"

He was thinking of this interchange when she joined him on the terrace, saying: *"Quite* abominable!" He was well aware by this time that her position was far more that of guardian than governess; and as he believed that she had too much intelligence not to have realized what was the end to which his dealings with Tiffany were directed he lived in daily expectation of being called to book. It seemed to him that Mrs Underhill viewed Julian's infatuation with complaisance. Far from demurring at his frequent visits she had begged them both to treat Staples as their own, standing upon

75

no ceremony. "For very uncomfortable it must be at Broom Hall, with builders working there, and plaster-dust in everything, as well I know it is!" she had said. "So take your pot-luck with us, Sir Waldo, whenever you fancy, and be sure you'll be very welcome!"

He said now, leading Miss Trent to one of the rustic seats on the terrace: "Very true! But do you think it will do your ravishing charge any harm to receive a few set-downs?"

"Oh, no!" she replied calmly. "I fear it won't do her any good either—but that, after all, is not your object, is it?"

He checked her, as she was about to sit down, saying: "One moment! You will have the sun in your eyes: I'll turn the seat a little."

She let him do so, but said, smiling faintly: "Trying to change the subject, sir?"

"No, no! Just sparring for wind, ma'am!"

"I imagine that to be some horrid boxing cant," she observed, seating herself. "I trust, however, that you don't think me such a ninny as to be blind to what *is* your object?"

He sat down beside her. "No, I don't," he confessed. "I'll own to you that I've been torn between the hope that you did know, and the dread of having a peal rung over me!"

If she blushed it was so slightly that he was unaware of it. She replied, ignoring the first part of his sentence: "Oh, I don't mean to scold!"

"Now you *have* surprised me!" he remarked.

"I suppose, under certain circumstances I might scold," she said thoughtfully. "But my situation is rather difficult. The thing is, you see, that Mrs Underhill doesn't wish Tiffany to marry your cousin any more than you do."

"In that case, it is a little astonishing that she should encourage Julian to run tame here," he said sceptically.

"I daresay it may seem so to you, not knowing Tiffany as well as I—we—do. I can assure you that if her mind is set on anything the least hint of opposition is enough to goad her into going her length, however outrageous that may be. And in general it *is* outrageous," she added candidly. "You will allow that an à suivie flirtation, conducted in my presence, or her aunt's, is by far less dangerous than clandestine meetings would be. For one thing, it is not so romantic; and, for another, such meetings would of necessity be infrequent, as well as brief, and that, you know, would preclude her becoming bored with Lord Lindeth."

He could not help smiling at her matter-of-factness, but he

76

said: "Yes, I will allow that, ma'am. I will even concede that the girl might prevail upon Lindeth to meet her in such a way. But when you talk of her becoming *bored* with him I think you are wide of the mark. I daresay she may be—but Lindeth would be a big prize for her to win."

She wrinkled her brow. "Well, it is very natural that you should think that, but *she* doesn't. She means to marry a Marquis."

"Means to—— Which Marquis?"

"*Any* Marquis," Ancilla replied.

"Of all the absurdities——!"

"I don't know that. When you consider that besides beauty she is possessed of a handsome fortune you must surely own that a brilliant match is by no means impossible. In any event, I beg you won't depress *that* one of her pretensions! I have suggested to her that to form a connection with a mere baron—and before she is even out!—would be perfectly bird-witted!"

He regarded her in some amusement. "Have you, indeed? What a very odd sort of governess you are, ma'am!"

"Yes, and you can't imagine what a worry I have been in, trying to decide what I ought to do in this troublesome situation," she said seriously. "I *think* I am right to scotch the affair, if I can; for while, on the one hand, the Burfords might welcome the match; on the other, Mrs Underhill would not, and Tiffany is too young to be contracted to anyone."

"Why wouldn't Mrs Underhill welcome the match?"

"Because she wants Tiffany to marry her cousin, of course."

"Good God! I should have said that the boy holds her in contempt and dislike!"

"Mrs Underwood thinks they will learn to love one another."

"Foolish beyond permission! Isn't he dangling after the pretty redhead?"

"Yes, and I should think they will make a match of it one day," she agreed. "Which would be a very good thing, for they suit wonderfully. And once Tiffany has left Staples, which will be next year, when her aunt Burford is pledged to bring her out, Mrs Underhill will very soon become reconciled. In the meantime, I do believe it to be my duty to do my possible to keep Tiffany quite—quite unattached!" She smiled kindly upon him, and added: "So I am very grateful to you for your assistance, Sir Waldo!"

"Even though—if the little minx has made up her mind to marry a Marquis!—it must be thought superfluous!"

"Oh, no! We can't foretell what *might* happen, you know. Tiffany is only a precocious child, and although she may indulge dreams of grandeur she doesn't *scheme*. Would you care to say that she won't take just enough fancy to Lord Lindeth to imagine herself in love? I promise you I wouldn't! He is very goodlooking, you know, besides having such engaging manners! Indeed, I am more than half in love with him myself!"

"Now, that I utterly forbid!" he declared.

She laughed. "I should rather think you might! I must be several years his senior. But in all seriousness, sir, a marriage between him and Tiffany would not do!"

"I am well aware of it."

"Even if her birth matched his!" she said earnestly. "It must seem shocking in me to say such a thing of her, but I feel it would be quite wicked of me not to put you on your guard!"

"You believe it to be necessary?"

"I don't know. I've seen how she can bring people round her thumb, and how charming she can be, when she chooses. But she hasn't a particle of that sweetness of disposition which is in your cousin, and nothing but misery could be the outcome of a marriage between them!"

"Let me assure you, ma'am, since you seem to think I might succumb to her wiles, that my taste runs to females of quite another complexion!"

"I am glad of it," she said, thinking, however, that he might well be courting more danger than he was yet aware of.

"That's the kindest thing you have yet said to me," he murmured.

She glanced at him, a puzzled expression in her eyes. They met his, and saw that they were quizzically smiling; and the suspicion flashed into her mind that he was trying to beguile her into flirtation. It was swiftly succeeded by the startling realization that she could very easily be so beguiled. That would never do, of course; so she said lightly: "I should be sorry to see anyone in Tiffany's toils. Which puts me in mind of something I had to say to you! Tell me, Sir Waldo, what do you think of this proposed expedition to Knaresborough?"

"Too far, and the weather too sultry," he replied, tacitly

accepting her rebuff. He thought she sighed faintly, and said: "Do you wish for it, then?"

"I own I should like to go, if it were possible. Your cousin's description of the Dripping Well made me long to see it. Tiffany, too. No sooner had Lord Lindeth told us of the wild, ragged rocks, and the cavern which was once the lair of bandits than she became mad after it!"

He smiled. *"Mysteries of Udolpho?"*

"Naturally! And I must own that it sounds most romantic. Isn't it odd that it should be Lord Lindeth, a stranger to the district, who should have told us about it?"

"Oh, no! Natives are never enraptured by their surroundings. *Over great familiarity*, you know, *genders despite*."

"Very true. I wish it were not too far to make an expedition eligible. I had not thought it about sixteen miles."

"Which would mean a ride of thirty-two miles."

"Nothing of the sort! Two rides of sixteen miles, with a long rest between for repose and refreshment! That's a very different matter."

"Out again, Miss Trent! Refreshment, certainly; but instead of reposing yourself you would spend your time clambering up rocky crags, and exploring caverns. Why don't you go by carriage, if go you must?"

"Because nothing would prevail upon Tiffany to sit beside me in a carriage, driving sedately along the road when she might be on horseback, enjoying a canter over the moor. To be honest with you, I should think it sadly flat myself! Do you picture us being quite knocked up? I know my own powers, and as for Tiffany, she is the most indefatigable girl imaginable. However, it *is* very hot, so I'll say no more."

"*You* may say no more, but if the Beautiful Baggage is indeed mad after it there will be not the least need for you to do so, will there?"

She choked, but replied awfully: "Sir Waldo, you go too far! Besides, you have only to drop a word in your cousin's ear to make him cry off, which will end the matter."

"My dear Miss Trent, if it would give you pleasure to go I withdraw my objection. In fact, I'll accompany you."

There could be no denying that it was very agreeable to be talked to in such a manner. Miss Trent was no self-deceiver, and she did not deny it; but she was uneasily aware of running the risk of forming far too strong an attachment to the Nonesuch. Commonsense told her that he was merely alleviating boredom with a little dalliance, probably thinking (for she was persuaded he would not wantonly trifle with any female's affections) that she was past the age of being taken in by his light advances; but although there was often a laugh in his eyes there was also a certain warmth, and, in his voice, a note of sincerity hard to withstand. She remembered that her aunt had told her once, in a moment of exasperation, that she was a great deal too nice in her requirements; and she thought, wryly, that poor Lady Trent had spoken more truly than she knew, and would have been as much surprised as dismayed to have learnt that her provoking niece, having repulsed two very eligible suitors, had discovered that no less a personage than the Nonesuch would do for her.

It would be fatal to indulge a tendre for him; and the wisest course to pursue would be to avoid his company; but as this, in the circumstances, was impossible, the next best thing would be to maintain a cool friendliness. So she said, with all the composure at her command: "Yes, it would be prudent in you to do so, no doubt. *Your* presence will divert Tiffany far more surely than mine."

"Oh, I've another reason than that!" he said.

She put up her brows, saying frigidly: "Indeed?"

The disarming twinkle was in his eyes. "Four is a more comfortable number than three, don't you think?" he suggested blandly.

She agreed to it, but with a quivering lip. Sir Waldo, duly noting this circumstance, continued to expatiate on the advantages of adding a second gentleman to the expedition, producing several which made it quite impossible for Miss Trent to keep her countenance. He was interrupted in this unchivalrous assault upon her defences by the reappearance on the scene of Tiffany, who came dancing out on to the terrace with Julian and Courtenay at her heels, and disclosed that the party of four had become a party of six.

"We have settled it between us to go to Knaresborough on Friday!" she announced, sparkling with delight. "It is to be a regular cavalcade, which will be such good fun! Lizzie Colebatch is to go with us, and Courtenay too, of course. And you, Sir Waldo—if you please?"

It was said so prettily, and with such an appealing smile, that he thought it no wonder that Julian should watch her in blatant admiration. He replied: "Thank you: I do please!"

"Miss Colebatch!" Ancilla exclaimed, taken aback.

"Tiffany, I don't think Lady Colebatch will permit her to go!"

"Yes, yes, she will!" Tiffany asserted, with a trill of laughter. "Lindeth and Courtenay have persuaded her, promising that *you* will be with us, you dear dragon!"

"Yes, but that's not what I mean," said Ancilla. "Miss Colebatch dislikes the hot weather so much that I should have thought her mama must have forbidden her to go on such an expedition. Does she perfectly understand where it is you mean to go?"

She was reassured on this point; but although Lady Colebatch's sanction made it improper for her to raise any further objection she could not feel at ease. Lady Colebatch was an indolent, good-natured woman who was much inclined to let her children overrule her judgment, but Ancilla knew how quickly Elizabeth wilted in the heat, and began to wish that the expedition had never been projected. Courtenay was confident that all would be well, for they meant to make an early start, so that they would have reached Knaresborough long before midday; and Tiffany said gaily that Lizzie only disliked the heat because it made her skin so red.

The three younger members of the party then began to discuss the route they should follow, the hour at which they should assemble, and the rival merits of the various inns in Knaresborough, Julian inviting the company to partake of a nuncheon at the Crown and Bell, and Courtenay asserting that the Bay Horse was superior.

"Well, as you wish!" Julian said. "You must know better than I do! Shall we ask Miss Chartley to go with us? Would she care for it?"

"Patience! Good gracious, no!" exclaimed Tiffany. "What put such a notion as that into your head?"

"You don't think she would like it? But she's an excellent horsewoman, and I know she loves exploring ancient places, for she told me so."

"Told you so? When?" demanded Tiffany.

"At Kirkstall, when we were wandering about the ruins. She knows almost as much as her father—do let us invite her to go with us!"

Miss Trent found herself digging her nails into the palms of her hands. It was irrational, but little as she wanted Tiffany to captivate Lindeth she could not help dreading the threatened tantrum. Since Courtenay was the one marriageable man whose devotion Tiffany neither desired nor demanded she was perfectly happy to include Miss Colebatch in the party, but that any one of her admirers should betray even the smallest interest in another lady invariably roused a demon of jealousy in her breast. She said now, with a glittering smile, well-known to her family: "Why? Do you like her so much?"

He looked at her in a little surprise. "Yes—that is, I *like* her, of course! I should think everyone must."

"Oh, if you have a fancy for insipid girls——!" she said, shrugging.

"Do you think her insipid?" he asked. "She doesn't seem so to me. She is very gentle, and persuadable, I agree, but not *insipid*, surely! She doesn't want for sense, you know."

"Oh, she has *every* virtue and *every* amiable quality! For my part, I find her prosy propriety a dead bore—but that's of no consequence! Do, pray, invite her! I daresay she will be able to recite you the whole history of the Dripping Well!"

Even Julian could not mistake the rancour behind the smile. Miss Trent saw the slight look of shock in his face, and decided that she could not bear to hear her charge expose herself any more. She said quietly: "I am afraid it would be useless to invite Miss Chartley, sir. I know that Mrs Chartley wouldn't permit her to go with us on such a long, fatiguing expedition. Indeed, I begin to wonder whether we should any of us attempt it."

This alarming apostasy caused an instant throw-up. Miss Chartley was forgotten in the more urgent necessity of alternately abusing Miss Trent for chickenheartedness, and cajoling her into unsaying her words. But before he left Staples Julian had received from Tiffany an explanation of her spiteful outburst which quite cleared the cloud from his brow. She owned her fault so contritely that he longed to take her in his arms and kiss away her troubled look. He perfectly understood how provoking it must be to have Patience Chartley held up to her continually as a model; and he thought her penitence so candid and so humble that by the time he took his leave he had not only assured her that she was not in the least to be blamed for flying into a pet, but also that he didn't care a rush whether or not Patience went with them to Knaresborough. Later, he tried to disabuse his cousin's mind of whatever unjust thoughts it might harbour: not because Waldo referred to the matter, but because it seemed to him that he carefully avoided doing so. He said rather haltingly:

"I daresay it may have seemed odd to you that Miss Wield was—that she shouldn't wish for Miss Chartley to accompany us on Friday."

"What, after such a slip-slop as you made?" said Sir Waldo, laughing. "Not in the least odd! You *did* grass yourself, didn't you? I hadn't believed you could be such a greenhorn."

Flushing, Julian said stiffly: "I don't understand what you mean! If you imagine that Miss Wield was—was cross because I wished to invite Miss Chartley—it wasn't so at all!"

"Wasn't it?" said Sir Waldo, amusement lurking beneath his too-obviously assumed gravity. "Well, take my advice, you young cawker, and never praise one woman to another!"

"You are quite mistaken!" said Julian, more stiffly than ever.

"Yes, yes, of course I am—being so green myself!" agreed Sir Waldo soothingly. "So, for God's sake, don't stir any more coals to convince me of it! I am convinced—wholly!— and I detest brangles!"

CHAPTER VII

Mr Underhill's optimistic plan of making an early start on Friday morning was not realized. He was certainly up betimes; but in spite of his having hammered on his cousin's door at an early hour, warning her to make haste, since it was going to be a scorching day, the rest of the breakfast-party, which included Sir Waldo and Lord Lindeth, had finished the handsome repast provided for them before Tiffany came floating into the parlour, artlessly enquiring whether she was late.

"Yes, you are!" growled Courtenay. "We've been waiting for you this age! What the deuce have you been about? You have had time enough to rig yourself out a dozen times!"

"That's just what she does," said Charlotte impishly. "First she puts one dress on, and decides it don't become her, and so then she tries another—don't you, cousin?"

"Well, I'm sure you look very becoming in that habit, love," interposed Mrs Underhill hastily. "Though if I was you I wouldn't choose to wear velvet, not in this weather!"

By the time Tiffany had eaten her breakfast, put on her hat to her satisfaction, and found such unaccountably mislaid articles as her gloves, and her riding-whip, the hour was considerably advanced, and Courtenay in a fret of impatience, saying that Lizzie must be supposing by now that they had forgotten all about her. However, when they reached Colby Place they found the family just getting up from the breakfast-table, and Lizzie by no means ready to set out. There was thus a further delay while Lizzie ran upstairs to complete her toilet, accompanied by her two younger sisters, who were presently heard demanding of some apparently remote person what she had done with Miss Lizzie's boots.

During this period Lindeth and Tiffany enjoyed a quiet flirtation, Sir Ralph gave the Nonesuch a long and involved account of his triumph over someone who had tried to get the better of him in a bargain, Courtenay fidgeted about the room, and Lady Colebatch prosed to Miss Trent with all the placidity of one to whom time meant nothing.

"Only two hours later than was planned," remarked Sir Waldo, when the cavalcade at last set forth. "Very good!"

Miss Trent, who had been regretting for nearly as long that she had ever expressed a wish to see the Dripping Well, replied: "I suppose it might have been expected!"

"Yes, and I did expect it," he said cheerfully.

"I wonder then that you should have lent yourself to this expedition."

"One becomes inured to the unpunctuality of your sex, ma'am," he responded.

Incensed by this unjust animadversion, she said tartly: "Let me inform you, sir, that *I* kept no one waiting!"

"But you are a very exceptional female," he pointed out.

"I assure you, I am nothing of the sort."

"I shall not allow you to be a judge of that. Oh, no, don't look at me so crossly! What can I possibly have said to vex you?"

"I beg your pardon! Nothing, of course: merely, I'm not in the mood for nonsense, Sir Waldo!"

"That's no reason for scowling at me!" he objected. "*I* haven't been boring you to death for the past half-hour! Of course, I may bore you before the day is out, but it won't be with vapid commonplaces, I promise you."

"Take care!" she warned him, glancing significantly towards Miss Colebatch, who was riding ahead of them, with Courtenay.

"Neither of them is paying the least heed to us. Do you always ride that straightshouldered cocktail?"

"Yes—Mrs Underhill having bought him for my use. He does very well for me."

"I wish I had the mounting of you. Do you hunt?"

"No. When Tiffany goes out with the hounds she is her cousin's responsibility, not mine."

"Thank God for that! You would certainly come to grief if you attempted to hunt that animal. I only hope you may not be saddle-sick before ever we reach Knaresborough."

"Indeed, so do I! I don't know why you should think me such a poor creature!"

"I don't: I think your horse a poor creature, and a most uncomfortable ride."

"Oh, no, I assure you——" She broke off, checked by a lifted eyebrow. "Well, perhaps he is not very—very easy-paced! In any event, I don't mean to argue with you about him, for I am persuaded it would be very stupid in me to do so."

"It would," he agreed. "I collect it didn't occur to your amiable charge to lend you her other hack? By the bye, what made your resolution fail the other day?"

She did not pretend to misunderstand him, but answered frankly: "I *couldn't* allow her to expose herself!"

He smiled. "Couldn't you? Never mind! I fancy she contrived to charm Lindeth out of his disapproval, but the image became just a trifle smudged, nevertheless. I added my mite later in the day—which is why I am being treated with a little reserve."

"Are you? Oh, dear, how horrid it is, and how very difficult to know what my duty is! Odious to be scheming against the child!"

"Is that what you are doing? I had no notion of it, and thought the scheming was all on my side."

"Not precisely scheming, but—but *conniving*, by allowing you to bamboozle her!"

"My dear girl, how do you imagine you could stop me?"

Miss Trent toyed with the idea of objecting to this mode of address, and then decided that it would be wiser to ignore it. "I don't know, but——"

"Nor anyone else. Don't tease yourself to no purpose! You are really quite helpless in the matter, you know."

She turned her head, gravely regarding him. "Don't you feel some compunction, Sir Waldo?"

"None at all. I should feel much more than compunction if I did not do my utmost to prevent Lindeth's falling a victim to as vain and heartless a minx as I have yet had the ill-fortune to encounter. Do I seem to you a villain? I promise you I am not!"

"No, no! But you do make her show her worst side!"

"True! Does it occur to you that if I employed such tactics against—oh, Miss Chartley—Miss Colebatch there—yourself —I should be taken completely at fault? You would none of you show a side you don't possess. What's more, ma'am, I don't *make* the chit coquet with me, or boast of her looks and her conquests to impress me: I merely offer her the opportunity to do so—and much good that would do me if she had as much elegance of mind as of person! All I should win by casting out such lures to a girl of character would be a well-deserved set-down."

She could not deny it, and rode on in silence. He saw that she was still looking rather troubled, and said: "Take comfort, you over-anxious creature! I may encourage her to betray her tantrums and her selfishness but I would no more *create* a situation to conjure up these faults than I would compromise her." He laughed suddenly. "A work of supererogation! If she could fly into a passion merely because Julian expressed a mild desire to include Miss Chartley in this party we shan't suffer from a want of such situations! Who knows! He may feel it incumbent upon him to pay a little attention to Miss Colebatch presently, in which case we shall find ourselves in the centre of a vortex!"

She was obliged to laugh, but she shuddered too, begging him not to raise such hideous spectres. "Though I've no real apprehension in this instance," she added, "Miss Colebatch is the one girl with whom Tiffany has struck up a friendship."

"Yes, I have observed that the redhead regards her with enormous admiration."

"I shall take leave to tell you, Sir Waldo," said Miss Trent severely, "that remark had better have been left unspoken!"

"It would have been, had I been talking to anyone but yourself."

Fortunately, since she could not think what to say in reply

to this, Courtenay came trotting back to them at that moment, to inform them of a slight change of plan. By skirting the cornfield that lay beyond the hedge to their right they could cut a corner, and so be the sooner out of the lane, and on to open ground, he said. The only thing was that there was no gate on the farther side: did Miss Trent feel she could jump the hedge?

"What, on that collection of bad points? Certainly not!" said Sir Waldo.

Courtenay grinned, but said: "I know, but there's nothing to it, sir! He'll brush through it easily enough—or she could *pull* him through it, if she chooses!"

"Oh, could she?" said Miss Trent, her eye kindling. "Well, she *don't* choose! By all means let us escape as soon as we may from this stuffy lane!"

"*I* knew you were a right one!" said Courtenay. "There is a gate on this side, where the others are waiting, and I'll have it open in a trice."

He wheeled his hack, and trotted off again. Miss Trent turned her fulminating gaze upon the Nonesuch, but he disarmed her by throwing up his hand in the gesture of a fencer acknowledging a hit, saying hastily: "No, no, don't snap my nose off! I cry craven!"

"So I should hope, sir!" she said, moving off in Courtenay's wake. She said over her shoulder, sudden mischief in her face: "I wish that handsome thoroughbred of yours may not make you look no-how by refusing!"

An answering gleam shone in his eyes. "You mean you wish he *may*! But I'm on my guard, and shall wait for you to show me the way!"

The hedge proved, however, to be much as Courtenay had described it, presenting no particular difficulty to even the sorriest steed, but Tiffany, who was leading the procession round the side of the field, approached it at a slapping pace, and soared over it with inches to spare. Miss Colebatch exclaimed: "Oh, one would think that lovely mare had wings! I wish I could ride like that!"

"I'm glad you *don't* ride like that!" said Courtenay. "Wings! She's more like to end with a broken leg!" He reined his horse aside, saying politely to Sir Waldo: "Will you go, sir?"

"Yes, if you wish—but rather more tamely! Your cousin is an intrepid horsewoman, and might become an accomplished one, but you should teach her not to ride at a hedge as if she had a stretch of water to clear. She'll take a rattling fall one of these days."

"Lord, sir, I've told her over and over again to ride *fast* at water, and *slow* at timber, but she never pays the least heed to what anyone says! She's a show-off—though I'll say this for her!!—she don't care a rush for a tumble!"

"And rides with a light hand," said Julian, with a challenging look at Sir Waldo.

"Yes, and such a picture as she presents!" said Miss Colebatch.

Miss Trent, following Sir Waldo over the hedge, observed, as she reined in beside him, that that at least was true. He shrugged, but did not reply. The rest of the party joined them; and as they were now upon uncultivated ground they rode on in a body for some way, and the opportunity for private conversation was lost.

It was when they had covered perhaps half the distance to Knaresborough that Miss Trent, herself uncomfortably hot, noticed that Miss Colebatch, who had started out in tearing spirits, had become unusually silent. Watching her, she saw her sag in the saddle, and then jerk herself upright again; and she edged her horse alongside her, saying quietly: "Are you feeling quite the thing, Miss Colebatch?"

A rather piteous glance was cast at her, but Elizabeth, trying to smile, replied: "Oh yes! That is, I—I have the headache a little, but *pray* don't regard it! I shall be better directly, and I would not for the world—— It is just the excessive heat!"

Miss Trent now perceived that under the sun's scorch she was looking very sickly. She said: "No wonder! I find it insufferably hot myself, and shall be thankful to call a halt to this expedition."

"Oh, no, no!" gasped Elizabeth imploringly. "Don't say anything—*pray*!" Her chest heaved suddenly, and her mouth went awry. "Oh, Miss Trent, I d-do feel so s-sick!" she disclosed, tears starting to her eyes.

Miss Trent leaned forward to catch her slack bridle, bringing both their horses to a halt. She had not come unprepared for such an emergency, and, thrusting a hand into her pocket, produced a bottle of smelling-salts. By this time the rest of the party had seen that something was wrong, and had gathered round them. Miss Trent, dropped her own bridle, supported Elizabeth's wilting frame with one arm while she held the vinaigrette under her nose with her other hand. She said: "Miss Colebatch is overcome by the heat. Lift her down, Mr Underhill!"

He dismounted quickly, very much concerned, and, with a little assistance from Lindeth, soon had poor Elizabeth out of the saddle. Miss Trent was already on the ground, and after directing them to lay their burden on the turf desired them to retire to a distance.

Elizabeth was not sick, but she retched distressingly for some minutes; and felt so faint and dizzy that she was presently glad to obey Miss Trent's command to lie still, and to keep her eyes shut. Ancilla remained beside her, shielding her as much as possible from the sun, and fanning her with her own hat. The gentlemen, meanwhile, conferred apart, while Tiffany stood watching her friend, and enquiring from time to time if Ancilla thought she would soon be better.

After a few moments the Nonesuch detached himself from the male group, and came towards Ancilla. He made a sign to her that he wished to speak to her; she nodded, and, leaving Tiffany to take her place, got up, and went to him.

"Just as you foretold, eh?" he said. "How is she?"

"Better, but in no cause to go on, poor girl! I have been racking my brains to think what were best to do, and can hit upon nothing. I think, if she could but get out of the sun she would revive, but there are no trees, and not even a bush to afford her some shade!"

"Do you think, if her horse were led, she could go on for half a mile? Underhill tells us that there's a village, and an inn: no more than a small alehouse, I collect, but he says the woman who keeps it is respectable, and the immediate need, as you say, is to bring Miss Colebatch out of the sun. What do you think?"

"An excellent suggestion!" she replied decidedly. "We must at all events make the attempt to get her there, for she can't remain here, on the open moor. I believe that if she could rest in the cool, and we could get some water for her, she will soon recover—but she must not go any farther, Sir Waldo!"

"Oh, no! There can be no question of that," he agreed. "We'll take her to the inn, and decide then how best to convey her home."

She nodded, and went back to the sufferer, who had revived sufficiently to think herself well enough to resume the journey. She was encouraged by Tiffany, who greeted Miss

Trent with the news that Lizzie was much better, and needed only a rest to make her perfectly ready to ride on. When she learned that they were to go to Courtenay's inn she said enthusiastically that it was the very thing. "We may all of us refresh there, and get cool!" she said. "You will like that, won't you, Lizzie?"

Miss Colebatch agreed to it, saying valiantly that she knew she would soon feel as well as any of them; but when she was helped to her feet her head swam so sickeningly that she reeled, and would have fallen but for the support of Miss Trent's arm around her. She was lifted on to her saddle, and was told by Courtenay, in a heartening voice, that she had nothing to do but hold on to the pommel, and sniff the vinaigrette if she felt faint. "No, you don't want the bridle: I'm going to lead White Star," he said. "And no need to be afraid of falling off, because I shan't let you!"

"Thank you—so very sorry—so stupid of me!" she managed to say.

"No such thing! Here, Tiffany, you know the way to Moor Cross! Lindeth is going to ride ahead to warn old Mrs Rowsely, so you'd best go with him!"

She was very willing to do this, announcing gaily that they would form the advance guard, and cantered off with Lindeth. When the rest of the party reached the village, she came dancing out of the little stone inn, crying: "Oh, it is the prettiest place imaginable! Do make haste and come into the taproom! Only fancy, I had never been in a taproom before, but there's no parlour, so I was obliged to! It is so diverting! You'll be enchanted, Lizzie!"

Miss Colebatch, whose headache had developed into a severe migrane, was only dimly aware of being addressed, and she did not attempt to respond. Courtenay's hand, which had been grasping her elbow, was removed, and she almost toppled into the arms of the Nonesuch, who was waiting to receive her. He carried her into the inn, where an elderly landlady, over-awed by this unprecedented invasion, dropped a nervous curtsy, and begged him to lay Miss down on the settle. She had placed a folded blanket over its uncompromising wooden seat, and fetched down a flock pillow: two circumstances to which Tiffany proudly drew his attention, saying that it was she who had directed Mrs Rowsely to do so.

"And while Lizzie rests we are going to sit on the benches outside, just as if we were rustics!" she said, laughing. "Lindeth has ordered *home-brewed* for you, but I am going to

90

drink a glass of milk, because Mrs Rowsley has no lemons. It seems very odd to me, and I detest milk, but I don't mean to complain! Do come out! Ancilla will look after poor Lizzie."

She flitted away again, but he lingered for a few moments, while Miss Trent desired the landlady to bring a bowl of water, and some vinegar. The door of the inn opened directly into the taproom, but there was no other ventilation, the tiny latticed windows resisting Sir Waldo's efforts to force them open. The room was low-pitched and stuffy, and a strong aroma of spirituous liquors pervaded the air. Sir Waldo said abruptly: "This won't do. I collect there's no other room than the kitchen on this floor, but there must be a bedchamber abovestairs. Shall I arrange to have her moved to it?"

"If I could be sure that no one will come in, I believe it would be better to remain here," she replied, in a low tone. "It would be far hotter, immediately under the roof, you know."

"Very well; I'll attend to it," he said.

Half-an-hour later she emerged from the inn. Three empty tankards and a milkstained glass stood on one of the benches against the wall of the house; of Tiffany and Sir Waldo there was no sign, but she saw Lindeth and Courtenay walking down the street. They hastened their steps when they caught sight of her, and came up, anxiously asking how Elizabeth did.

"Asleep," she answered. "Where is Tiffany?"

"Oh, she has gone off to look at the Church with Sir Waldo!" said Courtenay. "Lindeth and I have been enquiring all over for some sort of a carriage, but there's nothing to be had, so we've decided—that is, if you agree!—that I'd best ride to Bardsey, and see what I can come by there. Do you think Lizzie will be well enough to be driven home when she wakes, ma'am?"

"I hope so. I expect she will pluck up when she has had some tea." She smiled at Julian. "Poor girl, she is so much distressed at having spoilt your party! She made me promise to beg your pardon, and even suggested that we should continue without her!"

"What, abandon her in a common alehouse? I should rather think not!" exclaimed Courtenay.

"There's no question of that, of course," Julian said. "I am only sorry she should be feeling so poorly. I wish we might bring a doctor to her!"

Miss Trent assured him that matters were not very serious,

91

and recommended Courtenay to saddle up. He went off to the small stableyard to do this, just as Tiffany and the Nonesuch came strolling down the street. Tiffany had caught the sweeping skirt of her velvet habit over her arm, and from the sparkling countenance she had upturned to Sir Waldo's Miss Trent judged that he had been entertaining her very agreeably.

"Oh, is Lizzie better now?" she demanded, running up to Miss Trent. "Is she ready to go on?"

"Well, she's asleep at the moment, but I am afraid she won't be stout enough to ride any farther."

"Then what's to be done?" asked Tiffany blankly. "How can you say she won't be stout enough? I'm persuaded she would wish to do so!"

"Even if she did wish it, it would be very imprudent," Ancilla said. "Indeed, Tiffany, I couldn't permit it! You wouldn't wish her to run the risk of making herself really ill!"

"No, of course I shouldn't!" Tiffany said impatiently. "But what a fuss for nothing more than a headache! I should have thought she would have *tried* to be better!"

"My dear, she is quite determined to be better, not because she wishes to ride any more, but because she is so much distressed at the thought of spoiling the expedition. I have assured her that we are all agreed that it is a great deal too sultry——"

"You can't mean that it must be given up!" cried Tiffany, looking in dismay from Ancilla to Lindeth.

It was he who answered her, saying gently: "You wouldn't care to go without her. None of us would! Another day, when it isn't so hot——"

"Oh, *no*!" Tiffany interrupted imploringly. "I hate put-offs! I know what it would be—we should never go to the Dripping Well, and I *want* to!"

"Yes, we will go, I promise you," he said. "It is very disappointing that we can't go today, but——"

"We *can* go today!" she insisted. "Not Lizzie, if she doesn't care for it, but the rest of us!"

He looked slightly taken aback for an instant, but a moment later smiled, and said: "You don't mean that, I know. In any event, we can't go, because we've settled that your cousin is to ride to Bardsey, to see if he can come by a carriage there."

Her face cleared at that; she said eagerly, "So that Lizzie can drive the rest of the way? Oh, that's a capital scheme!"

"So that she can be driven home," he corrected.

"Oh! Yes, well, perhaps that would be best. I daresay he would much *prefer* to drive Lizzie home, too, and it will make Lizzie feel much more comfortable to know she hasn't spoilt the day for us after all. Only consider! She will be perfectly safe with Courtenay, and so we may be easy! *Do* say you will go, Lindeth! Ancilla? Sir Waldo?"

Ancilla shook her head, trying to frown her down; but Sir Waldo, apparently divorced from the scene, was pensively observing through his quizzing-glass the gyrations of a large white butterfly, and evinced no sign of having heard the appeal. But Courtenay, leading his horse out of the yard, did hear it, and it was he who answered.

"Go where? To Knaresborough? Of course not! We are none of us going there. I wonder you should think of such a thing!"

"Why shouldn't I? I don't mean *you*, either: you are to drive Lizzie home! We need not *all* go with her!"

"Miss Trent must! Ma'am, you surely won't leave Lizzie?"

"Of course not," she replied. "Don't say any more, Tiffany! You must know you cannot go without me, and that I cannot under any circumstances leave Miss Colebatch."

"I could go if Courtenay went," Tiffany argued.

"Well, I'm not going," said Courtenay. "I'm going to Bardsey, to try if I can find some sort of a vehicle there. But it ain't on a pike-road, so the odds are I shan't be able to get anything better than a gig. Would a gig serve, ma'am?"

"No, no, of course it wouldn't!" interposed Tiffany. "She would have the sun beating down upon her head, and that would never do! I don't think she should attempt the journey until it is cooler, do you, Ancilla? Poor Lizzie, I daresay she would liefer stay in this delightful inn! Then we can all ride home together, when the rest of us come back from Knaresborough! She will be quite well by that time, and Ancilla won't object to staying with her, will you, Ancilla?"

Lindeth, who was beginning to look extremely troubled, said: "I don't think you can have considered. It would be quite improper for two ladies to spend the day in a taproom!"

"Oh, fudge! *I* shouldn't care a rush, so why should Lizzie? She will have Ancilla to bear her company!"

"But you could not enjoy the expedition, knowing that they were so uncomfortably situated!" he suggested.

"Oh, couldn't she?" said Courtenay, with a crack of rude

laughter. "You don't know her! I can tell you this, Tiffany! you may as well stop scheming, because you won't cozen me into going to Knaresborough, and that's my last word!"

A flush rose to her cheeks; her eyes blazed. "I think you are the horridest, most disobliging *toad*!" she said passionately. "I *want* to go to Knaresborough, I *will* go!"

"Tiffany!" uttered Miss Trent, in despairing accents. "For heaven's sake——!"

Tiffany rounded on her. "Yes, and I think you're as disagreeable and unkind as he is, Ancilla! You ought to do what *I* want, not what Lizzie wants! She shouldn't have come with us if she meant to be ill!"

"Take a damper!" said Courtenay sharply, looking towards the door of the inn. "Hallo, Lizzie! Are you feeling more the thing now?"

Miss Colebatch, steadying herself with a hand on the door-frame smiled waveringly, and said: "Yes, thank you. I'm much better—quite well! Only so very sorry to have been such a bother!"

Tiffany ran to her. "Oh, you *are* better! I can see you are! I knew you would be! You don't wish to go home, do you? Only think how flat it would be!"

"Miss Colebatch, don't come out into the sun!" interposed Miss Trent, taking her hand. "I am going to ask the landlady to make some tea for us, so come and sit down again!"

"Yes, some tea will refresh you," agreed Tiffany. "You'll be as right as a trivet then!"

"Oh, yes! Only I don't think—I'm afraid if I tried to ride——"

"But you're not going to ride, Miss Colebatch," said Julian. "Underhill is to fetch a carriage for you, and we are none of us going to Knaresborough. It's far too hot!"

"Yes, that's right, Lizzie," corroborated Courtenay. "I'm just off—and I'll tell you what! I'll get an umbrella to shield you from the sun, even if I have to steal one! So just you stay quietly in the taproom with Miss Trent until I return! I shan't be gone much above an hour, I hope."

"An hour?" exclaimed Tiffany. "And what am *I* to do, pray? Do you imagine I'm going to sit in that odious, stuffy taproom for a whole hour? I won't!"

"Oh, so it's odious and stuffy now, is it?" said Courtenay. "I thought you said you wouldn't care a rush if you were obliged to spend the rest of the day in it? Yes, you can look daggers at me if you choose, but *I* know what you are, and

94

that's a selfish little cat! You never did care a button for any-one but yourself, and it's my belief you never will!"

Tiffany burst into tears; and Miss Colebatch, sympathetic tears starting to her own eyes, cried: "Oh, Courtenay, no! You mustn't—— It is all my fault for being so stupid! Oh, Tiffany, I *beg* your pardon!"

"*You* beg *her* pardon?" ejaculated Courtenay.

"Mr Underhill, will you please mind your tongue?" said Miss Trent, with all the authority of her calling. "Stop crying, Tiffany! If you don't care to stay here, I suggest you ride into Bardsey with your cousin. Then you may enjoy your quarrel without making the rest of us uncomfortable!"

Courtenay opened his mouth, encountered a quelling look, and shut it again.

"I won't!" sobbed Tiffany. "I hate Courtenay, and I don't *want* to go to Bardsey!"

Miss Trent, well aware of the ease with which Tiffany could lash herself into a fit of hysterics, cast a harassed look round in search of support. Lindeth, his lips rather firmly compressed, and his eyes lowered, neither spoke nor moved; but the Nonesuch, amusement in his face, strolled up to Tiffany, and said: "Come, come, my child! The beautiful Miss Wield with swollen red eyes? Oh, no, I beseech you! I couldn't bear to see it!"

She looked up involuntarily, hiccuping on a sob, but with her tears suddenly checked. "Swollen—— Oh, *no*! Oh, Sir Waldo, are they?"

He put a finger under her chin, tilting up her face, and scrutinizing it with the glinting smile so many females had found fascinating. "Thank God, no! Just like bluebells drenched with dew!"

She revived as though by magic. "*Are* they? Oh, how pretty!"

"Ravishing, I promise you."

She gave a delighted little trill of laughter. "I mean how prettily *said*!"

"Yes, wasn't it?" he agreed, carefully drying her cheeks with his own handkerchief. "What very long eyelashes you have! Do they ever become tangled?"

"No! Of course they don't! How can you be so foolish? You are trying to flatter me!"

"Impossible! *Don't* you wish to ride to Bardsey?"

Her face clouded instantly. "With Courtenay? No, I thank you!"

"With me?"

"With you! But—but you are not going—are you?"

"Not unless you do."

A provocative smile lilted on her lips. "Ancilla wouldn't permit it!" she said with a challenging glance cast at her preceptress.

"What, even though Courtenay goes with us?" He turned towards Miss Trent, interrogating her with one quizzical eyebrow. "What do you say, ma'am?"

She had been listening to this interchange with mixed feelings, torn between gratitude to him for averting a storm, and indignation at the unscrupulous methods he employed. Her answering look spoke volumes, but all she said was: "I am persuaded Mrs Underhill would raise no objection, if her cousin is to go with Tiffany."

"Then I'll go and saddle the horses again," he said. "You, Julian, will remain to keep watch and ward over the ladies!"

"Of course," Julian replied quietly.

"Unless you should choose instead to accompany us?" suggested Tiffany, blithely forgetting that it had been agreed that two defenceless females could not be abandoned in an alehouse.

"No, I thank you," he said, and turned from her to persuade Miss Colebatch, with his sweetest smile, to retire again into the taproom.

Miss Trent had seen the look of shocked dismay in his face when it had been so forcibly borne in upon him that his goddess had feet of clay; and her heart was wrung with pity. She might tell herself that his well-wishers might rejoice in his disillusionment, but she was conscious of an irrational and almost overpowering impulse to find excuses for Tiffany. She subdued it, strengthened by the saucy look her artless charge cast at Julian before she tripped off in Sir Waldo's wake. It was abundantly plain to her that Tiffany saw nothing in Julian's refusal to ride to Bardsey but an expression of jealousy, which in no way displeased her. Tiffany delighted in setting her admirers at loggerheads, and never wasted a thought on the pain she inflicted; and had she been told that Julian was as much hurt by his cousin's behaviour as by hers she would have been as incredulous as she was uncaring. But Miss Trent's heart had more than once been wrung by the puzzled look in Julian's eyes when he had watched Sir Waldo flirting with Tiffany, and she could not help longing to reassure him.

She stayed to see the riding-party off before joining Miss

Colebatch and Julian in the taproom. She found them already discussing a pot of tea, Elizabeth reclining on the settle and looking rather more cheerful, and Lindeth not seeming to be in need of reassurance. Miss Trent warmly, if silently, applauded the good manners which prompted him to appear very well satisfied with his situation; and at once seconded his efforts to divert Elizabeth. She, poor girl, was still far from being her usually lively self, for, in addition to an aching head, she was suffering the mortification of knowing that she had ruined what should have been a day of pleasure, and had made her dear friend cry. She could not help laughing when Julian, amongst other schemes for ensuring her privacy, announced his intention of borrowing an apron from the landlady, and carrying tankards out to any thirsty patrons of the Bird in Hand; but a moment later she was wondering whether Tiffany would ever forgive her, and saying, for perhaps the fiftieth time, that she could not conceive what had come over her, or how she could have been so stupid.

"Well, for my part," said Miss Trent, "I am glad that something did come over you! I was wishing I had never expressed a desire to visit the Dripping Well, and was never more thankful than when it was decided to abandon the scheme."

"You are always so kind! But Tiffany was so set on it!"

"My dear Miss Colebatch, if Tiffany suffers no worse disappointments than today's she may count herself fortunate!" replied Ancilla lightly. "I wish you won't tease yourself merely because she flew into one of her tantrums! You must know what a spoilt child she is!"

"It *is* that, isn't it?" Julian said eagerly. "Just—just childishness! She is so lovely, and—and engaging that it's no wonder she should be a trifle spoilt."

"No, indeed!" she said, adding with what she felt to be odious duplicity: "You must not blame Mrs Underhill, however. I daresay she should have been stricter, but her own nature is so gentle and yielding that she is no match for Tiffany. And she *does* so much dread her passions! I must own I do too! No one can be more enchanting than Tiffany, and no one that *I* ever met can more easily throw an entire household into discomfort! I can't tell you, sir, how very much obliged I am to your cousin for coming to our rescue as he did!"

He responded only with a quick, constrained smile, and she said no more, hoping that she had given him enough to digest for the present; and had perhaps made him wonder whether Sir Waldo's conduct had not sprung rather from a laudable impulse to nip a painful scene in the bud than from any desire to cut out his young cousin.

CHAPTER VIII

"I DON'T DENY that I was thankful to be spared a fit of strong hysterics," Miss Trent told the Nonesuch, when, at the end of that memorable day, Miss Colebatch had been safely restored to her parents, "and I can't doubt that *you* don't deny, sir, that your conduct was utterly unscrupulous!"

"Yes, I shall," he replied coolly. "I did nothing to promote the scene; I refrained from adding as much as one twig to the flames; and when I did intervene it was from motives of chivalry."

"From *what*?" she gasped.

"Motives of chivalry," he repeated, meeting her astonished gaze with a grave countenance, but with such a twinkle in his eyes that she was hard put to it not to laugh. "A look of such piteous entreaty was cast at me——"

"*No!*" protested Miss Trent. "Not *piteous*! I didn't!"

"Piteous!" said the Nonesuch remorselessly. "Your eyes, ma'am—as well you know!!—cried *Help me*! What could I do but respond to the appeal?"

"Next you will say that it went much against the pluck with you!" said Miss Trent, justly incensed.

"No service I could render you, ma'am, would go against the pluck!"

Her colour mounted, but she said: "I should have guessed you would have a glib answer ready!"

"You might also have guessed that I meant it."

She found herself suddenly a little breathless; and wished, for the first time, that she was more experienced in the art of dalliance. There was a note of sincerity in his voice; but caution warned her not to allow herself to be taken in by a man of the world whom she judged to be expert in flirtation. She managed to laugh, although rather shakily, and to say: "Very prettily said. Sir Waldo! I must give you credit too for having brought Tiffany back to us all compliance and good humour. A triumph indeed!"

"Fencing with me, Miss Trent?"

She was silent for a moment or two, and when she did speak it was with a good deal of constraint. "I think you forget my situation, sir."

"On the contrary: your situation chafes me too much to be forgotten."

She looked at him in astonishment. "Chafes you!"

"Beyond endurance! You stare! Does it seem so strange to you that I should very much dislike seeing you in such a position?"

"Good heavens!" she exclaimed. "One would suppose I was one of those unfortunate governesses who, for £24 a year, become drudges! But I'm no such thing! I'm excessively expensive, in fact."

"So you once told me."

"Well, it's true. I don't like to boast, but I can't allow you to suppose that I eke out a miserable existence on a pittance. I am paid £150 a year!"

"My dear girl, it would make no difference if you were paid ten times that sum!"

"That shows how little you know! It makes a great deal of difference, I promise you. Females who are paid very high wages are never used like drudges."

"You are at the beck and call of a woman I could more readily suppose to be your housekeeper than your mistress; you are obliged to endure impertinence from that abominable chit any time she is out of temper, and patronage from such mushrooms as——"

"Nonsense!" she interrupted. "Mrs Underhill treats me as if I were one of her family, and I won't have her abused! I think myself very fortunate, and if *I* don't dislike my position there can be no reason for anyone else to do so!"

"Oh, yes, there can be!" he retorted.

They had reached the gates of Staples, where the others had pulled up to wait for them. Miss Trent hardly knew whether to be glad or sorry that her tête-à-tête with the Nonesuch had come to an abrupt end; and when he and Lindeth had taken their leave she rode up the avenue to the house so lost in her own thoughts that Courtenay had to speak her name twice before she realized that she was being addressed.

He supposed her to be tired; and Tiffany, at her most caressing, was instantly all solicitude. Miss Trent was obliged to take herself to task for harbouring the uncharitable suspicion that her engaging manner sprang from a wish to avert a scold for her previous conduct.

Mrs Underhill said she was quite shocked to think of poor Lizzie's indisposition, but not at all surprised. She and Charlotte had taken a turn in the shrubbery, which had regularly exhausted her, so hot as it had been. Miss Trent made no mention of Tiffany's outburst, but when Courtenay came in he gave his mother a full and indignant account of it, stigmatizing his lovely cousin as a devil's daughter whom he was ashamed to own, and adding that she might as well stop setting her cap at Lindeth, since the veriest clodpole could have seen how outrageous he thought her behaviour.

This was all very dreadful, but, as Mrs Underhill presently confided to Miss Trent, every cloud had a silver lining. "For Courtenay told me, my dear, that his lordship was downright shocked, so I shouldn't wonder at it if he began to hedge off. Very likely it will have given him a disgust of her, for there's nothing gentlemen hate more than the sort of dust Tiffany kicks up when she flies into one of her miffs. Don't you think so?"

Miss Trent agreed. She also thought that Courtenay's disgust was considerably stronger than Lindeth's, but this she did not say.

"And it was Sir Waldo that stopped her from going her length, and took her off to Bardsey, which I'll be bound you were glad of, my dear, though whether it was what *he* wanted to do is another matter!"

The arch note in the good lady's voice was unmistakeable. Miss Trent's fine eyes turned towards her involuntarily, asking a startled question.

"Lor', my dear, as if I was such a nodcock as not to know it's you he's got a preference for!" said Mrs Underhill, with a fat chuckle. "To be sure, I did think at first that he was making up to Tiffany, but for all I haven't got book-learning I hope I've enough rumgumption to know he's trying to fix his interest with you!"

"You are mistaken, ma'am—you *must* be mistaken!" stammered Ancilla.

"Well, that's what I thought myself, when I first took the notion into my head," conceded Mrs Underhill. "Not that I mean you ain't genteel, as I hope I don't need to tell you, for

I'm sure anyone would take you for a lady of quality, such distinguished ways as you have, which even Mrs Mickleby has remarked to me more than once. But there's no denying it isn't to be expected that such a smart as Sir Waldo wouldn't be looking a great deal higher if he was hanging out for a wife, for from what Mrs M. tells me he's a gentleman of the first consequence, let alone being as rich as a new-shorn lamb, and has goodness knows how many fine ladies on the catch for him!"

"Ma'am!" interrupted Ancilla, in a stifled voice, "I am neither a fine lady, nor am I on the catch for Sir Waldo!"

"No, my dear, and well do I know it! I shouldn't wonder at it if it was that which took his fancy. If you was to ask me, I should say that there's nothing will make a gentleman sheer off quicker than the feel that he's being hunted! Lord! the females that set their caps at Mr Underhill! Of course, he wasn't a grand townbeau, like Sir Waldo, but he was thought to be a great catch, and might have had his pick of all the girls in Huddersfield. And what must he do but set his fancy on me, just because I didn't pay any more heed to him than I did to any of my beaux!"

Miss Trent, only too glad to encourage this divagation, said: "I don't think *that* was why he set his fancy on you, ma'am, but I can readily believe that you had any number of beaux!"

"Well, I had," admitted Mrs Underhill, gratified. "You wouldn't think it, to look at me now, but, though it don't become me to say so, I was used to be a very pretty girl, and had so many compliments paid me—— But *that's* not what I was wanting to say to you!"

Miss Trent, having learnt by experience that however far her employer might wander from the point she rarely lost sight of it, resigned herself.

"You won't take it amiss when I tell you, my dear, that when I saw the look in Sir Waldo's eyes whenever he had them fixed on you, which nobody could mistake, though I'd be hard put to it to describe it to you, if you was to ask me, it cast me into quite a quake, thinking that he was intending to give you a slip on the shoulder, as the saying is."

"Dear ma'am, I am—I am very much obliged to you for your concern, but indeed you have no need to be in a quake!"

"No, that's just what I think myself," said Mrs Underhill, nodding wisely. "I'd have dropped a hint in your ear otherwise, you being so young, for all you try to gammon everyone into thinking you are an old maid! But, 'no,' I said to myself, 'a libertine he may be'—not that I've any reason to suppose he is, mind!—'but he ain't making up to Miss Trent meaning nothing more than marriage with the left hand: not with her uncle being General Sir Mordaunt Trent, as he is!' Well, it stands to reason, doesn't it?" She paused, eyeing Ancilla in some bewilderment. "Now, whatever have I said to throw you into whoops?" she demanded.

"Oh, I beg your pardon, ma'am!" Ancilla said, wiping her streaming eyes. "But it is so—so absurd——!"

"Exactly so! But don't you tell me he ain't making up to you, because I'm not as blind as a beetle, which I'd have to be not to see what's going on under my nose!"

Ancilla had stopped laughing. She was rather flushed, and she said haltingly: "I think, ma'am—I think you refine too much on Sir Waldo's gallantry. I am persuaded he has no other intention than to amuse himself with a little flirtation."

Mrs Underhill's face fell; but after thinking it over for a minute, she brightened, saying: "No, you're out there, my dear. It's Tiffany he flirts with, which, of course, he oughtn't to do, but, lord, they all do it, even the Squire, and you can't blame them, so pretty and saucy as she is! But he don't look at her the way he looks at you—no, and he don't talk to you as he does to her either! What's more, if she ain't in the room he don't look up every time the door opens, hoping she's going to come in!"

Her cool composure seriously disturbed, Ancilla said involuntarily: "Oh, Mrs Underhill, d-*does* he do so when—— Oh, no! *Surely* not?"

"Lord bless you, my dear, of course he does!" replied Mrs Underhill, with an indulgent laugh. "And if it *is* you—well, often and often I've thought to myself that if he was to smile at me the way he does at you I should be cast into a regular flutter, as old as I am!"

Miss Trent felt her cheeks burning, and pressed her slim hands to them. "He—he has a very charming smile, I know!"

"I'll be bound you do!" retorted Mrs Underhill. "Mark my words if we don't have him popping the question before we've had time to turn round! And this I will say, my dear: I couldn't be better pleased if you was my own daughter! Not that he'd do for Charlotte, even if she was old enough, which, of course, she isn't, because, from all I can discover, he's nutty upon horses, and well you know that she can't abide 'em!"

Miss Trent gave a shaky laugh. "Yes, indeed I know it. But—— Dear Mrs Underhill, *pray* don't say any more! You mustn't encourage me to—to indulge ridiculous dreams! Sir Waldo knows exactly how to make himself very—very agreeable to females, and, I daresay, has broken many hearts. I am determined he shall not break mine! To suppose that he—a matrimonial prize of the first stare!—would entertain for as much as one moment the notion of contracting so unequal a match . . ." Her voice failed; she recovered it again to say, with an attempt at a smile: "You won't speak of this to anyone, I know!"

"Certainly not!" said Mrs Underhill. "But don't you behave missish, my dear, and start hinting him away because you think you ain't good enough for him! That's for him to decide, and you may depend upon it that a man of five- or six-and-thirty knows what will suit him. It would be a splendid thing for you, let alone making the Squire's lady and Mrs Banningham as mad as fire!"

On this invigorating thought she took her departure, leaving Miss Trent to her own reflections.

It was long before she fell asleep that night. Mrs Underhill's blunt words had forced her to confront the truth she had hitherto refused to acknowledge: she had been in love with the Nonesuch for weeks.

Like a stupidly romantic schoolgirl, she thought, dazzled by the aura of magnificence that hung about a Top-of-the-Trees Corinthian, and foolishly endowing him with heroic qualities because he had a handsome face and splendid figure, rode and drove his high-couraged horses with such effortless mastery, and bore himself with an unconscious assurance which cozened ninnyhammers like herself into thinking he was a demigod. Not that she was quite as idiotish as that, of course. She could scarcely help admiring his appearance, but she had not fallen in love with his face, or his figure, and certainly not with his air of elegance. He had considerable charm of manner, but she decided that it was not that either. She thought it might be the humour that lurked in his eyes, or perhaps his smile. But Lindeth had a delightful smile too, and she was not in the least in love with him. In fact, she didn't know why she loved the Nonesuch, but only that from the moment of first setting eyes on him she had felt so strong an attraction that it had shocked her, because he was clearly the exemplar of a set of persons whom she held in abhorrence.

Caution warned her not to place overmuch reliance on what Mrs Underhill had said. Far better than Mrs Underhill did she know how very unlikely it was that a man of Sir Waldo's eligibility, who could look as high as he pleased for a wife and must be thought to be past the age of contracting a rash engagement, should entertain the smallest intention of offering marriage to an obscure female who had neither consequence nor any extraordinary degree of beauty to recommend her. On the other hand, the things he had said to her that day, before they had parted at the gates of Staples, seemed to indicate that he had something other than mere flirtation in mind. If that had been all he sought she could not conceive why her inferior situation should chafe him, or why, if he had not been sincere, he should have told her that it did. Pondering the matter, she was obliged to own that she knew very little about the art of flirtation; and hard upon this thought came the realization that she knew very little about Sir Waldo either. He had shown himself to be most truly the gentleman, never above his company, nor betraying his boredom, and never seeking to impress the neighbourhood by playing off the airs of an exquisite. As for exerting an evil influence over his young admirers, she had it on the authority of the Squire that his coming to Broom Hall had done them all a great deal of good. Together with their extravagant waistcoats and their monstrous neckcloths they had abandoned such dare-devil sports as Hunting the Squirrel or riding their cover-hacks up the stairs of their parents' houses: the Nonesuch never wore startling raiment, and he let it be seen that he thought the Dashes and the Neck-or-Nothings not at all the thing. So instead of rushing into wild excesses as a result of his coming amongst them the youthful aspirants to Corinthian fame (said the Squire, with a chuckle) had now run mad over achieving what their hero would think a proper mode.

It was possible, however, that in his own element Sir Waldo might show another side to his character. Not for a moment did Ancilla believe that he would lead greenhorns astray; but she was bound to acknowledge that for anything she knew his path might be littered with wounded hearts. She could not doubt that he was a master of the art of flirtation; and she was only too well aware of his fatal fascination. She

104

decided that her wisest course would be to put him out of her mind. After reaching this conclusion she lay thinking about him until at last she fell asleep.

Upon the following day she was driven over to Colby Place in Mrs Underhill's smart new barouche to enquire after Elizabeth. Charlotte had been her companion designate, but as soon as Tiffany heard of the scheme she said that it was exactly what she had been meaning to do herself, and very prettily begged Miss Trent to grant her a place in the carriage. Forthright Charlotte, who suffered from few illusions, instantly cried off, saying that she preferred to bear Mama company at home than to occupy the forward seat in the barouche. So Tiffany went with Miss Trent, looking a picture of lovely innocence in a gown of sprig muslin, and a charming hat of chip straw, tied under her chin with blue ribbons. A parasol protected her complexion from the sun; and upon the forward seat reposed a basket of grapes. These were an offering from Mrs Underhill, whose succession-houses were the envy of her acquaintants; but Miss Trent, labouring under even fewer illusions than Charlotte, would not have hazarded a groat against the chance that Tiffany would not present them as the fruits of her own solicitude. Any doubts she might have cherished were dispelled by that damsel's disarmingly naïve explanation.

"So *no one* could think I was unkind to poor Lizzie, could they? and *also*, Ancilla, I have invited Patience to go with us to Leeds on Friday, because she wants to purchase new gloves and sandals for the Colebatches' ball next week, just as I do, and was in quite a puzzle to know how to manage, on account of Mrs Chartley's being laid up with one of her colicky disorders!"

"That *was* kind of you, Tiffany!" said Miss Trent admiringly.

"Well, I think it was," said Tiffany. "For there's nothing so uncomfortable as having a third person in one's carriage! It means you will be obliged to sit forward—— But I knew you wouldn't care a button!"

"No, indeed!" agreed Miss Trent, with great cordiality. "I am only too happy to be allowed to contribute my mite to your generosity."

"Yes," said Tiffany, sublimely unconscious of satire, "I was persuaded you would say I had done just as I ought!"

When they reached Colby Place they perceived that they were not the only visitors. A glossy phaeton, to which was harnessed a team once described by Courtenay as a bang-up set-out of blood and bone, was drawn up in the shade of a large elm tree. A groom in plain livery touched his hat to the ladies; and Tiffany exclaimed: "Oh, Sir Waldo is here!"

But it was not Sir Waldo, as they discovered when they entered the house, and found Lord Lindeth chatting to Lady Colebatch in her morning-parlour. He jumped up as they were ushered into the room, and when he saw Tiffany a warm light sprang to his eyes, and he said, in a low tone, as soon as she had greeted her hostess and turned to hold out her hand to him: "That's right! I knew you would come!"

"But of course!" she said, opening her eyes to their widest. "Poor Lizzie! Is she better, Lady Colebatch? I have brought some grapes for her."

Lady Colebatch, accepting the basket with thanks, replied placidly that there was nothing the matter with Lizzie that would not be amended by a day's repose, and invited Tiffany to run upstairs to join Miss Chartley at her bedside.

"Patience? Why, what brings her here?" demanded Tiffany, astonished, and by no means pleased to discover that the Rector's daughter had been before her in paying a visit of condolence.

Still less was she pleased when she learned that Patience, hearing the news of her friend's collapse through the mysterious but inevitable village-channels, had set out to walk the three miles that separated Colby Place from the village, but had been overtaken by Lindeth, driving his cousin's phaeton, and bent upon the same charitable errand. He had naturally taken her up beside him, which, said Lady Colebatch, with unruffled serenity, she was excessively relieved to know, because although she knew Patience to be an indefatigable walker it would have cast her into high fidgets to have thought of her having trudged so far in such warm weather.

Lindeth did not seem to have wasted his time during the short drive. Miss Chartley had chanced to mention the forthcoming shopping expedition to Leeds, and he had instantly proposed a capital plan to her, which he now propounded to Miss Trent. "I know my cousin has business in Leeds on Friday, so I am hereby issuing an invitation to you all to partake of a nuncheon at the King's Head!" he said gaily. "Do say you will come, ma'am! I've extracted a promise from Miss Chartley that *she* will, if her mama should not object!"

"*I* see!" said Miss Trent, quizzing him. "She *would* object if I were not there to chaperon the party! My dear Lord Lindeth, how can I find the words to thank you for your *very* flattering invitation? I am quite overcome!"

He laughed, blushing. "No, no, I didn't mean it so! You know I didn't! Miss Wield, what do you say?" He smiled at her, adding softly: "Instead of the nuncheon we *didn't* eat at Knaresborough! You won't be so cruel as to refuse!"

It piqued her to be the last to receive his invitation, but she was on her best behaviour, and she replied at once: "Oh, no! A delightful scheme! The very thing to revive us after all our shopping!"

She then went off, with every appearance of alacrity, to visit Elizabeth; and Lady Colebatch remarked that she didn't know what Lizzie had done to deserve such kind friends.

When Tiffany came down again she was accompanied by Miss Chartley, and the whole party took their leave. Miss Trent wondered whether his infatuation would prompt Lindeth to offer to take Tiffany up in place of Patience, and hardly knew whether to be glad or sorry when he made no such suggestion. It was Patience who hesitated, as he stood waiting to hand her up into the carriage, glancing towards Tiffany with a question in her eyes, and saying in her gentle way: "Wouldn't you prefer to go in the phaeton, Tiffany?"

Tiffany would infinitely have preferred it, and had Julian invited her she would have accepted, after a graceful show of reluctance. But Julian had not invited her, and he did not now add his voice to Miss Chartley's. That it would have been scarcely civil of him to have done so never occurred to Tiffany; if it had, she would have brushed such an excuse aside: he had chosen to be civil to Patience at *her* expense, and that, in her eyes, was an unpardonable offence. As for accepting a seat in the phaeton at Patience's hands, she would have chosen rather to walk back to Staples. She uttered a brittle laugh, and said: "No, I thank you! I detest riding in phaetons, and am in a constant quake—unless they are being driven by someone I *know* won't overturn them!"

Miss Trent, who had been stroking one of the leaders, said, in a voice that had in the past more than once abashed a pert pupil: "My dear Tiffany, surely you are able to distinguish between perch-phaeton and a *high*-perch phaeton?" She paid no further heed to Tiffany, but smiled at Lindeth: "The fact that you are driving your cousin's team tells me that you're no whipster, Lord Lindeth! Or did you steal them when his back was turned?"

He laughed. "No, I shouldn't dare! Waldo always lets me

drive his horses. He must, you know, for it was he who taught me to handle the reins in form. Only think of the wound his pride would suffer if he had to own that his pupil was not fit to be trusted with his horses! Don't be afraid, Miss Chartley! I'm not a top-sawyer, but I shan't overturn you!"

"Indeed, I haven't the smallest fear of that," she replied, glancing shyly up at him. "You drove me here so comfortably!"

"Thank you!" He saw that Tiffany was preparing to get into the barouche, and walked across to her, to hand her in. "I mean to make you unsay those words one of these days!" he said playfully. "The grossest injustice! I wish we hadn't to part so soon: I've scarcely exchanged half-a-dozen sentences with you. Did you find Miss Colebatch better? Her mama assured me we need not be afraid of a put-off of their ball next week. Will you dance the waltz with me?"

"*What?*" she exclaimed, her sulks instantly forgotten. "Lindeth, you can't mean we are to *waltz*? Oh, you're hoaxing me!"

He shook his head. "I'm not! Dashing, isn't it?"

"Oh, yes, and such fun!" she cried, clapping her hands. "I declare I'm ready to *dote* on Lady Colebatch! But how does she dare to be so dreadfully fast? Only think how Mrs. Mickleby will look!"

"It has her sanction—almost her blessing!"

"Impossible!"

"I assure you!" His eyes danced. "Lady Colebatch sought her counsel, and she—naturally!—applied to those tonnish London cousins of hers. They informed her that the waltz is now all the crack, and is even permitted at Almack's. Only rustics, they wrote, still frowned on it. *So——!*"

"Oh, famous, famous!" she giggled. "The great Mrs Mickleby a *rustic*? *Now* I understand!"

"And you'll stand up with me?"

"If my aunt permits!" she replied demurely.

He smiled, pressed her hand fleetingly, and went back to the phaeton. Tiffany was so much delighted with his news that she was not only able to bear with equanimity the sight of him driving off with Patience beside him, but to chat merrily to Miss Trent about the treat in store all the way back to Staples.

CHAPTER IX

MEANWHILE, LORD Lindeth, driving Miss Chartley home at an easy pace, naturally told her that the waltz would be danced at the Colby Place ball. She was quite as much surprised as Tiffany had been, but she received the news very differently, saying wistfully: "I have never learnt to waltz, but I shall enjoy watching it."

"You could learn the steps in a trice," he assured her. "*I* know how well you dance, Miss Chartley! Any caper-merchant could teach you in one lesson! Why, I could do so myself—though I'm no dab at it! Do let me!"

She smiled gratefully at him, but said simply: "I don't think Mama would permit it."

"Wouldn't she? Not even when she knows Mrs Mickleby sanctions it?"

She shook her head, but closed her lips on speech. A lady of true quality, said Mama, did not puff off her consequence: anything of that nature belonged to the mushroom class! Mama never mentioned the matter, but she was far better bred than the Squire's wife, and well did Patience know that she would be considerably affronted by any suggestion that she should accept Mrs Mickleby as a model.

"Does she believe it to be an improper dance?" asked Lindeth. "So too did my own mother, until she saw that it was no such thing. I shall see if I can't persuade Mrs Chartley to relent! It would be too bad if you were obliged merely to *watch* it!"

"I'm afraid you wouldn't succeed," she said, thinking there was no real intention behind his words.

She was mistaken. When they reached the Rectory Lindeth entered it with her, and was soon engaged in coaxing Mrs Chartley, recovering from her indisposition on the sofa in her drawing-room, to revise her opinion of the fast German dance which had become the rage in London.

She was by no means impervious to his charm, but her

109

sense of propriety was strict, and it is doubtful whether he would have prevailed upon her to relax it had he not received support from an unexpected quarter. The Rector, coming into the room and learning what was the subject under discussion, said that since the world began each generation had condemned the manners and customs of the next. For himself, he would not judge a dance he had never seen performed. Smiling kindly upon Julian, he invited him to show them the steps.

"Mr Chartley!" protested his wife, in half-laughing reproach.

"I was very fond of dancing when I was young," said the Rector reminiscently. "Dear me, what dashers we were! Always up to the knocker, as you young people would say!"

That made them all laugh; and when he told his wife that while he hoped no child of his would ever pass the line he found he could not wish his daughter to be a dowdy, Mrs Chartley flung up her hands in mock dismay, and consented to postpone judgment. The end of it was that Julian was persuaded to give Patience her first lesson, ably assisted by Miss Jane Chartley, who not only bullied her shrinking elder sister into standing up with him, but volunteered to play the music. This she did with great aplomb, strongly marking the time, in a manner which made her startled mama wonder who had taught her to play waltzes. It was certainly not her rather prim governess.

Patience (like her father) was very fond of dancing, and as soon as she had overcome her nervousness she showed herself to be an apt pupil, a trifle stiff, when she found Lindeth's arm round her for the first time, but quickly mastering the steps and the rhythm of the dance.

"Bravo!" applauded the Rector, gently clapping his hands. "Very pretty! Very pretty indeed!"

"Oh, do you think so, Papa?" Patience said eagerly. "I was dreadfully awkward, and kept missing my step! But, if you don't think it indecorous, I-I should like to learn to do it correctly. It *is* so exhilarating!"

It was this impulsive utterance which made Mrs Chartley say, later: "My dear John, I marvel at your countenancing this most improper dance! When they went down the room together, with his left hand holding her right one above their heads, *his* right hand was *clasping her waist!*"

"For guidance, my love!" said the Rector. "Lindeth had no *amorous* intention! I saw nothing improper. Indeed, I should have wished to see Patience a trifle less unyielding—but I daresay she was awkward from ignorance!"

"It's my belief," said Mrs Chartley severely, "that you would like to dance the waltz yourself!"

"No, no, not at my age!" he said guiltily. A smile crept into his eyes. "But if it had been in fashion when I was a young man, and not, of course, in orders, I *should* have danced it—and with you, my love! Would *you* have disliked it?"

A dimple quivered in her cheek, but she said: "My mother would never have permitted such a thing. Do you, in all sincerity, expect me to permit Patience to—to twirl round a ball-room in a male embrace—for I can call it nothing less than that!"

"You are the best judge of what she should do, my dear, and I must leave it to you to decide. I must own, however, that I should not wish to see Patience sitting against the wall while her friends are, as you phrase it, twirling round the room."

"No," agreed Mrs Chartley, forcibly struck by this aspect. "No, indeed!"

"Far be it from me to desire her to outshine her friends," said the Rector unconvincingly, "but I have sometimes thought that although she cannot rival little Tiffany's beauty she is by far the more graceful dancer."

These words afforded his wife food for considerable thought. She could not be perfectly reconciled, but her resolution wavered. The reference to Tiffany, little though the Rector knew it, had operated powerfully upon her. She was not, she hoped, a worldly woman, but neither was she so saintly (or so unnatural a parent) as to be unmoved by the spectacle of her daughter's being cast into the shade by an odiously precocious little baggage who was wild to a fault, as vain as she was beautiful, and wholly wanting in character and disposition. Mrs Chartley, in fact, did not like Tiffany Wield; and she had been thinking for some time that it was sad to see such a delightful young man as Lindeth in her toils. Heaven knew she was no matchmaking mother! Unlike certain of her husband's parishioners, she had made not the smallest attempt to throw her child in his lordship's way; but when she had watched him dancing with Patience the thought had flashed across her mind that they were a remarkably well-suited couple. Lindeth was just the sort of young man she would have chosen for Patience. It was one thing to make no push to engage his interest in the child, but quite another to throw obstacles in the way of his becoming better acquainted with her.

She was still in a state of indecision when the matter was clinched by an invitation to Patience from Mrs Underhill, to attend one or two morning dances at Staples, to practise the waltz.

"Morning dances!" she exclaimed. "Good gracious, what next?"

Patience, her eyes shining, and her cheeks in a glow, said: "It was Tiffany's suggestion, Mama, and Miss Trent says it is quite true that they have become the fashion in London. Just to enable people to practise waltzes and quadrilles, you know. And she has undertaken to play for us, and tell us all how to waltz in the correct manner. Mama, nearly all my friends are going! And even Courtenay Underhill, and the Banninghams, and Arthur Mickleby are determined to learn! And Lord Lindeth and Mr Ash have been so obliging as to promise to come too, to show us the way. And Mrs Underhill will be present, and——"

"My dear, how you do run on!"

"I beg your pardon, ma'am! Only, may I go? Not if you dislike it—but I *should* like to so very much!"

Mrs Chartley could not withstand such an appeal. "Well, my love, since your papa sees no harm in it, and the ball is to be a private one, not a public assembly,——"

"Oh, *thank you*, Mama!" breathed Patience. "Now I can look forward to it, which I didn't when I thought I should be obliged to sit down when the others were all dancing!"

"No, that would never do," agreed Mrs Chartley, visualizing such a scene with profound disapprobation.

"It is going to be a beautiful party!" confided Patience. "There are to be coloured lamps in the garden, and—but this is a great secret, Mama, which Lizzie whispered to me!—a firework display at midnight!"

"It's to be hoped, then, that it doesn't rain," said Mrs Chartley.

"Oh, don't suggest such a thing!" begged Patience. "Mama, would you think it very extravagant if I were to purchase a new reticule for it? I've been to so many parties that mine is looking sadly shabby."

"Not, not at all. You know, my dear, I have been thinking that if you were to bring back a length of satin from Leeds on Friday we could very easily make a fresh underdress for your gauze ball-dress. I never did like the green we chose. A soft shade of pink would become you. And if you can find some velvet ribbon to match it—— How vexatious it is that I can't go with you! But Dr Wibsey threatens me with all manner of evil consequences if I don't continue to be invalidish until the end of the week at least, so if I am to take you to this ball next week I suppose I must do what he tells me. Well, you will have Miss Trent to advise you! Let yourself be guided by her: she has excellent taste!"

What with the dissipation of waltzing at Staples all one rainy morning, and the prospect of an orgy of spending in Leeds, attended by a nuncheon-party, it was in a festive mood that Patience awaited the arrival of the Staples carriage on Friday morning. She had arrayed herself for the occasion in her best walking-dress of figured muslin, with long sleeves, and a double flounce round the hem; on her head she wore a pretty straw bonnet, trimmed with flowers; on her feet sandals of tan kid; in one hand she held a small parasol; and in the other (very tightly) a stocking-purse containing the enormous largesse bestowed on her by her Mama. It seemed quite profligate to spend so much money on her adornment, for although the Rector had been born to an independance which enabled him to command the elegancies of life he had reared his children in habits of economy, and in the belief that it was wrong to set store by one's appearance. "Going to waste your money on *more* finery?" he had said, smiling, but disapproving too. "My dear sir," had said Mama, "you would not wish your daughter to be seen in worn-out slippers and soiled gloves, I hope!" Afterwards she had explained the suppression of the pink satin and the velvet ribbon, saying in a confidential tone which made Patience feel suddenly very much more grownup that it was better not to talk to men about frills and furbelows, because they had no understanding of such things, and were merely bored by feminine chatter.

Miss Trent thought that she had seldom seen Patience in such good looks, and reflected that nothing became a girl so well as a glow of pleasurable excitement. She was inevitably dimmed by Tiffany, who was in great beauty, and wearing a dashing bonnet with a very high crown and a huge, upstanding poke framing her face, but there was something very taking about her countenance; and her eyes, though lacking the brilliance of Tiffany's, held a particularly sweet expression.

The drive into Leeds, once Patience had won a spirited argument with Miss Trent on which of them really *preferred* to

113

sit with her back to the horses, was accomplished in perfect amity. Tiffany took no part in a dispute which she felt to be no concern of hers, but she was very ready to discuss with her companions the various purchases she meant to make in the town, and to show a civil, if fleeting, interest in Patience's more modest requirements. Being a considerable heiress she had a great deal of pin-money allowed her; and as, unlike Patience, she had not the smallest notion of economy, it was enough for her to see something that took her fancy to make her buy it immediately. Her drawers were crammed with the expensive spoils of her visits to Leeds or Harrogate, most of which she had decided did not become her, or which were not as pretty as she had at first thought them. They ranged from innumerable pairs of rosettes for slippers to a Spartan diadem which (mercifully) was found to make her look positively haggish; and included such diverse items as an Angola shawl suitable for a dowager, a pair of Spanish slippers of sea-green kid, three muffs of spotted ermine, chinchilla, and swansdown, a tangle of spangled ribbon, and a set of head ornaments of silver filigree. She was obliged, at present, to apply to Mrs Underhill whenever she wanted to draw on her allowance. What would happen when she came into full possession of her fortune was a question which conjured up nightmarish visions in the mind of a conscientious governess; and Miss Trent had made persistent and extremely exhausting efforts to instil into her head some glimmerings of the value of money. She had failed, and as she was not one to fling her cap after the impossible there was nothing left for her to do but to check Tiffany's extravagance by whatever means her ingenuity might suggest to her; and to excuse her failure by the reflection that the control of that volatile damsel's inheritance would pass into the hands of her unknown but inevitable husband.

When they reached Leeds they alighted from the carriage at the King's Arms, and set forth on foot down the main shopping street. Leeds was a thriving and rapidly expanding town, numbering amongst its public edifices two Cloth Halls (one of which was of impressive dimensions, and was divided into six covered streets; five Churches; a Moot Hall; the Exchange (a handsome building of octangular design); an Infirmary; a House of Recovery for persons afflicted with infectious diseases; a Charity school, clothing and educating upwards of a hundred children, and over which (had they but known it) Sir Waldo Hawkridge was, at the time of their arrival in the town, being escorted by several of the Governors; a number of cloth and carpet manufactories; several cotton mills, and foundries; inns innumerable; and half-a-dozen excellent posting-houses. The buildings were for the most part of red brick, beginning to be blackened by the smoke of industry; and while none could be thought magnificent there were several Squares and Parades which contained private residences of considerable elegance. There was some very good shops and silk warehouses; and it was not long before Miss Trent's ingenuity was put to the test, Tiffany falling in love first with a pair of gold French shoe-buckles ornamented with paste; and next with a Surprise fan of crape, lavishly embellished with purple and gold devices. Miss Trent had never seen anything so exquisite as the buckles, and bemoaned the change in fashion which had made it impossible for anyone to wear them now without appearing perfectly Gothic. As for the fan, she agreed that it was a most amusing trifle: just what she would wish to buy for herself, if it had not been so excessively ugly!

These hazards successfully skirted, she steered her charges into a large and entrancing establishment, where both young ladies bought some gloves and some ribbons, and Tiffany several pairs of silk stockings, which aroused such envy in Miss Chartley's gentle bosom that she determined to save twelve shillings from the sum reposing in her purse so that she could buy just one pair to wear at the Colebatches' ball.

After this they visited the silk warehouse which enjoyed Mrs Chartley's patronage; and while Tiffany, who soon lost interest in the choice of a satin to furnish a new underdress for Patience's gauze ball-gown, wandered about, inspecting silks and velvets, with a dazed and slavishly admiring young shopman in attendance, Miss Trent placed her taste and experience at her young friend's disposal. A very reasonably priced satin of a charming shade of pink having been discovered, there was only enough time left before the ladies' assignation with Lord Lindeth for the purchase of Patience's new dancing-sandals. This was soon accomplished, and although it took several minutes to dissuade Tiffany from investing in a pair of pale blue silk sandals, they returned to the King's Arms before their host had begun to entertain any very serious fear that some accident must have overtaken them.

He was awaiting them in a private parlour, and it was evident from the array of cold meats, fruit, jellies, and creams on the table that he had taken great pains over their entertainment. Only one thing, in Miss Trent's view, was wanting. For no persuasion would she have betrayed the smallest interest in the whereabouts of the Nonesuch; but when Tiffany, who had few reserves, demanded to know why he was not present, she felt, for once, no desire to censure this unbecoming pertness.

"He'll be here presently," Lindeth answered. "We won't wait for him, however: he warned me not to—said I was to make his apologies, if he was detained. I daresay he is still interviewing bailiffs! From what I saw, that lawyer—what's his name?—Smeeth!—had a score of 'em drawn up in line for his inspection!"

"Oh!" Tiffany said, pouting. "Dull work!"

"Well——" He hesitated, and then said: "Yes, of course it is—dull work for a lady, I mean."

"I should suppose it must be very difficult," said Patience thoughtfully. "In particular, if you mean to leave the bailiff in sole charge. One hears of such shocking instances of tyranny, and neglect—though my father says the fault too often lies at the landlord's door."

"Yes, very true," he agreed. "Screws like old Joseph Calver, wringing every groat it will yield out of his land, and leasing his farms on short terms to thriftless get-pennies, because——" He stopped, seeing the frown that creased Tiffany's brow. "But I don't know why we should be talking about such things, and boring Miss Wield!"

"No, nor do I!" she said, all demure mischief. "*Tell* me why?"

He laughed. "Not for the world! I'll invite you to the table instead! I hope you are very hungry! Miss Trent, will you sit here, and may I carve you some chicken?"

"Misuse of language, Lindeth: *hack* is the word!" said Sir Waldo, entering the parlour at that moment. "How do you do, ma'am? Miss Chartley, your very obedient! Miss Wield, yours! I beg all your pardons: I'm late!"

"Now, that puts me in mind of a remark someone once made to me," said Miss Trent, apparently chasing an elusive recollection. "Something about becoming inured to unpunctuality . . . Who can have said that, I wonder? I have the wretchedest memory!"

"Then you should not attempt quotation, ma'am!" retorted Sir Waldo, a laugh in his eye. " 'To the unpunctuality of your sex' was what I said."

"Oh, no, did he, ma'am?" exclaimed Lindeth. "That's famous. *Hoist with his own petard!*"

"What does that mean, pray?" asked Tiffany.

"You must not ask me," responded Sir Waldo, with a reproving look. "Lindeth shouldn't say such things in the presence of ladies."

"Oh, is it improper?" she said innocently.

"Most improper!" he replied, his gravity unimpaired.

She saw that the others were laughing, and put up her chin, flushing slightly. But as Sir Waldo, taking his seat beside her at the table, asked her to tell him all about the morning's shopping expedition, showing a gratifying interest in her purchases, she very soon mended her temper, and prattled to him throughout the meal in the greatest good humour.

A new reticule for Patience, and velvet ribbon to match the pink satin had still to be found. When they rose from the table, Sir Waldo excused himself, and went away to resume his inspection of bailiffs; but Lindeth, declaring that he had a very good eye for colour, begged to be allowed to escort the ladies. Since the Nonesuch had devoted himself to Tiffany's entertainment at the table, Julian, wondering at this most unusual want of conduct in his cousin, had done his best to keep both his other guests amused; and he had succeeded very well. But Miss Trent, ably seconding his efforts, was assailed by apprehension. The faint suspicion, which had crossed her mind once or twice before, that Miss Chartley was more powerfully attracted to Lindeth than she would have wished anyone to guess was strengthened. The Rector's well-brought up daughter was behaving just as she ought, but the light in her soft eyes when she raised them to his lordship's face was, thought Miss Trent, unmistakeably tender. Like Mrs Chartley she could not help feeling that they would be very well-suited to one another; but while she knew, on the authority of chroniclers and poets, that it was by no means unusual for a gentleman to transfer his affections almost in the twinkling of an eye (witness the extraordinary revulsion of feeling experienced by young Mr Montague when he first clapped eyes on Miss Capulet!), she did not know whether the Nonesuch would look upon Patience with approbation. Miss Trent could not doubt that if he did not he would contrive to thrust a spoke into the wheel of a possible courtship. That realization, she thought, should have been enough to warn her that he was probably an unscrupulous man of whom she would do well to beware. The mischief was that while she was just able to admit this possibility in his absence she had only to meet his eyes across a room to become instantly convinced of his integrity.

He found an opportunity to exchange a few words with her before he left the King's Arms, asking abruptly: "Shall I see you at the Colebatches' ball?"

"Yes. I have been invited to go, and my kind mistress says I may—or, rather, insists that I must!"

"*En chaperon?*"

"No, she goes herself, so I am to enjoy a holiday."

"Then I shan't cry off from it."

He did not wait for an answer, but with a smile, and a brief handshake, took his departure.

The next hour was spent very agreeably by the rest of the party in various shops, where not only was a reticule found, and the satin exactly matched, but where Tiffany bought a pair of filigree earrings, and Miss Trent a spray of artificial flowers to wear with her only ball-dress. Lindeth's presence added a good deal of gaiety to the expedition. He took a keen interest in the various purchases, but as he knew very little about feminine fashions he made some wonderful blunders, which rapidly induced a mood of hilarity in his companions. He also discovered a pastrycook's shop advertizing ice-creams; and as the ladies were all feeling hot, and a trifle weary, he experienced no difficulty in persuading them to enter it. Tiffany, puffing off her knowledge, said that it was just like Gunter's: an inaccurate statement, but one which showed her to be in her best humour. Miss Trent thought that she had seldom spent a more pleasant day in her company.

After disposing of several lemon-flavoured ices, they left the pastrycook's, and began to retrace their steps to the King's Arms. The street was a busy one, and there was no room to walk four abreast, so the two girls went ahead, amicably discussing the latest modes, and Lindeth civilly offered his arm to Miss Trent. A picture hanging in the window of a print-shop caught his eye; he recognized the subject, which was the Dripping Well, and at once drew Miss Trent's attention to it. It was while they were studying it that the harmony of the day was suddenly and rudely shattered. Some kind of a stir was taking place further up the street; there were shouts of: "Stop thief!" and as they looked quickly round a ragged urchin came into view, darting towards them with an apple clutched in his hand, and an expression of hunted terror in his starting eyes. He was dodging between the passers-by, and had almost reached Patience and Tiffany when a middle-aged citizen thrust his walking-cane between his legs to arrest his progress. A crashing fall was the inevitable result: the child, swerving to avoid the over-zealous citizen, pitched forward, not on the flagway but on to the cobbled street. A cry of protest had burst from Patience; parcels, parasol, and purse were flung away; and under Miss Trent's horrified eyes she sprang into the road, snatching the urchin almost from under the hooves of a high-stepping chestnut harnessed to a tilbury, which was being driven at a spanking pace along the street. For a dreadful moment it seemed as if she must be trampled upon; then the chestnut reared up, snorting, and was miraculously swung to one side; and the driver of the tilbury, a natty young gentleman clad in raiment which, almost as clearly as his handling of the reins, proclaimed him to be a top-sawyer, added his voice to the general hubbub in a furious expletive. The next instant Lindeth had brushed past Miss Trent, racing forward to the rescue, and unceremoniously pushing Tiffany out of the way as he bent over Patience.

"Good God, Miss Chartley——! Are you hurt?"

She had dragged rather than lifted the urchin out of danger, and was on her knees, supporting him in her arms, and gazing down in horror at his face, down which blood was streaming from a gash on the forehead, but she glanced up, saying: "Oh, no, no! But this poor little boy——! Something to stop the bleeding—a handkerchief—*anything*!—— Oh, pray, *one* of you——!"

"Here, take mine!" Lindeth said, thrusting it into her hand. "Poor little devil! Knocked himself out!" He looked up at the driver of the tilbury, and said curtly: "I'm sorry, sir, and must thank you for acting so promptly. I trust your horse has suffered no injury."

By this time the natty gentleman had realized that the female kneeling beside the gutter was a young and very pretty girl of obviously gentle birth. Blushing hotly, he stammered: "No, no, not the least in the world! Beg you'll accept my apologies, ma'am! Agitation of the moment—forgot myself! By Jove, though! You might have been killed! Bravest thing I ever saw in my life! By Jove, it was!"

She looked up briefly, to say: "Oh, no! I am so much obliged to you! I don't wonder you were angry—but, you see, I *had* to do it!"

Miss Trent, who had succeeded in pushing her way through the fast-gathering crowd, bent over her, asking anxiously: "How badly is he hurt, my dear?"

"I don't know. His head struck the cobbles. I must take him to the hospital."

"Yes, for I fear this cut must be stitched," said Miss Trent, folding her own handkerchief into a neat pad, and pressing it over the wound. "Do you hold his head so that I can tie Lord Lindeth's handkerchief round it!"

At this point, a fresh voice intruded upon them. The owner of the stolen apple, a stout and breathless shopkeeper, had arrived on the scene, and was loudly announcing his intention of summoning a constable to take the young varmint in charge. He was in a blustering rage, and somewhat roughly told Patience that the gaol was the place for hedge-birds, not the hospital. She said imploringly: "Pray don't give him up to the constable! It was very wrong of him to steal from you, but you see what a little boy he is, and how wretched! And he's badly hurt, too."

"Not he!" retorted the shopkeeper. "Serve him right if he'd broke his neck! It's a shame and a scandal the way him and his like hang about waiting for the chance to prig something! I'll have this young thief made an example of, by God I will!"

"Here, you rascal, that's no way to speak to a lady!" exclaimed the gentleman in the tilbury indignantly. "What's more I'll go bail the brat ain't half as big a thief as you are! *I* know you shopkeepers! All the same: selling farthing-dips for a bull's eye apiece!"

Not unnaturally, the effect of this intervention was far from happy. The injured tradesman appealed to the onlookers for support, and although one or two persons recommended him to pardon the thief, several others ranged themselves on his side. The air was rent with argument; but Lindeth, who had never before found himself in the centre of so embarrassing a scene, collected his wits and his dignity, and in a voice which held a remarkable degree of calm authority bade the shopkeeper declare the worth of the stolen fruit.

The man seemed at first to be determined on revenge, but after some more argument, in which some six or seven members of the crowd took part, he consented to accept the coin held out to him, and withdrew, accompanied by several of his supporters. The crowd now began to disperse; the small thief, coming round from his swoon, started to cry for his home and his Mammy; and while Patience soothed him, assuring him that she would take him to his home directly, and that no one should lock him up in prison, or give him up to the beadle (an official of whom he seemed to stand in terror), Miss Trent, Lord Lindeth, and the gentleman in sporting toggery, who had descended from the tilbury to join in the discussion, held a hurried council.

Throughout this animated scene Tiffany had been standing neglected and alone, rigid with mortification, jostled by such low-bred persons in the crowd as wished to obtain a closer view of the group in the gutter; pushed out of the way by Lord Lindeth; sharply adjured by Miss Trent not to stand like a stock, but to pick up Patience's belongings; and left without chaperonage or male protection by those who should have made her comfort and safety their first concern. Even the sporting gentleman in the tilbury had paid her no heed! Patience—*Patience*—!—kneeling in the road, with her dress stained with blood, and a ragged and disgusting urchin in her arms, was the heroine of this most revolting piece, while she, the Beautiful Miss Wield, was left to hold as best she might two parasols, two purses, and a load of parcels.

She listened in seething fury to the plans that were being formulated. The sporting gentleman—he said that his name was Baldock, and that he begged to be allowed to place himself at their disposal—was offering to drive Patience and the dirty little boy to the infirmary; Lindeth was assuring her that he would himself convey the pair of them to the boy's home (no doubt a hovel in the back-slums of the town!), and Miss Trent was promising to proceed on foot to the infirmary immediately, there to render Patience all the aid and protection of which she was capable. Not one of them had a thought to spare for *her*! She was tired; she wanted to go home; out of sheer kindness of heart she had agreed to allow Patience (whom she had never liked) to accompany her to Leeds; she had submitted, without a word of protest, to being dragged all over the town in search of some stupid pink satin; her own companion—hired to take care of her!—instead of escorting her away from this degrading scene was merely concerned with Patience's welfare; and now she and Lindeth, without the slightest reference to her, were talking of driving that nasty child to his home in *her* carriage.

"I think I am going to faint!" she announced, in a penetrating voice which lent no colour to this statement.

Lindeth, who was lifting the boy out of Patience's arms, paid no heed; Miss Trent, assisting Patience to her feet, just glanced at her, and said: "I can't attend to you now, Tiffany!" and Mr Baldock, with no more than a cursory look at her, said: "Don't see why *you* should faint, ma'am! Shouldn't have wondered at it if *this* lady had, but not she! Didn't quite catch your name, ma'am, but shall take leave to say you're a regular trump! No—shouldn't have said that! Not the thing to say to a female! Beg your pardon: never been much of a lady's man! What I meant was, you're a—you're a——"

"Heroine!" supplied Lindeth, laughing.

"Ay, so she is! A dashed heroine!"

"Oh, pray——!" Patience protested. "I'm very much obliged to you, but indeed I'm nothing of the sort! If you will be so very good as to drive me to the infirmary, let us go immediately, if you please! He is still bleeding, and I'm afraid he may have injured his leg as well. You can see how it is swelling, and he cries if you touch it!" She looked round. "I don't know what became of my parcels, and my—— Oh, Tiffany, you have them all! Thank you! I am so sorry—so disagreeable for you!"

"Oh, *pray* don't mention it!" said Tiffany, quivering with fury. "I *like* picking up parcels and parasols for other people! I *like* being jostled by vulgar persons! *Pray* don't consider me at all! *Or* ask my leave to use *my* carriage for that odious, wicked boy!"

"Well, of all the shrews!" gasped Mr Baldock.

Lindeth, who had been staring at Tiffany, a queer look in his eyes, and his lips rather tightly compressed, turned from her, and said quietly: "Hand Miss Chartley into your tilbury, will you? I'll give the boy to her then, and we can be off."

"Yes, but it will be the deuce of a squeeze," responded Mr Baldock doubtfully.

"No, it won't: I'm going to get up behind." He waited until Patience had climbed into the carriage, and then deposited the whimpering child in her lap, saying gently: "Don't be distressed! There's no need, I promise you."

She was feeling ready to sink, and whispered: "I never thought—I didn't know—Lord Lindeth, stay with her! I shall do very well by myself. Perhaps you could hire a carriage for me? Oh, yes! of course that's what I ought to do! If you would direct the coachman to drive to the infirmary——"

122

"Stop fretting!" he commanded, smiling up at her. "We'll discuss what's best to be done presently. Meanwhile, Miss Trent will look after Miss Wield: I am coming with you!" He turned, as Miss Trent came up to give Patience her purse, and told her briefly what he meant to do, adding, in an under-voice: "Will you be able to come to the infirmary, ma'am? I think you should, don't you?"

"Of course I shall come," she replied. "Just as soon as I have taken Miss Wield back to the King's Arms!"

He looked relieved. "Yes, if you please. Then I'll find Waldo. He's the man we want in this situation!"

She had been thinking so herself, and although she was surprised that he should have said it she agreed cordially. It was then his lordship's turn to be a little puzzled, for he had spoken more to himself than to her, and (since Waldo very much disliked having his peculiar philanthropy puffed-off) was already regretting it. Before it could be established that they were talking at cross-purposes, Tiffany, almost beside herself with rage at their continued neglect, stalked up to them to demand in a voice vibrant with passion how much longer Miss Trent meant to keep her waiting.

"Not an instant!" replied her preceptress cheerfully, re-moving from her grasp the parasol and the various packages with which she was still burdened. Over her shoulder, she smiled reassuringly at Patience. "I'll join you at the infirmary directly, Miss Chartley. Now, Tiffany!"

"You will *not* join her at the infirmary!" said Tiffany. "I wish to go home, and it is your duty to stay with me, and if you don't do what *I* want I'll tell my aunt, and have you turned off!"

"Without a character!" nodded Miss Trent, tucking a hand in her arm, and firmly propelling her down the flagway. "And if I were to take you home, abandoning Miss Chartley, her mama would no doubt demand my instant dismissal too, so in either event I must be totally ruined. I am quite sick with apprehension! But if I were you, Tiffany, I would take care how I exposed myself!"

"How *I* exposed myself?" gasped Tiffany. "When it was that odious Patience Chartley, with her insinuating ways, be-having like a hoyden, just to make everyone think her a her-oine——"

"Do, Tiffany, strive for a little conduct!" interrupted Miss Trent. "I am not going to bandy words with you in public, so you may as well keep your tongue."

This, however, the outraged beauty was far too angry to do, delivering herself all the way to the King's Arms of a tirade which was as comprehensive as it was absurd. Miss Trent refused to be goaded into retort, but she could willingly have slapped her spoilt charge. She did indeed point out to her that she was attracting the undesirable notice of such passers-by who were privileged to overhear scraps of her diatribe; but although Tiffany lowered her voice she continued to scold.

It might have been supposed that the violence of her emotions would have exhausted her by the time the King's Arms was reached; but she was made of resilient fibre, and the recital of her wrongs and the condemnation of every one of her companions were merely the prelude to a storm which, as experience had taught Miss Trent, would involve her, when it broke, in embarrassment, startle everyone within earshot, and culminate in a fit of shattering hysterics. She knew it to be useless to reason with Tiffany; so when they reached the posting-house she almost dragged her into the parlour which Lindeth had hired for the day, and left her there, saying mandaciously that she was going to procure some hartshorn. Tiffany had already begun to cry in an ominously gusty way, but Miss Trent did not believe that she would work herself into hysterics if no one was present to be shocked or distressed by her passion. She was quite capable, of course, of doing something outrageous when she had lashed herself into one of these fits; but Miss Trent, after rapidly reviewing the circumstances, thought that the worst she could find to do in the middle of Leeds would be to order her aunt's coachman to put the horses to, and to have herself driven back to Staples immediately. When John-Coachman refused to obey this order, as he certainly would, there would really be nothing left for her to do but to smash the china ornaments on the mantelpiece.

Miss Trent might regard the situation in this practical light; but she was much more worried than she had allowed Tiffany to suspect. Her first duty was undoubtedly to that intransigent damsel, and by no stretch of the imagination could this duty be thought to include taking her into the back-slums of the town; but when Mrs Chartley had permitted her daughter to join the expedition she had done so in the belief that she would be respectably chaperoned. Neither she nor Miss Trent, of course, could have foreseen the accident which had made this double chaperonage so difficult; but that she would think it extremely reprehensible of Miss Trent to leave Patience to the sole protection and escort of Lord Lindeth was beyond doubt, or (in Miss Trent's own opinion) censure. Somehow the two conflicting duties must be reconciled. Try as she would, Miss Trent could hit upon no better solution to the problem than to enlist Sir Waldo's support, just as Lindeth had suggested. If he could be induced to keep Tiffany amused until Patience's protégé had been restored to his parents the unfortunate episode might yet end happily.

So it was not to procure hartshorn for Tiffany that Miss Trent hurriedly left the parlour, but to make all speed to the infirmary, whence she meant to send Lindeth off post-haste to find his cousin.

In the event, Sir Waldo entered the King's Arms just as she was about to leave the house. Never had she been more thankful, nor more relieved! She exclaimed impulsively: "Oh, how glad I am to see you! Sir Waldo, you are the *one* person who may be able to help me in this fix, and I do beg that you will!"

"You may be sure that I will," he replied, looking a little startled, but maintaining his calm. "What fix have you fallen into, and what must I do to extricate you from it?"

She gave a shaky laugh. "Oh, dear! I must seem to you to have flown into alt! I beg your pardon! It wasn't precisely I who fell into a fix, but——"

"Just a moment!" he interrupted. "Do you know that there is blood on your dress?"

She cast a cursory glance down her own person. "Is there? Yes, I see—but it's of no consequence!"

"Well, as you don't appear to have sustained any injury, I'll accept your word for that," he said. "Whose blood is it?"

"I don't know—I mean, I don't know what his name is! A little boy—but I must tell you how it all happened!"

"Do!" he invited.

As concisely as she could, she put him in possession of the facts, making no attempt to conceal from him that it was not the accident which had thrown her into disorder, but Tiffany's obstructive behaviour. "I know it must seem incredible that she should fly into one of her rages at such a moment," she said earnestly, "but you know what she is!"

"Of course I do! It is exactly what I should have expected of her. How could it be otherwise when the rôle of heroine in this stirring drama was snatched from her, and she found herself a mere spectator? Where is she now?"

"Upstairs, in the parlour where we ate luncheon. That was

the reason, of course, and I don't know what enraged her the more: your cousin paying no heed to her, or that absurd Mr Baldock saying he didn't see what cause *she* had to faint! Yes, it's all very well for you to laugh, sir! I own, I should think it very funny myself if it didn't concern me so nearly. Do you see *now* what a fix I'm in? I can neither leave Tiffany alone here for heaven only knows how long, nor can I abandon Miss Chartley! I never was more distracted! But your cousin said that you were the man to help us in this situation, and, although it surprised me a little that he should say so, I perceived immediately that he was perfectly right! Sir Waldo, will you be so *very* obliging as to stay with Tiffany—divert her, you know!—while I go with Patience to wherever the boy lives?"

"I don't think that was quite what Lindeth meant," he said dryly, "but certainly I'll take charge of Tiffany. Shall I find her indulging in a fit of hysterics?"

"No, for I came away before she had time to throw herself into one. There's no sense in having hysterics, you know, if one is quite by oneself."

He smiled, but said: "It's to be hoped that she doesn't have them for my edification, for I should be quite at a loss to know what to do!"

"She won't," said Miss Trent confidently. "Just flatter her —as you very well *do* know how to do!"

"I think that the best service I can render you will be to drive her back to Staples," he said. "You need not then be anxious on her account—I hope!"

The worried crease was smoothed from her brow. She said gratefully: "No, indeed! You know I shouldn't be! And there can be no objection—in an open carriage, and with your groom behind!"

"Yes, those circumstances will compel me to restrain any inclination I may feel to make violent love to her, won't they?" he agreed affably.

She laughed. "Yes—if that was what I had meant to say, which it was not! I know very well you don't feel any such inclination!"

"I imagine you might! Now, I have just one thing to say before we part, ma'am! From what you have told me, this urchin hails from the slums: either in the eastern part of the town, where the dyeing-houses and most of the manufactories are situated, or on the south bank of the river."

"I am afraid so. You are going to say that I shouldn't per-

126

mit Miss Chartley to go into such districts. I know it, but I don't think I can prevent her."

"No, I am not going to say that. But you must promise me you won't leave the carriage, Miss Trent! So far as I am aware there is no epidemic disease rife there at the moment, but most of the dwellings are little better than hovels, and there is a degree of squalor which makes it excessively imprudent for you—or Miss Chartley, of course—to enter them."

She looked wonderingly at him. "I have never been in the poorer part of the town. Have you, then?"

"Yes, I have, and you may believe that I know what I am saying. Have I your word?"

"Of course: I would not for the world expose Miss Chartley to the least risk!"

"Good girl!" he said, smiling at her. "Tell Julian I've left you in his charge—and that I've removed the worst of your embarrassments!"

He held out his hand, and, when she put hers into it, raised it to his lips, and lightly kissed her fingers.

CHAPTER X

TIFFANY DID NOT GREET Sir Waldo with hysterics; but he found her weeping in an angry, uncontrolled way which warned him that a more ticklish task lay before him than he had foreseen. Like a child suffering from over-excitement, she was as miserable as she was cross, and with the slightest encouragement she would have cast herself upon Sir Waldo's chest, and sobbed out her woes into his shoulder. With considerable skill he managed to prevent this without adding to her sense of ill-usage, but he soon saw that it was useless—indeed, perilous—to attempt to bring her to reason. The story she poured out to him bore little resemblance to the unembroidered account furnished earlier by Miss Trent. Tiffany never consciously deviated from the truth, but since she saw everything only as it affected herself the truth was apt to become somewhat distorted. Anyone unacquainted with the facts would have supposed from her version of the accident that Patience, having first, and with incredible selfishness, dragged her companions all over the town in search of her own needs, had next set her cap at Lindeth in a way that would have been diverting had it not been so unbecoming; and finally, in her determination to attract attention to herself, had created a ridiculous scene by dashing into the road to perform a spectacular and quite unnecessary rescue. For her part, Tiffany was persuaded that the nasty boy had been in no danger at all, but Patience, of course, had put on all the airs of a heroine, quite deluding Lindeth, as well as Mr Baldock, who was a very low, vulgar person, with the most disgusting manners of anyone Tiffany had ever met.

There was a good deal more in the same strain, culminating in the iniquity of all concerned in coolly, and without as much as a by-your-leave, appropriating Tiffany's carriage (for even if it did belong to her aunt it had been lent to her, not to Patience) for the conveyance of a dirty and thievish boy who ought rather to have been handed over to the constable. This was the crowning injury, and Tiffany's eyes flashed as she recounted it. She did not deny that she had lost her temper. She had borne everything else without uttering a single complaint, but that had been Too Much.

The Nonesuch, quick to seize opportunity, agreed that such conduct passed all bounds. He was astonished to learn that Lindeth and Miss Trent were so lost to all sense of propriety as to suppose that Tiffany could be left to kick her heels at the King's Arms while they jauntered about the town (with a dirty and thievish boy) in what was undoubtedly her carriage. He said that they would be well served if, when they at last returned to the King's Arms, they were to find that the bird had flown.

"Yes," agreed Tiffany, hiccuping on a sob. "Only, if I were to order John-Coachman to bring the carriage round he wouldn't do it, because he is a detestable old man, and treats me as if I were a child!"

"I'll take you home," said the Nonesuch, with his glinting smile.

She stared at him. "You? In your phaeton? *Now?*" He nodded: and she jumped up, exclaiming ecstatically: "Oh, *yes*! I should like that of all things! And we won't leave a message, either!"

"Oh, that will be quite unnecessary!" he said, with perfect truth.

Her tears ceased abruptly; and if the ill-usage she had suffered still rankled in her bosom it soon became at least temporarily forgotten in the elation of being driven by no less a person than the Nonesuch.

Mrs Underhill was very much shocked when she heard what had happened in Leeds, but although Sir Waldo left Tiffany to tell the story as she pleased the good lady's reception of it was not at all what her niece desired or expected. She said she wouldn't have had such a thing happen for the world. "Not with Mrs Chartley letting Patience go with you, as she did, which quite surprised me, for I never thought she would, and no more she would have, if it hadn't been for Miss Trent being there to take care of her. And what she'll say, when she hears about this—not that Miss Trent could have stopped it, by all I can make out, for it wasn't a thing anyone would *expect* to happen! Well, thank goodness Miss Trent had the sense to stay with Patience! At least Mrs Chartley won't be able to say we didn't do our best, *or* that she was left to be brought home by his lordship, which she wouldn't have liked at all! Not that I mean he wouldn't have kept the line, as I hope I don't need to explain to you, Sir Waldo, for I'm sure I never knew anyone more truly the gentleman—present company excepted, of course—but Mrs Chartley—well, she's nice to a fault, and very strict in her notions!"

This speech was naturally extremely displeasing to Tiffany. There were danger signals in her eyes, which her aunt viewed with apprehension. Mrs Underhill hoped that she was not going to fly into one of her miffs, and she said feebly: "Now, Tiffany-love, there's nothing to put you into high fidgets! To be sure, it was vexatious for you to be obliged to wait, when you was wanting to come home, but you wouldn't have wished to leave poor Miss Chartley with no carriage, now, you know you wouldn't! A very shabby thing that would have been! And Sir Waldo driving you home in his phaeton, which I'll be bound you enjoyed!"

"They should have *asked* me!" said Tiffany obstinately. "If they had done so——"

"*I* see what it is!" suddenly announced Charlotte, whose penetrating gaze had been fixed for some minutes on her cousin's face. "Nobody paid any heed to you! And you might

129

just as easily have rescued the boy as Patience, only you didn't, so it wasn't you that was brave and noble, but *her* and *that's* why you're in such a pelter!"

"How dare you?" gasped Tiffany, glaring at her.

"Charlotte, *don't*!" begged Mrs. Underhill, much agitated.

"*And*," pursued Charlotte, with acute if deplorable insight, "it's my belief the man in the tilbury didn't pay any heed to you either, and that's why you said he was rude and vulgar!"

"Now that's enough!" said Mrs Underhill, with a very fair assumption of authority. "Whatever must Sir Waldo be thinking of you? I don't know when I've been so mortified! You must please excuse her, sir!"

"I'll excuse them both, ma'am, and leave them to enjoy their quarrel!" he replied, looking amused.

"Oh, dear, and I was going to ask you if you wouldn't stop to eat your dinner with us!" exclaimed Mrs Underhill distressfully.

"Thank you: you are very good, ma'am, but I mustn't stay," he answered, smiling at her in a way which, as she afterwards told Miss Trent, made her feel all of a twitter.

He then took his leave, and went away. He reached Broom Hall as the shadows were lengthening, and strolled into the house, stripping off his gloves. The door leading into the book-room opened, and a slender sprig of fashion emerged, and paused on the threshold, saying with would-be jauntiness: "Hallo, Waldo!"

At sight of this unexpected visitor Sir Waldo had halted, one glove still only half drawn from his hand, a sudden frown in his eyes. He stood still for an instant; then the frown vanished, and he pulled off his glove, and laid it down on the table. "Dear me!" he said, in a tone of mild surprise. "And what brings you here, Laurie?"

Mr Calver, with the memory of his last encounter with his cousin uncomfortably in mind, was much relieved by the calm friendliness of this greeting. He had not expected to be met with an explosion of wrath, because Waldo never ripped up, or came the ugly; but he had feared that he might cut up a trifle stiff, perhaps. He came forward, saying awkwardly: "I've been visiting friends in York. Thought I'd come over to see how you go on."

"That's very kind of you," said Sir Waldo politely.

"Well, I—well—you know, I don't like to be at outs with you! The last time I saw you—— Well, I was in a damned bad skin, and I daresay I may have said things I don't mean! shouldn't wish you to think——"

"Oh, that's enough, Laurie!" Sir Waldo interrupted, a swift smile banishing the slightly stern look on his face. "Looby! Did you suppose I had taken an affront into my head? What a gudgeon you must think me!"

"No, I don't, but—— Well, I thought I'd post over to see you—beg your pardon, you know!"

"I'm much obliged to you. Come into the book-room! Has Wedmore done the honours of the house—such as they are?"

"Oh, yes! Well, I haven't been here much above half-an-hour, but he brought me some sherry, and took Blyth off to unpack my bags." He shot a sidelong look at his cousin, and ventured on a small joke. "I was pretty sure you wouldn't throw me out of doors even if you *had* nabbed the rust!"

"Very unlikely," agreed Sir Waldo, walking over to a side-table, and pouring himself out a glass of sherry. He drank a little, and stood thoughtfully regarding Laurence.

That exquisite, failing, not for the first time in a somewhat chequered career, to meet that steady, faintly amused gaze, cast himself into a chair, with an assumption of ease, and picked up his own glass from a table at his elbow, saying airily: "I hadn't thought you meant to remain here above a sennight. Everyone is wondering what's become of you! Is Lindeth still with you? Don't he find it devilish slow?"

"Apparently not. Tell me! Who are these friends of yours who live in York?"

"Oh, no one you're acquainted with!"

"I didn't think I was." He picked up the decanter, and walked across the room to refill Laurence's glass. "What is it you want, Laurie?"

"I told you! We came to cuffs, and——"

"No, don't sham it! You haven't travelled all the way from London merely to beg my pardon!"

"I've come from York!" said Laurence, reddening. "If you don't believe me you may enquire at the Black Horse, where I hired a chaise to bring me here!"

"I do believe you. I think you went to York on the Edinburgh mail. Or are you on the rocks again, and was it the stage? Stop trying to make a pigeon of me! You'll only be gapped, you know! What's the matter? Are you in the suds?"

"No, I am not!" replied Laurence angrily. "I may not be flush in the pocket, but I haven't come to ask you to pay any gaming debts!"

"Don't be so ready to sport your canvas! I didn't suppose that was it. There might be other debts which you forgot to mention when you were last down the wind."

"Well, there ain't!" growled Laurence. "Nothing to signify, that is! And if there was, I shouldn't ask you to dub up the possibles! Not after what you said a month ago! I daresay you think I'm a loose screw, but I don't run thin!"

"I wish you will come down from these high ropes! I don't think you a loose screw—though if I were to tell you what I *do* think you'd be ready to eat me! If you don't want me to dub up the possibles, what *do* you want me to do?"

"It may interest you to know, coz, that it's been make and scrape with me ever since you left London!" said Laurence bitterly. "And when I think of the shifts I've been put to—— Well, it's the outside enough for you to be suspecting me of having come to see you only to get you to tip over the dibs! It isn't that at all!" He paused. "At least," he amended, "it ain't debt! If you *must* know, I've hit upon a devilish good scheme—if I can but raise the recruits! Of course, if you don't care to frank me—though if it ain't so much franking me, mind, as *investing* your blunt!—there's no more to be said. But considering the times you've offered to buy me a pair of colours——"

"The offer still stands, Laurie."

"Yes, but I don't want it. It wouldn't suit me at all. I haven't any taste for the law, either. I didn't think of it at the time, but if you had suggested the Church to me, when I was up at Oxford, there would have been some sense in it. I daresay I shouldn't have liked it above half, but I wonder you shouldn't have thought of it, if you're so eager to thrust me into some profession or other. After all, I know you've several good livings in your gift! However, it's too late now."

"That's just as well, for I can think of few men less suited to the Church."

"No, very likely I should have found it a dead bore. Not but what a snug parsonage—— But it's of no consequence! I fancy I've hit on the very thing, Waldo! What's more, if the thing comes off right there's a fortune in it!"

Concealing his misgivings, Sir Waldo invited him to continue.

"Well, I hadn't meant to broach it to you so soon," said Laurence, rather naïvely. "But since you've asked me to— and there's no reason why you shouldn't care for the scheme: in fact, I'm persuaded you'll think it's the very thing——"

"You are filling me with foreboding, Laurie. Do put me out of suspense!"

"Of course, if you mean to set your face against it from the start I might as well keep my tongue!" said Laurence peevishly.

"We haven't reached the start yet. Cut line!" commanded his cousin.

Laurence looked offended for a moment, but he managed to swallow his spleen. "Yes—— Well—well, are you acquainted with Kearney, Waldo?"

"No." ·

"*Desmond* Kearney!" Sir Waldo shook his head. "Oh! I daresay he may not have come in your way, though I should have thought you must have met him. He's the devil of a man to hounds—a clipping rider! But you high sticklers are so top-lofty——" He broke off, and said hastily: "Not that it signifies! The thing is, Kearney is a friend of mine. Not a feather to fly with, but a first-rate man, and a capital judge of horseflesh! We mean to become partners."

"Partners in what?" asked Sir Waldo blankly.

"Hunters! Selling 'em, I mean."

"O my God!"

"I suppose I might have guessed you would—— No, do but listen, Waldo!" begged Laurence, suddenly altering his tone. "Only think of the blunt some of the Melton men drop on their hunters! Well, you're one yourself, so you should know! They say Lord Alvanley gave seven hundred guineas for one of the nags he bought last year, and I could name you a score of men who think nothing of shelling out five or six hundred for horses that were bought originally for no more than eighty or a hundred guineas! Why, if you was to put your own stud under the hammer—just your hunters and your hacks: not your driving-cattle, of course—they wouldn't fetch a penny under five thousand! I daresay you're thinking the scheme might not fadge, but——"

"Might not fadge!" interrupted Sir Waldo. "You'd find yourselves at point non-plus within a twelvemonth!"

"No, that we shouldn't! We have it all planned, and I'd be willing to lay you any odds we shall make an excellent hit. Of course, at first we shall be obliged to spend a good deal of blunt—no need to tell you that!—but——"

"No need at all!"

"Well, there's no doing anything unless one has some capital! The thing is——"

"Thank you, I know what the thing is!" said Sir Waldo acidly. "For God's sake, will you stop trying to tip me a rise? I never in my life listened to such an addle-brained scheme! Do you think me such a flat that I would provide the capital for such a crazy venture? Go into partnership with a man who hasn't a feather to fly with? Oh, no! Laurie! Coming it *too* strong!"

"If you would but *listen*——! Kearney ain't any plumper in the pocket than I am, but he's just come into some property! It was that circumstance which put the notion into his head! He's inherited a place in Ireland, from his uncle—Galway, I think. Sounds to me much like this place: gone to rack, and the house pretty well tumbling down. Seemed to him more of a liability than a honey-fall, for there's no getting rid of it as it stands."

"It seems like that to me too."

"Well, that's where you're out! We mean to put it to dashed good use! Kearney's been to look it over, and he says there's plenty of ground attached, and acres of stabling, which only needs repairing to furnish us with precisely what we need. Now, Waldo, you must know that Ireland's the place for picking up first-rate horses for no more than eighty pounds apiece! No cart-horse blood there! No black drop! A year's schooling, and you sell 'em over here for a couple of hundred at the least!"

"If you think that I'm going to set you up as a horsechanter——"

"No such thing!" exclaimed Laurence indignantly. "They won't be *unsound* horses!"

"They will be if you have anything to do with choosing them."

Laurence struggled with himself, and again managed to suppress his anger. "As a matter of fact, Kearney will attend to that side of the business: he knows the country, and which are the best fairs—and I shouldn't wonder at it if he's as good a judge of a horse as you are! *My* part will be to sell 'em over here."

"Laurie, are you seriously proposing to set up as a dealer?"

"No, of course not! I mean, I'm not going to have a sale-ring, or anything of that kind! I've got a much better notion: I'm going to sell 'em on the hunting-field!"

"*What?*" said Sir Waldo faintly.

"Lord, you know what I mean! You ride a goodlooking

134

hunter of the right stamp with one of the Hunts—the Quorn, for instance—and what happens?"

"You end up in the Whissendine."

"Oh, go to the devil! That's not what I mean! Someone takes a fancy to your horse—asks you if you'd care to sell him, and before you know where you are——"

"Not if he's seen you riding the horse!" interpolated Sir Waldo brutally.

Laurence flushed vividly. "Thank you! Upon my word, coz, of all the damnably unjust things to say——! I collect I'm a slow-top—a skirter—a——"

"No, no, I didn't mean that!" said Sir Waldo, relenting slightly. "You've plenty of pluck, but you sloven your fences, and you don't get the best out of your horses. Also—well, no matter! I'm sorry, but I'll have no hand in this project."

"Waldo, I'm not asking you to *give* it to me!" Laurence urged, rather desperately. "Only to *lend* it—and no more than five thousand! I swear I'd pay it back!"

"I doubt it! Oh, I don't doubt you think you would! But *I* think that so far from your paying me back I should be obliged to tow you out of the River Tick to the tune of a few more thousands. I won't do it."

There was a long silence. Laurence got up jerkily, and went over to stare out of the window. Presently he said: "I know you said—when you paid that debt for me last month —that it was the last time, but I never thought you'd refuse to help me when—when I'm trying to do what you've been urging me to for ever!"

Sir Waldo could not help smiling at this. "My dear Laurie, I really don't think I can be said to have urged you to take to horse-coping!"

"You want me to pursue some occupation. And now, when I'm determined not to be idle any longer, or to hang on your sleeve—you make it impossible!"

"Find a respectable occupation, and try me again! You think me a shocking nip-squeeze, but what you are asking me to do is to help you to break your back."

Laurence turned, forcing a smile to his drooping mouth. "No, I don't. You've been devilish generous to me: I know that! Only—— Oh, well! I suppose there's no more to be said. I'd best go back to London tomorrow. I know you don't want me here."

"Gammon! Do you wish to stay?"

"Well, I did rather think—I mean, everyone is going out of town now, and you know what Brighton costs in July! You told me I must stop wasting the ready——"

"So it clearly behoves me to house you! Stop playing off your tricks, you incorrigible dryboots! I haven't the smallest objection to your remaining here—but I don't think you'll like it above half! The builders are at work, you know."

"Oh, I don't care a straw for that!" Laurence assured him. "You seem to be pulling the place to bits—all for your ramshackle brats, I collect!"

"That's it," replied Sir Waldo cheerfully. "I must go and tell Wedmore we won't wait dinner for Julian: he's in Leeds, and is likely to be detained. That, by the way, is one of the disadvantages of the house: the only unbroken bell-wire is the one leading from our late lamented cousin's bedroom! There are some other drawbacks, too: your man will tell you all about them! I only hope he won't cut his stick. I live in constant dread of waking one morning to find that Munslow has abandoned me."

Laurence looked rather appalled, but said: "Oh, Blyth wouldn't serve me such a trick! As for your Munslow—I wish I may see him abandoning you! When do you dine? Should I change my rig?"

"Not on my account. We dine at the unfashionable hour of six."

"Oh, yes! country hours!" said Laurence, refusing to be daunted. "I'm glad of it, for, to own the truth, I'm feeling a trifle fagged. Been thinking lately that it was time I went on a repairing lease!"

He maintained this affability until nine o'clock, when, after trying in vain to smother a succession of yawns, he took himself off to bed. Sir Waldo was not in the least deceived. As little as he believed that Laurence had been visiting friends in York did he believe that Laurence either wanted to remain at Broom Hall or was resigned to the frustration of his preposterous scheme. He remembered, with a rueful smile, several previous occasions when, having refused some demand of Laurie's, he had allowed himself to be won over by just such tactics as Laurie was employing now. Laurie remembered them too; probably he had come prepared to meet with an initial rebuff; certainly he had not accepted it as final: that was betrayed by his meekness. When Laurie knew that he could not bring his cousin round his thumb he very rapidly fell into a rage, jealousy and self-pity overcoming his reason, and leading him to rant and complain until he really did believe in his illusionary grievances.

I ought to have sent him packing, Sir Waldo thought, knowing that in yielding to a compassionate impulse he was raising false hopes in Laurie's breast. But he could no more have done it than he could have left him to languish in a debtor's prison. He had little affection for Laurie, and he was well aware that Laurie had as little for him; but when he had told George Wingham that he had ruined Laurie he had spoken in all sincerity. Laurie's idleness, his follies, his reckless extravagance he set at his own door. By his easy, unthinking generosity he had sapped whatever independance Laurie might have had, imposing no check upon his volatility, but rather encouraging him in the conviction that he would never be run quite off his legs because his wealthy cousin would infallibly rescue him from utter disaster. "After all, it means nothing to you!" Laurie had once said to him, when he had been in his first year at Oxford. Sir Waldo, remembering, grimaced at his younger self. Laurie had said bitterly that it was easy for anyone rolling in gold to preach economy; and that younger Waldo, rich beyond most men's dreams, imbued with philanthropic principles imperfectly understood, morbidly anxious never to become clutchfisted, and only too ready to believe, with Laurie, that the difference between their respective circumstances was one of the grosser injustices of fate, had opened wide his purse for that predatory youth to dip into: not once, but so many times that Laurie had come to regard him as one on whom he had a right to depend. Only when he had taken to deep gaming had Sir Waldo put his foot down. He meant to keep it down, strengthened in his resolve by the storm of resentment he had roused in Laurence; but even at the height of exasperation his conscience told him that he was himself much to blame for this. He had often felt sorry for Laurie, but his pity had been mixed with contempt; and because he had never liked him he had given him money, which was an easy thing to do, instead of the very different services he had rendered Julian.

The cases were not, of course, parallel. Laurence was some years older than Julian, and he had not been left fatherless while still in leading-strings. But his father had been a cold-hearted man, bored by his children, and grudging every penny he was obliged to spend on them, so that Laurie had naturally enough turned to his cousin for help in any predicament.

It might have been wiser not to have told him that he might remain at Broom Hall, but Sir Waldo had found it impossible to treat him so unkindly. Moreover, Julian was staying at Broom Hall, and that circumstance alone made it imperative that he should also welcome Laurie. Laurie was jealous of his affection for Julian, not because of any fondness for him, but because he was obstinate in the belief that he lavished money on the boy. "If it had been Lindeth who had applied to you, you wouldn't have refused!" Laurie had flung at him once.

"Lindeth doesn't apply to me," he had answered.

"No! he ain't obliged to! Anything he wants he can get from you for the mere lifting of an eyebrow! We all know that!"

"Then you are all wonderfully mistaken," he had said.

But Laurie had not been mistaken in thinking that Julian was his favourite cousin; and just because it was true he would not turn Laurie away from his doors while Julian was at liberty to stay with him for as long as he chose.

He was thinking of Laurie's jealousy, and wondering how many days would pass before he and Julian came to cuffs, when he heard the sound of carriage-wheels, and Julian's voice calling good-night to someone. A few minutes later he came into the room, saying: "Waldo? Oh, there you are! Had you given me up for lost? I beg your pardon, but I knew you wouldn't be in a worry!"

"Not in a worry! When I have been pacing the floor for hours, in the greatest agitation——!"

Julian chuckled. "You look pretty comfortable to me!"

"Merely exhausted. Have you dined?"

"Yes, at the Rectory. They were just sitting down to dinner when we arrived, and Mrs Chartley *would* have me stay. Miss Trent declined it, but the Rector said I need not think I should be obliged to walk home, if I stayed, because his man should drive me here. So I did. I hadn't meant to remain for so long, but we got to talking about everything under the sun —you know how it is!—and I never noticed the time. You didn't wait for me, did you?"

"No, not for a second. Did you restore your young Hemp to his parents?"

"Yes, but as for calling the poor little devil a young Hemp—— Good God, he's only six years old, and all he stole was one apple! Miss Trent told you what happened, didn't she? It was the most frightful moment!"

"It must have been. I collect that Miss Chartley showed the greatest presence of mind."

"Yes, and such courage! She made nothing of it: her only concern was for the boy. I could only wonder at her, for she is so quiet and shy that one would never have supposed that she could behave with such intrepidity, or remain so composed! If the danger she had been in had not been enough to overset her you'd have thought that the people who crowded round would have done it! She paid no heed to them—didn't even shrink from the fellow who ranted at her that he was going to hand the boy over to the Law. Lord, Waldo, I never wanted you more in my life!"

"Why? Couldn't you deal with the bloodthirsty citizen without my assistance?"

"That! Of course I could! But I didn't know what the devil ought to be done with the brat. However, Miss Chartley knew—yes, and just what to say to the mother and father, too! The only thing that did overset her—for a few minutes——" He broke off abruptly.

"I can guess," said Sir Waldo helpfully.

Julian shot him a quick, defensive look; but after a slight pause he said, with a forced smile and a mounting colour: "I suppose so—since you drove her back to Staples! I'm very much obliged to you, by the way. Did she—did she rip up to you about it?"

"Oh, yes, but no more than I expected! Accredited beauties, you know, can rarely bear to be eclipsed. It was clearly incumbent upon me to remove her from the scene, but I own I shall always regret that I was denied the privilege of meeting the low, vulgar, and disgustingly ill-mannered young gentleman in the tilbury!"

That drew an involuntary laugh from Julian. "Baldock! First he said he didn't see why *she* should faint, and then he called her a shrew! I don't know why I should laugh, for the lord knows I didn't feel like laughing at the time! But what a clunch!" He was silent again for a minute, and then said, with a little difficulty: "You think I'm a clunch too, don't you? But I've known, ever since that ill-fated expedition to Knaresborough. . . . I thought, at first, that it was just—just because she was so young, and had been so much indulged, but—but, there's no *heart* behind that lovely face, Waldo! Nothing but—oh, well! What a fellow I am to be saying such things! Even to you! But I daresay you may have suspected that she—she did bowl me out, when I first saw her!"

"I should have been astonished if she hadn't," replied Sir Waldo, in an indifferent tone. "I don't recall when I've seen a more beautiful girl. It's a pity she has neither the wits nor the disposition to match her beauty, but I've no doubt she'll do very well without them. If her fortune is sufficiently substantial she may even catch her Marquis!"

"Catch her Marquis?" exclaimed Julian blankly. "Which Marquis?"

"Whichever offers for her. Yes, I know it may seem absurd, but she seems to have set her heart on becoming—at the least!—a Marchioness. It won't surprise me at all if she achieves her ambition. What, by the way, did the Chartleys think of this stirring adventure?"

"*She* was very much shocked, of course," Julian replied, "but the Rector said that Patience—Miss Chartley, I mean! —had done just as she ought! Naturally Mrs Chartley couldn't but wish it hadn't happened: she didn't *blame* anyone! In fact, neither she nor the Rector made much more of it than Miss Chartley did herself! You may depend upon it that I took care to assure them that she had not entered that dreadful hovel which was the boy's *home*!—Miss Chartley told me there were many worse to be seen, but I swear to you, Waldo, my pigs are better housed!—but Mrs Chartley only said that a clergyman's daughter was used to go amongst the poor. I had thought she would be very much vexed, but not a bit of it! We spent such a comfortable evening! Yes, and only imagine my surprise when I discovered that she was a Yateley! Somehow or other we had got to talking about Timperley, and Mrs Chartley told me that she had been born not so very far from it! Well, in the next county, at all events: Warwick! When she mentioned her previous name, you may guess how I stared!"

"Forgive me!" apologized Sir Waldo. "I'm either very dull, or very forgetful, but I haven't the least guess! Who *are* the Yateleys?"

"Oh, a Warwickshire family! I don't know much about 'em, but you must have heard Mama talk of her great friend, Maria Yateley! She's Lady Stone—a regular fusty mug!— but Mama has known her for ever, and she always speaks of her as Maria Yateley. Well, would you believe it? Mrs Chartley is her first cousin!"

There did not seem to Sir Waldo to be much cause for satisfaction in this discovery, but he responded suitably; and Julian chatted away happily, his sad disillusionment forgotten in

140

telling his cousin all about the very pleasant evening he had spent, and in trying to persuade him that Miss Chartley's protégé, at present domiciled with both his parents and one of his grandmothers, was an eligible candidate for entrance to the Broom Hall Orphanage. Failing in this, he said that he must discuss the matter with the Rector: perhaps the boy could be admitted to the Charity School. "For I feel one ought to do *something*," he said, frowning over the problem. "After Miss Chartley saved him from being trampled on it seems a pity that he should be put to work in one of the manufactories, poor little rat! I daresay if *you* were to speak to the Governors, or the Warden, or whatever they call themselves——"

"No, you talk it over with the Rector!" said Sir Waldo.

"Well, I will." He yawned. "Lord, I am sleepy! I think I'll go to bed, if you've no objection."

"None at all. Oh, by the bye! Laurie is here. He went to bed early too."

Julian had walked over to the door, but he wheeled round at that, exclaiming: *"Laurie?* What the devil brings him here?"

"He told me he had been visiting friends in York, and drove over to see how we go on here."

"Gammon!" said Julian scornfully. "What a damned thing! What does he want?"

Sir Waldo raised his brows. "You had better ask him," he replied, a faint chill in his voice.

Julian reddened. "I didn't mean—I know it's your house, and no concern of mine whom you invite to stay in it, but—oh, lord, Waldo, what a dead bore! You didn't invite him, either, did you?"

"No, I didn't," admitted Sir Waldo, with a smile that was a trifle twisted. "I'm sorry, Julian, but I couldn't turn him away, you know!"

"No, I suppose not. Oh, well! As long as he don't start abusing you——!"

"I don't think he will. But if he *should* happen to pick out a grievance, oblige me by keeping two circumstances in mind! That he will not be doing so under any roof of yours, and that I am really quite capable of fighting my own battles!"

"Don't I know it!" Julian retorted. *"And* of giving nasty set-downs! Very well! I'll behave with all the propriety in the world—if I can!" He opened the door, but looked over his shoulder, grinning, as a sudden thought assailed him. "Oh, by Jupiter! *Won't* our Bond Street bean stagger the neighbourhood?"

CHAPTER XI

IF JULIAN'S DEMEANOUR, when he met his cousin Laurence on the following morning, put Sir Waldo forcibly in mind of a stiff-legged terrier, not aggressively inclined but giving warning by his slightly raised bristles that he was prepared to repel any attack, this wary hostility soon vanished. Laurence greeted him in the friendliest manner, with apparently no memory of their last stormy encounter; so Julian, naturally sunny-tempered, immediately responded in kind. Laurence was very full of liveliness and wit, giving a droll account of his valet's horror at the privations of life at Broom Hall, and describing the various hazards he had himself encountered. "Not that I mean to complain, coz!" he assured Sir Waldo. "After all, I *know* where the rotten floorboard is now, and even if the ceiling does come down I daresay I may not be lying helpless in bed at the time. I don't regard a few scraps of plaster descending on me as anything to make a dust about! To think that I should have been as cross as crabs because old Joseph left the place to you! You're very welcome to it, Waldo!"

This was clearly so well-intentioned that Julian instantly regaled him with a highly-coloured account of his own first night in the house, when he had put his foot through the sheet; and before very long they were both of them roasting Sir Waldo in lighthearted, if temporary, alliance.

"Jackstraws!" he remarked. "A little more, and you'll find yourselves cast upon the world! Laurie, if you want to ride I can mount you, but if you prefer to drive the matter becomes more complicated. There's my phaeton, and there's a gig, and there's a tub of a coach which I imagine old Joseph must have inherited from his grandfather. We rumble to balls and rout-parties in that: Julian thinks it's just the thing. You

142

won't—and nor, for that matter, do I. You can have the phaeton when I'm not using it myself, but——"

"Oh, lord, no!" Laurence interrupted. "I shouldn't think of taking your horses out! The gig will do well enough, if I should want to drive myself anywhere."

"No, I'll tell you what, Waldo!" said Julian. "The Buffer at the Crown has a whisky, which he lets out on hire: that's the thing for Laurie! He won't like the look of the gig."

"What you mean is that you're afraid he will want it when you do," said Sir Waldo. "Take him into the village, and hire the whisky!"

"I will. I mean to call at the Rectory, too, to see how Miss Chartley does after yesterday's adventure. Are you using the phaeton this morning," Julian asked hopefully.

"No, you may have it."

"Much obliged! Have you driven Waldo's bays, Laurie?"

"Oh, I shall leave driving them to you! *I'm* not a pupil of the great Nonesuch!" said Laurence, with a titter.

"I daresay you are a better fiddler than I am, however," replied Julian, with determined civility.

"Waldo would not say so!"

"Fudge! What do you think, Waldo?"

Sir Waldo was reading one of his letters, and said, without looking up from it: "Think about what?"

"Our handling of the reins. Which of us is the better whip? You are to decide!"

"Impossible! Two halfpennies in a purse!"

"Of all the knaggy things to say!" Julian exclaimed indignantly. "If that's what you think us I wonder at your letting either of us drive your precious bays!"

"Yes, so do I," agreed Sir Waldo, getting up from the breakfast-table. "Have you a fancy to attend a ball, Laurie?"

"Good God, coz, do you have *balls* in these rural parts? What do they dance? minuets?"

"Country-dances and reels—but this one is to be a waltzing-ball, isn't it, Julian?"

Julian laughed. "*Some* waltzing, at all events. You'd be surprised if you knew how gay we've been, Laurie!"

"I think you had better take him to visit Lady Colebatch," said Sir Waldo.

"Puffing him off to the neighbourhood? Very well!"

Laurence was by no means sure that he wished to become acquainted with his cousins' new friends. He was much addicted to ton parties, where all the guests were of high fashion, but country entertainments he thought abominably dull. However, when he learned that his cousins were engaged for almost every evening for some time to come he realized that unless he joined them in these rural festivities he would be condemned to solitude, so he yielded, and went away to change the frogged and braided dressing-gown in which he had chosen to breakfast for raiment more suited to paying country morning-visits.

Julian, who had been mischievously looking forward to the effect his dandified cousin's usual costume was likely to have on the neighbourhood, was disappointed to see, when Laurence came strolling into the stableyard, that he was not wearing the town-dress of a Bond Street beau, but had exchanged his delicately hued pantaloons and his mirror-bright Hessian boots for breeches of pale yellow and white-topped riding-boots; and his exaggeratedly long-tailed coat of superfine for a redingote. However, this garment was raised above the ordinary by its stiffly wadded shoulders and its enormous breast flaps; and both the Mathematical Tie which Laurence wore, and the height of his shirt-points, left nothing to be desired. Furthermore, the driving-coat which he tossed negligently into the phaeton bore upwards of a dozen capes. Julian advised him earnestly to put it on, warning him that the roads were very dusty. "You'll be smothered in it!" he prophesied. "It would be too bad, for you look *very* dapper-dog!"

"I regret I can't return the compliment, coz!" said Laurence, surveying him through his quizzing-glass. "If you don't object to my saying so, your rig is more that of a hayseed than of a Nonesuch!"

"Oh, I gave up aping Waldo's fashions when I found I couldn't ape his skill!" retorted Julian, with the blandest of smiles.

Fortunately for the harmony of the day, Laurence recollected that a quarrel with Julian would do nothing to advance his cause with Waldo; so he suppressed a pretty stinging answer, and merely laughed, and said: "How wise!" He then languidly waved aside an offer to yield the reins up to him, and climbed into the phaeton. No conversation was exchanged for the first few minutes; but after critically watching Julian's handling of the mettlesome pair harnessed to the carriage, Laurence said: "You're growing to be a regular dash. Pretty lively, ain't they? What's keeping Waldo here for so long?"

"Why, you know, don't you? He's turning Broom Hall into another orphanage."

"Oh, yes, I know that! He did the same with that place he bought in Surrey, but if he ever spent as much as one night in it it's the first I've heard of it."

"That was different!" objected Julian. "There's the estate to be thought of here, and I can tell you it's in a shocking way! No bailiff, either. Waldo is determined to bring it into good order before he leaves, which means the devil of a lot of work, you know."

"Lord, he must have a dozen men he could employ on that!" Laurence said impatiently.

"Well, he don't choose to. Hallo, here comes the Squire! A very good sort of a man: wife all pretension: one son and two daughters!" explained Julian, in a hurried undervoice, as he pulled up his horses. "Good-morning, sir! Not so hot today, is it? May I present my cousin to you? Mr Calver—Mr Mickleby!"

The Squire, acknowledging Laurence's graceful bow with a brief nod, stared very hard at him, and ejaculated: "Ha! Calver! Ay, you 've got a look of old Joseph."

Laurence had never seen Joseph Calver, but he resented this remark: and told Julian, when the Squire had trotted off on his stout cob, that if his manners were a sample of what was to be expected in this uncouth district he would as lief be spared any more introductions. However, when the hire of the whisky had been arranged, he consented to accompany Julian to the Rectory. Leaving the phaeton at the Crown, they walked down the village street, reaching the Rectory just as Mrs Underhill was stepping into her barouche, which was drawn up at the gate.

Mrs Underhill had driven from Staples to enquire after Patience, and to tell Mrs Chartley how sorry she was that such a disagreeable adventure should have befallen her while she had been in Miss Trent's charge; and she had arrived at the Rectory in as flustered a state of mind as was possible in one of her calm temperament, her headstrong niece having flatly refused to accompany her on this visit of reparation. She might know little about fashionable manners, but one thing (she said) she did know, and that was that Tiffany behaved very badly to Miss Chartley, and owed her an apology. Upon which, Tiffany, after declaring in a torrent of angry words that it was Patience who owed her an apology, for exposing her to a scene of odious embarrassment, had slammed

145

out of the room and locked herself into her bedchamber. So Mrs Underhill, much agitated, had been obliged to excuse her to Mrs Chartley. She said that she was laid down with a headache; but when Patience exclaimed that she was so sorry, because it must have been quite horrid for poor Tiffany to be jostled and stared at by a crowd of people, she had abandoned all pretence, and said bluntly: "It's like you to say so, my dear, but by what I can discover she behaved in a very unbecoming way, and I'm so mortified as never was! And if she won't beg your pardon—which she won't, for bring her to own she's ever at fault you can't, tell her so till Doomsday, —*I* will, and so I do!"

Perceiving that she was very much upset, Mrs Chartley made a sign to Patience to leave them, and applied herself to the task of soothing the poor lady's ruffled sensibilities. She succeeded so well that before long Mrs Underhill was pouring out to her the difficulties and discomforts attached to the guardianship of a spoiled beauty who didn't seem to have a scrap of affection in her. Mrs Chartley listened sympathetically, agreeing that she would have grown up very differently if her uncle had not sent her to school, and encouraging Mrs Underhill's wistfully expressed belief that her tantrums were merely childish, and that she would improve when she was a little older.

Mrs Underhill felt much better after unburdening herself. A glass of ratafia, and a comfortable gossip with her hostess still further restored her; and by the time the two Chartley ladies escorted her to her barouche she was her placid self again, and able to meet Lord Lindeth without suffering any recrudescence of mortification. He performed the introductions, and while Laurence exchanged civilities with the Chartleys he enquired politely after Tiffany, expressing his regret that the previous day's accident should have proved too much for her nerves.

"Nerves!" said Mrs Underhill, rejecting this tactful effort. "She hasn't got any, my lord! A nasty, spiteful temper is what she's got, and wears us all to death with it! Not that she can't be as sweet as a nut when she chooses, but if things don't fall out just the way she wants them to she flies into the boughs directly." She then lowered her voice, and said, with a significant glance cast at Laurence: "Did you say he was your cousin?"

"Yes, ma'am: my cousin Calver."

"Well!" she uttered. "I'm sure we all thought there was

never anyone as modish as Sir Waldo, so elegant and trim as he is, but he's nothing to Mr Calver, is he? Why, he's as fine as a star! I'll be bound he's one of the London smarts?"

"Yes, indeed!" said Julian, his eyes dancing. "A real Pink of the Ton!"

"I can see that," she nodded, much impressed. "I hope you'll bring him with you when you come to my turtle-dinner next Friday, if he won't think it a bore."

"He will be very much obliged to you, ma'am," Julian answered promptly. He turned his head toward his cousin. "Laurie, Mrs Underhill has been so kind as to invite you to dine at her house next Friday!"

Laurence, executing one of his exquisite bows, said all that was proper, for he prided himself on his social address, but not even Mrs Underhill's evident admiration reconciled him to the prospect of dining in her house. He described her as a vulgar mushroom, and wondered that his cousins should not have kept her at a proper distance.

"We're not as niffy-naffy as you—or, of course, of such consequence!"

Laurence reddened, and said peevishly: "You needn't ride grub because I don't care for low company! Who *is* the creature?"

"She is a wealthy widow, with a son, a daughter, and a very beautiful niece. She owns the largest house in the neighbourhood, and may be depended on to set a capital dinner before us. She's a cit, but excessively good-natured, and has been particularly kind in giving us an open invitation to dine at Staples whenever we choose—or whenever the builders make Broom Hall intolerable! We have been in the habit of going there quite frequently, so, if you don't want one of Waldo's set-downs, I advise you not to speak of Mrs Underhill to him as a vulgar mushroom!"

"One of Waldo's eccentricities, I collect. Or has he got up a flirtation with the beautiful niece? Is that what's keeping him in Yorkshire?"

"I've told you already what's keeping him. As for Miss Wield, she's no more than seventeen, and if you think Waldo would——"

"Oho!" interrupted Laurence, his curiosity roused. "Have you an interest there yourself?"

Julian flushed, and answered stiffly: "No. I admire her, as everyone must, but I am not one of her suitors. She has dozens of 'em!" He continued, in an easier tone: "She's a dia-

147

mond of the first water, I promise you! But there are several very pretty girls to be seen—Miss Colebatch is one of them. I hope she may be at home when we get to Colby Place."

"Don't hope it on my account!" said Laurence, yawning. "*I'm* not in the petticoat-line!"

Inasmuch as he was too self-absorbed ever to have contracted even the mildest passion for any lady, this was true; but provided that he was not expected to run errands, or to dance attendance, or, in fact, to put himself out in any way, he was rather fond of feminine society. He was also responsive to flattery, and of this he received full measure at Colby Place. Not only was Miss Colebatch at home, but her two younger sisters were sitting with their mama when the visitors were announced; and from the moment of his entering the room they seemed unable to drag their eyes from the elegant Mr Calver. Awe was writ large on their youthful countenances; and when he was kind enough to address a word or two to one or other of them they showed by their blushes, nervous giggles, and stammering replies how appreciative they were of his condescension. Miss Colebatch, though she did not betray it, was a good deal impressed by his air of à la modality; and her mama, not content with begging him to honour her ball with his presence, gratified him by asking his advice on various questions concerning it, because she said that she was persuaded he must be familiar with all the latest kicks of high fashion.

He was shortly to be still more gratified. The news that the Nonesuch had another cousin staying with him, and one who was an out-and-out dandy, rapidly spread, and was productive of a spate of notes directed to Sir Waldo, and carrying the assurances of the various hostesses to whom he and Lindeth were engaged that they would be most happy to include Mr Laurence Calver amongst their guests.

Laurence affected unconcern, but he was secretly as much exhilarated as surprised by his sudden and unexpected rise to importance. In London, amongst men of more natural parts and longer purses than his, it was almost impossible to make a hit: particularly (as he had often and resentfully thought) if one had the misfortune to be overshadowed by so magnificent a cousin as the Nonesuch, who, besides being universally acknowledged as Top-of-the-Trees, commanded as much liking as admiration. Far too frequently had Laurence been presented to strangers as Sir Waldo Hawkridge's cousin; and although he had not scrupled to use this relationship to gain the entrance to certain exclusive circles it galled him very much to know that he was accepted merely because of the respect in which Waldo was held. He would have repudiated with scorn any suggestion that he should seek fame in a rural district remote from the hub of fashion; but having been compelled by circumstances to visit his cousin he did not find it at all disagreeable to have become a star in this lesser firmament. Elderly and bucolic gentlemen might look upon him with disfavour; their hard-riding sons were welcome to make Waldo their model: to be admired or despised by dotards and schoolboys were matters of equal indifference to him while he was courted by the ladies, and enjoyed the exquisite satisfaction of knowing that his hair-style, his neckties, and many of his mannerisms were being copied by several aspirants to dandyism. His success made it possible for him to bear, with tolerable equanimity, his cousin's tacit refusal to allow him to reopen the discussion which had brought him to Yorkshire. He had only once attempted to do so. He had been foiled, and he had thought that he had been a trifle too precipitate, perhaps, and must allow Waldo more time for consideration. He meant to have another touch at him after a discreet interval; meanwhile he was very well pleased to bridge the gap with whatever entertainments were offered him.

His appearance at the Colebatches' ball transcended all expectations, and quite eclipsed the local smarts. The beautiful arrangement of his pomaded locks, the height of his shirt-points, the intricacies of his neckcloth, the starched frill which protruded between the lapels of his tightly-fitting coat, with its short front and its extravagantly cutaway tails, the fobs and the seals which hung from his waist, and even the rosettes on his dancing-pumps, proclaimed him to be a Tulip of the first stare. His bow was much admired; if he was not precisely handsome, he was generally held to be goodlooking; and when he led Tiffany Wield on to the floor for the first waltz even the most hostile of his critics acknowledged him to be a most accomplished dancer. The Squire went further, setting Sir Ralph Colebatch off into an alarming choking fit by growling in his ear: "Damned caper-merchant!"

The eyes that followed his progress round the room might have remained fixed in his direction had they not been drawn off by a less agreeable but far more startling sight.

"*Look!*" ejaculated Mrs Banningham to Mrs Mickleby, in throbbing accents.

The Broom Hall party had arrived just as the opening set

149

of country-dances had come to an end. Having greeted his hostess, Sir Waldo passed on, pausing to exchange a word or two with various acquaintances, unhurried, but scanning the room searchingly as he moved from group to group. His height enabled him to see over many heads, and it was thus that he discovered Miss Trent, who was seated beside Mrs Underhill against the wall on one side of the room. She was wearing a ball-dress of pale orange Italian crape, trimmed with lace, and cut low across the bosom; and instead of the demure braids she considered suitable for a companion-governess she had allowed her natural ringlets to fall becomingly from a knot placed high on her head. She looked very much younger, and, in Sir Waldo's eyes, beautiful.

He made his way towards her, reaching her as the musicians were about to strike up. A smile, and a brief how-do-you-do Mrs Underhill, and he was bowing to Miss Trent, and saying: "May I have the honour, ma'am?"

He had told her that he should ask her for the first waltz, but she had expected him rather to invite her to dance with him later in the evening. She hesitated, feeling that she ought not to be the first lady to stand up with him. "Thank you, but —Miss Colebatch? Should you not——"

"No, certainly not!" he replied. "That's Lindeth's privilege."

"Oh! Yes, of course. But there are many other ladies who have a claim to——"

"No," he interrupted. He smiled down at her, holding out his hand. "With you or no one! Come!"

"That's right, Sir Waldo!" said Mrs Underhill, beaming up at him. "Don't you take no for an answer, that's my advice to you! And as for you, my dear, just you say *thank you kindly, sir,* and no more nonsense!"

Ancilla could not resist. She rose, giving Sir Waldo her hand. Her eyes laughed into his. "Thank you kindly, sir!" she repeated obediently.

His right hand lightly clasped her waist; he said, as he guided her round the room: "That woman is a constant refreshment to me!"

"Indeed!" she said quizzing him. "How quickly your opinions change, sir! I seem to recall that when you last spoke of her it was in very different terms!"

"I did her an injustice. I now recognize that she is a woman of great good sense. How well you dance!"

It was true, but very few of the onlookers derived any

pleasure from the spectacle. Matrons who had brought their daughters to the ball felt their bosoms swell with wrath as they watched Tiffany Wield's companion (or whatever she called herself) gliding over the floor in the Nonesuch's arms, not finding it necessary to mind her steps, but performing the waltz gracefully and easily, and apparently enjoying an amusing conversation with him while she did it.

The Rector was one of those who watched with approval. He said to his wife: "Now, my love, we see how unexceptionable this new dance is! Charming! charming, indeed!"

"Well, I cannot quite like it, but I own that it is very pretty when it is danced correctly," she replied. "I understand that Mr Calver is the best dancer here, but for my part I prefer Sir Waldo's more restrained style. Miss Trent, too, dances as a lady should, but you may depend upon it that as soon as ever they become familiar with the steps Tiffany Wield, and Lizzie Colebatch, and the Mickleby girls will turn it into a romp. I should be sorry indeed to see a daughter of mine led into such impropriety."

He laughed gently. "It would reflect sadly on her upbringing, would it not? I fancy we need feel no apprehension! She is dancing very prettily. It may be my partiality, but I am of the opinion that, saving only Miss Trent, she performs the waltz better than any other lady present."

"Yes," agreed his wife, "but Arthur Mickleby is too clumsy a partner for her."

She saw that Mrs Underhill was quite alone, and went to her, sitting down beside her, and saying: "What do you think of the waltz, Mrs Underhill? My husband is in raptures over it, and thinks me very old-fashioned for not liking it as much as he does!"

"Well, I wouldn't like to be seen dancing it myself," said Mrs Underhill, "but I'm sure I never saw anything so pretty as the way Sir Waldo and Miss Trent glide and twirl about the room so elegantly! What has me in a puzzle is how she knows when he means to go down the room, and when he means to go round and round, for he don't seem to push her or pull her, which you'd think he'd be obliged to, and which he certainly would be, if it was me he had his arm round!"

Mrs Chartley smiled. "They certainly dance very well together."

"Ay, don't they?" nodded Mrs Underhill, watching them complacently. "So well-matched as they are, Miss Trent being so tall, and the both of them so handsome! When she came downstairs this evening, with her hair dressed the way you see it, and that gown on, which she says she's had laid up in lavender ever since she left the General's house, though little would you think it, 'Well,' I said to her, 'I declare I've never seen you in greater beauty!' I said. And no more I have." She lowered her voice, and added conspiratorially: "What's more, Mrs Chartley, I wasn't the only one to be knocked bandy! Oh, no! 'With you or no one!' he said, when she was telling him he should ask another lady to stand up with him!"

"Sir Waldo?" asked Mrs Chartley, startled.

"Sir Waldo!" corroborated Mrs Underhill, with immense satisfaction. "Mind you, it didn't come as any surprise to me! A pea-goose I may be, which Mr Underhill was used to call me—joking me, you understand!—but I've got eyes in my head, and I don't need to wear spectacles either! Nor I'm not such a pea-goose as to think it's for the pleasure of *my* company that Sir Waldo comes to Staples as often as he does. I *did* think it was Tiffany he was dangling after, but it ain't. Not but what he flirts with her: that I can't deny. But, to my way of thinking, it's no more than playfulness. It's Miss Trent who brings him to Staples."

Mrs Chartley was disquieted by this confidence; and after a moment's hesitation, said: "That he should feel some degree of preference for Miss Trent is very understandable. To a certain extent they belong to the same world—the London world—and no doubt they have acquaintances in common. Then, too, she is not a girl, but a woman of five or six-and-twenty, with a well-informed mind, and the habits of easy intercourse which come with increasing years. She doesn't want for sense, but when a man of Sir Waldo's address and experience makes a woman the object of his gallantry——"

"Lor', ma'am, whatever are you thinking of?" broke in Mrs Underhill. "It's not marriage with the left hand he has in his mind! Not with her uncle being a General!"

"No, indeed! You mistake me! I meant only to say that it would be unwise to—to encourage Miss Trent to cherish what I am persuaded must be false hopes. Forgive me, dear ma'am, but I feel you are refining too much upon a mere flirtation!"

Mrs Underhill smiled indulgently at her. "Ay, well, he who lives the longest will see the most!" she prophesied.

CHAPTER XII

As SHE HAD LOOKED forward to the ball with mixed feelings, so did Ancilla loon back upon it. It had been with misgiving that she had accepted Lady Colebatch's invitation, believing, with a sense of guilt, that in doing so she was allowing her desire to overcome the principles she had laid down for herself when she had first stepped deliberately out of her own sphere to become a schoolteacher.

It had been a hard decision to reach, for although her family was not affluent it was respected, and she had been accustomed all her life to move in the first circles of Hertfordshire. Her father's death, coupled as it had been with unlucky investments, had left the family, not in penury, but in uncomfortably straitened circumstances, and no doubt existed in the minds of all those who were acquainted with the Trents that it was incumbent upon Ancilla to relieve her eldest brother of the burden of providing for her by contracting a suitable marriage. It was generally agreed that although she was then in her twenty-fourth year, and had no fortune, her case was not hopeless. She was very goodlooking, with an air of distinction that always attracted attention; she was accomplished; her disposition was charming; though she was not vivacious she had a lively mind, and a witty tongue; and if she had rather too much reserve, and a composure that made her seem sometimes a little cold, her graceful manners always ensured her a welcome at any social function. It was a thousand pities she had not liked any of her admirers well enough to encourage their advances; but it was hoped that now, when she had been out for more than four years and must be fearful of dwindling into an old maid, she would not spurn a respectable offer.

That was what her aunt had hoped, when she had invited her to London for a whole season. Lady Trent, who was sincerely attached to her, had really done her best for her, introducing her to the ton, taking her to Almack's, and even presenting her at one of the Queen's Drawing-Rooms, but it had been to no avail. Ancilla would not marry where she did not love; and until she encountered the Nonesuch her heart had never experienced the smallest flutter.

Unwilling to marry, and resolved neither to add to the expenses of her brother's household nor to hang upon her uncle's sleeve, she had made her difficult decision, against the loudly expressed wishes of her family, and in the full realization that if she became a schoolmistress she would, to all intents and purposes, have renounced the world. It had been a hard duty, but she saw it as inescapable; and when she had accepted the post offered her by Miss Climping she had put the social life which she enjoyed behind her, and moulded herself into the form of a governess. By the time she had been fortunate enough to exchange her situation at Bath for the highly paid and privileged one which she now held she had thought herself inured to the disadvantages of her position. It had not been long before that position had become far more agreeable than she had ever supposed possible; but however much her kind employer might urge her to think herself one of the family, discretion, and a strong sense of propriety had prevented her from stepping across the invisible line she had drawn for herself. Her place was in the background, ready to fill a social need, but never putting herself forward. If Mrs Underhill were indisposed, she was perfectly willing to escort Tiffany to a party, where she took her place amongst the chaperons; but when, as had occasionally happened, she had herself received an invitation she had been steadfast in her refusal.

Until the arrival on the scene of the Nonesuch. Within a fortnight of their first meeting—or had it been within a minute?—he had destroyed her calm, undermined her resolution, and utterly demolished her comfort. She had believed herself to be a rational woman, with a well-regulated mind and a temperate disposition; but since his coming into Yorkshire she had swung from breathless happiness to doubt and despondency. Her heart had never previously opposed her mind: they seemed now to be in eternal conflict, the one warning her to take care, the other urging her to throw care and discretion to the wind.

Mind had suffered a severe set-back over the invitation to Lady Colebatch's ball. The correct Miss Trent, who had long since outgrown her love of dancing, desperately wanted to go to the ball. *Just this once!* she pleaded. *What harm can there be in it, when Mrs Underhill particularly wishes me to accept? I have too much sense to let it turn my head!* Her well-regulated mind replied uncompromisingly: *You have none at all. You want to go to this ball because Sir Waldo will be there, and if you had a grain of sense you would hint him away before he has ruined your peace.*

Heart had won. She had gone to the ball, meaning to behave with the utmost circumspection; but no sooner had she dressed her hair in her former style than circumspection fled. She felt young again, as excited as a girl going to her first party, a little reckless.

The recklessness, encouraged by the lights and the laughter, and the music, had grown. She had retained enough prudence to demur when Sir Waldo had asked her to dance the first waltz with him, but none thereafter, she thought. She had felt the exquisite happiness of knowing herself to be sought after by the man of her choice; and when he had asked her to waltz with him a second time she had not hesitated. He had taken her in to supper, too; and when they had gone into the garden to watch the firework-display it had been he who had fetched her shawl, and put it round her shoulders. So heedless had she been, so lost in enchantment, that she had not spared a thought for what might be the opinions of the matrons who watched her so jealously, and was shocked when an acid comment from Mrs Banningham made her realize that she was considered by that lady, and some others too, to be setting her cap at the Nonesuch. She knew it to be spite, but she felt ready to sink; and when Lady Colebatch had said to her, laughingly: "All this dangerous flirting with Sir Waldo——! Fie on you, Miss Trent!" her enjoyment was at an end, and her fears and doubts again assailed her.

She knew herself to be inexperienced in love, and guessed that Sir Waldo was not. It was beyond question that he was strongly attracted to her, but whether he had anything but flirtation in mind she could not tell. When their eyes met, and he smiled, she thought that surely he could not look at her and smile just so if the feeling he had for her was not deeper and more enduring than a mere passing fancy. Then she remembered that she was not the only woman to be charmed by his smile; and wondered if she was flattering herself in believing that that particular smile was one which no one but she had seen. But it was rumoured that he had had many loves: she supposed that a squire of dames must necessarily possess the power of making one believe that he was very much in love with one.

Almost as painful as these doubts was the thought that by allowing the Nonesuch to single her out she, who had so often preached propriety to Tiffany, should herself have set the neighbourhood in a bustle. Her conduct must have been very bad, she thought, for even Courtenay had remarked on it, saying, with a grin: "Lord, ma'am, won't Tiffany be as mad as fire to see the Nonesuch making up to you!"

But it had not entered Tiffany's head that any man, far less a man of Sir Waldo's consequence, could feel the smallest tendre for a governess. In talking over the ball she had spoken quite casually of Sir Waldo's having danced two waltzes with Miss Trent, and disclosed, as a very good joke, that some of the old cats had taken snuff at it; because they fancied him to be dangling after her. "You and *Sir Waldo*, Ancilla——!" she gurgled, "I was very nearly in whoops, as you may imagine! Of all the absurdities!"

"I don't think it would be at all absurd!" stated Charlotte belligerently. "Not nearly such an absurdity as for anyone to suppose that he was dangling after *you!* I suppose you're jealous because he didn't ask you to stand up with him first of all!"

"Oh, he couldn't!" said Tiffany, with a saucy look. "Mr Calver was before him! He was obliged to wait for the second waltz with me! And poor Lindeth for the third!"

Miss Trent regarded her thoughtfully for a moment, before lowering her gaze again to the handkerchief she was hemming. She had not been so much absorbed in her own affairs as to have had no leisure to observe Tiffany's behaviour at the ball. Being fairly well conversant with Tiffany's methods of punishing and still further enslaving any member of her court who had displeased her, she had not been surprised when she had seen her at her dazzling best with all the admirers whose noses had been put out of joint by Lord Lindeth, raising melting eyes to Mr Calver's face, and treating Lindeth with careless indifference. Miss Trent had been amused rather than shocked, for these tactics, she thought, betrayed Tiffany's extreme youth. They might answer well enough with callow boys, but they were not at all likely to inspire Lindeth with anything but disgust. She hoped they would do so, but she hoped also that they were not as blatant to others as they were to her.

To one person they were perfectly obvious. Laurence Calver's intellect was not superior, but he had a certain quickness of perception, and a decided talent for discovering scandals and frailties. He went to the ball suspecting that his cousin Lindeth had a considerable interest in the unknown Beauty, and it did not take him long to become convinced of this, or to realize that some tiff had occurred to rupture what had no doubt been a promising *affaire*. That was very interesting, and opened out all sorts of possibilities. The girl was a minx: bang-up to the echo, of course, but not at all the thing for Lindeth. Waldo must know that, so what was he doing to prevent such a shocking alliance? Or was he at a stand? And if so would he be grateful if his other cousin were to intervene? Yes, thought Laurence: if the thing were serious, he would be. It would be very amusing, and not at all difficult: the Beauty had already thrown out unmistakeable lures to him, and he was perfectly ready to accept these. No doubt she was on the catch for Lindeth; and no doubt either that she thought to bring him to the scratch by making him mad with jealousy. Possibly she would succeed in making him jealous—and that would be amusing too—but if she supposed that by flirting outrageously with another man she would goad Lindeth into popping the question she must be as bird-witted as she was beautiful. Too vulgar by half for young Julian!

All this was pleasantly intriguing. It was satisfactory too to have discovered why Waldo was lingering in this God-forsaken district: he had set up a new flirt. Not very like him to make a female who appeared to be some sort of a governess the object of his gallantry, but girls who were just out never took his fancy, and apart from them the only females in the neighbourhood seemed to be fussocks, like Lady Colebatch, or regular worri-crows, like Mrs Banningham and the Squire's wife.

Critically surveying Miss Trent, Laurence doubted whether she would prove a satisfactory flirt. Not striking *au fait de beauté*, and too much of a Long Meg for his taste, but a distinguished-looking woman: nothing of the dasher about her! If Waldo didn't take care he'd find himself riveted, and a rare kettle of fish that would be! The last of the Hawkridges leg-shackled to a nobody who earned her bread by teaching provincial schoolgirls to write and to cipher and to stitch samplers! Devilish funny that would be! But it was odd of Waldo to raise false expectations. Come to think of it, all his flirts were married women of the world, well up to snuff; and he had some pretty Gothic notions about trifling with females on the catch for eligible husbands. Still odder that he shouldn't have seen that this Long Meg of his was badly love-bitten.

Hot on the scent of this really succulent on-dit, Laurence sought information of his younger cousin, saying casually: "You didn't tell me that Waldo had set up a new flirt. Who is she?"

Julian stared at him. "New flirt? Waldo?"

"Running rather sly, ain't you?" drawled Laurence. "Tall female—somebody's governess, I collect. Lord, Julian, do you take me for a flat?"

"Miss Trent! Good God, what next? New flirt, indeed! She's Miss Wield's companion: a most agreeable woman, but as for being Waldo's *flirt*——! You should know him better!"

"No need to take a pet! All *I* know is that between the pair of 'em they set all the tabbies in an uproar last night!"

"I daresay! They live on scandal-broth!"

"But who is she?" insisted Laurence. "Or is that one of those questions one shouldn't ask?"

"Not in the least. You are probably acquainted with her cousin, Bernard Trent. Her father was killed in the assault on Cuidad Rodrigo, and left the family all to pieces, I fancy. General Trent is her uncle."

"Is he, though?" said Laurence, his eyes widening a little.

He asked no more questions, because he didn't want Waldo to think he was prying into his affairs, and Julian was such a bagpipe that you never knew what he might blurt out, in his artless way. Besides, Julian probably didn't know any more. He had said enough to put quite a different complexion on the matter: it began to look as though Waldo was thinking of becoming a tenant-for-life at last. Nothing wonderful about that: he was bound to marry one day. The wonder was that with the pick of the ton to choose from he should throw the handkerchief to a mere Miss Trent, who might be well-enough born, but who was quite unknown, and hadn't rank, fortune, or any extraordinary degree of beauty to recommend her. Lord, what a sensation it would cause! Laurence knew of several top-lofty beauties who would look blue when they heard of it, one of whom had once rudely snubbed him. It would be pleasant to whisper the news in her ear.

Of course, it might not be true; he would be better able to judge when he had seen them together again. He hoped Miss

Trent would be present at Mrs Underhill's turtle-dinner: it seemed likely that she would be; and if she was he had every intention of making himself very agreeable to her. If there was the least chance of her becoming Waldo's wife, it was a matter of the highest importance to stand well with her. Really, it was very fortunate that he had come to Yorkshire!

Miss Trent was present at the dinner, but had she been able to do so without disarranging Mrs Underhill's carefully planned table she would have excused herself. She did indeed venture to suggest that since Charlotte was suffering from severe toothache, and would make no appearance in the drawing-room, it would be better if she remained upstairs with her, but Mrs Underhill would not hear of it. Where she demanded, was she to find a lady to take Miss Trent's place?

"I thought, perhaps, since the Micklebys are coming, ma'am, you might invite the elder Miss Mickleby," suggested Ancilla, but without conviction.

"Don't talk so silly!" begged Mrs Underhill. "As though you didn't know as well as I do that Mrs Mickleby takes an affront into her head if anyone invites one of those dratted girls without t'other! Yes, and so she would if I was to invite either of them at the last minute, like this is, and I can't say I blame her, for a very poor compliment that would be!"

So Miss Trent submitted, and no one could have supposed, observing her cold composure, that she was suffering from acute embarrassment. To a proud woman of her upbringing the imputation of setting her cap at the Nonesuch was so abhorrent that she was nauseated every time she thought of it. Like some vulgar, scheming creature, without delicacy or conduct, throwing out her every lure to snare a husband! Worse!—a husband so wealthy and so distinguished as to be considered one of the biggest prizes to be won! And she the penniless daughter of an officer in a marching regiment! She could not accuse herself of having thrown out lures, but when she looked back over the past month it was upon a vista of rides with the Nonesuch, evenings spent in his company, strolling walks with him in the gardens of Staples, tête-à-tête, with him, jokes shared with him: all culminating in that disastrous ball, which she ought never to have attended. How indiscreet she had been! It must have appeared to everyone that she had gone to the ball, breaking her own rule, for no other purpose than to dance with the Nonesuch, and the dreadful truth was that she had. And who, seeing her waltz with him twice, and go in to supper on his arm, and allow him to fetch her shawl, would believe that she had committed these imprudencies unthinkingly, because she loved him, and had been too happy in his company to remember the delicacy of her situation, or even common propriety? She might as well have tied her garter in public!

It was a severe ordeal to be obliged to appear at Mrs Underhill's dinner-party, knowing that Mrs Mickleby's sharp eyes would be watching her: perhaps, even, Mrs Chartley's? She chose from her slender wardrobe the most modest and sober-hued of her few evening-dresses, and set a cap over her tightly braided locks, to which Mrs Underhill took instant exception, exclaiming: "Whatever made you put on a cap, as if you was an old maid of forty? For goodness' sake, go and take it off! There'll be time enough for you to wear caps when you're married!"

"I have no expectation of being married, ma'am, and you know it is customary for a gover——"

"No, and nor you will be if you don't prettify yourself a bit!" interrupted Mrs Underhill tartly. "If you aren't wearing that old, brown dress, too, which is enough to give anyone the dismals! I declare you're as provoking as Tiffany, Miss Trent!"

So Miss Trent went away to remove the offending cap, but she did not change her dress, or come downstairs again until the guests had all arrived, when she slipped unobtrusively into the drawing-room, responding to greetings with smiles and slight curtsies, and sitting down in a chair as far removed from Sir Waldo as was possible.

She was seated at dinner between the Squire and the Rector, and with these two uncritical friends she was able to converse as easily as usual. It was more difficult in the drawing-room, before the gentlemen joined the ladies. Mrs Mickleby talked of nothing but the waltzing-ball, and contrived, with her thin smile, to plant quite a number of tiny daggers in Miss Trent's quivering flesh. Miss Trent met smile with smile, and replied with a calm civility which made Mrs Mickleby's eyes snap angrily. Then Mrs Chartley, taking advantage of a brief pause in these hostilities, moved her seat to one beside Ancilla's, and said: "I am glad of this opportunity to speak to you, Miss Trent. I have been meaning for weeks to ask you if you can recall the details of that way of pickling mushrooms which you once described to me, but whenever I see you I remember about it only when we have parted!"

Ancilla could not but be grateful for the kindness that prompted this intervention, but it brought the colour to her cheeks as Mrs Mickleby's barbs had not. She promised to write down the recipe, and bring it to the Rectory; and wished very much that she could retire to the schoolroom before the gentlemen came in. It was impossible, however: Mrs Underhill expected her to pour out tea later in the evening.

A diversion (but a most unwelcome one) was created by Tiffany, who suddenly exclaimed: "Oh, I have had a famous notion! Do let us play Jackstraws again!"

Since she had broken in not only on what Patience was saying to her, but on what Mrs Mickleby was saying to Mrs Underhill, this lapse from good manners made Miss Trent feel ready to sink, knowing that Mrs Mickleby would set the blame at her door. Worse was to come.

"I was hoping Miss Chartley would give us the pleasure of hearing her sing," said Mrs Underhill. "I'll be bound that's what we should all like best, such a pretty voice as you have, my dear!"

"Oh, no! Jackstraws!"

"Tiffany," said Miss Trent, in a quiet but compelling voice.

The brilliant eyes turned towards her questioningly; she met them with a steady gaze; and Tiffany went into a trill of laughter. "Oh! Oh, I didn't mean to be uncivil! Patience knows I didn't, don't you, Patience?"

"Of course I do!" replied Patience instantly. "I think it would be much more amusing to play Jackstraws. But Miss Trent will beat us all to flinders—even Sir Waldo! If you and he engage in another duel, ma'am, I shan't bet against you this time!"

Miss Trent could only be thankful that at that moment the door opened, and the gentlemen came in. She was able to move away from the group in the middle of the room on the pretext of desiring one of the footmen to open the pianoforte and to light the candles in its brackets; and she remained beside the instrument, looking through a pile of music. After a minute or two she was joined by Laurence, who came up to her, and said very politely: "Can I be of assistance, ma'am? Allow me to lift that for you!"

"Thank you: if you would put it on that table, so that the instrument may be opened——?"

He did so, and then said, with a winning smile: "You must let me tell you how delighted I am to have the pleasure of making your acquaintance, ma'am. With *one* member of your family I'm already acquainted: I believe Bernard Trent is your cousin, is he not?"

Miss Trent inclined her head. It was not encouraging, but Laurence persevered. "A first-rate man! The best of good company! We are quite old friends, he and I."

"Indeed!" said Miss Trent.

He was not unnaturally daunted, for her tone was arctic, and the look in her eyes contemptuous. He wondered what the devil was the matter with her, and felt aggrieved. Anyone would have supposed that she would have been glad to meet someone who knew her cousin, but instead she had snubbed him! Pretty well for a governess! he thought indignantly.

She realized that she had spoken curtly, and added, with a slight smile: "I daresay you are better acquainted with him than I am, sir. He has never come very much in my way."

She turned away, to adjust one of the candles, and as she did so looked up, to find that Sir Waldo was standing within easy earshot. Her eyes met his, and saw that they were alight with amusement, and involuntarily she smiled. It was only for an instant, but Laurence caught the exchange of looks, and was so much pleased to find his suspicion confirmed that he forgot his indignation. If ever two people were head over ears in love! he thought, and tactfully moved away.

Sir Waldo strolled up to the pianoforte, and picked up the snuffers. As he trimmed one of the candlesticks he murmured: "He *meant* well, you know! Of course, I ought to have warned him."

"I'm afraid I was uncivil," she owned.

"No, no, merely quelling!" he assured her.

She could not help laughing, but she was aware of Mrs Mickleby's eyes upon her, and said: "That was very bad! Excuse me—I must speak with Miss Chartley!"

She walked away immediately, and contrived to remain at a distance from him until the tea-tray was brought in. She was ably assisted by Mrs Mickleby, who kept him at her side, and maintained a flow of vivacious small-talk until Patience had been persuaded to sing. After that, Tiffany renewed her demand that they should play at Jackstraws, which enabled Miss Trent to retire into the back drawing-room, where she became busy, finding the straws, and settling the four youngest members of the party round the table. Sir Waldo made no attempt to follow her; but when she was obliged to return to the front drawing-room, to dispense tea, he came up to the table to receive his cup from her, and asked her quietly if he had offended her.

No, but people are saying that I have set my cap at you!

Unthinkable to utter such words! She said: "Offended me? No, indeed! How should you?"

"I don't know. If I did, I should be begging you to forgive me."

Her eyes smarted with sudden tears; she kept them lowered. "How absurd! To own the truth, I have the headache, and should perhaps be begging *your* pardon for being cross and stupid! This is Mr Chartley's cup—would you be kind enough, Sir Waldo, to give it to him?"

He took it from her, but said: "If that's the truth I am sincerely sorry for it, but I don't think it is. What has happened to distress you?"

"Nothing! Sir Waldo, *pray*——!"

"How intolerable it is that I should be forced to meet you always in public!" he ejaculated under his breath. "I shall drive over tomorrow—and hope to find you, for once, alone!"

That made her look up. "I don't think—I mean, it is not —that is, I cannot conceive, sir, why——"

"I wish for some private conversation with you, Miss Trent. Now, don't freeze me with *Indeed*! as you froze poor Laurie, or tell me that you can't conceive why I should hope to find you alone!"

She forced her lips to smile, but said with a good deal of constraint: "Very well—though it is true! But you must know, sir, that it would be quite improper for me—in my situation—to be receiving visitors!"

"Oh, yes! I know that. But mine won't be a *social* call!" He saw the guarded look in her face, and his eyes twinkled. "I have a—a certain proposition to lay before you, ma'am! No, I shan't tell you what it is tonight: I can see you would bite my nose off!"

CHAPTER XIII

BUT WHEN SIR WALDO called at Staples next day he entered upon a scene of disorder. He did not see Miss Trent at all, but he did see Mrs Underhill; and when she had explained why he should have found them all in an uproar, as she phrased it, he made no attempt to see Miss Trent. He had clearly chosen the wrong moment for declaring himself.

Miss Trent, withdrawing from the party as soon as she had poured out tea, had gone upstairs to find Charlotte looking flushed and heavy-eyed, and obviously suffering a good deal of pain. Her old nurse was ministering to her; and she made it plain that while Miss Trent was at liberty to instruct her nurseling, neither her advice nor her assistance was required when Miss Charlotte was feeling poorly. She had several infallible remedies for the toothache to hand; and although she was sure it was very obliging of Miss Trent to offer to sit up with Miss Charlotte there was not the least need for her to put herself out.

Correctly understanding this to mean that any attempt on her part to lend Nurse her aid would be regarded by that lady as a gross encroachment, Miss Trent retired, not unthankfully, to her own room, and to bed.

But not to sleep. She was tired, but her brain would not rest. The evening, which was fast assuming the proportions of a nightmare, had culminated in a brief exchange with the Nonesuch which provided her with much food for thought, and was open to more than one interpretation.

It was during the small hours that she was roused from a fitful doze by the creaking of a floor-board. She raised herself on her elbow, thrusting back the curtain round her bed, and listened. A heavy footfall, which she instantly recognized, came to her ears, and the creek of the door that led into the servants' wing; and without troubling to light her candle from the tinder-box that stood on the table by her bed, she got up quickly, groping in the dim dawn light filtering between the

164

blinds for her slippers, and shrugging herself into her dressing-gown. She saw, when she went out on to the broad passage, that the door into Mrs Underhill's room was open; and she went at once to Charlotte's room, where, as she had feared, a most distressing sight confronted her. Charlotte, having stoutly declared when she bade her governess goodnight that she was better, and would be as right as a trivet by morning, was walking up and down the floor in her nightdress, her cap torn off, and tears pouring down her face. Nurse's infallible remedies had failed; Charlotte's toothache had grown steadily worse, until she had been unable to bear it with fortitude any longer. She was obviously almost crazy with pain; and Miss Trent, perceiving that the glands in her neck were swollen, and recalling a hideous night spent in ministering to her brother Christopher in just the same circumstances, had little doubt that an abscess was the cause of her agony. Nurse had tried to apply laudanum to the affected tooth, but Charlotte screamed when she was touched, and behaved so wildly that Nurse had taken fright, and gone away to rouse her mistress.

Mrs Underhill was a devoted parent, but she had very little experience of illness, and could scarcely have been thought an ideal sickroom attendant. Like many fat and naturally placid persons, she became flustered in emergency; and as her sensibility was far greater than her understanding the sight of her daughter's anguish upset her so much that she began to cry almost as much as Charlotte. An attempt to cradle Charlotte in her arms had been fiercely repulsed; her fond soothings had had no other effect than to make Charlotte hysterical; but thankful though she was to see Miss Trent come into the room she was quite indignant with her for showing so little sympathy, and for speaking to Charlotte so sternly.

"However, she did it for the best, and I'm bound to say she made Charlotte sit down in a chair, telling her that to be rampaging about the room, like she was doing, only served to make the pain worse. So then Nurse set a hot brick under her feet, and we wrapped a shawl round her, and Miss Trent told me she thought it was an abscess, and not a bit of use to put laudanum on her poor tooth, but better, if I would permit it, to give her some drops to swallow in a glass of water, so as to make her drowsy. Which it did, after a while, but such a work as it was to get Charlotte to open her lips, or even take the glass in her hand, you wouldn't believe!"

"Poor child!" said Sir Waldo. "I expect she was half mad with pain."

"Yes, and all through her own fault! Well, I hope I'm not unfeeling, but when she owned to Miss Trent that she had had the toothache for close on a sennight, and getting worse all the time, and never a word to a soul, because she was scared to have it drawn,—well, I was so vexed, Sir Waldo, after all that riot and rumpus, that I said to her: 'Let it be a lesson to you, Charlotte!' I said."

"I should think it would be, ma'am. I own I have every sympathy with those who dread having teeth drawn!"

"Yes," agreed Mrs Underhill, shuddering. "But when it comes to letting things get to such a pass as last night, and *still* crying, and saying she wouldn't go to Mr Dishforth, no matter what, it's downright silly! Well, I don't mind saying that it put me in a regular quake only to think of taking her to him, for I can't but cry myself when I see her in such misery, and a nice thing that would have been—the pair of us behaving like watering-pots, and poor Mr Dishforth not knowing what to do, I daresay! Not but what I would have gone with her, only that Miss Trent wouldn't have it, nor Courtenay neither. Miss Trent took her off first thing, and Courtenay went along with them, like the good brother he is. And just as well he did, for they were obliged to hold her down, such a state as she was in, and how Miss Trent would have managed without him I'm sure I don't know. So then they brought her home, and Courtenay's ridden off to fetch Dr Wibsey to her, for she's quite knocked up, and no wonder!"

Decidedly it was not the moment for a declaration. Expressing an entirely sincere hope that Charlotte would soon be herself again, Sir Waldo took his leave.

He was not to see Miss Trent again for five days. Charlotte, instead of making the swift recovery to be expected of such a bouncing girl, returned from Harrogate only to take to her bed. Her feverish condition was ascribed by Dr Wibsey to the poison that had leaked into her system; but Mrs Underhill told Sir Waldo with simple pride that Charlotte was just like she was herself.

"It's seldom I get a screw loose," she said, "for, in general, you know, I go on in a capital way. But if there's the least little thing amiss, such as a colicky disorder, it throws me into such queer stirrups that many's the time when my late husband thought to see me laid by the wall for no more than an epidemic cold!"

Sir Waldo called every day at Staples to enquire after Charlotte, but not until the fifth day was he rewarded by the sight of Miss Trent, and even then it was under inauspicious circumstances. The invalid was taking the air on the terrace, seated in a comfortable chair carried out for her accommodation, with her mother on one side; and her governess, holding up a parasol to protect her from the sun, on the other; and with Mrs Mickleby and her two eldest daughters grouped round her. When Sir Waldo was ushered on to the terrace by Totton Mrs Mickleby had already learnt from her hostess that he had been a regular visitor to Staples. She drew her own conclusions, rejecting without hesitation the ostensible reason of his daily visits.

"So kind as he's been you'd hardly credit!" Mrs Underhill told her, not without complacency. "Never a day passes but what he comes to enquire how Charlotte goes on, and it's seldom that he don't bring with him a book, or some trifle to amuse her, isn't it, love? Well, Charlotte hasn't any more of a fancy for reading than what I have, but she likes Miss Trent to read aloud to her, which she does beautifully, and as good as a play. Well, as I said to Sir Waldo only yesterday, it isn't only Charlotte that's very much obliged to him, for Miss Trent reads it after dinner to us, and I'm sure I couldn't tell you which of us enjoys it the most, me, or Charlotte, or Tiffany. Well, it's so lifelike that I couldn't get to sleep last night for wondering whether that nasty Glossin would get poor Harry Bertram carried off by the smugglers again, or whether the old witch is going to save him—her and the tutor —which Tiffany thinks they're bound to do, on account of its being near the end of the last volume."

"Oh, a novel!" said Mrs Mickleby. "I must confess I am an enemy to that class of literature, but I daresay that you, Miss Trent, are partial to romances."

"When they are as well-written as this one, ma'am, most certainly!" returned Ancilla.

"Oh, and he brought a dissected map!" Charlotte said. "I had never seen one before! It is all made of little pieces which fit into each other, to make a map of Europe!"

The Misses Mickleby had not seen one either, so Miss Trent, feeling that she had a score to pay, advised their mama, very kindly, to procure one for them. "So educational!" she said. "And *quite* exceptional!"

Then Sir Waldo arrived, and although he did not single Miss Trent out for any particular attention Mrs Mickleby, who was just as quick as Mr Calver to recognize the signs of an *affaire*, was convinced that if she had not outstayed him he would have found an excuse to take Miss Trent to walk round the gardens, or some such thing.

"And it's my belief, sorry though I am to think it, that she would have gone with him," she told Mrs Banningham later. "I was watching her closely, and I assure you, ma'am, she coloured up the instant his name was announced. I never saw anyone look more conscious!"

"It doesn't astonish me in the least," replied Mrs Banningham. "There was always something about her which I couldn't like. *You*, I know, took quite a fancy to her, but for my part I thought her affected. That excessive reserve, for instance, and her airs of gentility——!"

"Oh, as to that," said Mrs Mickleby, a trifle loftily, "the Trents are a very good family! That is what makes it so distressing to see her showing such a want of delicacy. All those rides! Of course, she was *said* to be playing propriety, but I thought at the time it was very odd, very imprudent!"

"Imprudent!" said Mrs Banningham, with a snort. "Very sly, *I* call it! She has been on the catch for him from the outset. A fine thing it would be for her, without a penny to bless herself with! *If* he makes her an offer, which I don't consider a certain thing at all. A *carte blanche*, possibly; marriage, no!"

"Someone should warn her that he is merely trifling. I should not wish her to be taken in, for however much I may deplore her conduct in luring him on to sit in her pocket, I do not think her *fast*."

"If it isn't fast to dance *twice* with him—the waltz, too!— besides going in to supper with him, and sending him to fetch her shawl, not to mention the way she looked up at him over her shoulder when he put it round her, which quite put *me* to the blush——!"

"Most unbecoming!" agreed Mrs Mickleby. "But you must own that before Sir Waldo came to Broom Hall she behaved with all the propriety in the world. I fear that he may have deceived her into believing that he was hanging out for a wife, merely because he paid her attention; and in her situation, you know, it must have seemed to her worth a push to bring him to the point. One can only pity her!"

Mrs Banningham was easily able to refrain. She said acidly: "I dislike ninnyhammers, and that she must certainly be if she imagines for one moment that a man of his consequences would entertain the thought of *marriage* with her!"

"Very true, but I fancy her experience of the Corinthian set is not large. It would be useless, of course, to suppose that Mrs Underhill would ever give her a hint."

"That vulgar female! She does not give her own niece a hint! I should be sorry to see any daughter of mine behave as Tiffany does. Wild to a fault! There is something very disgusting, too, in her determination to attach every man she meets to her apron-strings. First it was Lord Lindeth, now it is Mr Calver: he, if you please, is teaching her to drive! I saw them with my own eyes. No groom, no Miss Trent to chaperon her! Oh, no! Miss Trent only thinks it her duty to chaperon her when Sir Waldo is with her!"

"I shall be thankful when that wretched girl goes back to her uncle in London! As for Miss Trent, I have always said that she was by far too young for her position, but in this instance it must be allowed that her time has been taken up by Charlotte. If Mrs Underhill preferred her to devote herself to Charlotte rather than to Tiffany, the blame is hers. Far be it from me to suggest that Sir Waldo's daily visits have anything to do with the case! And so Tiffany is playing fast and loose with Lord Lindeth, is she? I daresay Mr Calver is much more in her style. A Macaroni merchant is what Mr Mickleby calls him, but no doubt she thinks him quite up to the nines."

In this she was right: Tiffany was greatly impressed by Laurence, whom she had recognized instantly as belonging to the dandy-set. During her brief sojourn in London she had seen several of these exquisites on the Grand Strut in Hyde Park, and she was well aware that to win the admiration of an out-and-out Pink of the Ton added enormously to a lady's consequence. It was not an easy thing to do, because in general the dandies were extremely critical, more likely to survey with boredom, through an insolently lifted quizzing-glass, an accredited beauty than to acclaim her. She was impressed also by his conversation; and flattered by his assumption that she was as familiar with the personalities and the on-dits of the ton as he was himself. Had it been he, and not Lindeth, who was a Peer, she would have preferred him, because he was so much more fashionable, and because he never bored her by talking about his home in the country, as Lindeth too often did. She would, in any event, have tried to attach him to her apron-strings, because it was torment to her if any young man, even so negligible a one as Humphrey Colebatch, either showed himself to be impervious to her charms, or betrayed a preference for some other girl. In Laurence's case there was an added reason for encouraging his advances: Lindeth, in whom she had detected, since the Leeds adventure, a certain reserve, probably discounted such rivals as Mr Ash, Mr Jack Banningham, and Mr Arthur Mickleby, but she could not believe that he would be indifferent to the rivalry of his fashionable cousin. She had realized almost immediately that he did not like Laurence: not because he uttered a word in his disparagement, but because, when questioned, he spoke of him in a temperate manner far removed from the eager enthusiasm which any mention of his other cousin kindled in him. Since Tiffany much admired Laurence she had no hesitation in ascribing Lindeth's dislike of him to jealousy; it did not so much as cross her mind that Lindeth might be contemptuous of Laurence; and had anyone suggested such a solution to her she would have been utterly incredulous.

When Lindeth called at Staples to leave compliment cards, she told him, with a provocative look under her lashes, that his cousin, learning that although she was an accomplished horsewoman in the saddle she had never found anyone capable of teaching her how to handle the reins in form, had begged to be allowed to offer his services.

He stared at her blankly. "Mr Calver says he will teach me to drive to an inch," she added, with one of her sauciest smiles.

"*Laurence?*" he demanded, the oddest expression on his face.

"Why not?" she countered, lifting an eyebrow at him.

He opened his mouth, shut it again, and turned away to pick up his hat and gloves.

"Well?" persisted Tiffany, pleased with the success of her gambit. "Pray, have you any objection?"

"No, no, not the least in the world!" he said hastily. "How should I? I only—but never mind that!"

That was quite enough to confirm Tiffany in her belief that she had roused a demon of jealousy in his breast. She never knew that his lordship, whom Laurence stigmatized as a bagpipe, snatched the first opportunity that presented itself of admitting his cousin Waldo into a joke which was much too rich to be kept to himself. "I don't know how I contrived to keep my countenance! *Laurie!* Driving to an inch! Oh, lord, I shall be sick if I laugh any more!"

But Tiffany, with no suspicion that she had afforded Lindeth food for laughter, was very well satisfied. Her former suitors, who had gloomily but unresentfully watched Lindeth's star rise, were roused to violent jealousy by Laurence; and she saw no reason to suppose that Lindeth would not be similarly stirred. For several days she was intoxicated by success, believing herself to be irresistible, and queening it over her court with ever-increasing capriciousness. And since, like Mrs Mickleby, she discarded without hesitation the ostensible reason for the Nonesuch's daily visits, and had never for an instant suspected that he might prefer her companion to her peerless self, she was sure that he too was unable to stay away from her. This seemed so obvious that she did not pause to consider that his behaviour, when he came to Staples, was not in the least that of a man dazzled by her charms. She had always found him incalculable, and if she had thought about it at all she would have supposed that he was content merely to look at her.

Courtenay, revolted by her self-satisfaction and indignant with his friends for making such fools of themselves, told her that she was no better than a vulgar lightskirt, and prophesied that she was riding for a fall; and when she laughed said that Lord Lindeth was only the first man to become disgusted: there would be others soon enough.

"Pooh!"

"Mighty pot-sure, aren't you? But it seems to me that we don't see so much of Lindeth these days!"

"When I want him," boasted Tiffany, smiling in a way which made him want to slap her, "I shall just lift a finger! Then you'll see!"

That sent him off in a rage to represent to his mother the absolute necessity of curbing Tiffany's flirtatious antics. "I tell you, Mama, she's *insufferable*!" he declared.

"Now, Courtenay, for goodness' sake don't go upsetting her!" begged Mrs Underhill, alarmed. "I own I wouldn't wish to see Charlotte being so bold as she is, but she always *was* caper-witted, and it ain't as though she was carrying on with strange gentlemen that mightn't keep the line. If I was to interfere, she wouldn't pay a bit of heed to me—and you know what she is when she's crossed! There's enough trouble in the house, with Charlotte being so poorly, without us having to bear one of Tiffany's tantrums!"

He turned appealingly to Miss Trent, but she shook her head. "I'm afraid the only remedy is for her admirers to grow cool," she said, smiling. "She is too headstrong, and has been allowed to have her own way for too long to submit to restraint. What would you have me do? Lock her in her room? She would climb out of the window, and very likely break her neck. I think, with you, that her behaviour is unbecoming, but she has done nothing scandalous, you know, and I fancy she won't—unless she is goaded to it."

"How Greg, and Jack, and Arthur can make such cakes of themselves——! Lord, it puts me in such a pelter to think they should be such gudgeons that there's no bearing it!"

"I shouldn't let it tease you," she said. "It's the fashion amongst them to worship Tiffany, and fashions don't endure for long."

"Well, I only hope she has a rattling fall!" he said savagely. "And what have you to say to this Calver-fellow? Teaching her to drive indeed! How do we know he ain't a loose screw?"

"We don't, of course, but although I should prefer her not to drive out alone with him every day I have very little apprehension of his taking advantage of her childishness."

"No, indeed!" said Mrs Underhill. "When he asked my permission, and told me I could trust him to take good care of her! He's a very civil young man, and I'm sure I don't know why you should have taken him in dislike!"

"Civil young man! A Bartholomew baby! It's my belief he's a dashed fortune-hunter!"

"Very possibly," agreed Miss Trent, quite unmoved. "But since she's under age we needn't tease ourselves over that. If you imagine that Tiffany would fling her cap over the windmill for a mere commoner you can't know her!"

Oddly enough, at that very moment, Sir Waldo, lifting an eyebrow at Laurence, was saying: "Having a touch at the heiress, Laurie?"

"No, I ain't. If you mean the Wield chit!"

"I do. Just started in the petticoat line, I collect!"

"Well, I haven't. *Is* she an heiress?"

"So I'm given to understand. I rather think she told me so herself."

"Sort of thing she would do," said Laurie. He thought it over for a moment, and then added, "I don't want to be legshackled: wouldn't suit me at all! Not but what I may be forced into it."

"I'm reluctant to blight your hopes, Laurie, but I think it only right to warn you that I have reason to suppose that your suit won't prosper. Miss Wield is determined to marry into the Peerage."

"Exactly so!" exclaimed Laurence. "*I* saw at a glance! She means to catch Lindeth, of course. I imagine you wouldn't like that above half!"

"Not as much," said Sir Waldo, in a voice of affable agreement.

"No, and my aunt wouldn't like it either!" said Laurence. "What's more, I wouldn't blame her! No reason why *he* should make a cream-pot marriage: *he* ain't under the hatches!"

"I don't think he has any such intention."

"I know *that*! The silly chub was bowled out by her face. Well, you won't cozen *me* into thinking that young Julian is not your cosset-lamb! You'd give something to see him come safe off, wouldn't you?"

Sir Waldo, who had drawn his snuff-box from his pocket, opened it with an expert flick of one finger, and took a pinch. He looked meditatively at Laurence, amused understanding in his eyes. "Alas, you've missed your tip!" he said.

Laurence stared at him. "If you're trying to bamboozle me into believing that Julian ain't dangling after that girl it's you who have missed your tip, Waldo! You won't tell me that he——"

"The only thing I shall tell you," interposed Sir Waldo, "is that you're after the fair! Oh, don't look so affronted! Console yourself with the reflection that as little as I discuss Julian's business with you do I discuss yours with him!"

He said no more, leaving Laurence puzzled and aggrieved. He had his own reasons for believing that Julian had been cured of his passing infatuation; but if Laurie, bent on detaching Tiffany, had not discovered that his young cousin now had his eyes turned towards a very different quarry so much the better, he thought, profoundly mistrusting Laurie's mischief-making tongue. If Julian's interest in Miss Chartley became fixed, nothing could more surely prejudice his mother against the match than to learn of it from Laurie. The first news of it must come from Julian himself; after which, he reflected wryly, it would be his task to reconcile the widow. She would be bitterly disappointed, but she was no fool, and must already have begun to doubt whether her cherished son would gratify her ambition by offering for any one of the damsels of rank, fortune, and fashion in whose way she had thrown him. She was also a most devoted parent; and once she had recovered from her initial chagrin Sir Waldo believed that she would very soon take the gentle Patience to her bosom. A pungent description of the beautiful Miss Wield would go a long way towards settling her mind.

For himself, he was much inclined to think that after his various tentative excursions Julian had found exactly the wife to suit him. Just as Patience differed from Tiffany, so did Julian's courtship of her differ from his eager pursuit of Tiffany. He had begun with liking; his admiration had been kindled by the Leeds episode; and he was now, in Sir Waldo's judgment, quietly and deeply in love. From such references to Patience as he from time to time let fall, his cousin gathered that she had every amiable quality, a well-informed mind, and a remarkable readiness to meet Julian's ideas, and to share his every sentiment. Sir Waldo guessed that he was a frequent visitor at the Rectory, but there were none of the rides, picnics, and evening parties which had attended his transitory passion for Tiffany. Probably that was why Laurence seemed not to have realized that he had suffered a change of heart; no doubt Laurie supposed him to be in his elder cousin's company when he found him missing from Broom Hall; and was misled by the innate civility which made him continue to call at Staples into thinking him still Tiffany's worshipper.

It was during one of these morning visits that Julian learned that the al fresco ridotto which Tiffany had coaxed her aunt to hold in the gardens was to be postponed. Charlotte still continued to be languid and out of spirits; the doctor recommended a change of air and sea-bathing; so Mrs Underhill was going to take her to Bridlington, where she had a cousin living with his wife in retirement. She explained apologetically to Lindeth, and to Arthur Mickleby, whom Lindeth had found kicking his heels in the Green Saloon, that she hoped they wouldn't be vexed, but she didn't feel able for a ridotto when Charlotte was so poorly. Both young men expressed their regrets, and said everything that was polite; and Arthur reminded Mrs Underhill, in a heartening way, of how he had been taken to Bridlington after the measles, and how quickly he had plucked up there.

In the middle of this speech Tiffany came in wearing her driving-dress, and with Laurence at her heels. "Bridlington? Who is going to *that* stupid place?" she demanded. She extended a careless hand to Lindeth. "How do you do? I haven't seen you this age! Oh, Arthur, have you been waiting for me? Mr Calver has been teaching me how to loop a rein. *You* are not going to Bridlington, are you? It is the dullest, horridest place imaginable! Why don't you go to Scarborough?"

" 'Tisn't me, it's Charlotte," explained Arthur. "I was telling Mrs. Underhill how much good it did me when *I* was in queer stirrups."

"Oh, Charlotte! *Poor* Charlotte! I daresay it will be the very thing for her. When does she go, ma'am?"

"Well, my dear, I believe I'll take her this week," said Mrs Underhill nervously. "There's no sense in keeping her here, so low and dragged as she is, and Cousin Matty for ever begging me to pay her a visit, and to bring Charlotte along with me. I've been asking his lordship's pardon, and Arthur's too, for being obliged to put off the ridotto."

"Put off my ridotto!" exclaimed Tiffany. "Oh, *no*! you can't mean to be so cruel, ma'am!"

"I'm sure I'm as sorry as I can be, love, but you can't have a party without I'm here, now, can you? It wouldn't be seemly."

"But you must be here, aunt! Send Nurse with Charlotte, or Ancilla! Oh, pray do!"

"I couldn't be easy in my mind, letting the poor lamb go without me, and I wouldn't have the heart for a ridotto, nor any kind of party. But there's no need to get into a fidget, love, for I don't mean to stay above a sennight—that is, not if Charlotte's going on well, and don't dislike to be left with Cousin George and Cousin Matty, which I daresay she won't. But she made me promise her I'd go with her, and so I did. Not that I intended otherwise."

"How can she be so abominably selfish?" cried Tiffany, flushing. "Making you go away when she knows that *I* need you! Depend upon it, she did it for spite, just to spoil my ridotto!"

Arthur looked rather startled, but it was Lindeth who interposed, saying: "It is very natural that she should wish for her mama, don't you think!"

"No!" Tiffany replied crossly. "For she would as lief have Ancilla! Oh, *I* know! Ancilla shall be hostess in your stead, aunt! Famous! We shall do delightfully!"

But Mrs Underhill was steadfast in refusing to entertain this suggestion. Observing the rising storm signals in Tiffany's eyes, she sought to temper the disappointment by promising to hold the ridotto as soon as she returned from Bridlington but this only made Tiffany stamp her foot, and declare that she hated put-offs, and marvelled that her aunt should be taken in by Charlotte's nonsense. "For my part, I believe she could be perfectly stout if she chose! She is putting on airs to be interesting, which I think quite odious, and so I shall tell her!"

"Here!" protested Arthur, shocked. "That's coming it a bit strong! I beg pardon, but—but you shouldn't say that!" He added haltingly: "And although *I* should have enjoyed it, there—there are several people who don't take to the notion. Well—Mrs Chartley won't permit Patience to come, and, as a matter of fact—Mama won't let my sisters either. Not to a moonlight party in the gardens!"

"There! if I didn't say it wasn't the thing!" exclaimed Mrs Underhill.

"Who cares whether they come or not?" said Tiffany scornfully. "If they choose to be stuffy, I promise you *I* don't!"

Arthur reddened, and got up to take his leave. Mrs Underhill, acutely embarrassed, pressed his hand warmly, and gave him a speaking look; but Tiffany turned her shoulder on him, saying that he was quite as stuffy as his sisters.

"I must be going too, ma'am," Lindeth said. "Pray tell Charlotte how sorry I am to hear that she's so much pulled, and tell her to take care she don't get her toes pinched by a crab when she goes sea-bathing! . . . Are you coming, Laurie?"

"Oh, don't wait for me! I have been thinking, Miss Wield, if we might perhaps get up a party to dance at one of the Assemblies in Harrogate—instead of the ridotto. Would you countenance it, ma'am? With Miss Trent, of course, or some older lady, if any might be persuaded?"

Tiffany's eyes lit up, but Mrs Underhill looked dismayed, and faltered: "Oh, dear! No, no, don't suggest it, Mr Calver, for it's the very thing Mr Burford—that's Tiffany's uncle, and her guardian, you know—don't wish for! Because she ain't out yet, and he won't have her going to public dances, for which, of course, he can't be blamed."

"It wasn't he, but Aunt Burford!" said Tiffany. "The greatest beast in nature! Why shouldn't I go to an Assembly in Harrogate! I *will* go. I *will*!"

Lindeth went quietly away, hearing the storm break behind him. Miss Trent was coming down the stairs, and paused, looking enquiringly at him. "How do you do? Tell me at once! The ridotto?"

He burst out laughing. "Well, yes! Coupled with Mrs Underhill's saying she might not go to a Harrogate Assembly."

Miss Trent closed her eyes for an anguished moment. "I see. How prudent of you to slip away, sir! Would that I could do so too! She will sulk for days!"

CHAPTER XIV

THAT TIFFANY refrained from sulking was due to Miss Trent, who waited only until they were alone in the room to utter words which provided her with food for reflection. She said cheerfully that she did not wonder at it that Tiffany was bored with her admirers, but that she thought she might have chosen a better way of being rid of them. Tiffany stared at her.

"Nothing, of course, makes a gentleman retire more quickly than a fit of the tantrums; but you should recollect that a reputation for being ill-tempered would be most prejudicial to your success. As for being rude and unkind to your aunt—indeed, Tiffany, I had not thought you such a wet-goose! What will become of you if you drive off *all* your admirers?"

"I d-don't! I *c-couldn't*!" Tiffany stammered.

"It can be done more easily than you know," replied Ancilla. "You have accomplished it with Lord Lindeth; and, unless I am much mistaken, we shan't see Arthur Mickleby at Staples for some time to come. Your aunt tells me that you spoke slightingly of his sisters. How *stupid* of you, Tiffany! and how dreadfully ill-bred! How came you to do such a thing?"

"I don't care! I only said they were stuffy, and they are! And I don't care a button for Arthur either! And I didn't

177

drive Lindeth off! I *didn't*! He's jealous, because his cousin is teaching me to drive! I have only to smile at him—— How dare you look like that? I tell you——"

"You will be wasting your breath," interrupted Miss Trent. "Try to believe that I am rather more up to snuff than you! I am, you know. Don't glare at me! When your aunt Burford engaged me to be your companion, she particularly desired me to teach you how to go on in society, and if I didn't warn you that your conduct lately has been such as to give people a disgust of you, I should be failing in my duty."

"Disgust! Of *me*? It's not true!" Tiffany gasped, white with rage.

"If you will stop preening yourself on your beauty, and allow yourself the indulgence of a few moments' reflection, I think you must realize that it *is* true," responded Miss Trent. "Before you began to fancy yourself to be a Nonpareil beyond criticism you were used to take care not to fly into unbecoming rages when any stranger was present; but during these past weeks you have grown to be so puffed up in your own conceit that you seem to think you may go your unbridled length and still command everyone's admiration. Well, you were never more mistaken! That is all I have to say to you—and I've said it only because I can't reconcile it with my conscience not to warn you to mend your ways."

She then opened a book, and apparently became so absorbed in it that the furious tirade directed at her did not cause her to betray by the flicker of an eyelid that she heard a word of it. Tiffany slammed out of the room, and was not seen again until she came down to dinner; but as she then seemed to be in her softest mood, even speaking affectionately to Charlotte, and politely to her aunt, Miss Trent was encouraged to suppose that her words had not failed of their intended effect. Towards her, Tiffany adopted a manner of frigid disdain, which had not abated by the following morning, when she refused every offer made by her companion to minister to her entertainment. So Miss Trent, unabashed, left her to her own devices, or (as she suspected) to the attentions of Mr Calver, and seized the opportunity to pay a call on Mrs Chartley, with a copy of the recipe for pickling white mushrooms tucked into her reticule. Charlotte was fretful, and would not go with her, so she went to the village alone, and, having delivered a large parcel at the Crown, to be picked up by the carrier, drove the gig into the Rectory stableyard.

She found Mrs Chartley in her morning-parlour, and received the usual kind welcome from her. Mrs Chartley thanked her for the recipe, enquired after Charlotte, and, when Ancilla would have taken her leave, begged her to sit down for a few minutes.

"I am very glad to see you, Miss Trent," she said, "because I fancy you can perhaps answer a question which is teasing me a good deal." She smiled. "Rather an odd question, you may think—but I know I may depend upon your discretion."

"Certainly you may, ma'am."

Mrs Chartley hesitated. "Yes. If I did not—Miss Trent, I find myself in a quandary! I daresay you are aware that Lord Lindeth is growing extremely particular in his attentions to Patience?"

"I wasn't aware of it, ma'am. I have been constantly with Charlotte, you know. But I am not at all surprised. He always liked her, and I have frequently thought that he and Miss Chartley might have been made for one another. I hope you don't dislike it? I have a great regard for Lord Lindeth —as far as I know him—and I believe him to be really worthy of Miss Chartley."

"No. No, I don't dislike it—though I own to some feelings of doubt at the outset. He appeared to me to be violently in love with Tiffany, which argues a volatility I cannot like."

"I had rather say that he was dazzled by her, as so many have been. He might have loved her if her disposition had matched her face, which, alas, it does not! You are thinking that the change in his sentiments was very sudden, but I fancy he began to be disillusioned quite early in their acquaintance. There were several occasions when—— But I should not be talking of them!"

"You need not scruple to speak frankly: if her conduct at Leeds is anything to judge by, I can readily understand Lindeth's disillusionment. But to turn so soon from Tiffany to Patience does disquiet me! The Rector, however, sets very little store by it. Indeed, he seems to think it perfectly natural that a young man, when he is *ripe for falling in love* (as he puts it), should transfer his affection to another, when he finds he has mistaken his own heart. It seems very odd to me, but I am well aware, of course, that men *are* odd, even the best of them!"

"And Miss Chartley, ma'am?" Ancilla said, smiling.

"I am very much afraid that she is in danger of forming a lasting attachment," replied Mrs Chartley, with a sigh. "*She* is not volatile, you know, and if he were again to discover that he had mistaken his heart——"

"Forgive me!" Ancilla interposed. "I collect that you believe Lindeth to be fickle. But I have been a great deal in his company, and I have had the opportunity to observe his *infatuation*. As I have said, it might have deepened into *love*, but it never did so. And—I do assure you, ma'am, that it would have been wonderful indeed if an ardent young man, having at that time formed no real attachment, had not succumbed to Tiffany's beauty, and to the encouragement he received from her."

Mrs Chartley's face lightened a little. "So the Rector says. I own, there is no *infatuation* in question now. I don't leave them alone together, I need hardly say, but even if I allowed my daughter the license Tiffany has I am persuaded Lindeth would not *flirt* with her. Indeed, I have been agreeably surprised in him! Under the gaiety which makes his manners so taking, there is a strong vein of seriousness. He feels as he ought on all important subjects, and the tone of his mind is particularly nice."

"But in spite of this you do not wish for the connection, ma'am?" Ancilla asked, a little puzzled.

"My dear, a very strange creature I should be if I did not wish for such an advantageous connection for my daughter! If he is sincere, nothing would please me more than to see her so well-established. But although they are not unequal in birth they are unequal in consequence. Nor is Patience an heiress. She will have some four thousand pounds, but that, though it is a respectable portion, might be thought paltry by Lindeth's family. From things he has let fall, about disliking *ton* parties, and being the *despair of his mother*—in his funning way, you know!—I suspect that the family wish him to make what is called a brilliant marriage, and might be strongly opposed to his marriage to a country clergyman's daughter." She paused, and rather aimlessly shifted the position of a book lying on the table at her elbow. "I had fancied that Sir Waldo had been his guardian, but I understand this was not the case. At the same time, there can be no doubt that he has stood in much that position. Nor that his influence over Lindeth is great. That, my dear Miss Trent, is why I have been anxious to have the opportunity of talking to you. If there is any fear that Sir Waldo might exert himself to prevent the marriage—even if he should merely dislike it—I would not upon any account continue to permit Lindeth to visit us as he now does. Neither the Rector nor I would countenance the alliance if it had not the approbation of Lindeth's family. You will understand, I am persuaded, why I am in a quandary, and why I made up my mind to admit you into my confidence. Tell me! What are Sir Waldo's sentiments upon this occasion?"

Miss Trent felt her colour rising, but she responded in a steady voice: "I am honoured by your confidence, ma'am, but Sir Waldo has not taken me into his. I wish I might be able to help you, but it is not in my power."

Mrs Chartley raised her eyes, directing a slightly sceptical look at her. "If that is so, there is no more to be said, of course. I ventured to put the question to you because I know you to be far better acquainted with him than anyone else in the district."

There was silence for a few moments. Then Miss Trent drew a breath, and said: "I have been obliged to be a good deal in his company, ma'am, but I do not stand upon such intimate terms with him as—as you seem to suggest." She managed to smile. "My sins have found me out! I allowed myself to be persuaded to accept Lady Colebatch's invitation, and was imprudent enough to waltz with Sir Waldo, twice. I have been made to regret it. I'm afraid the pleasure of dancing again, after such a long time, went to my head!"

Mrs Chartley's face softened; she leaned forward, and briefly clasped one of Ancilla's hands. "No wonder! I perfectly understand. But—— My dear, will you permit me to speak frankly to you? You are a young woman, in spite of your sober ways! And you have not your mama at hand to advise you, have you? I am most sincerely fond of you, so you must forgive me if I seem to you to take too much upon myself. I have been feeling a little anxious about you, for I'm afraid you may be cherishing hopes which are unlikely to be fulfilled. Don't think that I blame you! Sir Waldo's attentions have been marked: it is even common knowledge that not a day has passed since Charlotte has been laid up without his calling on you at Staples."

"To enquire after her progress—to bring her what he thought might entertain her!" Ancilla uttered, her throat constricted.

"My dear!" protested Mrs Chartley, with a slight laugh.

"Ma'am, I only once saw him—and then in company!"

"If you tell me so, I believe you, but it will be a hard task to convince others."

"I am aware of it, ma'am," said Ancilla bitterly. "I am held to be setting my cap at him, am I not?"

"We need not concern ourselves with expressions of spite. That is not at all *my* opinion. What makes me uneasy is *his* pursuit of *you*. If it had been any other man than Sir Waldo, I should have known it to be a determined courtship, and I should have been expecting every day to be able to wish you happy—for you cannot conceal from me, my dear, that you are by no means indifferent to him. That doesn't surprise me in the least: I fancy there are few women strongminded enough to withstand him. Even I—and he does not make up to me, you know!—am very conscious of his charm. I think him dangerously attractive, and don't for a moment doubt that a great many females have fallen in love with him."

"Did Mrs Mickleby tell you so, ma'am?"

"On the authority of her cousin in London. I should be sorry to place too much reliance on mere gossip, but it has been to some extent borne out by Lindeth—not, you may be sure, with any intention of traducing his cousin. Indeed, the reverse! He often talks about Sir Waldo, and always with admiration—I had almost said, with pride! And one must bear in mind, my dear Miss Trent, that Sir Waldo belongs to a certain set which is considered to be the very height of fashion. In fact, he is its leader, and very much a man of the world. You must know, perhaps better than I do, that the manners and too often the conduct of those who are vulgarly called Top-of-the-Trees are not governed by quite the same principles which are the rule in more modest circles."

"Are you trying to warn me, ma'am, that Sir Waldo is a libertine?" asked Ancilla bluntly.

"Oh, good gracious! No!" exclaimed Mrs Chartley. "You must not think—my dear, I beg you won't say that I said that! No doubt he has had his—shall we say his adventures? —but pray don't imagine that I suspect him of—of——"

"Offering me a *carte blanche*? That, I believe, is the term, is it not? I promise you I should not accept it!"

Mrs Chartley was thrown still more off her balance by this, and said: "No, no! I don't suspect him of meaning to do you the least harm! What I fear is that he may harm you unwittingly, not realizing that you might fall far more deeply in love with him than he knew, or intended. He is accustomed to associate, recollect, with fashionable females who understand the rules of flirtation as you, I am happy to say, do not. Very likely he has been a trifle misled into thinking you are

182

as worldly wise as any of his London flirts: you are *posée* beyond your years, you know! He would not, I am persuaded, tamper with the affections of a girl whom he knew to be inexperienced."

"But you don't hold him in very high esteem, do you, ma'am?" said Ancilla, with a painful smile.

"Oh, you are quite mistaken! In some respects, I hold him in the highest esteem!" Mrs Chartley replied quickly. "I have every reason——" She checked herself, colouring, and added: "All I wish to say to you, my dear, is that you should be on your guard. Don't refine too much upon his gallantry, but recollect that he is a man of five or six-and-thirty, handsome, rich, very much courted—and still a bachelor!"

Miss Trent began to pull on her gloves. "I do recollect it," she said, in a low voice. "I am very much obliged to you for your kindness in—in warning me, ma'am, but I beg you to believe that it was unnecessary! You have told me nothing that I haven't told myself." She rose. "I must go. I wish I might have been able to give you the assurance you want. I cannot—but I don't think Sir Waldo would ever stand in the way of what he saw to be Lindeth's happiness."

"Thank you: I hope you may be right. Did you come in the gig? I'll walk with you to the stables. By the bye, what has been the outcome of Mr Calver's Harrogate scheme? I can picture your dismay! We heard of it from Lindeth, and from what he did *not* say I collect that Tiffany was—sadly disappointed by her aunt's refusal to countenance it!"

Ancilla laughed. "Not sadly, ma'am! Furiously! Lord Lindeth made good his escape when he saw the storm about to break. I fancy we shall hear no more of the scheme."

"You must be thankful for it! A very rackety suggestion to have put forward! I daresay you will be glad to see the last of that young man."

"Well, I own that I can't like Mr Calver, but I should be doing him less than justice if I didn't tell you that when he saw that Mrs Underhill disliked the scheme he let it drop immediately. I must say, too, that I have felt very much more cordial since he confessed to me that he had spoken without reflection, meaning only to divert Tiffany's mind, and was sincerely sorry for it. He assured me I might depend upon him to discover a hundred reasons, if it should be necessary, why the scheme was ineligible! He was extremely civil—as, indeed, he has always been."

They had reached the stables; and they parted on this

183

lighter note. Mrs Chartley stayed only until Ancilla had stepped up into the gig, and then walked back to the house, along the garden-path. Ancilla drove out of the stable-gate, and turned into the village street. Before the cob had broken into a trot a phaeton, drawn by a team of chestnuts, swept round the bend immediately ahead. Knowing herself to be in full view of the Rectory, Miss Trent saw with dismay that Sir Waldo was checking his team, with the evident intention of pulling up alongside the gig. There seemed to be nothing to do but to follow suit, since to urge the cob into a trot at that moment would be so uncivil as to make Sir Waldo think that she was trying to avoid a meeting.

The next instant the phaeton had stopped beside the gig, driven up so close that if she had not known how expert was the driver she would have feared that the wheels would be locked; the groom had jumped down, and run to the wheelers' heads; and Sir Waldo was raising his hat, and smiling at her. "How do you do, ma'am? I must have been born under a lucky star! A moment earlier, and I should have missed you. I have been thinking myself singularly *un*lucky for the past sennight, you know."

She replied, as easily as she could: "So, too, has poor Charlotte. Are you on your way to Leeds?"

"Yes; have you any commissions for me?"

"No, I thank you, none. I must not detain you."

"I have the impression that it's I who am detaining you," he said quizzically.

She smiled, but said: "Well, I certainly ought not to linger: I have been with Mrs Chartley, and stayed longer than I meant to. And you, I expect, have a great deal of business to attend to in Leeds."

"Not so very much. I'm happy to say that I am nearing the end of it."

"You must be heartily tired of it," she agreed. "Have the builders finished their work?"

"No, not yet. I am having—rather extensive alterations made."

She laughed. "No need to tell me that, Sir Waldo! Your alterations are a matter of the greatest interest in the neighbourhood, I promise you!"

"Yes, so I've been told. Speculation is rife, is it? I should have known better than to suppose that no one would care a rush what I did with the house, for my own home is in the country. That's the worst—and sometimes the best—of country-life: intense interest in one's neighbours!"

"Very true. And you, I would remind you, are an exceptionally interesting neighbour in these backward parts! Besides which, you have whetted curiosity by not choosing to disclose whether you mean to sell Broom Hall, or to keep it as a suitable house to stay in when the York Races are run. This reserve, sir, is felt to indicate that there is some mystery attached to your alterations, which you are afraid to make known!"

She spoke in a tone of raillery, and was surprised to see that although he smiled he looked rather rueful. "I think I am," he admitted. "My purpose *will* be known, but I prefer that it should remain a secret while I remain in the district."

She said: "I was only joking you! Not trying to pry into your concerns!"

"I'm well aware of that. But I have every intention of making a clean breast of the matter to you, Miss Trent. I am afraid that I shall fall under the displeasure of the majority of my neighbours, but I fancy your voice won't swell the chorus of disapproval. You have too liberal a mind. I shall do myself the honour of coming to visit you in the very near future—as I warned you I should, an æon ago!"

She could not believe that these were the words of a man with nothing but idle dalliance in mind; but she felt obliged to demur. "I should be very happy, but—I don't think—Sir Waldo, Mrs Underhill is to take Charlotte to Bridlington, and will be away from home for a sennight, or more!"

He made a sign to his groom, and said, with his glinting smile, as he gave his horses the office: "I know it. I may at last contrive to see you alone, Miss Trent!"

CHAPTER XV

MISS TRENT drove home in a happy dream, no longer caring whether her meeting with the Nonesuch had been observed by Mrs Chartley, or not; and able to dismiss that lady's earnest warning with a light heart. Mrs Chartley, she now believed, had misjudged Sir Waldo. So too, indeed, had she: probably they had each of them been prejudiced by their mutual dislike of the Corinthian set; almost certainly (and very strangely) they had been misled by commonsense. Neither she nor Mrs Chartley was of a romantic turn of mind; and she at least had learnt, early in life, the folly of indulging fantastic dreams which belonged only to the realm of fairytales. Nothing could be more fantastic than to suppose that the Nonesuch bore the least resemblance to the handsome nursery-prince whose wayward fancy had been fixed on Cinderella, so perhaps they were not so very much to be blamed for their doubts. Inexperienced though she knew herself to be in the art of dalliance, Miss Trent could no longer doubt: she could only wonder. Try as she would she could discover no reason why she should have been preferred to all the noble and lovely ladies hopeful of receiving an offer from the Nonesuch. It seemed so wildly improbable as to be unreal. But when she had tried in vain to place a different construction upon the things he had said to her, it flashed into her mind that nothing, after all, was so wildly improbable as her own headlong tumble into love with the epitome of all that she held in contempt; and that that was precisely what she had done there was no doubt whatsoever.

She returned to Staples treading on air. Even Mrs Underhill, not usually observant, was struck by the bloom in her cheeks, and the glow in her eyes, and declared that she had never seen her in such high beauty. "Never tell me he's popped the question?" she exclaimed.

"No, no, ma'am!" Ancilla replied, blushing and laughing.

"Well, if he hasn't done it now, I'll be bound you know he means to, for what else is there to cast you into alt?" demanded Mrs Underhill reasonably.

"Am I in alt? I didn't know it! Dear Mrs Underhill, pray —*pray* don't ask me questions I cannot answer!"

Mrs Underhill very kindly refrained, but she could not help animadverting on the perversity of fate, which had decreed that she should be away from Staples just as she would have most wished to be at home. "For gentlemen are so unaccountable," she said, "that he may need to be nudged on, and that I *could* have done!"

Miss Trent, albeit profoundly thankful that her employer would not be at hand to perform this office, recognized the kindly intention that had inspired her daunting speech, and thanked her with what gravity she could command, but told her that she would as lief receive no offer from a gentleman who required nudging.

"Yes, that's all very well," retorted Mrs Underhill, "and very easy for you to talk like that, when all you've got to say is yes, or no, as the case may be! As though it didn't stand to reason that a gentleman that's screwed himself up to the point, and very likely hasn't had a wink of sleep all night for making up a pretty speech and learning it off by heart, needs a bit of encouragement, because he's bound to feel bashful, on account of not wishing to make a figure of himself, which gentlemen, my dear, can't abide!"

Miss Trent could not picture the Nonesuch overcome by bashfulness, but she kept this reflection to herself. She had no wish to prolong a discussion which she felt to be unbecoming, so after murmuring an agreement she directed Mrs Underhill's thoughts into a different channel, by producing a list of all the things that must be attended to before that lady could leave Staples with a quiet mind. Fortunately the list was a long one, and included problems of great complexity, chief amongst which loomed the vexed question of the new winter curtains for the drawing-room. These were being made by an indigent widow, living in a village some miles distant from Staples: an arrangement which, owing partly to the dilatory disposition of the widow, and partly to the folly of the silk warehouse in sending silk for the linings which in no way matched the opulent brocade chosen by Mrs Underhill, had already been productive of considerable annoyance.

"If it isn't one thing it's another!" declared Mrs Underhill. "*Faithfully* did they promise to send me another pattern this week! And did they do it? Answer me that!"

"No, ma'am," said Miss Trent obediently. "They sent you a civil letter, explaining why there must be a little delay. Would you perhaps wish me to write to the warehouse, desiring them to send the new pattern to Mrs Tawton, so that she may judge——"

"No, that I wouldn't!" interrupted Mrs Underhill. "*She* judge? She wouldn't know black from white, for a sillier creature I never met! And so slow that—— Well, there! I knew how it would be when Mrs Chartley asked me if I'd put some work in her way, for I never yet employed anyone out of kindness but what it cost me more and was worse done than if I'd sent all the way to London to have it made for me! I'd liefer by far have dipped my hand in my pocket, and made her a present of the money, and so I would have done if Mrs Chartley hadn't warned me not, for fear of hurting the silly woman's pride. Which is another thing I don't hold with. Don't you ever, my dear, send out work to anyone that has claims to gentility, for if they don't do it in their time instead of yours ten to one they'll do it wrong, and very likely look as if you'd insulted 'em if you tell 'em it's not been done to your satisfaction!"

"I won't," said Miss Trent. "If you think I may be trusted to judge, I'll take the lining-silk to Mrs Tawton, and look at it beside the brocade. If the pattern is sent before your return, that is. Or would you prefer to let it stand until you can take it yourself?"

"No, that I wouldn't!" said Mrs Underhill. "It's this winter I want my new curtains, not next! Though I don't like to be asking you to run *my* errands, which you might well take offence at!"

"I'm not so genteel, ma'am! So that is settled. Then there is the fruit to be given to——"

"Oh, my goodness, if that hasn't put me in mind of old Matthew!" exclaimed Mrs Underhill. "Well, I'm sure it's no wonder I should have forgot, with all the fuss and worry about Charlotte, and the packing, and such! He's laid up with his rheumatism, and there's a bottle of liniment, and a bit of flannel to be taken to his cottage, which I'll have to find the time to do, because he's a pensioner, and Mr Underhill was always very particular not to neglect any of them."

"I shall be glad of a walk, and I'll go tomorrow morning, as soon as I have seen you and Charlotte safely into the carriage," promised Ancilla.

Since Mrs Underhill, who rarely spent a night away from Staples, was rapidly becoming distracted, this duty proved to be more arduous than might have been expected, and entailed much hurried unpacking to discover whether various indispensable comforts had been included in the numerous trunks and portmanteaux, as Mrs Underhill's maid asserted they had; or whether they had been overlooked, as Mrs Underhill feared they must have been. However, after only one false start, because Charlotte found that she had forgotten her travelling chessboard, the travellers at last drove away, leaving behind them a somewhat breathless and exhausted household.

"Phew!" uttered Courtenay, restoring the handkerchief he

188

had been waving to his pocket. "You'd think they were bound for the Antipodes!" He turned to his giggling cousin, and said, with all the air of a young gentleman virtuously mindful of his mother's parting injunctions: "I'm riding over to Crawshays, and if you care to go with me you may. Only don't keep me kicking my heels for ever while you rig yourself out!"

Having no other engagement, and apprehending that Miss Trent might bear her off to visit the aged Matthew, Tiffany accepted this handsome invitation, and ran into the house to put on her riding-dress. Relieved of responsibility for one morning at least, Miss Trent presently set forth with a basket over her arm, glad of the exercise after her close attendance on Charlotte, and only too happy to be alone with her thoughts.

It was on her way back to Staples that she was overtaken by Lindeth, driving the late Mr Calver's gig. He pulled up beside her, his eyes dancing with amusement. "Good-morning, ma'am! You have missed *such* a capital sight! Do get up beside me, and let me drive you home!"

She smiled up at him. "Why, thank you, but I enjoy walking, you know! What sight have I missed?"

He laughed. "I'll tell you—but you must let me drive you! I think it's going to rain, and you have no umbrella."

"Very well," she replied, taking the hand he stretched down to her, and mounting nimbly into the gig. "Though *I* think the clouds are too high for rain. Don't keep me in suspense another moment! *What* did I miss?"

"Arthur Mickleby, trying to catch the thong of his whip over his head!" he said, still laughing. "I missed it too, but if you'd seen him——! What must he do but practise the trick half-a-mile back on this lane, just where the trees overhang the road! *What* a cawker!"

She began to laugh too. "Oh, no! Did it get caught up?"

"I should rather think it did! By the time I came along he was in such a rage, cursing the tree, and the whip, and that nappy gray of his, that I couldn't have helped laughing if it had been to save my life! Every time he got hold of the butt, and tried to twitch the thong free, the gray took fright, and started forward, so of course Mickleby was obliged to let the whip go while he got the hard-mouthed brute quiet again. So there he was, backing under the tree with the whip swinging like a pendulum, and knocking his hat off!"

Miss Trent, much enjoying this story, said: "To think I should have missed it! Did he succeed in freeing it?"

"Oh, lord, no! It's still there—but I'll lay you odds it won't be for long! Mickleby's gone off home: to fetch a ladder, *I* think! Before anyone comes along and sees the whip dangling, and starts making enquiries! I would, too. He was ready to murder me, but there was nothing I could do about it."

"Poor Arthur! I expect you were perfectly odious!"

"Not a bit of it! I picked up his hat for him! Of course, the whole thing was Waldo's fault: Mickleby must have seen him catch his thong over his head. I tell Waldo that if he stays here much longer he'll get to be so puffed up that there'll be no bearing it! Mickleby, and the rest of them, copy every single thing he does, you know. If he took to wearing his coat inside out they'd do the same!"

"Yes, I think they would," she agreed. "Fortunately, he never does anything extravagant! Indeed, he has exerted a very beneficial influence over his devout worshippers—and has won great popularity amongst their parents in consequence!"

He grinned. "I know he has. He is the most complete hand! But he won't be popular with 'em when they find that he only wanted Broom Hall for his wretched brats!"

"Wretched brats?" repeated Miss Trent, in a queer tone.

"Well, that's what my cousin George calls 'em!" chuckled his lordship. "He don't approve of them at all! He's a very good fellow, but a trifle too full of starch and propriety. Always in the established mode, is George! He told Waldo that to be housing the brats in a respectable neighbourhood is carrying his eccentricity too far. I must say, I wouldn't dare do it myself. Well, even the Rector was pretty taken aback when Waldo broached it to him, and I fancy he's in a bit of a quake over what people like Mrs Mickleby will say to him when they learn that he was in Waldo's confidence!" He became aware suddenly that Miss Trent was curiously silent, and stopped short in the middle of his cheerful rattle, and glanced round to find that her eyes were fixed on his face. There was a blank look in them, which made him say uneasily: "Waldo told you about his children, didn't he, ma'am?"

She looked away, saying stonily: "No. He hasn't mentioned them."

"Oh, lord!" exclaimed Lindeth, in the liveliest dismay. "I had a notion that—— Now I am in the suds! For God's sake, ma'am, don't betray me! I don't want one of Waldo's trimmings!"

He spoke half-laughingly; she forced her lips into a faint smile, and replied: "You may be easy on that head, sir. I shall certainly not speak of it."

"He warned me he didn't want it talked of," said Lindeth remorsefully. "He never does himself, you know, except, of course—— But I'm not going to say another word!" An alarming thought suddenly assailed him; he said apprehensively: "*You* aren't scandalized, are you, ma'am? I mean, I know all the old tabbies will nab the rust at having brats of that sort planted at Broom Hall, but *you* don't hold up your nose at what you don't think *quite the thing*! After all, most men wouldn't care a straw what became of the poor little devils, much less squander a fortune on housing them, and feeding them, and educating them! You may say that he's so full of juice that it can't signify to him, but——"

Miss Trent, feeling herself to be on the verge of strong hysterics, interrupted him. "My dear Lord Lindeth, I assure you that you have not the smallest need to say more! I collect that you and Sir Waldo will soon be leaving Yorkshire?"

He hesitated, before saying: "Yes—that is, I am not perfectly sure! I must go home, of course, but—I hope to be in Yorkshire again as soon as—well, *soon*!"

"Next month, for the York Races," she agreed. "I daresay you have frequently attended them. This will be the first time I have had that opportunity. Mrs Underhill has the intention of getting up an agreeable party for the event, you know."

He followed this lead readily enough; and the rest of the short drive was beguiled with innocuous chattery, in which his lordship bore decidedly the major part. He would have turned in at the gates of Staples, but Miss Trent would not permit it, saying that if he would set her down at the lodge she would enjoy the walk up the avenue to the house. Her command over both her voice and her countenance was such as to banish from his mind any lingering fear that his indiscreet tongue might have wreaked more mischief than had ever been in his head; and he drove off with a cheerful wave of his beaver.

She walked up the avenue, keeping to the carriageway by instinct rather than by sight, her eyes looking blindly ahead; and the empty basket weighing heavily on her arm. Her thoughts were chaotic; before she could attempt to marshal them into even the semblance of order some period of quiet and solitude would be necessary to enable her to recover from the shock of Lindeth's artless disclosure.

Mercifully, it was granted to her. When she entered the house, it was wrapped in an unusual silence. Tiffany and Courtenay had not returned from their ride; and the servants, all sweeping and dusting finished, were in their own quarters. No one observed her return, and no one disturbed her when she reached the refuge of her bedchamber. She untied the strings of her bonnet, and mechanically smoothed them, before restoring the bonnet to the shelf in her wardrobe. As she turned away she became aware of the trembling of her limbs, and sat down limply, resting her elbows on the dressing-table before her, and sinking her head between her hands. She had not known that shock could affect one in a manner unpleasantly reminiscent of a feverish illness she had suffered years before.

It was long before she could compel her brain to consider rather than to remember. It might be useless to recall everything the Nonesuch had said to her, everything he had done, but there was no helping it. So many of his words had assumed a new significance! He had had a *certain proposition* to lay before her; and *every intention of making a clean breast of the matter* to her; he had known that he would fall under the displeasure of his neighbours, but had fancied that her voice would not swell the chorus of disapproval, because she had *too liberal a mind.* She wondered, in the detachment of despair, what she could have said or done to imbue him, and Lindeth too, with so false an estimate of her character.

The first impulse of her mind had been to reject as incredible the disclosure that Sir Waldo was a hardened libertine; and even when she grew calmer, and was able to think rather than to feel, there still persisted in her brain, beyond reason, the conviction that it could not be true. Had anyone but Lindeth told her that Sir Waldo had fathered nameless children she would not have lent the tale a moment's belief. But Lindeth would never slander his cousin, and what he said could not be scornfully dismissed. She had been amazed that he should speak so lightly of the matter, for she could not doubt that he was himself a young man of principle. Then she thought of what Mrs Chartley had said to her, and realized what strong support her warning gave to Lindeth's words. It was rather dreadful to know that so strict and upright a woman could condone what she had called "adventures". She knew the truth, but she plainly thought little the worse of Sir

Waldo. She had uttered her warning not to prevent a marriage, but in the fear that no offer of marriage would be made. She might, like Mrs Mickleby, be scandalized by the arrival in the neighbourhood of Sir Waldo's bastards, but she did not consider them a bar to his marriage with a young woman who was far removed from the wantons with whom he had enjoyed his *adventures*. This attitude of mind would have seemed as incredible to Ancilla as all the rest if she had come to Staples straight from her home, where loose conduct was regarded with abhorrence; but Ancilla had spent some months in London, and she had learnt that in fashionable circles promiscuous conduct was regarded by many with amusement, not with horror. The most surprising people talked openly of the latest *crim. cons.*, and still more surprising were the several haughty ladies of high position who were known to have foisted other men's children on to their husbands. Provided one was discreet in that exclusive world, one might take as many lovers as one chose, and still maintain an accepted respectability. The only unforgiveable crime was to cause a scandal. As for the gentlemen, few people thought the worse of them for rakishness. Even Lady Trent, quite as virtuous as Mrs Chartley, could survey, critically, but without disgust, some Drury Lane vestal well-known to be the latest mistress of a gentleman whom she would entertain in her house that very evening with the greatest cordiality.

But Miss Trent had not been reared in this accommodating morality. She was as much revolted by a libertine as by a prostitute, and she would as soon have contemplated becoming such a man's mistress as his wife.

CHAPTER XVI

By THE TIME TIFFANY returned to Staples Miss Trent had regained sufficient command over herself to be able to meet her with at least the semblance of composure. There was a stricken look in her eyes, but Tiffany, very full of her own concerns, did not notice it. She was in sparkling good-humour, for on their way home she and Courtenay had met Lady Colebatch and Lizzie, tooling along the road to the village in a dowdy landaulette. "And Lady Colebatch asked us if we cared to dine at Colby Place this evening—just Courtenay and me! It is not a party—only the Mickleby girls and Arthur, and Jack Banningham! So I may, Ancilla, mayn't I? Oh, she said she would be glad to see you, if you liked to go with us! But I daresay you won't, for all we mean to do is to play games, and there won't be any *strangers* there, so there *can't* be any objection to my going without you! Now, can there?"

"No, none, if Courtenay goes with you."

"*Dear* Ancilla!" Tiffany said, embracing her. "Shall you accompany us? You *need* not, you know!"

"Then I won't," said Miss Trent, faintly smiling.

Courtenay, who had entered the room in Tiffany's wake, cried out at this. Miss Trent pleaded a headache; which made Tiffany say instantly: "I thought you were not looking quite the thing! *Poor* Ancilla! You will be glad of a quiet evening, I daresay: you should go to bed, and I'll bring some lemon peel to put on your temples!"

Miss Trent declined this; so Tiffany, all eager solicitude, offered to find the pastilles her aunt burned whenever she too had the headache; or to mix a glass of hartshorn and water for her to drink.

"Thank you, Tiffany, no!" said Miss Trent firmly. "And I don't want a cataplasm to my feet either! You know I never quack myself!"

Tiffany was rather daunted by this; but after searching her memory for a moment, her brow puckered, she pronounced triumphantly: "Camphorated spirits of lavender!" and ran out of the room, calling to old Nurse.

Miss Trent raised her brows enquiringly at Courtenay. "Why is she so anxious to render me bedfast? If you know of any reason, pray don't keep it from me!"

He grinned. "Well, I don't—except that Lady Colebatch said that she was going to invite Lindeth as well, and I rather fancy Tiffany means to lift her finger. So, of course, she don't want a chaperon!"

"Means to do *what*?" demanded Miss Trent.

His grin broadened. "Lift her finger! That's what she told me she'd do when she wanted to bring Lindeth back to heel; but for my part I think she's mistaken her man! *She* thinks he must be in flat despair because she's been flirting with that

194

court card of a cousin of his, and turning a cold shoulder on him, but *I* think he don't care a rush! In fact,—but mum for that!"

"Mum indeed for that!" said Miss Trent, roused to speak with unusual earnestness. "I do *beg* of you,——"

"Oh, no need for that!" declared Courtenay virtuously. "I told Mama I wouldn't stir the coals, and no more I will. Unless, of course, *she* comes the ugly," he added, after a thoughtful pause.

Miss Trent could only hope that her charge would refrain. Her humour at the moment seemed sunny, but there was no depending upon its continuance; and although she and her cousin rarely quarrelled when they rode together, each favouring much the same neck-or-nothing style, and Courtenay admitting that with all her faults Tiffany was pluck to the backbone, at all other times they took a delight in vexing one another.

However, they presently set off together in perfect amity, in Courtenay's phaeton, each agreeing that since the party was no dress affair this conveyance was preferable to the rather outdated carriage drawn by a pair of horses kept largely for farmwork which was the only other closed vehicle available during Mrs Underhill's absence from home. Miss Trent, whose opinion of young Mr Underhill's ability to drive a team was not high, noted with relief that he had only a pair harnessed to his phaeton, reflected that the moon was at the full, thus rendering it unlikely that he would drive into a ditch, and retired to grapple with her own melancholy problem.

Not the least perplexing feature of this, as she soon discovered, was her inability to think of the rake whose love-children were to be foisted cynically on to an unsuspecting society and of the delightful man whose smile haunted her dreams as one and the same person. It was in vain that she reminded herself that charm of manner must necessarily form the major part of a rake's stock-in-trade; equally in vain that she lashed herself for having been so stupidly taken in. From this arose the horrifying realization that however tarnished in her eyes might be Sir Waldo's image her love had not withered, as it ought to have done, but persisted strongly enough to make her feel more miserable than ever in her life before.

For on one point her resolution was fixed: there could be no question of marriage with him, even if marriage was what he had in mind, which, in the light of Lindeth's revelations, now seemed doubtful. But when she thought it over she could not believe that he meant to offer her a less honourable alliance. A libertine he might be, but he was no fool, and he must be well aware that she was no female of easy virtue. She wondered why he should wish to marry her; and came to the dreary conclusion that he had probably decided that the time had come for him to marry, and hoped that by choosing a penniless nobody to be his wife he would be at liberty to continue to pursue his present way of life, while she, thankful to be so richly established, turned a blind eye to his *crim. cons.* and herself behaved with all the propriety which he would no doubt demand of the lady who bore his name.

By the time Tiffany and Courtenay returned from Colby Place her headache was no longer feigned. Only a sense of duty kept her from retiring to bed hours earlier; and she could only feel relief when Tiffany, instead of prattling about the party, yawned, shrugged up her shoulders, said that it had been abominably insipid, and that she was fagged to death. An expressive grimace from Courtenay informed Miss Trent that he had a tale to disclose; but as she felt herself to be quite incapable of dealing with Tiffany's problems at that moment she did not stay to hear what the tale was, but went upstairs with her wayward charge.

Tiffany put in no appearance in the breakfast-parlour next morning. Her maid told Miss Trent that she was suffering from a headache: a statement interpreted by Nurse as "in one of her dratted miffs." So Courtenay, cheerfully discussing an enormous breakfast, was able to regale Miss Trent with the history of the previous night's entertainment.

"Lindeth wasn't there," he said, cracking his second egg. "Told Lady Colebatch he was already engaged. Deepest regrets: all that sort of flummery! *But*, ma'am, Patience wasn't there either! *She* had a previous engagement too, and if you can tell me what it could have been but Lindeth's being invited to the Rectory, it's more than anyone else can! Because Arthur Mickleby and his sisters were at Colby Place, and Sophy and Jack Banningham, *and* the Ashes, so where did Lindeth go if it wasn't to the Rectory? Plain as a pikestaff! But what must Mary Mickleby do but—no, it wasn't Mary! it was Jane Mickleby, and just the sort of thing she *would* do! —well, she said, with that silly titter of hers, that she was sure *no one* could give the least guess as to why Patience and Lindeth were both engaged on the same evening. And, if you

196

ask *me*, ma'am," concluded Courtenay, in a very fairminded spirit, "she didn't say it *only* to pay off a score with Tiffany, but because she's as cross as crabs herself that Lindeth never showed the least preference for *her*! But, however it may have been, you should have seen Tiffany's face!"

"I am thankful I did not!" responded Miss Trent.

He chuckled. "Ay, so you may be! Lord, what a ninny-hammer she is! It's my belief she'd never had the least suspicion that Lindeth had a tendre for Patience—and, I must say, I felt quite *sorry* for her!"

"That was kind of you," said Miss Trent politely.

"Well, I think it was," owned Courtenay. "For I don't like her, and never did! But she's my cousin, after all, and I'm dashed if I wouldn't as lief have her for a cousin as an antidote like Jane Mickleby!" He paused, his fork spearing a vast quantity of ham, halfway to his mouth and said, in portentous accents: "But that wasn't the whole!"

Miss Trent waited with a sinking heart while he masticated this Gargantuan mouthful. "Well?"

"Arthur!" he pronounced, a trifle thickly. He washed down the ham with a gulp of coffee, and handed her his cup to be replenished. "Mighty cool to her!"

"Very likely. She didn't speak of his sisters as she ought."

"I know that, but I've got a notion there was more to it than that. Seemed to me—— Well, you know what cakes he, and Jack, and Greg have been making of themselves over that chit, ma'am?"

"Yes?"

"Seemed to me they weren't. Don't know why, but I daresay Jack will tell me, even if Greg don't. Not that they were uncivil, or——or—— Dashed if I know what it was! Just struck me that they weren't any of 'em so particular in their attentions. Good thing! For," said Courtenay, about to dig his teeth into a muffin, "they were getting to be dead bores!"

Miss Trent could not share his satisfaction. Since she knew no more than he did what had happened to cause Tiffany's local admirers to grow suddenly cold, she could only hope either that he had been mistaken, or that these ill-used gentlemen were trying a change of tactics in their attempts to attach her.

"Was Mr Calver present?" she asked.

"No, but he wasn't invited," replied Courtenay. "Sir Ralph can't abide him: he told me. Said he wouldn't have any man-milliners running tame at Colby Place!"

It was in a mood of considerable foreboding that Miss Trent presently went upstairs to visit Tiffany. Never before had that turbulent beauty sustained a rebuff, and what the repercussions might be Miss Trent could only, shudderingly, guess.

She found Tiffany seated, partially clothed, at her dressing-table, while her maid, who was looking aggrieved, brushed out her lustrous black locks. Tiffany made no mention of the previous night's party, but complained of a sleepless night, of a headache, and of unutterable boredom. "I want to go back to London!" she said. "I hate Yorkshire! I declare I had liefer by far be with the Burfords than at Staples, which is dowdy, and slow, and horrid!"

Miss Trent did not think it worth while to remind her that the Burfords were hardly likely to be in Portland Place in the middle of July, or that they had evinced no desire to have their niece restored to them. Instead, she reminded Tiffany that she had the Ashes' party to look forward to, and, not so very far ahead, the York Races. Tiffany disclaimed any interest in either event; so, after trying several more gambits with as little success, Miss Trent left her, hoping that one at least of her admirers would present himself at Staples that day, to restore the discontented beauty to good humour.

At the foot of the staircase she encountered Totton, who informed her that Sir Waldo had called, to enquire if any tidings had yet been received from Mrs Underhill.

"He asked for Miss Tiffany, ma'am, but I told him Miss had the headache," disclosed Totton. "So he said if you was at home he would like to see you instead. I was just coming to find you, ma'am. Sir Waldo is in the Green Saloon."

It was on the tip of her tongue to tell the butler to deny her, but she mastered the impulse. The interview must be faced, since she could not run away from Staples, deserting her post, as she longed to be able to do. She had made up her mind that she must be prepared to meet the Nonesuch, and to conduct herself, when she did so, with calm and dignity.

She entered the Green Saloon to find him standing by the table in the middle of the room, and glancing through the latest issue of the *Liverpool Mercury*. He looked up as the door opened, and at once laid the paper down, saying with the smile that made her heart tremble: "At last!"

"I beg your pardon! Have you been waiting for long?" she returned, determined to maintain an attitude of friendly civility, and desperately hoping that he would understand from

198

this that it would be useless to make her any sort of declaration.

"More than a sennight! Yes, I know you feel that the delicacy of your position makes it ineligible for you to receive visitors, but I have been very discreet, I promise you! I told the butler that I came to enquire after the travellers—and even went so far as to ask first if Miss Wield was at home."

"We have had no news yet."

"You could scarcely have done so, could you? It was the only excuse I could think of." He paused, the laughter arrested in his eyes as they searched her face. "What is it?" he asked, in quite another tone.

She answered with forced lightness: "Why, nothing!"

"No, don't fob me off! Tell me!" he insisted. "Something has happened to distress you: has that spoilt child been plaguing you?"

She had known that it would be a dreadful interview, but not that he would rend her in two by so instantly perceiving the trouble in her face, or by speaking to her in that voice of concern. She managed to summon up a laugh, and to say: "Good gracious, no! Indeed, sir,——"

"Then what?"

How could you ask a man if it was true that he had several love-begotten children? It was wholly impossible: not even the boldest female could do it! Besides, it would be useless: she knew the answer, and her knowledge had not come to her from a doubtful, or a spiteful source: Lindeth had said it, not dreaming of mischief, treating it as only a slightly regrettable commonplace. The thought stiffened her resolution; she said, in a stronger voice: "Nothing more serious than a headache. I fancy there's thunder in the air: it always gives me the headache. Tiffany isn't feeling quite the thing either. Indeed, I should be with her, not talking to morning-visitors! I hope you may not think it uncivil in me to run away, Sir Waldo, but——"

"I don't think you uncivil: merely untruthful! Why do you call me a morning-visitor, when you know very well I've been awaiting the opportunity to see you privately—and certainly not with the object of uttering social inanities?" He smiled at her. "Are you fearful of offending against the proprieties? You're not so missish! And even the most strictly guarded girl, you know, is permitted to receive an offer of marriage unchaperoned!"

She put out her hand, in a repelling gesture, averting her

199

head, and saying imploringly: "No, don't say it! pray don't!"

"But, my dear——!"

"Sir Waldo, I am very much obliged to you—much honoured—but I can't accept your—your very flattering offer!"

"Why not?" he asked quietly.

Dismayed, she realized that she ought to have foreseen that he would say something quite unexpected. She had not, and was betrayed into incoherence. "I don't—I could never —I have no intention of—no thought of marriage!"

He was silent for a moment, a crease between his brows, his eyes, fixed on her profile, a little puzzled. He said at last: "Don't you think that you might perhaps bring yourself to give marriage a thought? It's quite easy, you know! Only consider for how many more years than you *I* never gave it a thought. And then I met you, and loved you, and found that I was thinking of very little else! Forgive me!—I don't mean to sound presumptuous—but I can't believe that you are as indifferent to me as you'd have me think!"

She flushed. "I am aware that I—that I gave you reason to suppose that it would not be disagreeable to me to receive this offer. Even that I have encouraged you! I didn't mean it so. Circumstances have thrown us a good deal together, and —and I found you amusing and conversable, and was led, I am afraid, into—into treating you with a familiarity which you mistook for something warmer than mere liking!"

"You are wrong," he replied. "So far from encouraging me, or treating me with familiarity, you have been at pains to hold me at arm's length. But there has been a look in your eyes—I can't explain, but I couldn't mistake it, unless I were blind, or a green youth, and I'm neither!"

"I don't doubt that you have had a great deal of experience, sir, but in this instance I assure you you have been misled."

"Yes, I have had experience," he said, looking gravely at her. "Is that what's in your mind?"

"No—that is,—Sir Waldo, I must be frank with you, and tell you that even if I wished to be married, I could never wish for marriage with a man whose tastes—whose mode of life—is so much opposed to everything which I have been taught to hold in esteem!"

"My dear girl," he said, between hurt and amusement, "I'm really not quite as frippery a fellow as you seem to think! I own that in my grasstime I committed a great many follies and extravagances, but, believe me, I've long since out-

200

grown them! I don't think they were any worse than what nine out of ten youngsters commit, but unfortunately I achieved, through certain circumstances, a notoriety which most young men escape. I was born with a natural aptitude for the sporting pursuits you regard with so much distrust, and I inherited, at far too early an age, a fortune which not only enabled me to indulge my tastes in the most expensive manner imaginable, but which made me an object of such interest that everything I did was noted, and talked of. That's heady stuff for greenhorns, you know! There was a time when I gave the gossips plenty to talk about. But do give me credit for having seen the error of my ways!"

"Yes—oh, yes! But—Sir Waldo, I beg you to say no more! My mind is made up, and discussion can only be painful to us both! I have been very much at fault—I can only ask your forgiveness! If I had known that you were not merely flirting with me——"

"But you did know it," he interposed. "You're not a fool, and you can't have supposed that when I told you I wanted to be private with you, because I had a proposition to lay before you, I was *flirting* with you! You didn't suppose it. Something has occurred since I met you in the village which has brought about this change in you—and I fancy I know what it must have been!"

Her eyes lifted quickly to his face, and sank again.

"Tell me!" he said imperatively. "Have you been accused of setting your cap at me? Yes, that's an outrageous question, isn't it? But I know very well that a certain weasel-faced lady of our acquaintance *has* said it, for she did so within my hearing, and I daresay she would not scruple to say it within yours. Has she done so? *Could* you be so absurd as to reject me for such a reason as that?"

"No! If I returned your regard, it would not weigh with me!"

"I see. There doesn't seem to be anything more I can say, does there?"

She could only shake her head, not daring to trust her voice. She saw that he was holding out his hand, and she reluctantly laid her own in it. He lifted it, and kissed her fingers. "I wish you did return my regard," he said. "More than I have ever wished anything in my life! Perhaps you may yet learn to do so: I should warn you that I don't easily despair!"

CHAPTER XVII

THE NONESUCH HAD GONE, and Miss Trent's only desire was to reach the refuge of her bedchamber before her overcharged emotions broke their bonds. Sobs, crowding in her chest, threatened to suffocate her; tears, spilling over her eyelids, had to be brushed hastily aside; she crossed the hall blindly, and as she groped for the baluster-rail, setting her foot upon the first stair, Tiffany came tripping down, her good humour restored by the news that Sir Waldo had come to visit her. "Oh, were you coming to find me?" she said blithely. "Totton sent a message up, so you need not have put yourself to that trouble, Ancilla dearest! Is he in the Green Saloon? I have had *such* a capital notion! Now that Mr Calver has taught me to drive so well, I mean to try if I can't coax Sir Waldo to let me drive his chestnuts! Only think what a triumph it would be! Mr Calver says no female has ever driven *any* of his horses!"

It was surprising how swiftly the habit of years could reassert itself. Miss Trent was sick with misery, but her spirit responded automatically to the demands made upon it. She had thought that any attempt to speak must result in a burst of tears, but she heard her own voice say, without a tremor: "He has gone. He came only to discover if we had yet had news of our travellers, and would not stay."

"Would not stay!" Tiffany's expression changed ludicrously. "When I *particularly* wished to see him!"

"I expect he would have done so had he known that," said Ancilla pacifically.

"*You* must have known it! It is too bad of you! I believe you sent him away on purpose to spite me!" said Tiffany, pettishly, but without conviction. "*Now* what is there for me to do?"

Miss Trent pulled herself together. Wisely rejecting such ideas as first occurred to her, which embraced a little much-needed practice on the pianoforte, a sketching expedition, and an hour devoted to the study of the French tongue, she sought in vain for distractions likely to find favour with a damsel determined to pout at every suggestion made to her. Fortunately, an interruption came just in time to save her temper. A carriage drove up to the door, and presently disgorged Elizabeth Colebatch, who came in to beg that Tiffany would accompany her and her mama to Harrogate, where Lady Colebatch was going to consult her favourite practitioner. Elizabeth, still faithful in her allegiance, eagerly described to Tiffany a programme exactly calculated to appeal to her. Besides a survey of the several expensive shops which had sprung up in the town, it included a walk down the New Promenade, and a visit to Hargroves Library, which was the most fashionable lounge in either High or Low Harrogate, and necessitated an instant change of raiment for Tiffany, and the unearthing from a bandbox, where it reposed in a mountain of tissue-paper, of her very best hat. Since the season was in full swing, and all the inns and boarding-houses bursting with company, it was safe to assume that the progress through the town of two modish young ladies, one of whom was a striking redhead, and the other a dazzling brunette, would attract exactly the kind of notice most deprecated by Tiffany's Aunt Burford; but as Miss Trent knew that Mrs Underhill would regard Lady Colebatch's casual chaperonage as a guarantee of propriety she did not feel it incumbent on her to enter a protest. But she did feel it incumbent on her to not to be backward in attention to Lady Colebatch; so, much as she longed for solitude, she went out to beg her to come into the house while Tiffany arrayed herself in her finest feathers. Lady Colebatch declined this, but invited Miss Trent to step into the carriage instead, to indulge in a comfortable coze. Miss Trent bore her part in this with mechanical civility; but little though she relished it, it proved beneficial, in that by the time Elizabeth and Tiffany came out to take their places in the carriage her disordered nerves had grown steadier, and the impulse to sob her heart out had left her.

Her rejected suitor, though in no danger of succumbing to even the mildest fit of hysterics, would also have been glad to have been granted an interval of solitude; but hardly had he entered the book-room at Broom Hall than he was joined by his younger cousin, who came in, asking, as he shut the door: "Are you busy, Waldo? Because, if you're not, there's something I want to say to you. But not if it isn't quite convenient!" he added hastily, perceiving the crease between Sir Waldo's brows.

Mastering the impulse to tell Lord Lindeth that it was extremely inconvenient, Sir Waldo said: "No, I'm not busy. Come and sit down, and tell me all about it!"

The tone was encouraging, and even more so the faint smile in his eyes. It was reflected, a little shyly, in his lordship's innocent orbs. He said simply, but with a rising colour: "I daresay you know—don't you?"

"Well, I have an inkling!" admitted Sir Waldo.

"I thought very likely you had guessed. But I wanted to tell you—and to ask your advice!"

"Ask my advice?" Sir Waldo's brows rose. "Good God, Julian, if you want my advice on whether or not you should offer for Miss Chartley, I can only say that until my advice or my opinion are matters of complete indifference to you——"

"Oh, not *that*!" interrupted Julian impatiently. "I should hope I knew my own mind without your advice, or anyone's! As for your opinion——" He paused, considering, and then said, with a disarmingly apologetic smile: "Well, I *do* care for that, but—but not very much!"

"Very right and proper!" approved Sir Waldo.

"Now you're roasting me! I wish you won't: this is *serious*, Waldo!"

"I'm not roasting you. Why do you need my advice?"

"Well . . ." Julian clasped his hands between his knees, and frowningly regarded them. "The thing is . . . Waldo, when we first came here I daresay you may have guessed—well, I told you, didn't I?—that I was pretty well bowled out by Tiffany Wield." He glanced up, crookedly smiling. "You'll say I made a cake of myself, and I suppose I did."

"Not such a cake that you offered for her hand."

Julian looked at him, suddenly surprised. "Do you know, Waldo, I never thought of marriage?" he said naïvely. "I hadn't considered it before, but now you've mentioned it I don't think that I *ever* thought of it until I met Miss Chartley. In fact, I never thought about the future at all. But since I've come to *know* Patience, naturally, I've done so, because I wish to spend the rest of my life with her. And, what's more, I'm going to!" he stated, his jaw hardening.

"My blessing on the alliance: she will make you an excellent wife! But wherein do you need my advice? Or are you merely trying to wheedle me into breaking the news to your mama?"

"No, of course not! I shall tell her myself. Though it *would* be helpful if you supported me," he added, after a reflective moment.

"I will."

Julian smiled gratefully at him. "Yes. I know: you *are* such a right one, Waldo!"

"Spare my blushes! And my advice?"

"Well, that's the only thing that has me in a worry!" disclosed his lordship. "I want to come to the point, and although the Chartleys have been as kind and affable as they could be—not hinting me away, or anything of that nature!—I can't but wonder whether it may not be too soon to ask the Rector for permission to propose to Patience! I mean, if he thought I was a regular squire of dames, because I dangled after Miss Wield, he'd be bound to send me packing—and then it would be all holiday with me!"

"I hardly think that he will judge you quite as harshly as that," replied Sir Waldo, with admirable gravity. "After all, you are not entangled with Tiffany, are you?"

"Oh, no!" Julian assured him. "Nothing of that sort! In fact, she brushed me off after what happened in Leeds, so I don't think I need feel myself in any way bound to her, do you?" He chuckled. "Laurie cut me out! I was never more glad of anything! Well, it just *shows* you, doesn't it? Only think of being grateful to Laurie! Lord! But tell me, Waldo! What should I do?"

Sir Waldo, whose private opinion was that the Rector must be living in the hourly expectation of receiving a declaration from Lord Lindeth, had no hesitation in answering this appeal. He recommended his anxious young cousin to make known his intentions at the earliest opportunity, very handsomely offering, at the same time, to reassure the Rector, if he should be misled into believing that his daughter's suitor was a hardened roué. Julian grinned appreciatively at this; and for the following half-hour bored Sir Waldo very much by expatiating at length on Miss Chartley's numerous virtues.

He departed at last, but his place was taken within ten minutes by Laurence, who came in, and stood irresolutely on the threshold, eyeing his cousin in some doubt.

Sir Waldo had sat down at the desk. There were several papers spread on it, but he did not seem to be at work on them.

His hands were clasped on top of the pile, and his eyes were frowning at the wall in front of him. His expression was unusually grim, and it did not lighten when he turned his head to look at Laurance. Rather, it hardened. "Well?"

If his demeanour had not warned Laurence already that he had chosen an inauspicious moment to seek him out, the uncompromising tone in which this one word was uttered must have done so. Laurence was still holding the door, and he backed himself out of the room, saying hurriedly, as he drew the door to upon himself: "Oh, nothing! I only—— Beg pardon! Didn't know you was busy! Some other time!"

"I advise you not to cherish false hopes! At no time!" Sir Waldo said harshly.

Under any ordinary circumstances Laurence would have been provoked into lengthy retort, but on this occasion he did not venture to reply at all, but effaced himself with all possible speed.

The door safely shut between himself and his suddenly formidable cousin, he let his breath go in an astonished: "Phew!" Indignation warred with curiosity in his breast, but curiosity won. After looking speculatively at the door for several moments, as though he could see Waldo's face through its stout panels, he walked away, his somewhat ferret-like brain concentrated on the new and unexpected problem which had presented itself.

It did not take him long to decide that the only possible cause of Waldo's unprecedented behaviour must be a disappointment in love. It was absurd to suppose that he might be faced with pecuniary difficulties; and, in Laurence's view, only love or penury could account for so bleak an aspect. At first glance it seemed equally absurd to suppose that his courtship of Miss Trent could have suffered a setback; but after some moments of reflection Laurence came to the conclusion that this must be the answer. It might seem incredible that a female in her circumstances should rebuff so opulent a suitor, but there could be no doubt that Miss Trent was a very odd creature. But no doubt either that she was as deeply in love with Waldo as he with her. No forbidding frown had marred Waldo's countenance at the breakfast-table: he had been in particularly good spirits. Then he had driven off, tossing a joking remark over his shoulder to Julian; and although he had not disclosed his destination only a lobcock could have doubted that he was bound for Staples. Julian, wrapped up in his own affairs, might not know that Waldo had visited

Staples every day for more than a sennight, but his far more astute cousin knew it. It looked very much as if Waldo had popped the question, and had been rejected. But why?

Cudgel his brains as he might, Laurence could arrive at no satisfactory answer to this enigma. Had any man but Waldo been concerned he would have been inclined to think that someone had traduced him to Miss Trent: he rather supposed her to be pretty straitlaced. But so was Waldo straitlaced, and what the devil could the most arrant scandalmonger find to say of him that would disgust any female? And was his Long Meg fool enough to believe a story fabricated by one of the jealous tabbies of the parish?

It was all very perplexing, but an answer there must be, which it might be well worth his while to discover. His first scheme to win his affluent cousin's gratitude had gone awry —it had not taken him very long to realize that no assistance from him had been needed to wean Julian from his attachment to Tiffany Wield—but it might well be that in this new, and very odd, situation lay the means he had been seeking. If, through his agency, the starcrossed lovers became reconciled, it was difficult to see how Waldo—no nip-squeeze, give him his due!—could fail to express his gratitude in a suitable and handsome manner.

Laurence's spirits had been rapidly sinking into gloom, but they now rose. It had been vexatious to find that his admirable plan to detach the Wield chit from Lindeth had been labour wasted. He did not regret it, precisely, for to have stolen the Beauty from under the noses of her ridiculous swains had been amusing, and as good a way as any other of whiling away the time he had been obliged to spend in an excessively boring place. He had even toyed for a day or two with the thought of wooing Tiffany in earnest, but had soon abandoned the scheme. The idea of tying himself up in wedlock was distasteful to him; and although he might have overcome his reluctance for the sake of Tiffany's fortune he could not feel that there was the least likelihood of obtaining her guardians' consent to the match, much less of their relinquishing into his hands the control of her fortune a day before she attained her majority. So however pleasant it might be to flirt elegantly with such an out-and-out beauty the affair was really a waste of time. Its only value was that it now provided him with an excuse for visiting Staples, to see for himself how the land lay there. It might not be easy to coax Miss Trent to confide in him; but although her manner towards him held a good deal of reserve, she had lately begun to show him rather more friendliness; and if she was as blue-devilled as Waldo over the rift between them she might, Laurence considered, be glad to be offered the opportunity to unburden herself. Certainly she would be, if she and Waldo had quarrelled: positively burning to state her grievances, if he knew anything of women! A quarrel, however, seemed highly unlikely: she did not look to be the sort of female to fly into the boughs, or to take affronts into her head; and Waldo's even temper was proverbial. On the whole, Laurence was more inclined to believe that the trouble must be due to some misunderstanding. Very probably each was too proud to seek an explanation of the other, and no one would be more welcome to them than a tactful mediator. Acting as a go-between might prove to be a wearing task, but in the pursuit of his own ends Laurence grudged no expenditure of effort.

Accordingly, he drove over to Staples that very day, ostensibly to visit Tiffany. He was met by the intelligence that Tiffany had gone to Harrogate, and that Miss Trent was laid down on her bed with the headache. He left cards and compliments, and drove off, by no means cast down by this setback. Laid down with the headache, was she? Promising! That was the excuse females always put forward whenever they had been indulging in a hearty fit of crying: he would have been far more daunted had he found her in excellent spirits.

Waldo's behaviour that evening was satisfactory too: he wasn't exactly cagged, but he wasn't what one could call chirping merry. Agreeable enough when addressed, but for the most part he was in a brown study. Julian had gone off somewhere with Edward Banningham, so there was very little conversation at dinner, Laurence not being such a cawker as to irritate Waldo with idle chatter when it was plain that he didn't want to talk. When they rose from the table, Waldo shut himself up in the book-room, saying that he was sorry to be such bad company, but that a vexatious hitch had occurred in his arrangements for installing a suitable warden at Broom Hall. Humdudgeon, of course, but Laurence replied sympathetically, and said that there was no need for Waldo to trouble his head over him: he would be happy enough with a book.

It was less satisfactory, on the following morning, to find neither Tiffany nor Miss Trent at home, when he called at Staples, but the evening, which was spent by him at the

Ashes' house, was more rewarding. Miss Trent had brought Tiffany to the party, and it was easy to see she'd got the hips. She might smile, and converse with her usual tranquillity, but she was suspiciously pale, and there were tell-tale shadows under her eyes. As soon as she could do so, she went to sit beside a mousy little woman whom Laurence presently discovered to be governess to the children of the house. She was taking care not to glance in Waldo's direction: rather too much care, thought Laurence. Out of the tail of his eye he watched Waldo cross the room towards her. He couldn't hear what passed between them, of course, but he was perfectly well able to draw conclusions. He had a pair of sharp eyes, and he saw how tightly her hands were gripping her reticule, and how swiftly the colour rushed into her cheeks and ebbed again. Then Waldo bowed—the bow of a man accepting a rebuff: no question about that!—and went off with Sir William Ash to the card-room. Miss Trent's eyes were downcast, but they lifted as he turned away, and followed him across the room. Lord! thought Laurence, startled, who would have thought that such a cool creature could look like that? Flat despair! But what the devil had happened to set the pair of them at outs?

The sound of a fiddle being tuned obliged him to drag his mind from this intriguing problem. The first set was forming; and as the dance was of an informal nature, Lady Ash having announced that since all the young people knew one another she meant to leave them to choose their own partners, it behoved him to look about him for an unattached lady. He saw Tiffany, talking vivaciously to Miss Banningham, and to Lindeth, who was clearly waiting to lead the eldest daughter of the house into the set. It did vaguely occur to Laurence that it was unusual to find Tiffany without an eager crowd of admirers clamouring for the privilege of dancing with her, but although he bowed, and smirked, and solicited the honour of leading her on to the floor, his mind was still too much preoccupied to allow of his paying more than cursory heed to this circumstance. Nor did he notice that the lady who was being besieged by suppliants was Miss Chartley.

But Miss Trent noticed it, and she thought that it set the seal on an evening of unalleviated misery. Too well did she know that glittering look of Tiffany's, that over-emphatic gaiety; and if she was relieved to see, as the evening progressed, that Tiffany was never left without a partner, her relief was soon tempered by the spectacle of Mr Wilfred Butterlaw, a pimply youth suffering from unrequited adoration of the Beauty, leading her charge into a set. Mercifully for what little peace of mind was left to Miss Trent, she could not know that Mr Butterlaw's evil genius prompted him to blurt out, when he and Tiffany came together in the dance: "I d-don't care a s-straw what anyone says, Miss Wield! *I* think you're *p-perfect*!"

But although she never knew of this essay in tactlessness she was not at all surprised, during the drive back to Staples, to find that Tiffany was in her most dangerous mood, which found expression, not in one of her stormy outbursts, but in brittle laughter, and the utterance of whatever damaging animadversions on the manners or looks of her acquaintances first occurred to her. Miss Trent preserved a discouraging silence, and devoutly hoped that Courtenay, seated opposite to the ladies, would refrain from adding fuel to the fire. So he did, until Tiffany reached the most galling cause of her discontent, and said, with a trill of laughter: "And Patience Chartley, looking like a dowd in that hideous green dress, and putting on die-away airs, and pretending to be *so* shy, and *so* modest, and casting down her eyes in that ridiculous way she uses when she wants to persuade everyone that she's a saint!"

"If I were you," interposed Courtenay bluntly, "I wouldn't be quite so spiteful about Patience, miss!"

"Spiteful? Oh, I didn't mean to be! Poor thing, she's close on twenty and has never had an offer! I'm truly sorry for her: it must be odious to be so—so *insipid*!"

"No, you ain't," said Courtenay. "You're as mad as fire because it wasn't you that got all the notice tonight but *her*! And I'll tell you this!——"

"Don't!" said Miss Trent wearily.

The interpolation was unheeded. "If you don't take care," continued Courtenay ruthlessly, "you'll find yourself in the suds—and don't think your precious beauty will save you, because it won't! Lord, if ever I knew such a corkbrained wagfeather as you are! First you drove Lindeth off with your Turkish treatment, then it was Arthur, and to crown all you hadn't even enough sense to keep your tongue about what happened in Leeds, when it was Patience that showed what a game one she is, not you! All you did was to scold like the vixen you are!"

"A game one?" Tiffany said, in a voice shaking with fury. "Patience? She's nothing but a shameless show-off! I collect you had this from Ancilla! She positively *dotes* on dear, demure little Patience—exactly her notion of a well-brought-up girl!"

"Oh, no, I didn't! Miss Trent never told us anything but that Patience had snatched some slum-brat from under the wheels of a carriage, with the greatest pluck and presence of mind! Nor did Lindeth! And as for Patience, she don't talk about it at all! *You* did all the talking! You was afraid one of the others would describe the figure *you* cut, so you set it about that Patience had created an uproar just so that people should think she was a heroine, but that it was all a fudge: no danger to the brat or to herself!"

"Nor was there! If Ancilla says——"

"Wasn't there? Well, *now*, coz, I'll tell you something else! Ned Banningham was in York t'other day, staying with some friends, and who should be one of the people who came to the dinner-party but the fellow who nearly drove over Patience? I don't recall his name, but I daresay you may. Very full of the accident he seems to have been! Told everyone what a trump Patience was, and how she didn't make the least fuss or to-do, and what a stew he was in, thinking she was bound to be trampled on. Described you too. Jack wouldn't tell me what he said, and I'd as lief he didn't, because you *are* my cousin, and I ain't fond of being put to the blush. But Ned told Jack, and of course Jack told Arthur, and then Greg got to hear of it—and *that's* why you got the cold shoulder tonight! I daresay no one would have cared much if you'd said cutting things about Sophy Banningham, because she ain't much liked; but the thing is that everyone likes Patience! What's more, until you came back to Staples, and peacocked all over the neighbourhood, she and Lizzie were the prettiest girls here, *and* the most courted! So take care what you're about, Beautiful Miss Wield!"

CHAPTER XVIII

By the time Miss Trent was at liberty to seek her own bed after that memorable party she was so much exhausted that she fell almost instantly into a deep, yet troubled sleep. The drive back to Staples had ended with Tiffany in floods of tears, which lasted for long after she had been supported upstairs to her bedchamber. Miss Trent, thrusting aside her own troubles, applied herself first to the task of soothing Tiffany, then to that of undressing her, and lastly to the far more difficult duty of trying to point out to her, while she was in a malleable condition, that however brutal Courtenay might have been he had spoken no more than the truth. Bathing Tiffany's temples with Hungary Water, she did her best to mingle sympathy with her unpalatable advice. She thought that Tiffany was attending to her; and found herself pitying the girl. She was vain, and selfish, and unbelievably tiresome, but only a child, after all, and one who had been flattered and spoilt almost from the day of her birth. She had met with a severe check for the first time in her headlong career; it had shocked and frightened her; and perhaps, thought Miss Trent, softly drawing the curtains round her bed, she might profit by so painful a lesson.

She did not come down to breakfast, but when Miss Trent went to visit her she did not find her lying in a darkened room with a damp towel laid over her brow and smelling-salts clasped feebly in her hand, as had happened on a previous and hideous occasion, but sitting up in bed, thoughtfully eating strawberries. She eyed Miss Trent somewhat defensively, but upon being bidden a cheerful good morning responded with perfect amiability.

"No letters yet from Bridlington," said Miss Trent, "but Netley has just brought up a package from the lodge. I couldn't conceive what it might be until I saw the label attached to it, for a more unwieldy parcel you can't imagine! My dear, those idiotish silk merchants haven't sent patterns, but a whole roll of silk! They must have misunderstood Mrs Underhill—and I only hope it may match the brocade! I shall have to take it to Mrs Tawton in the gig. Will you go with me? Do!"

"No, it will take *hours*, and I can't, because I've made a plan of my own."

"Well, that's not very kind! Abandoning me to the company of James, who can never be persuaded to say anything but *Yes, miss!* and *No, miss!* What is this plan of yours?"

"I'm going to ride into the village," said Tiffany, a hint of defiance in her voice. She cast a sidelong glance at Miss Trent, and added: "Well, I mean to call at the Rectory! And you know that pink velvet rose I purchased in Harrogate? I am going to wrap it up in silver paper, and give it to Patience! *Especially* to wear with her gauze ball-dress! Do you think that would be a handsome present? It was very expensive, you know, and I haven't worn it, because though I did mean to, last night, I found it didn't become me after all. But Patience frequently wears pink, so I should think she would feel very much obliged to me, shouldn't you? And that will just *show* people! And *also* I shall invite her to go for a walk with us tomorrow—just you and me, you know!"

"That would indeed be a noble gesture!" said Miss Trent admiringly.

"Yes, *wouldn't* it?" said Tiffany naïvely. "It will be horridly dull, and you may depend upon it Patience will be a dead bore, going into raptures over some weed, and saying it's a rare plant, or—— But I mean to bear it, even if she moralizes about nature!"

Miss Trent was unable to enter with any marked degree of enthusiasm into these plans, but she acquiesced in them, feeling that they did at least represent a step in the right direction, even though they sprang from the purest self-interest. So she went away to prepare for her long and rather tedious drive to the home of the indigent Mrs Tawton, while Tiffany, tugging at the bell-rope, allowed her imagination to depict various scenes in which her faithless admirers, hearing of her magnanimity, and stricken with remorse at having so wickedly misjudged her, vied with one another in extravagant efforts to win her forgiveness.

It was an agreeable picture, and since she really did feel that she was being magnanimous she rode to the Rectory untroubled by any apprehension that she might not meet with the welcome which she was quite sure she deserved.

The Rector's manservant, who admitted her into the house, seemed to be rather doubtful when she blithely asked to see Miss Chartley, but he ushered her into the drawing-room, and said that he would enquire whether Miss Chartley was at home. He then went away, and Tiffany, after peeping at her reflection in the looking-glass over the fireplace, and rearranging the disposition of the glossy ringlets that clustered under the brim of her hat, wandered over to the window.

The drawing-room looked on to the garden at the rear of the house. It was a very pretty garden, gay with flowers, with a shrubbery, a well-scythed lawn, and several fine trees. Round the trunk of one of these a rustic seat had been built, and in front of it, as though they had just risen from it, Patience and Lindeth were standing side by side, confronting the Rector, who was holding a hand of each.

For a moment Tiffany stood staring, scarcely understanding the significance of what she saw. But when Lindeth looked down at Patience, smiling at her, and she raised her eyes adoringly to his, the truth dawned on her with the blinding effect of a sudden fork of lightning.

She was so totally unprepared that the shock of realization turned her to stone. Incredulity, fury, and chagrin swept over her. *Her* conquest—her most triumphant conquest!—stolen from her by Patience Chartley? It wasn't possible! Patience to receive an offer of marriage from Lindeth? The thought flashed into her mind that he had never so much as hinted at marriage with herself, and she felt suddenly sick with mortification.

The door opened behind her; she heard Mrs Chartley's voice, and turned, pride stiffening her. She never doubted that Mrs Chartley hoped to enjoy her discomfiture, and because the thought uppermost in her mind was that no one should think that she cared a rush for Lindeth she achieved a certain dignity.

She said: "Oh, how do you do, ma'am? I came to bring Patience a trifle I purchased for her in Harrogate. But I must not stay."

She put out her hand rather blindly, proffering the silver-wrapped parcel. Mrs Chartley took it from her, saying in some surprise: "Why, how kind of you, Tiffany! She will be very much obliged to you."

"It's nothing. Only a flower to wear with her gauze dress. I must go!"

Mrs Chartley glanced uncertainly towards the window.

"Won't you wait while I see whether I can find her, my dear? I am persuaded she would wish to thank you yourself."

"It's of no consequence. The servant said he fancied she was engaged." Tiffany drew in her breath, and said with her most glittering smile: "That's true, isn't it? To Lindeth! Has he offered for her? I—I have been expecting him to do so this age!"

"Well—if you won't spread it about, yes!" admitted Mrs Chartley. "But there must be nothing said, you know, until he has told his mother. So you must not breathe a word, if you please!"

"Oh, no! Though I daresay everyone has guessed! Pray—pray offer her my felicitations, ma'am! I should think they will deal extremely together!"

On this line she took leave of Mrs Chartley, declining her escort to the stableyard, but hurrying out of the house, the flowing skirt of her habit caught over her arm, and one hand clenched tightly on her whip. She was uplifted by the feeling that she had acquitted herself well, but this mood could not last. By the time she reached Staples, all the evils of her situation had been recollected. It no longer mattered that she had behaved so creditably, at the Rectory, for even if Mrs Chartley believed that she was indifferent to the engagement no one else would. Her rivals, Lizzie only excepted, would rejoice in her downfall. She had boasted too freely of being able to bring Lindeth back to her feet by the mere lifting of a finger. She writhed inwardly as she remembered, knowing that it would be said she had been cut out by Patience Chartley. People would laugh at her behind her back, and say sweetly spiteful things to her face; and even her admirers could not be depended on to uphold her.

When she thought of this, and of what had been the cause of their defection, it had the unexpected effect of drying the tears which till then had been flowing fast. Her predicament was too desperate for tears. She could see nothing but humiliation ahead, and by hedge or by stile she must avoid it. In her view there was only one thing to be done, and that was to leave Staples immediately, and to return to London. But London meant Portland Place, and although she could not suppose that even her aunt Burford would send her back to Staples, where she had been unhappy and ill-used, there was no saying that she might not try again to confine her to the schoolroom, until she brought her out in the following spring.

Pacing up and down the floor of her bedroom, Tiffany

cudgelled her brains, and not in vain. She remembered all at once the existence of her other guardian, bachelor Uncle James, who lived, with an old housekeeper to look after him, somewhere in the City. That, of course, was undesirable, but might, perhaps, be mended. James Burford, on the few occasions when they had met, had behaved much as all the other elderly gentlemen of her acquaintance did: chuckling at her exploits, pinching her ear, and calling her a naughty little puss. If he should not be instantly delighted to receive his lovely niece he could very easily be brought round her thumb. Either she would remain under his roof until the spring, or he must be persuaded to represent to Aunt Burford the propriety of bringing her out during the Little Season. Far less than Aunt Burford would he be likely to insist on her returning to Staples. Indeed, the more Tiffany thought of the wrongs she had suffered the more convinced did she become that no one could possibly blame her for running away. Aunt Underhill had deserted her, not even inviting her to go to Bridlington too; Courtenay had been unkind and boorish to her from the outset; and Miss Trent, whose sole business it should have been to attend her, had neglected her for Charlotte; and had shown herself to be so wholly wanting in conduct as to have allowed her to be exposed to the Mob in Leeds, going off in *her* carriage with an odious girl to whom she owed no duty at all, and leaving her precious charge alone in a public inn, to be conveyed back to Staples, unchaperoned, by a single gentleman.

The difficulty was to decide how the flight could be achieved. Forgetting for a moment that she had cast Miss Trent for the rôle of villainess in this dramatic piece, Tiffany wondered whether it would be possible to cajole that lady into escorting her to London immediately. Very little consideration sufficed to make her abandon this solution to her problem. Miss Trent was too insensitive to appreciate the necessity of an instant departure; and nothing was more certain than that she would refuse to do anything without first consulting Aunt Underhill. It was even possible that she would advise her charge to live down her humiliation: as though one would not rather die than make the attempt!

No: Miss Trent could only be a hindrance—in fact, it would be wise to be gone from the house before she returned to it. But how was she to get to Leeds? She could ride there: they were too well-accustomed in the stables to her solitary rides to raise any demur; but she thought it would be impossible to carry even the smallest piece of baggage, in which case she would be obliged to drive all the way to London in her habit. Useless to desire the under-coachman to drive her there in the barouche: he would refuse to do it unless she had Miss Trent with her, or her maid. Equally would Courtenay's groom refuse to let her drive herself in his phaeton.

A less determined girl might have been daunted at this point; but it had been truly observed of Miss Wield that there were no lengths to which she would not go to achieve her ends. Rather than have abandoned her project she would have walked to Leeds. Indeed, she was trying to make up her mind whether to pursue this dreary course, carrying a bandbox; or to ride, carrying nothing, when a welcome sound came to her ears. She ran to the window, and saw Mr Calver driving up to the house in his hired whisky.

Tiffany flung up the window, and leaned out to hail him. "Oh, Mr Calver, how do you do? Have you come to take me out? I shall be with you directly!"

He looked up, sweeping off his high-crowned beaver. "Very happy to do so! No need to bustle about, however: I must pay my respects to Miss Trent, you know."

"Oh, she has gone to Nethersett, and won't be home for hours!" Tiffany answered. "Only wait for ten minutes!"

This was not at all what he had hoped to hear; nor had he much desire to sit beside Tiffany while she tooled the whisky round the immediate countryside. There seemed to be no object to be gained by dangling after her any longer; and teaching her to drive was an occupation which had begun to pall on him. However, he could think of no better way of passing the time, so he resigned himself.

He was rather startled, when she came running out of the house some twenty minutes later, to see that she was arrayed in a modish pelisse, with a hat embellished by several curled ostrich plumes on her head, and a large bandbox slung by its ribbons over her arm.

"Here——!" he expostulated. "I mean to say—what the dooce——?"

Tiffany handed the bandbox to him, and climbed into the whisky. "You can't think how glad I am that you came!" she said. "I was quite in despair! For I must go to Leeds, and Ancilla set off in the gig quite early, and I don't know where Courtenay may be!"

"Go to Leeds?" he repeated. "But——"

"Yes, it is the most vexatious thing!" she said glibly. "The dressmaker had sent home my new ball-dress, which I particularly wish to wear at the Systons' party, and the stupid creature has made it too tight for me. And how to get to Leeds, with the coachman away, and no one to accompany me, I'd not the least notion, until you came driving up the avenue! You'll take me, won't you? That will make everything right!"

"Well, I don't know," he said dubiously. "I'm not sure I ought. Seems to me Miss Trent might not think it quite the thing."

She laughed. "How can you be so absurd? When I have been driving with you for ever!"

"Yes, but——"

"If you don't escort me, I shall go alone," she warned him. "I shall ride there, and *that* won't be the thing at all. So if you choose to be disobliging——"

"No, no! I suppose I'd better drive you there, if you're so set on it. You can't go alone, at all events," he said, giving his horse the office. "Mind, though! it won't do if you mean to remain for hours with this dressmaker! I should think it will take us close on a couple of hours to get to Leeds and back again. Did you tell anyone where you was off to?"

"Oh, yes!" she assured him mendaciously. "Ancilla won't be in a worry, so you need not be either. And I shan't be with Mrs Walmer above half-an-hour, I promise you!"

He was satisfied with this; and although he had little faith in her ability to emerge from a dressmaker's establishment in so short a space of time, he reflected that he must be certain of finding Miss Trent at home if it was three or more hours before he brought Tiffany back to Staples.

Tiffany beguiled the drive with lighthearted chatter. Having surmounted the first obstacle to her flight, she was in high good-humour, her eyes glowing with excitement, laughter never far from her lips. Already, in her imagination, she was the petted darling of her Uncle James, and had prevailed upon him to remove from the City to a more fashionable quarter of the town. The humiliation of the previous evening's party, and the shock of discovering that Lindeth had become engaged to Patience, were rapidly fading from her mind, and would be wholly forgotten as soon as she had put Yorkshire behind her. Fresh, and far more dazzling conquests lay ahead. She had never cared a button for Lindeth, after all; and as for the rest of her court, they were a set of bumpkins whom she would probably never set eyes on again.

Arrived in Leeds, Laurence, who was unfamiliar with the

town, requested her to direct him to a decent posting-house, where the whisky could be left, and the horse baited. "Then I'll escort you to the dressmaker. It won't do for you to be jauntering about this place alone," he said, surveying the crowded street with disfavour.

This put Tiffany in mind of something which, in her large dreams of the future, she had overlooked. Never having travelled except in the company of some older person, who made all the arrangements, she was ignorant of where, and under what conditions, post-chaises were to be hired; or, failing this, the only mode of travel to which she was accustomed, how one obtained a seat on the stage, or the Mail; and at what hour these humbler conveyances left Leeds for London. She stole a glance at Laurence's profile, and decided that it would be necessary to enlist his help. It might require some coaxing to obtain it; but she could not doubt that he was one of her more fervent admirers. Courtenay had jeered at her for being taken in by a fortune-hunter; and if Courtenay was right in thinking that the exquisite Mr Calver was hanging out for a rich wife she thought that it would not be difficult to persuade him to render her a signal service. She directed him to the King's Head, adding that she would like some lemonade, and that there were several private parlours to be hired at this hostelry.

Laurence was perfectly ready to regale her with lemonade, but he thought it quite unnecessary, and even undesirable, to hire a private parlour. However, since she seemed to take it for granted that he would do so, he kept his objections to himself. But when, in the inn's yard, he picked up her bandbox, it occurred to him that it was extraordinarily heavy. When Tiffany had first handed it up to him, he had been too much astonished by her festal raiment to pay any heed to the weight of the bandbox, but he now directed a look at her which was sharp with suspicion, and said: "Very heavy, this dress of yours, ain't it?"

"Well, there are some other things in the box," she confessed.

"I should rather think there must be! Seems to me there's something pretty smokey going on, and if there is——"

"I am going to explain it to you!" she said hastily. "But in private, if you please!"

He regarded her with misgiving; but before he could say more she had flitted away from him, into the inn; and it was not until they had been ushered into the same parlour which

219

Lindeth had hired for his memorable nuncheon-party that he was able to demand the explanation.

Tiffany bestowed upon him her most devastating smile, and said simply: "Well, I told you a bouncer! It isn't a ball-dress. It's—oh, all manner of things! I am going to London!"

"Going to London?" repeated Laurence blankly.

She fixed her glorious eyes to his face in a melting look. "Will you escort me?"

Mr Calver's carefully arranged locks were too lavishly pomaded to rise on end, but his eyes showed a tendency to start from their sockets. He replied, unequivocally: "Good God, no! Of course I won't!"

"Then I must go alone," said Tiffany mournfully.

"Have you taken leave of your senses?" demanded Laurence.

She sighed. "You must know I haven't. I am going to—to seek the protection of my Uncle James Burford."

"What do you want that for?" asked Laurence, unimpressed.

"I am very unhappy," stated Tiffany. "My aunt has not used me as she should. Or Ancilla!"

Mr Calver's intelligence was not generally thought to be of a high order, but he had no difficulty in interpreting this tragic utterance. He said gloomily, and with a regrettable want of tact: "Lindeth's offered for the parson's daughter, has he? Oh, well! I guessed as much! No use going to London, though: he wouldn't care a straw!"

"Nor do I care a straw!" declared Tiffany, her eyes flashing. "*That's* not why I am determined—*determined!*—to go to my uncle!"

"Well, it don't signify," said Laurence. "You can't go to London today, that's certain!"

"I can, and I will!"

"Not with my help," said Laurence bluntly.

No one had ever responded thus to Tiffany's demands; and it cost her a severe struggle to keep her temper. "I should be *very* grateful to you!" she suggested.

"I daresay you would," he replied. "Much good that would do me! Lord, what an after-clap there would be if I was to do anything so ramshackle as to drive off to London with a chit of your age—and nothing but a dashed bandbox between the pair of us!" he added, looking with profound disapproval at this object.

"I didn't mean we should go in the whisky! How can you be so absurd? A post-chaise, of course!"

"Yes, and four horses as well, no doubt!"

She nodded, surprised that he should have thought it necessary to have asked.

Her innocent look, far from captivating Laurence, exasperated him. "Have you the least notion what it would cost?" he demanded.

"Oh, what can that signify?" she exclaimed impatiently. "My uncle will pay for it!"

"Very likely, but he ain't here," Laurence pointed out.

"He will pay all the charges when I reach London."

"You won't reach London. Who's to pay the first post-boys? Who's to pay for the changes of teams? If it comes to that, who's to pay for your lodging on the road? It's close on two hundred miles to London, you know—at least, I collect you *don't* know! What's more, you can't put up at a posting-house, travelling all by yourself! I shouldn't wonder at it if they refused to take you in. Well, I mean to say, who ever heard of such a thing? Now, do but consider, Miss Wield! You can't do such a jingle-brained thing: take my word for it!"

"Do you care what people may say?" Tiffany asked scornfully.

"Yes," he answered.

"How paltry! *I* don't!"

"I daresay you don't. You're too young to know what you're talking about. If you're so set on going to London, you ask Miss Trent to take you there!"

"Oh, how *stupid* you are!" she cried passionately. "She wouldn't do it!"

"Well, that quite settles it!" said Laurence. "You drink your lemonade, like a good girl, and I'll drive you back to Staples. No need to tell anyone where we've been: just say we went farther than we intended!"

Curbing the impulse to throw the lemonade in his face, Tiffany said winningly: "I *know* you couldn't be cruel enough to take me back to Staples. I had rather die than go back! Go with me to London! We could pretend we were married, couldn't we? That would make everything right!"

"You know," said Laurence severely, "you've got the most ramshackle notions of anyone I ever met! No, it would not make everything right!"

She looked provocatively at him, under her lashes. "What if I *did* marry you? Perhaps I will!"

"Yes, and perhaps you won't!" he retorted. "Of all the outrageous——"

"I am very rich, you know! My cousin says that's why you dangle after me!"

"Oh, does he? Well, you may tell your precious cousin, with my compliments, that I ain't such a gudgeon as to run off with a girl who won't come into her inheritance for four years!" said Laurence, much incensed. "Yes, and another thing! I wouldn't do it if you was of age! For one thing, I don't wish to marry you; and, for another, I ain't a dashed hedge-bird, and I wouldn't run a rig like that even if I were all to pieces!"

"Don't *wish* to marry me?" Tiffany gasped, and suddenly burst into tears.

Horrified, Laurence said: "Not a marrying man! If I were —— Oh, lord! For God's sake, don't cry! I didn't mean— that is, any number of men wish to marry you! Shouldn't wonder at it if you became a *duchess*! I assure you—most beautiful girl I ever set eyes on!"

"*Nobody* wants to marry me!" sobbed Tiffany.

"Mickleby! Ash! Young Banningham!" uttered Laurence.

"*Those*!" Tiffany said, with loathing. "Besides, they *don't*! I wish I were dead!"

"You're above their touch!" said Laurence desperately. "Above mine too! You'll marry into the Peerage—see if you don't! But *not*," he added, "if you go beyond the line!"

"I don't care! I want to go to London, and I *will* go to London! If you won't escort me, will you lend me the money for the journey?"

"No——Good God, no! Besides, I haven't got it! And even if I had I wouldn't lend it to you!" Strong indignation rose in his breast. "What do you suppose my cousin Waldo would have to say to me if I was to do anything so cockbrained as to send you off to London in a post-chaise-and-four, with nothing but a dashed bandbox, and not so much as an abigail to take care of you?"

"Sir Waldo?" Tiffany said, her tears arrested. "Do you think he would be vexed?"

"Vexed! Tear me in pieces! What's more," said Laurence fairly, "I wouldn't blame him! A nice mess I should be in! No, I thank you!"

"Very well!" said Tiffany tragically. "Leave me!"

"I do wish," said Laurence, eyeing her with a patent want of admiration, "that you wouldn't talk in that totty-headed fashion! Anyone would think you was regularly dicked in the nob! Leave you, indeed! A pretty figure I should cut!"

She shrugged. "Well, it's no matter to me! If you choose to be disobliging——"

"It may not be any matter to you, but it is to me!" interrupted Laurence. "Seems to me nothing matters to you but yourself!"

"Well, it seems to me that nothing matters to you but *your*self!" flashed Tiffany. "Go away! Go away, go away, go *away*!"

Her voice rose on every repetition of the command, and Laurence, in the liveliest dread of being precipitated into a scandalous scene, swallowed his spleen, and adopted a conciliatory tone. "Now, listen!" he begged. "You don't want for sense, and you must see that I can't go away, leaving you here alone! What the deuce would you do? Tell me that! And don't say you'll go to London, because for one thing you haven't enough blunt to pay for the hire of a chaise, and for another I'd lay you long odds there ain't a postmaster living that would be such a clunch as to oblige you! If you was to try to tip him a rise, he'd be bound to think you was running away from school, or some such thing, and a rare hobble he'd be in if he aided and abetted you! What *he'd* do would be to send for the constable, and then your tale would be told!" He perceived that her eyes had widened in dismay, and at once enlarged on this theme. "Before you knew where you were you'd be taken before a magistrate, and if you refused to tell him who you was he'd commit you. A pretty piece of business that would be!"

"Oh, no!" she said, shuddering. "He wouldn't—he *couldn't*!"

"Oh, yes, he would!" said Laurence. "So, if you don't want everyone to know you tried to run away, and had to be bailed out of prison, you'd best come home with me now. No need to fear I'll tell a soul what happened! I won't."

She did not answer for a minute or two, but sat staring at him. Miss Trent would instantly have recognized the expression on her face; Laurence was less familiar with it, and waited hopefully for her capitulation. "But if I were to go on the stagecoach, or the Mail," she said thoughtfully, "no one would try to stop me. I know *that*, because several of the girls used to come to Miss Climping's school on the stage.

I'm very much obliged to you for warning me! Yes, and the Mail coaches travel all night, so I shan't have to put up at a posting-house! How much will it cost me to buy a ticket, if you please?"

"I don't know, and it don't signify, because I'm not going to let you go to London, post, stage, or Mail!"

She got up, and began to draw on her gloves. "Oh, yes! You can't prevent me. I know just what to do if you try to —and it won't be of the least use to stand leaning against the door like that, because if you don't open it for me *at once* I shall scream for help, and when people come I shall say that you are abducting me!"

"What, in an open carriage, and you hopping down in the yard as merry as a cricket? That won't fadge, you little pea-goose!"

"Oh, I shall say that you deceived me, and I never knew what your intentions were until—until you made *violent* love to me, just now!" said Tiffany, smiling seraphically.

Laurence moved away from the door. It seemed more than likely that she would put this threat into execution; and although it would be open to him to explain the true circumstances to such persons as came running to her rescue, not only did he shrink from taking any part at all in so vulgar and embarrassing a scene, but he doubted very much whether his story would be believed. He would not have believed it himself, for a more improbable story would have been hard to imagine. On the other hand, Tiffany's story, backed by her youth, her staggering beauty, and the private parlour, was all too probable. He said mildly: "No need to kick up a dust! I ain't stopping you. But the thing is that it will cost you a deal of money to buy a seat on the Mail, and I can't frank you— haven't above a couple of guineas in my purse!"

"Then I shall go by the stage. Or even in a *carrier's cart!*" replied Tiffany, her chin mulishly set.

"Wouldn't take you," said Laurence. "Of course, you could go by the stage, but they're deucedly slow, you know. Bound to be overtaken. Nothing that cousin of yours would like better than to go careering after a stage-coach in that phaeton of his!"

"No! How should he guess where I was going? Unless you told him, and *surely* you wouldn't be so wickedly treacherous?"

"Well, I should have to tell him! Dash it all——"

"Why?" she demanded. "You don't care what becomes of me!"

"No, but I care what becomes of *me*," said Laurence frankly.

Some dim apprehension that she had met her match dawned on Tiffany. She regarded Laurence with a mixture of indignation and unwilling sympathy, annoyed with him for considering no interest but his own, yet perfectly able to appreciate his point of view. After a reflective pause, she said slowly: "People would blame you? *I* see! But you'd help me if no one knew, wouldn't you?"

"Yes, but they're bound to know, so——"

"No, they won't. I've thought of a capital scheme!" interrupted Tiffany. "You must say that I hoaxed you!"

"I shall. It's just what you did do," said Laurence.

"Yes, so it will be *almost* true. Only, you must say that I went off to the dressmaker, and you waited, and waited, but I didn't return, and though you looked all over for me you couldn't find me, and you hadn't the least notion what had happened to me!"

"So I drove back to Broom Hall——just taking a look-in at Staples, to tell Miss Trent I'd lost you in Leeds!"

"Yes," she agreed happily. "For by that time I shall be out of reach. I've quite made up my mind to go by the Mail, and I know precisely what to do about paying for the ticket: I'll sell my pearls—or do you think it would be better to pawn them? I know *all* about that, because when I was at school, in Bath, Mostyn Garrowby, who was my *first* beau, though *much* too young, pawned his watch to take me to a fête in the Sydney Gardens one evening!"

"You don't mean to tell me you was allowed to go to fêtes?" said Laurence, incredulously.

"Oh, no! I had to wait until everyone had gone to bed, of course! Miss Climping never knew."

This artless confidence struck dismay into Laurence's soul. He perceived that Miss Wield was made of bolder stuff than he had guessed; and any hopes he might have cherished of convincing her that her projected journey to London would be fraught with too much impropriety to be undertaken vanished. Such a consideration could not be expected to weigh with a girl audacious enough to steal away from school at dead of night to attend a public fête in the company of a roly-poly youth without a feather to fly with.

"What do you advise?" enquired Tiffany, unclasping the single row of pearls she wore round her neck.

He had been pulling uncertainly at his underlip, but as she turned to the door, shrugging her shoulders, he said: "Here, give 'em to me! If you *must* go to London, I'll pawn 'em for you!"

She paused, eyeing him suspiciously. "I think I'll do it myself—thank you!"

"No, you dashed well won't!" he said, incensed. "You don't suppose I'm going to make off with your pearls, do you?"

"No, but—— Well, it wouldn't surprise me in the least if you went galloping back to Staples! Though I must own that if I could trust you—— Oh, I know! I'll come with you to the pawnbroker! And then we must discover where to find the Mail, and when it leaves Leeds, and——"

"Very well! You come—but don't blame *me* if we walk smash into someone who knows you!"

The change in her expression was almost ludicrous. She exclaimed: "Oh, no! No, no, surely not?"

"Nothing more likely," he said. "Seems to me the tabbies spend the better part of their time jauntering into Leeds to do some shopping. Not that I care—except that I should be glad if we did meet the Squire's wife, or Mrs Banningham, or——"

She flung up protesting hands. "Oh, how odious you are! You—you would positively *like* to betray me!"

"Well, if that's not the outside of enough!" he said. "When I've *warned* you——!"

Still rampantly suspicious, she said: "If I let you go alone, and you met one of those horrid creatures, you'd tell them!"

"Give you my word I wouldn't!" he replied promptly.

She was obliged to be satisfied, but it was with obvious reluctance that she dropped her string of pearls into his outstretched hand. He pocketed them, and picked up his hat. "I'll be off, then. You stay here, and don't get into a pucker, mind! I daresay it will take me some little time to arrange matters. I'll tell 'em to send up a nuncheon to you."

He then departed, returning nearly an hour later to find Miss Wield so sick with apprehension that she burst into tears at sight of him. However, when he handed her a ticket, and informed her that he had obtained a seat for her on the next Mail coach bound for London, her tears ceased, and her volatile spirits soared again. They were slightly damped by the news that it was not due to arrive in Leeds, coming from Thirsk, for another two hours, but agreeably diverted by the restoration to her of her pearls. "Thought it best to spout my watch instead," explained Laurence briefly.

She accepted them gratefully, saying, as she clasped them round her neck again: "I am *very* much obliged to you! Only, if I must wait so long for the Mail, perhaps I should travel on the stage, after all."

"Not a seat to be had!" responded Laurence, shaking his head. "Way-bills all made up! Besides, the Mail will overtake the stage—no question about that! You'll be set down at the Bull and Mouth, in St Martin's Lane, by the bye. Plenty of hacks to be had there: nothing for you to do but to give the jarvey your uncle's direction."

"No," she agreed. "But I do wish—— Where must I go to meet the Mail?"

"Golden Lion: no need to tease yourself over that! I'll take you there."

The anxious furrow vanished from her brow. "You don't mean to leave me here alone? Then I am most *truly* obliged to you! I misjudged you, Mr Calver!"

He cast her a slightly harried glance. "No, no! That is, told you at the outset I'd have nothing to do with it!"

"Oh, yes, but *now* everything will be right!" she said blithely.

"Well, I hope to God it will be!" said Laurence, with another, and still more harried glance at the clock on the mantelshelf.

CHAPTER XIX

Miss Trent, returning from a long, dull drive, which had afforded her far too much opportunity to indulge in melancholy reflection, reached Staples in a mood of deep depression. Relinquishing the reins to the monosyllabic groom who had accompanied her on the expedition, she descended from the gig, and rather wearily mounted the broad steps that led to the imposing entrance to the house. The double-doors stood open to the summer sunshine, and she passed through them into the hall, pulling off her gloves, and hoping that she might be granted a respite before being obliged to devise some form of entertainment to keep her exacting charge tolerably well amused during an evening void of any outside attraction. She was momentarily blinded by the transition from bright sunlight to the comparative darkness of the hall, but her vision cleared all too soon; and a lowering presentiment assailed her that no period of repose awaited her. At the foot of the stairs, and engaged in close colloquy, were Mr Courtenay Underhill and Miss Maria Docklow, abigail to Miss Tiffany Wield. Both turned their heads quickly to see who had come into the house, and one glance was enough to confirm Miss Trent's forebodings.

"Oh, dear!" she said, with a faint, rueful smile. "*Now* what's amiss?"

"That damned resty, rackety, caper-witted cousin of mine ——!" uttered Courtenay explosively. He saw Miss Trent's delicate brows lift slightly, and reddened. "Oh——! Beg pardon, ma'am, but it's enough to make anyone swear, by God it is!"

Miss Trent untied the strings of her straw bonnet, and removed it from her flattened locks. "Well, what has she done to vex you?" she asked, laying the bonnet down on the table.

"Vex me! She's run off with that man-milliner, Calver!" declared Courtenay.

"Nonsense!" said Miss Trent, preserving her calm.

"Well, it ain't nonsense! She's been gone for three hours, let me tell you, and——"

"Has she? Some accident to the carriage, I daresay, or perhaps the horse has gone lame."

"Worse, miss!" announced Miss Docklow, in sepulchral accents.

"Why, how can you know that?" Miss Trent asked, still undismayed.

"Ay! that's what I said!" said Courtenay grimly.

"But," interposed the abigail, determined to hold the centre of the stage, " 'if that, sir, is what you think,' I said, 'come upstairs, and see what I have seen, sir!' I said."

"And what did you see?" asked Miss Trent.

Miss Docklow clasped her hands to her spare bosom, and cast up her eyes. "It gave me a Spasm, miss, my constitution being what it is, though far be it from me to utter any word of complaint, which anyone acquainted with me will testify!"

"Oh, never mind that!" said Courtenay angrily. "There's no need for you to put on those die-away airs: no one is blaming *you*! Tiffany has gone off with all her night-gear, and her trinket-box, ma'am!"

"Packed in the box where I had her best hat put away!" said Miss Docklow. "The one she wore to Harrogate, miss; the Waterloo hat, ornamented with feathers! And her China blue *pelisette*, with the silk cords and tassels! And her riding-habit—the *velvet* habit, miss!—left on the floor! Never will it be the same again, do what I will!" Startled at last, yet incredulous, Miss Trent hurried up the stairs, Miss Cocklow and Courtenay in her wake. She was brought up short on the threshold of Tiffany's bedchamber, and stood blinking at a scene of the utmost disorder. It bore all the signs of a hasty packing, for drawers were pulled out, the wardrobe doors stood open, and garments had been tossed all over the room. "Good God!" said Miss Trent, stunned.

"*Now*, ma'am, perhaps you'll believe me!" said Courtenay. "Pretty, ain't it? Rare goings-on! Just one of dear little Tiffany's whisky-frisky pranks, eh? By God, it's past all endurance! It ain't enough for her to set us all at odds: oh, no! nothing will do for *her* but to kick up the most infamous scandal——"

"Quiet!" begged Miss Trent. "I do beg of you——!"

"It's all very well for you to say *quiet*," retorted Courtenay savagely, "*I'm* thinking of my mother! And when I consider the way she's cosseted that little viper, and pandered to her——"

"I perfectly understand your feelings," interrupted Miss Trent, "but railing won't mend matters!"

"Nothing can mend *this* matter!"

Looking round the disordered room, her spirit failed for a moment, and she was much inclined to agree with him. She pulled herself together, however, and said: "I can't tell what may be the meaning of this, but I'm certain of one thing: she has not run off with Mr Calver."

"That's where you're out, ma'am! She did go with him! He was seen waiting for her in that carriage he hired from the Crown."

"True it is, miss, though I blush to say it! With his own eyes did Totton see him!"

"He could hardly have seen him with anyone else's eyes!" snapped Miss Trent, her temper fraying. She controlled it, and said in a cooler tone: "You had better put all these garments away, Maria, and make the room tidy again. I am persuaded I need not tell you that we rely upon your discretion. Mr Underhill, pray come downstairs! We must try to think what is best for us to do."

He followed her rather sulkily, saying, as he shut the door of the morning parlour: "I know what *I* am going to do—and if you hadn't come in just then I should be gone by now, for there's no time to be wasted!"

She had sunk into a chair, her elbows on the table, and her hands pressed to her temples, but she raised her head at this: "Gone where?"

"Harrogate, of course!"

"*Harrogate?* For heaven's sake, why?"

"Lord, ma'am, the fellow can't drive all the way to the Border in a whisky! Depend upon it, he's hired a chaise, and where else could he do that but in Harrogate?"

"Good God, are you suggesting that they are eloping to Gretna Green?" she exclaimed incredulously.

"Of course I am! It's just the sort of thing Tiffany *would* do—you can't deny that!"

"It is not at all the sort of thing Mr Calver would do, however! Nor do I think that Tiffany could by any means be persuaded to elope with a mere commoner! She has far larger plans, I assure you! No, no: *that's* not the answer to this riddle."

"Then what *is* the answer?" he demanded. "Yes, and why didn't she go with you to Nethersett? You told me at breakfast that you meant to take her along with you!"

"She wished to visit Patience. . . ." Miss Trent's voice faltered, and died.

Courtenay gave a scornful snort. "That's a loud one! Wished to visit Patience, indeed! To beg her pardon, I daresay?"

"To make amends. When you told her that Mr Edward Banningham had spread the true story of what happened in Leeds—— Oh, how much I wish you'd kept your tongue! You might have known she would do something outrageous! But so should I have known! I should never have left her: I am shockingly to blame! But she seemed so quiet this morning, scheming how to overcome her set-back——"

"Ay, the sly cat! Scheming how to be rid of you, ma'am, so that she could run off with Calver!"

She was silent, staring with knitted brows straight before

her. She said suddenly: "No. She *did* go to the Rectory: recollect that her riding-habit was lying on the floor, with her whip, and her gloves! Something must have happened there. Patience—no, Patience wouldn't rebuff her! But if Mrs Chartley gave her a scold? But what could she have said to drive the child into running away? Mr Underhill, I think I should go to the Rectory immediately, and discover——"

"*No!*" he interrupted forcefully. "I won't have our affairs blabbed all round the district!"

"It's bound to be talked of. And I'm persuaded Mrs Chartley——"

"Not if I fetch her back! Which I promise you I mean to do, for my mother's sake!" He added rather grandly: "I shall be obliged to call that fellow out of course, but I shall think of some pretext for it."

At any other time she must have laughed, but she was too busy racking her brains to pay much heed to him. "Something must have happened," she repeated. "Something that made her feel she couldn't remain here another instant. Oh, good God, Lindeth! He must have offered for Patience—and she told Tiffany!"

Courtenay gave a whistle of surprise. "So that's serious, is it? Well, by Jove, if ever I expected to see her given her own again! Lord, she'd be as mad as fire! No wonder she ran off with Calver! Trying to hoax everyone into thinking it was him she wanted all along!"

She was momentarily daunted, but she came about again, "Yes, she might do that, in one of her wild fits, but he would not. Wait! Only let me think!" She pressed her hands over her eyes, trying to cast her mind back.

"Well, if she isn't going to Gretna Green, where else can she be going?" he argued.

Her hands dropped. "What a fool I am! To London, of course! That's what she wanted—she begged me to take her back to the Burfords! Of course that's the answer! She must have persuaded Mr Calver to take her to Leeds—perhaps even to escort her to London!" She read disbelief in Courtenay's face, and said: "If she made him believe that she was being hardly used here—you know how she always fancies herself to be ill-treated as soon as her will is crossed! Recollect that he doesn't know her as we do! She has shown him her prettiest side, too—and she can be very engaging when she chooses! Or—or perhaps he has done no more than put her on the stage, in charge of the guard."

"Stage!" exclaimed Courtenay contemptuously. "I wish I may see Tiffany condescending to a stage-coach! A post-chaise-and-four is what she'd demand! And much hope I have of catching it!"

"She couldn't go post," said Miss Trent decidedly. "She spent all her pin-money in Harrogate. And I must think it extremely unlikely that Mr Calver could have been able to oblige her with a loan. She would need as much as £25, you know, and how should he be carrying such a sum upon him when all he meant to do was to take her out for a driving-lesson? And I fancy he's not at all beforehand with the world." She thought for a moment, and then said, in a constricted voice: "Mr Underhill, I think—I think you should drive over to Broom Hall, to consult Sir Waldo. He is Mr Calver's cousin, and—and I think he is the person best fitted to handle this matter."

"Well, I won't!" declared Courtenay, reddening. "I'm not a schoolboy, ma'am, and I don't need him to tell me what I should do, or to do it for me, I thank you! I'm going to tell 'em to bring the phaeton up to the house immediately. If that precious pair went to Leeds they must have passed through the village, and someone is bound to have seen them. And if they did, trust me to have Tiffany back by nightfall! If you ask me, I'd say good riddance to her, but I'll be *damned*—begging your pardon!—if I'll let her shab off to the Burfords as if we had made her miserable here!"

Miss Trent had no great faith in his ability to overtake a truant who had had three hours' start; but since she felt quite as strongly as he did that every effort must be made to do it, and realized that to persist in urging that Sir Waldo should be consulted would be a waste of breath and time, she resigned herself to the prospect of an uncomfortable, and possibly nerve-racking drive. He was relieved to learn that she meant to accompany him, but he warned her that he was going to *put 'em along*. That she would do better to be content with putting his horses well together was an opinion which she kept to herself.

When she found that he had had a team harnessed to the phaeton her heart sank. His leaders were new acquisitions, and he was not yet very expert in pointing them, or, indeed of sticking to them, as she very soon discovered. Observing that there was not a moment to be lost, Courtenay sprang his horses down the avenue to the lodge-gates. Since it was not only rather narrow, but had several bends in it as well, Miss

Trent was forced to hold on for dear life. The sharp turn out of the gates was negotiated safely, though not, perhaps, in style, and they were soon bowling along the lane that led to the village. Courtenay, exhilarated by his success in negotiating the difficult turn out of the gate, confided to Miss Trent that he had been practising the use of the whip, and rather thought he could back himself to take a fly off the leader's ear.

."I beg you won't do any such thing!" she replied. "I have no wish to be thrown out into the ditch!"

Nettled, he determined to show her that he was at home to a peg, and it was not long before her worst fears were realized. Within less than a quarter of a mile from Oversett, feather-edging a bend in the lane, his front-wheel came into sharp collision with a milestone, partially hidden by rank grass, and the inevitable happened. Miss Trent, picking herself up, more angry than hurt, found that one wheel of the phaeton was lying, a dismal wreck, at some distance from the carriage, that one of the wheelers was down, a trace broken, and both the leaders plunging wildly in a concerted effort to bolt. Blistering words were on the tip of her tongue, but she was a sensible woman, and she realized that there were more urgent things to do than to favour Courtenay with an exact and pithy opinion of his driving-skill. She hurried to his assistance. Between them, they managed to quieten the frightened leaders, backing them gently to relieve the drag on the crippled phaeton from the remaining trace. "Cut it!" she commanded. "I can hold this pair now. Do you get that wheeler on his feet!"

Speechless with rage and chagrin, he had just freed the leaders when, sweeping round the bend towards them, came the Nonesuch, his team of chestnuts well in hand, and his groom seated beside him. The team was pulled up swiftly, every rein holding as true as if it had been single, the groom jumped down, and ran to the wheelers' heads; and the Nonesuch, his amused gaze travelling from Courtenay, beside his struggling wheeler, to Miss Trent, who had led the two sweating leaders to the side of the lane, said: "Dear me! Do what you can, Blyth!"

The groom touched his hat, and went to Courtenay, who was suffering such agonies of mortification at being found in such a situation that he would have been hard put to it to decide whether he wished himself dead or the Nonesuch. He blurted out, scarlet-faced: "It was that curst milestone! I never saw it!"

"Very understandable," agreed Sir Waldo. "But if I were you I would attend to my horses! You really need not explain the circumstances to me." He looked smilingly at Miss Trent. "How do you do, ma'am? Quite a fortunate encounter! I was on my way to visit you—to invite you to go with me to Leeds."

"To Leeds!" The exclamation was surprised out of her; she stood staring up at him, her embarrassment forgotten.

"Yes: on an errand of mercy!" He glanced towards the phaeton, and saw that the fallen wheeler was up. "Very good, Blyth! Now take those leaders in hand!"

The groom, who had been running a hand down one of the unfortunate wheeler's legs, straightened himself, saying: "Yes, sir. Badly strained hock here."

"So I should imagine. Render Mr Underhill all the assistance you can!"

"Sir!" uttered Courtenay, between gritted teeth. "I—we—were on our way to Leeds too! That was how it came about that I—I mean, it is a matter of—of great urgency! I *must* get there! I can't tell you why, but if you are going there yourself, would you be so very obliging as to take me with you?"

"Well, no!" said the Nonesuch apologetically. "Phaetons, you know, were not built to carry three persons, and I have been particularly requested to bring Miss Trent with me. Oh, don't look so distressed! Believe me, the matter is not of such great urgency as you think! You may also believe that Miss Trent is far more necessary to the success of my mission than you could hope to be."

Miss Trent, having relinquished the reins she had been holding into Blyth's hands, stepped quickly up to the phaeton, and said, in an undervoice: "You know, then? But how? Where are they?"

"In Leeds, at the King's Head." He leaned across the empty seat beside him, and held down his hand to her. "Come!"

She looked at it, thinking how strong and shapely it was; and then up, meeting his eyes, smiling into hers. She felt helpless, knowing it was her duty to go to Tiffany, longing to be with Sir Waldo, dreading to be with him, afraid, not of his strength but of her own weakness. Before she had made up her mind what to do, Courtenay, whose worshipful regard for the Nonesuch was rapidly diminishing, broke in, saying in a furious voice: "Your pardon, sir! But Miss Trent can't discharge *my* errand, which is of *immediate* urgency, I promise you! I don't care if he *is* your cousin—I—I have a very ardent desire to meet Mr Calver!"

"Yes, yes!" said the Nonesuch soothingly. "But you can express your gratitude to him at a more convenient time. Your *immediate* duty is to your horses."

"My *gratitude?*" ejaculated Courtenay, so far forgetful of his immediate duty as to abandon his wheelers, and to stride up to Sir Waldo's phaeton. "That—that damned rip makes off with my cousin, and you expect me to be *grateful?* Well, let me tell you, Sir Waldo,——"

"My amiable young cawker," interrupted Sir Waldo, looking down at him in considerable amusement, "you are fair and far off! To whom, do you suppose, do I owe my information?"

Nonplussed, Courtenay glared up at him. "I don't know! I——"

"Well, think!" Sir Waldo advised him. He looked again at Miss Trent, his brows lifting enquiringly.

"Is Tiffany with Mr Calver?" she demanded.

"Well, I trust she may be. She was with him when he sent off his impassioned plea for help, but he seemed to entertain some doubt of his ability to hold her in—er—check for any considerable period. I don't wish to be importunate, ma'am, but are you coming with me, or are you not?"

"I *must* come!" she said, gathering up her skirt in one hand, and holding the other up to him.

He grasped it, drawing her up into the phaeton, and saying softly: "Good girl! Pluck to the backbone! Were you tumbled into the ditch?"

"I collect you've guessed as much from my appearance!" she said, with asperity, and putting up her hands to straighten her bonnet.

"Not a bit of it! A mere knowledge of cause and effect: you are, as ever, precise to a pin—and an enduring delight to me!" He turned his head to address Courtenay once more. "I'll leave Blyth to assist you, Underhill. Indulge no apprehensions! just look to your horses! Miss Wield will very soon be restored to you."

As he spoke, he drew his leaders back gently, and gave the would-be top-sawyer an effortless demonstration of how to turn to the rightabout in a constricted space a sporting vehicle drawn by four high-bred lively ones.

Miss Trent, deeply appreciative of his skill, was moved to

235

say: "You *do* drive to an inch! I wish I could turn a *one*-horse carriage as easily!"

"You will: I'll teach you," he said. "You shall take the shine out of all our fair whips!"

She had no particular desire to take the shine out of anyone, but the implication of these words conjured up a vision of the future so agreeable that it was with great difficulty that she wrenched her mind away from it. Rigidly confining it to the matter in hand, she said: "I hope you mean to explain to me, sir, how it comes about that you are so exactly informed of Tiffany's whereabouts. *I* could only guess what must be her intention, for I have been away from Staples for the better part of the day, and she left no message for me."

"What an abominable girl she is!" he remarked. "My information came, as I told you, from Laurie. He sent off one of the post-boys with a note for me, from the King's Head. As far as I understand the matter——but he wrote in haste, and, to judge from the manner of it, in an extremely harassed state of mind!——Tiffany induced him to drive her to Leeds, by some fetch or wheedle, and only on arrival there divulged her intention of travelling to London. I can't tell you why she should have suddenly taken this notion into her head. All I know is that Laurie has hoaxed her into believing that there is not a place to be had in any of the stage-coaches, and that the Mail doesn't reach Leeds until four o'clock. I should have thought that rather too improbable an hour to have chosen, but Tiffany seems to have accepted it without question."

"Of course it's perfectly ridiculous! But Tiffany knows nothing about Mails or stages. Well! it's some comfort to know that I was right. Mr Underhill *would* have it that she and your cousin had gone off in a post-chaise-and-four, but I couldn't suppose that Mr Calver would be carrying a large enough sum of money on his person."

"Very unlikely," he agreed. "Still more unlikely that he would have disgorged a penny of it for Tiffany's benefit. I'll say this for Laurie: he had her measure from the outset."

"Indeed? It would be interesting to know, then, why he has been so assiduous in his attentions to her!"

He smiled. "Oh, that was to detach her from Julian! He came after the fair, but it was quite a good notion."

"Your own, in fact!" she said, somewhat tartly. "I find it very hard to believe that Mr Calver takes the smallest interest in Lord Lindeth's happiness."

"Oh, he doesn't! He knows, however, that I do; and unless

236

I'm much mistaken his scheme was to win my gratitude. Poor Laurie! It was some time before he realized that his labour was thrown away. Still, it kept him occupied, and did neither of them any harm."

"I think it utterly unscrupulous!" said Miss Trent indignantly. "It would have done a great deal of harm if Tiffany had fallen in love with him!"

"On the contrary, it might have done a great deal of good. It's high time that young woman suffered a shake-up. To own the truth, I rather hoped she might develop just enough tendre for him to enable her to bear more easily the shock of finding that Lindeth had offered for Miss Chartley. Not for her sake, but for yours. I can readily imagine what you will be made to suffer, my poor girl!"

She disregarded this, but asked eagerly: "Has he done so? Oh, I am so glad! I hope you don't dislike it, Sir Waldo?"

"Not at all. An unexceptionable girl, and will make him an admirable wife, I daresay."

"I think that too. She has as little worldly ambition as he, and quite as sweet a disposition. But his mother? Will she like it?"

"No, not immediately, but she'll come round to it. She has all the worldly ambition Julian lacks, and has lately been doing her utmost to interest him in various diamonds of the first water. However, I fancy she has begun to realize that it's useless to try to bring him into fashion. In any event, she is by far too fond a parent to cast the least rub in the way of his happiness. Julian informs me, moreover, that Mrs Chartley is related to one of my aunt's oldest friends. His description of this lady—unknown to me, I'm thankful to say!—wouldn't lead one to suppose that my aunt would regard the relationship as an advantage, but he seems to think it will. As far as I remember, he said she was a regular fusty mug—but I daresay he exaggerated!"

A ripple of laughter broke from her. "What a boy he is! Tell me, if you please: when did this event take place, sir?"

"This morning. I had the news from him barely half-an-hour before I received Laurie's message."

"Then I know why Tiffany ran away," said Miss Trent, with a despairing sigh. "She was at the Rectory this morning, and they must have told her. You may say she's abominable —and, of course, very often she *is!*—but one can't but pity her, poor child! So spoiled as she has been all her life, so pretty, and so much petted and admired——! Can't you understand what it must have meant to her, coming, as it did, after the ball last night?"

He glanced down at her. "The ball last night? What happened to overset her then?"

"Good God, surely you must have noticed?" she exclaimed. "All those foolish boys who have been dangling after her ever since I brought her to Staples clustered round Miss Chartley—almost showed Tiffany the cold shoulder!"

"No, I didn't notice," he answered. "I was in the card-room, you know. But I can readily understand her feelings upon being shown a cold shoulder: I was shown one myself, and I assure you I am filled with compassion." Again he glanced down at her, his smile a little wry. "That, Miss Trent, is why I sought refuge in the card-room."

CHAPTER XX

SHE TURNED AWAY HER FACE, aware of her rising colour. He said reflectively: "I can't recall that I was ever so blue-devilled before."

She knew that it was unwise to answer him, but she was stung into saying: "That, Sir Waldo, is—as you would say yourself—doing it rather too brown! You do not appear to me to be suffering from any want of spirits!"

He laughed. "Oh, no! Not since it occurred to me that you were blue-devilled too!"

"To be thrown into a ditch is enough to blue-devil anyone!" she retorted.

"What, *twice*?" he exclaimed. "I had no notion that such an accident had befallen you on the way to the *ball*!"

"It didn't. Last night," she said carefully, "I was not feeling at all the thing. I had the headache."

"Again?" he said, in a voice of deep concern. "My dear Miss Trent, I'm persuaded you should consult a physician about these recurrent headaches of yours!"

She did her best to stifle it, but he caught the sound of the tiny choke of laughter in her throat, and said appreciatively:

"Do you know, I think that of all your idiosyncrasies that choke you give, when you are determined not to laugh, is the one that most enchants me. I wish you will do it again!"

Only the recollection that he must of necessity be expert in the art of seduction prevented her from complying with this request. Appalled to discover that in despite of upbringing and principles her every fibre was responsive to the Nonesuch's wicked charm, she said, apparently addressing the ears of his leaders: "Sir Waldo, circumstance compelled me to accept a seat in your carriage. When I consented to go with you to Leeds, I trusted that chivalry—a sense of propriety—would prohibit you from entering again upon this subject."

"Did you?" he said sympathetically. "Only to find your trust misplaced! Well, that is a great deal too bad, and one must naturally shrink from shattering illusions. At the same time—where *did* you pick up such a ridiculous notion?"

The Reverend William Trent, whose mind was of a serious order, had several times warned his elder sister that too lively a sense of humour frequently led to laxity of principle. She now perceived how right he was; and wondered, in dismay, whether it was because he invariably made her laugh that instead of regarding the Nonesuch with revulsion she was obliged to struggle against the impulse to cast every scruple to the winds, and to give her life into his keeping.

"What is it that troubles you, my heart?" he asked gently, after a short pause.

The change of tone almost overset her, but she managed to say, though faintly: "Nothing!"

"No, don't say that. What did I do to bring about this alteration in your sentiments? I've racked my brain to discover the answer—searched my memory too, but quite in vain. God knows I'm no saint, but I don't think I'm more of a sinner than any other man. *Tell* me!"

She realized from these words that they must be poles apart. She thought it would be useless to enter upon any discussion, even if she could have brought herself to broach a subject of such delicacy. She said, with as much composure as she could command: "Sir Waldo, pray leave this! I don't wish to be married."

"Why not?"

She ought to have guessed, of course, that he would disconcert her. Casting wildly in her mind for an excuse, she produced, after a betraying pause: "I am an educationist. No

239

doubt it seems strange to you that I should prefer to pursue that profession, but——but so it is!"

"My dear girl, so you might, with my goodwill!"

"You would hardly wish your wife to be employed as a teacher in a school!"

"No, certainly not, but if superintending the education of the young is your ambition I can provide you with plenty of material on which to exercise your talents," he said cheerfully.

For a moment she could hardly believe her ears. She turned her head to stare at him; and then, as she saw the familiar glint in his eyes, wrath at his audacity surged up in her, and she gasped: "How *dare* you?"

The words were no sooner uttered than she regretted them; but she had at least the satisfaction of seeing the glint vanish from his eyes. It was succeeded by a look of astonishment. Sir Waldo pulled up his team. "I *beg* your pardon?" he said blankly.

Furiously blushing, she said: "I should not have said it. I didn't intend—— Pray forget it, sir!"

"Forget it! How could I possibly do so? What the devil did I say to make you rip up at me? You don't even know what I was talking about, for I haven't yet told you my dark secret! Do you remember that I promised I would do so?"

"I do remember," she replied, in a stifled voice. "You said that you would *make a clean breast* of it, but it is unnecessary. I know what your——your *dark secret* is, Sir Waldo."

"Do you indeed? Which of my cousins took it upon himself to enlighten you?" he asked grimly. "Laurie?"

"No, no! He has never mentioned it to me, I promise you! Don't ask me more!"

"I need not. Julian, of course! I might have known it! If ever there was a prattle-box——! But I can't for the life of me understand why——"

She broke in rather desperately on this. "Oh, pray——! He asked me particularly not to tell you! It was very wrong of me to have said what I did. He thought I knew—he meant no harm! I don't think he dreamed that I should not look upon it as—as lightly as he does himself—as *you* do! You told me that you believed I had too liberal a mind to disapprove. You meant it as a compliment, but you were mistaken: my mind is not so liberal. I am aware that in certain circles—the circles to which you belong—such things are scarcely regarded. It is otherwise in my circle. And my family—oh, you would not understand, but you must believe that I *could* not marry a man whose—whose way of life fills me with repugnance!"

He had listened to the first part of this speech in frowning bewilderment, but by the time she reached the end of it the frown had cleared, and a look of intense amusement had taken its place. "So that's it!" he said, a quiver of laughter in his voice. He set his team in motion again. "I'll wring Julian's neck for this! Of all the leaky, chuckleheaded rattles———! Just what *did* he tell you?"

"Indeed, he said nothing more than you told me yourself!" she said earnestly. "Only that people would be bound to disapprove of the use to which you mean to put Broom Hall! He said nothing in your dispraise, I do assure you! In fact, he said that although one of your cousins thinks it not at all the thing to—to house children of that sort in a respectable neighbourhood———"

"George," interpolated Sir Waldo. "Are you sure he didn't refer to them as *Waldo's wretched brats*?"

"I believe he did," she replied stiffly.

"You shouldn't tamper with the text. Go on!"

She eyed his profile with hostility. "There is nothing more to say. I wished merely to make it plain to you that Lord Lindeth spoke of you with as much admiration as affection."

"I daresay. Heaven preserve me from affectionate and admiring relations! Laurie couldn't have served me a worse turn! So you won't help me to set up schools for my wretched brats, Miss Trent?"

"*Schools?*" she repeated, startled.

"In course of time. Oh, don't look so alarmed! Only one at the moment! Those of my brats who are established in Surrey are already provided for."

Dazed, she demanded: "How many children have you?"

"I'm not perfectly sure. I think they numbered fifty when I left London, but there's no saying that there may not be one or two more by now."

"*Fifty?*"

"That's all. I expect shortly to double the number, however," he said affably.

Her eyes kindled. "I collect that you think it a joking matter, Sir Waldo! I do not!"

"I don't think it anything of the sort. It is, in fact, one of the few matters which I take seriously."

"But you cannot possibly have fif——" She broke off

241

abruptly, her eyes widening. "Schools—wretched brats—carrying eccentricity too far—and only the Rector knew——! Oh, what a *fool* I've been!" she cried, between laughter and tears. "And Lindeth said, when we took that child to the infirmary, that *you* were the man we wanted in such a situation! But how *could* I guess that you were interested in *orphans*?"

"Easier to think that I was a loose-screw, was it?" said Sir Waldo, who had once more halted his team. "Let me tell you, my girl, that I'm swallowing no more of your insults! And if I hear another word from you in disparagement of the Corinthian set it will be very much the worse for you!"

Since he palliated this severity by putting his arm round her she was undismayed. Overwhelming relief making her forgetful of the proprieties, she subsided thankfully into his embrace, clutching a fold of his driving-coat, and saying into his shoulder: "Oh, no, you never will! But I *didn't* find it easy to believe! Only people said such things—and you talked of making a clean breast of it—and then Lindeth! Don't scold me! If you *knew* how unhappy I've been——!"

"I do know. But what *you* don't know is that if you don't take your face out of my coat, and look at me, you will be still more unhappy!"

She gave a watery chuckle, and raised her head. The Nonesuch, his arm tightening round her, kissed her. The phaeton jerked forward, and back again, as Sir Waldo, who had transferred the reins to his whip-hand, brought his restive wheelers under control. Miss Trent, emerging somewhat breathlessly from his embrace, said, in shaken accents: "For goodness' sake, take care! If I'm thrown into a ditch a second time I'll never forgive you!" .

"You must teach me sometime how to handle my cattle," he said. "I imagine your lessons—Miss Educationist!—will bear a close resemblance to Laurie's efforts to instruct Tiffany."

"Good God! Tiffany!" she exclaimed. "I had quite forgotten her! Waldo, this is *no* time for dalliance—and it isn't the place, either! What William would say if he knew——! You *are* an atrocious person! Since the day I met you I have become steadily more depraved. No, no, don't! We *must* make haste to Leeds: you know we must! There's no saying what Tiffany may do, if she becomes impatient."

"To be honest with you," said Sir Waldo, "I have very little interest in what she may do."

242

"No, but I cannot cast her off so lightly. She was left to my guardianship, and if anything were to happen to her how dreadfully to blame I should be!"

"Yes, the sooner you're rid of her the better. Is this fast enough for you, or do you wish me to spring 'em?"

"Oh, no! Not that I would venture to dictate to you, dear sir! Tell me about your orphanage! Lindeth said that you squandered a fortune on your wretched brats, and, indeed, I should think you must, if you mean to support a hundred of them. Is it for infants?"

"No, I don't encroach on the Foundling Hospitals. Nor do I squander a fortune on my brats. Broom Hall, for instance, will be largely self-supporting; subsisting on rents, you know."

She smiled. "Don't think me impertinent!—But I am not *wholly* devoid of intelligence! What will it cost you to bring that estate into order?"

"No more than I can well afford!" he retorted. "Are you fearful of finding yourself in ebb-water if you marry me? You won't! Lindeth misled you: only *half* my fortune is devoted to my favourite charity! My aunt Lindeth will inform you that the whole is *indecent*—if she doesn't describe it in rather stronger terms, which, in moments of stress, she is prone to do."

"My mind now being relieved of care, I wish you will tell me what prompted you to found an orphanage?"

He said reflectively: "I don't know. Tradition, and upbringing, I suppose. My father, and my grandfather before him, were both considerable philanthropists; and my mother was used to be very friendly with Lady Spender—the one that died a couple of years ago, and was mad after educating the poor. So you may say that I grew up amongst charities! This was one that seemed to me more worth the doing than any other: collecting as many of the homeless waifs you may find in any city as I would, and rearing them to become respectable citizens. My cousin, George Wingham, swears they will all turn into hedge-birds, and, of course, we've had our failures, but not many. The important thing is to enter them to the right trades—and to take care they're not bound to bad masters." He stopped, and said, laughing: "What induced you to mount me on my pet hobby-horse? We have matters of more immediate importance to discuss than my wretched brats, my little educationist!—my mother, by the way, will welcome you with open arms, and will very likely egg you on to bully me into starting an asylum for female orphans: she's got

243

about a dozen of 'em already, down at Manifold. How soon may you leave Staples? I warn you, I don't mean to wait on Mrs Underhill's convenience, so if you've any notion of remaining there until Tiffany goes back to London——"

"I haven't!" she interrupted. "Nor, I assure you, would Mrs Underhill ask it of me!"

"I'm happy to hear it. The devil of it is that I must leave with Julian, on Monday: I told the boy I would support his cause with my aunt, and I think I must. I should have wished to have postponed my departure until I could have escorted you to Derbyshire, but as things have fallen out I shall be obliged to leave you here until Julian's affairs are settled, and one or two other matters as well. I'll return as soon as I can, but——"

"I had as lief you did not," she said. "And liefer by far that we should tell no one at Oversett, except Mrs Underhill (whom I hope to heaven I can pledge to secrecy!), of our intentions. Think me foolish if you will, but I don't feel I could bear it! It will be so very much disliked, you know, and —well, I need not tell you what things will be said by certain ladies of our acquaintance! Then there is Tiffany. Waldo, *she* mustn't know until she has recovered a little from Lindeth's engagement! It would be too cruel—when you encouraged the poor child by flirting with her! Besides, I shudder to think of what life at Staples would be if she knew that you had preferred me to her! We should all of us be driven distracted. I must give Mrs Underhill time to fill my post—don't ask me to leave her in the lurch, for I couldn't do it: I have had nothing but kindness from her, remember! But as soon as she has done so I'll go home to Derbyshire, and we may meet there. Oh, how much I long to make you known to Mama and William! But as for *escorts*——! My dear, how can you be so absurd as to suppose that at my age I should need one? The journey will be nothing—no more than fifty miles! I have only to go by the stage to Mansfield, and from there——"

"You will not go by the stage anywhere at all," said Sir Waldo. "I'll send my chaise to fetch you, with my own boys, of course."

"To be sure!" she said instantly. "Outriders, and a courier too, I hope! Now, do, do be sensible, my dear sir!"

They were still arguing the matter when they reached the King's Head. Leaving the Nonesuch in the stableyard, Miss Trent walked into the inn. She had on several occasions refreshed there with Mrs Underhill, and the first person she encountered was an elderly waiter who was well-known to her. Greeting him with a smile, and speaking with studied coolness, she said: "Good-day to you, John! Are Miss Wield and Mr Calver still here, or have they given me up in despair? I should have been here long since, but was most tiresomely delayed. I hope they may not have left?"

Even as she said it she became aware of tension, and of curious glances cast in her direction, and her heart sank. The waiter coughed in obvious embarrassment, and replied: "No, ma'am. Oh, no, they haven't *left*! The gentleman is in one of the parlours—the same one as you was in yourself, ma'am, when you partook of a nuncheon here the other day."

"And Miss Wield?"

"Well, no, ma'am! Miss is in the best bedchamber—being as she is a trifle out of sorts, and the mistress not knowing what else to do but to persuade her to lay down on the bed, with the blinds drawn, till she was more composed, as you might say. Very vapourish, she was—but the mistress will tell you, ma'am!"

Sir Waldo, entering the house at that moment, encountered an anguished look from Miss Trent, and said: "What's amiss?"

"I couldn't take it upon myself to say, sir," responded the waiter, casting down his eyes. "But the gentleman, sir, is in the parlour, the mistress having put some sticking-plaster over the cut, and one of the under-waiters carrying a bottle of cognac up to him—the *best* cognac, sir!—the gentleman, as I understand, having sustained an accident—in a manner of speaking!"

"We will go up to him!" said Miss Trent hastily.

"Sinister!" observed Sir Waldo, following her up the narrow stairs. "Where, by the way, is the heroine of this piece?"

"Laid down upon the bed in the best bedchamber," replied Miss Trent, "with the landlady in attendance!"

"Worse and worse! Do you suppose that she stabbed poor Laurie with a carving-knife?"

"Heaven knows! It is quite *appalling*—and no laughing matter, let me tell you! Mrs Underhill is very well known here, and it is perfectly obvious to me that that atrocious girl has created a dreadful scandal! The *one* thing I was hopeful of avoiding! Whatever you do, Waldo, don't let her suspect that you regard me even with *tolerance*!"

245

"Have no fear! I will treat you with civil indifference!" he promised. "I wonder what she *did* do to Laurie?"

He was soon to learn the answer to this. Mr Calver was discovered in the parlour, reclining on a sofa of antiquated and uncomfortable design, a strip of sticking-plaster adorning his brow, his beautifully curled locks sadly dishevelled, a glass in his hand, and a bottle of the King's Head's best cognac standing on the floor beside him. As she stepped over the threshold, Miss Trent trod on splinters of glass; and on the table in the centre of the room was an elegant timepiece, in a slightly battered condition. Miss Wield had not stabbed Mr Calver: she had thrown the clock at his head.

"Snatched it off the mantelpiece and dashed well *hurled* it at me!" said Laurence.

The Nonesuch shook his head. "You must have tried to dodge it," he said. "Really, Laurie, how could you be such a cawker? If you had but stood still it would have missed you by several feet!"

"I should rather think I did try to dodge it!" said Laurence, glaring at him. "So would you have done!"

"Never!" declared the Nonesuch. "When females throw missiles at my head I know better than to budge! Er—would it be indelicate to ask *why* she felt herself impelled to throw the clock at you?"

"Yes, I might have known you would think it vastly amusing!" said Laurence bitterly.

"Well, yes, I think you might!" said Sir Waldo, his eyes dancing.

Miss Trent, perceiving that her beloved had allowed himself to fall into a mood of ill-timed frivolity, directed a quelling frown at him, and said to the injured dandy: "I am so sorry, Mr Calver! I wish you will lie down again: you are not looking at all the thing, and no wonder! Your cousin may think it a jesting matter, but *I* am excessively grateful to you! Indeed, I cannot conceive how you were able to hold that tiresome child in check for so long!"

Slightly mollified, Laurence said: "It wasn't easy, I can tell you, ma'am. It's my belief she's queer in her attic. Well, would you credit it?—she wanted me to sell her pearl necklet, or put it up the spout, just to pay for the hire of a chaise to carry her to London! I had to gammon her I'd pawned my watch instead!"

"How very wise of you!" said Miss Trent sycophantically.

"Pray do sit down, sir! I wish you will tell me—if you feel able—what caused her to—to take a sudden pet?"

"To do *what*?" interpolated the Nonesuch.

Miss Trent, turning her back on him in a marked manner, sat down in a chair by the sofa, and smiled at Laurence encouragingly.

"You may well ask, ma'am!" said Laurence. He glanced resentfully at his cousin. "If you are fancying I was trying to make love to her, Waldo, you're no better than a Jack Adams! For one thing, I ain't in the petticoat-line, and for another I wouldn't make love to that devil's daughter if I was!"

"Of course you would not!" said Miss Trent.

"Well, I didn't. What's more, it wasn't *my* fault at all! Mind you, I had the deuce of a task to keep her here! Still, we were going on prosperously enough until she suddenly took it into her head she must drink some tea. Why she should want to maudle her inside with tea at this time of day the lord knows, but I'd no objection, as long as it stopped her from riding grub. Which I daresay it would have done if she hadn't asked the jobbernoll who brought in the tray what time the London Mail was expected to arrive in the town. Couldn't catch the fellow's eye—wasn't close enough to give him a nudge! The silly bleater told her there wouldn't be another till tomorrow morning. That brought the trap down! Talk of ringing a peal——! She scolded like a cat-purse! You'd have supposed I was a regular Bermondsey boy! And the waiter standing there with his mouth at half-cock, until I told him to take himself off—which I wish I *hadn't* done!" Shuddering at the memory, he recruited his strength with a sip or two of cognac. "The names she called me! It beats me where she learned 'em, I can tell you that, ma'am!"

"What *did* she call you, Laurie?" enquired Sir Waldo, much interested.

"I wonder," said Miss Trent, in a voice of determined coldness, "if you would be so obliging, sir, as to refrain from asking quite unimportant questions? Mr Calver, what can I say but that I am deeply mortified? As Miss Wield's governess, I must hold myself to blame, but I trust——"

"Learned them from you, did she, ma'am?" said Sir Waldo irrepressibly.

"Very witty!" snapped Laurence. "You wouldn't be so full of fun and gig if *you'd* been in my shoes!"

"Pray don't heed your cousin!" begged Miss Trent. "Only tell me what happened!"

"Well, she twigged I'd been hoaxing her, of course, and it didn't take her above a minute or two to guess *why* I'd kept her kicking her heels here. I give you my word, ma'am, if she'd had a dagger about her she'd have stuck it into me! Not that I cared for that, because I knew she hadn't one. But the next thing was that she said she was going off to spout her pearls that instant, so that she could be gone from the place before you reached us! She'd have done it, too! What's more, I wish I'd let her!"

"I don't wonder at it. But you did not—which was *very* well done of you, sir!"

"I don't know that," he said gloomily. "She wouldn't have raised such a breeze if I'd had the sense to have taken off my bars. The thing was she'd put me in such a tweak by that time that I was hanged if I'd cry craven! Told her that if she tried to shab off I'd squeak beef—what I mean is, tell the landlord who she was, and what she was scheming to do. So then she threw the clock at me. That brought the landlord in on us, and a couple of waiters, and the boots, and a dashed gaggle of chambermaids—and it's my belief they'd had their ears to the door! And before I could utter a word the little hussy was carrying on as though she thought she was Mrs Siddons! Well, she'd threatened to tell everyone I'd been trying to give her a slip on the shoulder if I wouldn't let her leave the room, and, by God, she did it!"

"Oh, *no!*" exclaimed Miss Trent, changing colour. "Oh, how *could* she?"

"If you was to ask me, ma'am, there's precious little she couldn't do! So there was nothing for me to do but tell the landlord she was Mrs Underhill's niece—which he knew— and that she was trying to run off to London, and all I was doing was holding on to her till you arrived to take her in charge. Which he believed, because I'd hired one of the post-boys to carry a message to Waldo. So, as soon as she saw he did believe it, off went her ladyship into hysterics. Lord, you never heard such a commotion in your life!"

"I have frequently heard just such a commotion!" said Miss Trent. "Where is she, sir?"

"I don't know. The landlady took her off somewhere. No use asking me!"

She got up. "I will go and find the landlady, then. But you must let me thank you, Mr Calver! Indeed, I am so *very* much obliged to you! You have had the most disagreeable time imaginable, and I am astonished you didn't abandon the wretched child!"

"Well, I couldn't do that," said Laurence. "I ain't such a rum touch! Besides—— Well, never mind that!"

He watched her cross the room towards the door, and his cousin move to open it for her. In deepening gloom, he observed the punctilious civility of Sir Waldo's slight bow, and the rigidity of Miss Trent's countenance.

Sir Waldo shut the door, and strolled back into the middle of the room. Drawing his snuff-box from his pocket, he tapped it with one long finger, and flicked it open. Taking an infinitesimal pinch, he said, his amused gaze on Laurence's face: "Do tell me, Laurie! Why did you send for me rather than for Underhill?"

Laurence shot him a resentful look. "Thought I could do you a good turn, that's why! And well you know it!"

"But how kind of you!" said Sir Waldo. "I never had the least guess that you had my interests so much at heart."

"Oh, well!" said Laurie awkwardly. "I don't know that I'd say that, precisely, but we're cousins, after all, and it was easy to see your affair was hanging in the hedge, so——"

"What affair?"

Laurence set his empty glass down rather violently. "I know you, coz!" he said angrily. "So don't think to bamboozle me! It's as plain as a pikestaff——"

"And don't *you* think to bamboozle *me*!" said Sir Waldo, quite pleasantly. "All you wish to do is to put me under an obligation to you, so that I shall be moved to set you up in the horse-coping line. I'm familiar with your tactics."

"Well, damn it, what else can I do?" demanded Laurence in an aggrieved tone. "Who the devil do you suppose is going to dub up the possibles if you don't?"

Sir Waldo's mouth quivered. "I shouldn't think anyone is going to," he replied.

"Yes, that's just like you!" Laurence said, his resentment flaring up. "You're so full of juice you don't know what it is to be bushed—and don't care, either! It wouldn't mean any more to you to lend me five thousand than it would mean to me to tip over a bull's eye to a waiter. But will you do it?——"

"No," said Sir Waldo. "I'm far too hard-fisted. So don't waste any more time or effort in trying to put me under an obligation! You won't do it. You're awake upon some suits, but not on all! And you can't know me as well as you think you do if you imagine I'm not very well able to manage my affairs without your assistance."

"You didn't seem to me to be managing them so very well. No, and even when I threw you and Miss Trent together, you must have made wretched work of it! And you ain't even grateful to me for *trying* to bring you about! When I think of all the trouble I've taken since I came into Yorkshire—let alone being obliged to put up with the infernal racket those builders make!—damme if I don't think you *owe* me that paltry five thousand! Because you came the concave suit over me, Waldo, and don't you deny it! Oh, yes, you did! You let me pretty well wear myself out, drawing off that vixen from Lindeth, and it's my belief you knew all along that he was tired of her! And just look what it's led to! Let alone the riot and rumpus I've had to endure, and the blunt I laid out on hiring this parlour, and giving her tea, and lemonade, and buying a ticket for the Mail, my head's been laid open, and I shall very likely carry a scar for the rest of my life!"

"But what have all these misfortunes to do with me?"

"They've got everything to do with you! They'd none of 'em have happened if you hadn't behaved so scaly! Yes, you laugh! It's just what I expected you'd do!"

"You might well!" replied Sir Waldo. "What a hand you are! You know perfectly well that that's nothing but a bag of moonshine!"

"No, I—oh, Waldo, be a good fellow, and oblige me just this once!" Laurence said, with a sudden change of tone. "You wouldn't be so shabby as to refuse, when it was you who made it impossible for me to come by the ready by my own exertions!"

"Now, what in the name of all that's marvellous——"

"You *did!*" insisted Laurence. "You made me give you my word I wouldn't play for more than chicken-stakes! I daresay you think I'll run thin, but that's where you're mistaken!"

"I know very well you won't."

Laurence looked at him in quick surprise, flushing. He said, with a short laugh: "Much obliged to you! It's more than George does!"

"George doesn't mean all he says."

"He can mean it or not for anything I care. Waldo, if I asked you to buy me a cornetcy, would you do it?"

"Tomorrow!"

"Would you expect me to pay it back?"

"Good God, no! Of course I shouldn't!"

"Then why won't you *lend* me the blunt for something I *want*? You'll say a cornetcy wouldn't cost you much above seven or eight hundred pounds, but you wouldn't get it back, remember! Whereas if you was to invest in my scheme you'd make a *profit!*"

Sir Waldo sighed. "I've already told you, Laurie, that——" He broke off, as the door opened, and Miss Trent came in, accompanied by Tiffany.

"Oh, so you've recovered, have you?" said Laurence, surveying Tiffany with acute dislike. "In prime twig, I daresay! Never stouter in your life!"

Tiffany was looking rather pale, and decidedly tear-stained, but she was evidently restored to good-humour. Paying no heed to Laurence, she smiled seraphically upon the Nonesuch, and said: "*Thank* you for coming to rescue me! I might have known you would do so, and I'm glad now, though I didn't wish anyone to come after me, at first. But Ancilla says I have made *such* a scandal that there's nothing for it but to take me back to my Uncle Burford, which is exactly what I want! She says she shall write to Aunt Underhill immediately, and as soon as Aunt sends back her consent we shall be off."

"God help your Uncle Burford!" said Laurence.

"You needn't think I have *anything* to say to you, because I haven't!" Tiffany informed him. "And I won't beg your pardon for throwing the clock at you, whatever Ancilla says, because you told lies, and cheated me, and you deserved to have it thrown at you! And, in any event, everything has turned out for the best, and I *am* going to London! So I'm not sorry about anything. When are *you* going to London, Sir Waldo?"

"Almost immediately!" he replied promptly.

For an instant his eyes met Miss Trent's, brimful of laughter. So fleeting was the silent message that passed between them that Tiffany was unaware of it. She looked up at Sir Waldo through her lashes. "I thought you might be," she said demurely.

But Laurence had not missed that swift, revealing exchange of glances, and he ejaculated: "So I *didn't* miss my tip! Well, I had a notion you was shamming it, coz! Now perhaps you'll own——"

"Laurie!" interrupted Sir Waldo. "I should warn you, perhaps, that if you wish to succeed as a horse-coper you must learn to keep your tongue between your teeth!"

Laurence looked at him. "Are you bamming me?" he asked suspiciously.

"No: merely warning you!"

"I don't understand what you're talking about!" complained Tiffany, by no means pleased at being overlooked.

"Well, who wants you to?" retorted Laurence. "It's coming to something, so it is, if I can't talk to my cousin without having an uppish scrub of a brat prying into what don't concern her!"

"*Scrub?*" cried Tiffany, colour flaming into her cheeks. "How dare you speak to me like that? I'm not a scrub! I'm not, I'm *not*!"

"A scrub!" repeated Laurence, with relish. "Distempered into the bargain!"

"Quiet!" commanded Sir Waldo.

"Oh, very well!" said Laurence, subsiding.

"I'd liefer be anything but a Bartholomew baby, which is what Courtenay says *you* are! And also a——"

"I said, *Quiet!*"

Tiffany was so much startled by this peremptory reminder that she gasped, and stood staring up at the Nonesuch as though she could not believe that he was speaking not to his cousin, but actually to her. She drew in her breath audibly, and clenched her hands. Miss Trent cast a look of entreaty at Sir Waldo, but he ignored it. He strolled up to the infuriated beauty, and pushed up her chin. "Now, you may listen to me, my child!" he said sternly. "You are becoming a dead bore, and I don't tolerate bores. Neither do I tolerate noisy tantrums. Unless you want to be soundly smacked, enact me no ill-bred scenes!"

There was a moment's astonished silence. Laurence broke it, seizing his cousin's hand, and fervently shaking it. "I *knew* you was a right one!" he declared. "A *great* gun, Waldo! Damme, a *Trojan!*"